Moribund

T.S. Petersen

Moribund: An Evanee Sheperd Novel

Copyright © Tammy S. Petersen 2019

The moral right of the author has been asserted.

This is a work of fiction. Names, characters, places, and incidents are either the product of the author's imagination or are used factiously, and any resemblance to the actual persons, living or dead, business establishments, events or locales is entirely coincidental.

Cover art © by Amanda Pillar of Smoking Hot Covers

To David and our two babies, who patiently stood beside me as I undertook this epic journey. You sacrificed time spent together and supported my dream. This made me love you all the more.

To Jenna, who's been a constant source of support and information. I would be lost without your direction and brilliant editing skills. Thank you.

CHAPTER 1

Salty popcorn and freshly baked chocolate chip cookies scented the air, drifting lazily through the cosy, open plan cottage. A lone lamp in the dining area cast a gentle glow around the snug interior, the only other light coming from the flickering television.

Outside in the evening's gloom, mist snuck its way through winding streets, creeping across lawns to lap gently at closed windows—the perfect evening for a date with my TV boyfriends.

When you lived in a smallish town like Murder Point Bay, whose only source of evening entertainment included a night out at one of the two local pubs; the 24hr drive-thru fast-food chain, where local teenagers hung out; and any harebrained schemes the locals thought of, evening fun was in short supply. If you were single and had workaholics for friends as I did, well, evening fun was even more limited. Not that I minded too much. I usually worked on weekends, and on the rare occasions that I had a night off, I tried to catch up with my workaholic friends for a night of drinks and laughter.

Tonight, however, I wanted some peace. I needed some time with two of my main men—Dean and Sam. Oh, I had others, but tonight was their time to shine.

I had all thirteen seasons of Supernatural lined up and ready to go, with the first disk of season two already playing. I turned the sound up; the scene unfolding with Dean being all tough man after losing his father, while

Sam was attempting to deal with his loss in a more therapeutic way, which pissed Dean off to no end.

Bliss. Pure bliss.

~

I was jerked from my reverie when someone knocked sharply on the front door. I was loathed to get up from the horizontal position I was occupying on my super comfortable couch. No one could resist *the couch* once they sat in it, no one.

Assessing my energy levels, I debated whether I wanted to rise when another series of knocks sounded.

"Come on, Evanee, I know you're in there. I can hear the TV. Don't make me stand out here in the cold." Cassandra's whine crept through the spaces in the door frame, shattering my relaxed mood.

Damn it. I thought she was out partying with Jared tonight, not bloody harassing me.

I took my time hauling my backside off the couch. I didn't bother to hit pause as I placed my bowl of popcorn onto the coffee table. I'd already watched all the seasons of Supernatural enough times to quote most of the lines.

Feet dragging along the fluffy caramel carpet, I took my sweet time, hoping she would give up and leave.

Tiptoeing across the cool, dark wooden floors, I stood at the front door, hesitant to open it. There were only a few steps between my lounge room and the front door.

A third series of impatient knocks echoed in the little hallway.

"I'm coming, I'm coming. Keep your panties on."

Impatient woman.

"I don't have any on, another reason my butt is freezing out here." Her high-pitched whine scraped at me as nails would on a chalkboard, grating every one of my nerves.

I wasn't in the mood for any company tonight. I'd had a long week and just wanted some veg-out time.

"Well, whose bloody fault is that, Cass?" I didn't bother hiding my annoyance, hoping she might take the hint and go?

Although this was Cassandra—she never listened. Not anymore, anyway.

Unlocking and pulling the door open, crisp fresh air raised goosebumps along my exposed arms. There, in all her glory, stood Cassandra. Her ebony hair was down and tousled to perfection. She had a figure enough to make even the most seasoned model jealous.

Looking her over, I noticed she was dressed to party. A gold metallic dress clung to what little curves she had, somehow enhancing them; whilst her legs were on full display, amplified by a pair of black stilettoes any stripper would cry over.

"I can't wear underwear with this dress," she complained. "Besides, Jared likes it when I keep him guessing what's underneath."

I just bet he does.

"Yeah, yeah. Are you coming in, or you going to stand out there and give Steve across the street a heart attack?" I could see him nosing through the curtain as I spoke.

Steven Mors worked in Security at the same hospital as me, Acrasin General Hospital. We'd known each other since my first day of work placement at the hospital morgue, during high school. He'd taken me under his wing my first day, showing me where all the best vending machines were and which café to get my lunch from.

Cass stepped through the door and I waved to Steve before gently closing the door.

"What can I do for you, Cassandra? I'm in the middle of something."

Picking my way back to the couch, I flopped back into it and grabbed my bowl of popcorn.

"Oh, I can see that. Is this how you're planning on spending your Friday night?"

Nodding in response, I stuffed more popcorn into my mouth.

"Haven't you seen this like a thousand times already?" Said with exasperation.

She glided towards the two-seater against the wall. Dropping gracefully, she arranged herself as a Queen might on her throne. Me, I was going for the sloth look.

"Yes I have, but a thousand and one times never hurt a girl," I spoke through a mouthful of popcorn.

Poor Sam was getting his ass kicked by a demonic clown. He never could catch a break.

"Oh, come on, Eve, it's not even that good of a show. Never mind the lack of talent." Cassandra bitched.

"You're treading on thin ice, Cassandra James. I'll put up with you showing up at my front door with no text or phone call. I'll even put up with you walking into my clean house in your dirty stilettoes. What I won't put up with is you throwing shade at Supernatural. Some things should never be messed with and my favourite show is one of them." Arching my neck, I looked back at her. My cranky expression must have been enough, as she raised her hands in surrender.

"Okay, okay, sorry. Psycho much?" she sniffed.

She pursed lips and raised eyebrows, hinting at how she couldn't care less about the fact that she'd just insulted me.

"Why are you here, Cassandra? I thought you and Jared had a party to go to?" I mumbled distractedly as I hit the skip button, bypassing the credits for the episode.

Cassandra picked at non-existent fibres on her pristine dress, her boredom coming through loud and clear, as she pouted, "Yeah, we're still going. I was intending to go after I came here and checked if you wanted to tag along? I knew you wouldn't answer your phone or a text, so I thought I'd show up in person. Besides, I thought it might do you good to get out and socialise."

5

"Hey, I socialise, thank you very much. Almost every night, in fact." I objected weakly.

I wasn't interested in going to any party. I knew who would be there. Thinking about it left a nasty taste in my mouth.

"Socialising with other staff members at the hospital does not count and you know it, Evanee. Now get your butt off the couch and into something pretty so we can go celebrate," Cassandra ordered.

"Celebrate what? There's not a lot going on our lives that needs celebrating at this point. Is there?" I looked over at her, waiting for her answer.

"There may or may not be something to celebrate, but I'll only tell you if you get off that couch and into something other than that atrocious nightie."

The little minx, she knew my weakness all too well. Curiosity. It had been my ultimate flaw since childhood.

"Can't you just tell me here? You don't need me to go to a party just to tell me good news, do you?" I whined.

I don't want to leave my couch, and I like this atrocious nightie!

"Nope. You want to know the secret, you need to come with me to the party. Look, don't consider it as just a party, consider it a celebration. Come on, Eve, you also know you want to know my secret," she taunted.

Damn it, she has me backed into a corner. Damn you, curiosity.

"Humph, fine, I'll come." I relented, to Cass' obvious glee. "But I'm only staying for an hour or two. You also have to tell me your big secret while I'm getting dressed."

Sitting up, I stood to turn the TV off, already mourning the loss of my peaceful evening. Clapping with delight, Cassandra followed me into my bedroom.

I flicked the light switch, and I shuffled in, smiling to myself at the sight that greeted me. I loved how everything had come together. It was a haven and my sanctuary after a busy night at work.

"Now what's this big secret you have to tell me?" I called back as I retreated into my walk-in closet.

The closet was a thing of perfection. Colour co-ordination at its best. Flicking through my dresses, I was looking for something specific—a dress my mother had sent. It'd arrived on Monday.

I wasn't particularly interested in fashion per se, but this dress had caught my eye. It was edgier than I normally went for, but the cut was beautiful, as was the midnight fabric. No one knew my figure better than my mother.

Placing the dress on the back of the door, I went to grab the black stiletto knee-high boots that had accompanied it. They were divine. The heel of the boots were silver-coated, with the rest of the boot made up of supple, genuine leather.

Sliding the boots just under the dress, I stood back to admire the effect.

Stunning.

I returned to an impatient Cass.

"Don't keep me waiting," I chided as I made my way to the ensuite bathroom. "A deal's a deal. What's the big news?"

Starring at my bedraggled reflection in the mirror, I pondered what makeup and hairstyle to do.

My eyes drifted from where I stood to a hovering Cassandra, who, if I wasn't mistaken, looked rather shy.

What on earth would make Cassandra shy?

She hadn't done shy since before year 12. *Intriguing.*

Clicking my finger, I pointed at her. "Out with it, woman, don't make me beg."

I watched and waited as she twisted her hands. Whatever it was, it was big. It surprised me she'd kept it in this long.

"The thing is... Um... You see, Jared kind of asked me to move in with him when he moves back to Acrasin." She spoke hesitantly.

Well colour me blind, I did not see that coming. Quick, say something reassuring before she sees!

I knew it was only a matter of time before my disgust for her newest boyfriend peeked through.

I'd met Jared Miller at the hospital two years ago when he'd taken up a position as one of the many researchers at the newly established Aeternum Ltd. Scientific Research Department at Acrasin General Hospital. Coincidentally, Cassandra had met him the same night I had. She'd paid a surprise visit to my office one Friday evening asking if she could bum a ride with me back home after my shift.

My dislike, well, that had grown over time. There was something off about him, and I couldn't quite put my finger on it, but every inch of my skin crawled whenever he was in my presence.

"That's wonderful news. It is, isn't it?" I checked to be sure she was happy with this recent development in their relationship. After all, she'd flittered between men more times than a butterfly between flowers.

"Yes, of course, its wonderful news. I'm thrilled about it. I'll be getting out of Murder Point Bay, what more could I ask for?" Her hands went into the air in exasperation, as if I'd asked a stupid question.

"What about love? You could ask for love."

"That's the thing. I… I think I might love him. I'm not sure. I mean, it's not like I've ever been in love before! He makes me feel special, like I'm the only woman in the world for him. That's love, isn't it?" Her uncertainty had returned, and now I understood why. She was nervous, almost scared of taking such a monumental step, even though it was something she'd been aiming for since graduation.

I stepped up to her, knowing right now she needed reassurance that she was making the right decision.

I placed both hands on her tiny shoulders and smiled the most reassuring smile I had in my arsenal. "It sounds like love to me. I'm thrilled for you. I know you'll love living in Acrasin. Now help me with my hair, woman, and I'll do my makeup, while you tell me all about your plans."

I prayed she hadn't seen through my smile.

~

For the next half hour, we chatted about her plans to play house. Cassandra wasn't sure when they were intending to move, but it was likely to be sooner rather than later. Nothing was tying Jared or her to Murder Point Bay. She'd already begun looking for a job in the city, hopefully, close enough to the area Jared had said they should start looking for an apartment.

Happiness radiated from her with the intensity of the sun.

With my hair straightened and secured in a high ponytail and my makeup applied to perfection, I made my way back to my walk-in wardrobe.

"I'll wait for you in the lounge room, Eve. I'm just going to call Jared and let him know we'll be leaving soon," Cassandra called out as she left the room, not waiting for my response.

Cassandra was impatient.

Sliding my dress from the coat hanger, I slipped the exquisite material over my head. Stepping into my boots, I turned carefully towards the full-length mirror in the corner of the room.

I'll be damned. Mum, it looks like I owe you a serious thank you for this one.

The dress not only made me look slimmer, but it also made me look taller, with the help of the heels. The simple cut and plunging neckline did wonders for all my assets; including giving me a semblance of cleavage—an unusual thing. The long sleeves were perfect for a cool evening like this one. Opting for understated jewellery, the necklace my mother had gifted me on my eighteenth birthday nestled snuggly against my chest.

It had shocked me the day my mother, Reagan, had presented me with the scale pendant. It'd been the first time she'd mentioned her family and the significance of the pendant as a crest worn only by those born into the family. I'd loved it with all its intricately woven strands of white and yellow gold.

Until my eighteenth birthday, my mother had never once spoken about her family. I'd mistakenly asked about her side, after being tasked with an ancestry assignment in primary school. Reagan had gone pale before walking out of the room.

Distraught at the fact that I'd done something wrong, my father had sat beside me soothing me, whilst calmly explaining that her family had disowned my mother for choosing to marry him. I'd found it difficult to understand how anyone could disown someone they loved over who they married.

The grief and guilt that had hung over the family that day had been bad enough for me to never question my heritage again; although the curiosity had lingered well into my adulthood, I'd respected my mother and father's decision to not broach the topic. That and the fact that Reagan's temper was just as bad as mine, if not worse.

Clutch in hand, my heels click-clacked quietly on the wooden floors as I made my way to the lounge room. Cassandra's slack-jawed expression was confirmation enough that I was in fine form tonight.

"Wow, Evanee, you look fantastic! Is that a new dress, and if so, where d'you get it? I need to be shopping in the same shop." She made a circling motion, and I complied, turning around so she could get the full effect. "Add to that the place where you got those heels. You look like sex on legs, girl."

Rolling my eyes at the absurdity that I could ever look like sex on legs, I made my way towards the front door, snagging my keys from the bowl on the cabinet by the door.

"The shoes and dress arrived on Monday, courtesy of my mother. I can only imagine she purchased it from one of her designer friends' latest collections. Are you ready to head off?" I called out.

Cool night air rushed in when I opened the door. Cassandra was already striding past before I could snatch my jacket from the coat stand, and a cloud of the latest Chanel perfume trailed behind her.

"Yeah, I'm ready. Jared took the day off to help Desmond, and the boys set up."

Oh goody, Desmond will be there. He must have swapped his shift. It's not enough I have to see the arse at work, now I have to see him on my night off too. Awesome.

Deflating just a little, I tried hard to keep my voice perky. "Sounds good. Look, I'm going to take my car just in case I get bored and decide to come home early." Holding up my hand before she could object, I continued, "I promised I would go for a couple of hours and you know I don't go back on my promises. Now let's go, before we freeze to death on my doorstep."

"You know the way to Jared and Desmond's place, right?"

"Yep. I think everyone knows where their place is. I won't be far behind you." I scoffed as I locked up and made my way towards my little Audi hatchback.

Sliding in, I looked up in my rear-view mirror in time to notice Cassandra's Lexus pull off. I hated driving with her. She scared the hell out of me with her inability to focus on what was going on around her.

Reversing out, I braced myself for the night ahead, and the inevitable interaction I'd be forced to endure with Desmond.

Desmond Reilly had transferred to Acrasin General Hospital Mortuary Facility roughly six months after I'd started. We never worked directly with each other, and I was grateful for it. I usually came in to do my night shift as he was finishing his shift. I'd taken an instant disliking to him the first shift I'd worked with him.

As part of his induction during his first week of work, I'd been required to acquaint him with the facility and AGH's procedures. One of the forensic assistants had fallen, twisting her ankle. He'd politely offered to examine her ankle, while I rushed to grab a seat for her to sit in, but upon returning I'd walked in on the young woman crying, begging him to stop touching her. The unfriendly smile he'd worn had chilled me to the bone; it was almost as if he'd enjoyed the assistant's pain.

After that day I'd been weary and grateful to never be on the same shift as him. The problem was it hadn't taken long after he'd arrived before he decided a working relationship wasn't enough. I'd put up with his obnoxious flirting for two months, politely declining his invitations before I'd lost my limited amount of patience and told him in no uncertain terms I was not interested.

That proved to be more of a challenge than a deterrent to him. I'd eventually had to call the regional boss, Bob Johnston, last week after I'd noticed Desmond sitting in the car park, watching me from his car. To say I was a little weirded out would be an understatement. Bob assured me he would personally deal with the situation.

His anger and frustration at Desmond's actions had come across loud and clear during our conversation on the phone the other evening.

I'd loved working for Bob from the moment I'd stepped foot in the morgue during my work placement in high school. That he was a family friend helped. He'd been the one to suggest I complete my placement at the morgue after picking up on my love of forensics and the many forms of decomposition during a family barbeque before my Dad had died.

I'd been curled up on the couch watching a medical documentary when he and Aunty Marg had arrived. He'd also persuaded me to qualify as a Forensic Pathologist and had been delighted when I'd put in for a transfer to my old haunt.

Not long after settling in, he'd taken a position as regional manager of Far North Queensland, confident I could handle the job on my own. He lived in Brisbane and still consulted on the particularly troublesome cases; although they didn't pop up all too often in the outer towns and smaller cities.

How Desmond secured a spot at Acrisin General was beyond me. I wasn't even sure Bob knew how he arranged a transfer. His work was sloppy and rushed; his disrespect for his charges well known amongst his colleagues.

I sighed heavily and drove away from the house, already missing my date night, popcorn and freshly baked cookies.

CHAPTER 2

Pulling into a spot not too far from the front door, I sat looking up at the crowd assembled on the steps. Bodies were huddled together against the chill, laughing, smoking and swigging at whatever drink was in their hand.

Rubbing my lower back, I debated whether to go inside. It'd started as a dull ache about five kilometres from Desmond's house, and now the pain felt as if it was about to burn a hole through my dress. Taking another look around, I forgot all about it as I noticed a familiar-looking black ute parked not too far from me.

"Oh yes, yes! Brad, you beautiful man. When I see you, you're so getting an extra big hug." I exhaled on a relieved sigh.

Brad's personalised number plates were a dead giveaway. SBH15, Science Before Hoes, was a standing joke between my best friend Ellie, Brad, and I. His work came first, with girls sitting somewhere at the bottom whenever he was in the zone.

Brad Reign was one of the few best friends I had. Like me, he worked at the hospital. He and Ellie Arnam worked for the same private company as Jared — Aeternum Ltd. I'd met the two of them their first day on the job which was around the same time I'd transferred back to my old haunt.

Climbing out of the car, my heels sunk slightly into the damp grass.

Please, please don't let me fall ass over heels. I prayed.

Tip-toeing, I made it safely to the front stairs with no incident, stopping briefly I smiled at the song blasting from the sound system.

On the plus side, if the party sucked, at least the music would be good. I dodged the party-goers spilling out of the front door, and no one paid attention to me—frankly, that's the way I liked it.

Sweat and alcohol permeated the air, along with something a little more pungent—smoke, and the cigarette kind.

The scents of the room disappeared when a sudden sharp pain stabbed at my birthmark, the area heating as though it had been burned. Rubbing at it, the renewed ache refused to ease up.

I scanned the room to distract myself.

Bodies writhed and ground together in time to some techno song. Couples all but screwed each other against any flat surface available, which in this case was limited to the walls and floors. They had removed the furniture in anticipation of the crowd that would turn up this evening.

Making my way towards the kitchen, I eyed off the open eskie in the corner. I needed something cool, and it didn't matter what it was, as I'd only be slapping it on my back to stop my bitch of a birthmark from searing my skin off.

With the pain came thoughts of that night three and a half years ago. It triggered a searing ache within my ribs, a snippet of a memory of a face I'd rather forget flashing through my mind.

I fought the urge to double over. The acidic taste of fear filled my mouth and adrenaline raced its way through my veins.

Anxiety jumped into the driver's seat, about to take me for a ride when a high-pitched squeal from right behind me jerked my mind and body from the personal hell that was my past, dumping me right back into reality.

I shook slightly, taking longer than it should have to turn and look for the women responsible for the ear-splitting shriek.

For a petite woman of 5'5", my best friend and partner in crime, Ellie, really could clear a path.

I watched, a weak smile working its way onto my face when she shouldered her way through the crowd. Her stunning blonde hair stood out from a mile away.

Behind her, towering at 6'3", auburn locks sticking out at all angles, trailed Brad. It never ceased to amaze me he could get his hair to stick like that without the help of hair products. Not to mention, that for a nerd, his vibe was completely off. He came across as more of a billionaire who knew no one could touch him because he was at the top of his game. For the life of me, I couldn't fathom why someone hadn't snapped him up already.

"You're here!" Ellie yelled over the blaring musing.

Ellie's pale arms locked around my neck, her hug calmed my shattered nerves better than any pill could.

I looked past her to Brad, who raised his beer in a silent salute and smiled warmly at me.

"Yes, yes, I'm here. Cassandra dragged my backside out of my date night," I giggled, letting her go when I stepped back.

Ellie's usual sour look at the mention of Cassandra always amused me. She truly disliked her, and I guess the feeling was mutual for Cassandra.

"Suppose she's good for something." Ellie sullen tone had my eyes rolling in exasperation.

"Okay, okay. Let's find me a drink and some ice." I pointed towards the kitchen, stepping lightly to avoid touching party goers as I went.

The sensation of eyes tracking my movements across the room stopped me short. Searching the room for the owner, the sensation of those eyes roaming up and down my body sent shivers up my spine.

Finally, I spotted him almost hidden in the shadows near the doorway.

Our eyes locked for the briefest of moments. I smiled at him briefly and his eyebrows rose in surprise as if he hadn't anticipated being caught in the act.

With a slight shrug, I dismissed the stranger, and I turned to follow Ellie and Brad into the kitchen.

Scooping up a bottle of Apple Cider, a sudden movement in my peripheral vision drew my attention to a figure standing in the doorway of what I assumed was the garage. It only took me a second to realise who it was—Desmond. His bloodshot eyes roamed my body as if they owned me. Covering me in maggots would have been more appealing than feeling as exposed as I did in his presence.

I'm out of here.

Fleeing out the nearest door, my breath came out in small white clouds when I hit the coolness of the fresh outdoor air. This was better. Truthfully, anything was better than being in the same room as Desmond.

"You okay?" Ellie appeared at my side, studying me with concern.

"Yeah, sorry. Desmond was freaking me out just a little. He's been getting worse lately."

I hope Bob talks to him soon. I don't think I can take much more.

"Did Bob say he would talk to him?" Brad's asked in concern.

Brad's gaze darted between my rigid form and the kitchen behind me.

"Yep, whenever he was next up. He mentioned that he needed to pop up to check on some issues the hospital has raised with him. I'm hoping that means he'll be here next week sometime."

"Well, let's go down to the gazebo and chill out. Did you drive?" Ellie suggested.

I laughed to myself. In other words, Ellie wanted to know if I could legally hit the piss with her or was she on her own.

"I drove. Sorry, Chicky. Besides, I have work tomorrow night and I am so not turning up hungover. It didn't end well the last time." I shuddered lightly.

Setting off along the concrete path, we made our way towards the outdoor lounge chairs in the gazebo.

I thought of Ellie's birthday last year, which saw the three of us reliving drinking games from our uni days. I'd passed out on the couch during the evening, only to wake with the world's worst hangover.

Work had been wretched, and I'd thrown up after only one cut. Steve had chosen that precise moment to walk in, at which point he had laughed his arse off, before walking back out to grab a bucket and mop. The bastard had stood there, his deep bellied laugh ringing in my ears, while I dry heaved and cleaned at the same time.

"Oh, come on, it wasn't that bad," Brad laughed.

"Not that bad? I only just missed losing what was left of my dinner all over poor old Mrs Misty." Index finger and thumb coming together, I emphasised how close it'd been. "She deserved better than that. Not to mention I had to finish the damned autopsy with a bucket on the actual table. Steve stood there the whole time laughing at me while wiping my brow." I said with exasperation.

Uproarious laughter was the only thing I was getting out of the two of them.

Bastards.

I sipped on my cider, raising my right hand in a one-finger salute.

"Arseholes. I hate you both," I groused.

Despite my words, a grin tugged at the corners of my lips. A giggle slipping through, signalling an end to all seriousness.

It took a while before any of us could talk without erupting into new laughter. We really were a morbid lot.

Enjoying the night air, I sipped at my cider. The glass walls of the gazebo kept the chill of the wind out, allowing us to sit in comfort.

I looked out over the lawn at the small groups of party-goers and noticed my mysterious stranger once again hovering in the shadows. This time, however, he had company—a giant of a man and a lean gentleman.

Our eyes locked once more, familiarity tickling the back of my mind, a memory trying to resurface.

My curiosity was interrupted when Ellie's body grew rigid beside me. Frowning at her, my internal alarm bells shrieked in warning, something they'd only ever done once before.

Brad and I reached for her simultaneously.

My fear that Ellie might be having a fit vanished when birthmark flared to life. I was halfway across the space separating us when I dropped to the cold, tiled floor, curling into a ball.

The intensity of the pain tore a ragged moan from my lips. Ellie's scream of anguish sliced at my pain riddled body, my cries silent against my clenched jaw.

Brad's pained yell barely registered over Ellie's screams and my ringing ears.

The glass walls surrounding us splintered audibly before they buckled under an unseen pressure.

They gave way, and the glass shattered, spraying outwards and into the garden bed bordering the gazebo, as Ellie's high-pitched screech sought freedom.

For a moment, there was silence, a blessed peace that allowed a dazed Brad to crawl over to where the two of us lay. His shaking hand touched my shoulder.

His touch may as well have been a hot poker straight out of the blacksmith's forge. So intense was the pain, I was sure that if you stood close enough, you'd have smelt my skin burning under his palm. The sensation accompanied by the burning from my birthmark had tears streaming from my unseeing eyes, while darkness danced enticingly at their corners.

It would be so easy to give in to the encroaching darkness. Let it take me away to the land of quietness, calm and bliss. I was close enough to that darkness that I was sure I heard a voice calling to me from within.

The fire ripping my shoulder to shreds ceased when Brad's hand lifted abruptly, only to be replaced by a heavy cooler touch.

Respite was instantaneous, and my soul fairly weeping in relief. The sudden weightlessness of my body left me confused and even more lightheaded. A soft cushion supported my back before cool hands framed my face, gently caressing my icy cheeks.

A man whispered my name gently into my ear, beckoning me back to reality.

I fought that beautiful voice, fought to slip into the darkness. My eyes drifted shut, and I was one step closer to oblivion. The man whose voice promised seductive nights spent wandering beneath the stars and silk sheets, lovingly caressing bare skin, wouldn't release me. His grip on my mind was total, as he gently entranced me, pulling me slowly towards the surface. I fought that grip, fought with what little strength I had left.

No! No more pain, please! Just let me rest, let me sink into her arms. She'll protect me. I beseeched.

'That darkness can't have you now. We need here you. Your friends are anxious, especially Brad.' The man soothed. Yet there was the impression of steel that flashed through my mind. That steel gave me pause, warning me of a man whose will was strong and wouldn't bend easily.

My hackles rose. If he thought I was some weak-willed female who'd obey his every command, he had another thing coming. Just because I wanted to pass out didn't mean I was weak.

Fire flashed through my mind. Steel might be strong, but I'd be quite happy to show him just how pliable it was when met with heat. I sure as hell would not be bossed around by some random, albeit sexy as hell, voice. Amusement fluttered at the edges of my mind as the fog sluggishly cleared, despite my best attempts.

"She is fighting me. Your friend is strong-willed."

"That's our Evanee, she'll fight till her last breath. She'd probably keep on fighting after that too," Brad chuckled nervously.

His worry helped to drag me just that bit further to the surface. I certainly wasn't going to give the strange man the benefit of being the one to wake me fully.

"She's surfacing slowly. Jordan, clear an area around the gazebo and get rid of the crowd. They'll only unsettle the women once they are fully conscious," the sexy voice ordered. His tone making it clear he would not accept anything other than what he'd just commanded.

A deep and gravelly males voice responded, "On it."

"Tristan, what progress have you made?"

"She's not as resistant as your ward, sire, but she appears to have a powerful will—and some very un-ladylike comments."

Sire? Are you kidding me? Did I travel back in time or something?

'It's my title. Why does it offend you?' Amusement once again infiltrated my mind.

'You're not serious? I shouldn't need to tell you how medieval that sounded. And excuse me, just what the

hell are you doing in my thoughts? I must have hit my head, that's the only logical explanation for me having a random conversation with a random male in my mind of all places.' I rationalised.

'You were checked for concussions and other injuries you may have sustained. You're fine physically, what I can't determine is why you're in a state of semi-consciousness. Perhaps you could come back fully so we can determine what caused this episode?' He sounded worried, which I grudgingly admit was kind of sweet.

Fine, I'll come back, but if I'm in any pain, and you are in fact real, I will punch you. I didn't care that I sounded stubborn and sullen.

I can accept that deal. The sexy bastard was laughing at me. Oh, he had no idea just how hard I could punch when I scared or in pain. He'd learn.

CHAPTER 3

Mentally bracing myself, I gently swim back to the surface. Eyelids fluttering, a pale face with somewhat familiar blazing emerald eyes framed by black-winged eyebrows loomed over me. With weighted limbs and a body lethargic, I was thankful my birthmark was no longer shooting mind-numbing pain through my body. The pain had been replaced by a soothing warmth radiating from the area.

The fire burning in my chest, on the other hand, was not soothing, drawing my attention to the fact that my body was starved of oxygen. My mouth opened to draw in precious air and nothing happened. Back arching, my head snapped backwards, eyes widening in panic.

How am I not breathing? Am I going to die?

My mind fought my body as it tried to remember how to breathe. A large, smooth hand weighted my chest, as a smooth cool cheek pressed gently to my cold one.

Soft lips caressed my ear, my mystery man whispering one word, "Breath."

Just like that my body obeyed, drawing in lengthy heaving breaths, lungs inflating with precious oxygen. After several gasps, my stampeding heart settled from a gallop into a trot.

I rotated my head to my left, and I noticed Ellie lying on her back, fear etched into her delicate features. Bracing, I attempted to sit up, only to be restrained.

"Rest, you're not strong enough to move yet. Your friend is fine, she's just in shock. Tristan will look after her. You need to recover first, okay. How much have you had to drink this evening?" The man soothed.

He was handsome and somehow familiar, but I would not admit that out loud.

"I'm fine. Really." I reassured him.

Scepticism creased his gorgeous face. He wasn't buying into my brave attitude one bit.

I sighed and rolled my eyes. "Look, I'm fine, okay. If you must know, I've barely had one drink this evening. I also have no clue what happened, so let's not go there, please."

Cause if I go there, I will freak out and this is neither the place nor time for that.

Pulling myself into a sitting position to prove my point, my gaze took in the surrounding carnage. My mouth clenched at the sight of the chunks of shattered glass circling the gazebo.

My attention turned back to my rescuer if you could call him that, it occurred to me I hadn't thanked him for helping me yet.

"Sorry. I didn't mean to sound like a bitch just then. It's just that the damsel in distress thing is not my gig. My name's Evanee, by the way." I offered.

"Evanee, it's a pleasure to meet you. I'm Erick." His face gave nothing away, yet a spark of something in his eyes hinted at the humour he held in check.

"Erick?" Why did that name ring so many bells?

Now's not the time to wonder. Just thank the guy, for goodness' sake.

"Thank you for your help. I'm sure I speak for all of us when I say that." I fought the urge to cringe at the primness of my thank you.

Brad stood in the corner watching the scene unfold before him, concern and anxiety fairly rolling off him. The poor bugger did not understand how to handle whatever was going on in front of him. Truth be told, neither did I.

"You're very welcome. I believe another one of your friends has arrived and is determined to see you." His sentence had barely finished before an irritated Cassandra descended upon the gazebo.

"Eve, what the hell is going on here? You've got the whole damn party harping on about you and Ellie? Des will flip when he sees what's happened to his gazebo!" She chortled.

Taking in the carnage that used to be the gazebo, it took a moment before she finally registered that Ellie and I were not alone. I could see the gears turning in that calculating mind of hers.

"Hi, Cass, nice of you to worry. I'm fine, by the way. Why don't you go back inside," I snapped?

Cass's reaction to the scene was not one I would have expected from a friend.

Beside me, an intrigued Erick watched on, a delectable eyebrow raised.

Damn, that's hot. The bimbo purred within me.

She was one of the two versions of myself who occupied my mind, bringing balance to my control-freak nature. The bimbo, as I liked to call her on account of her brain being between her thighs, only ever came out to perv or whisper naughty thoughts and ideas.

"Oh Eve, don't be silly I am worried about you. What happened, do you need an ambulance?" Cass purred.

Crouching down in front of me, she positioned herself, ensuring the three men a magnificent view of her figure. Always thinking about how she presented, that was the new Cassandra.

"Thanks, Cass, but I'm fine. I think I'm just going to make my way home. I've had enough excitement for one night." I replied stiffly.

I looked past her to where Brad still stood.

"You okay to go, Brad?"

"Yeah Evie, I'm all good. You need me to give you a lift?" Brad nodded.

His clenched fists hung loosely at his sides, yet his eyes depicted kindness and brotherly love.

I shook my head and cringed at the stiffness of my neck, as I murmured, "Nah, I'll drive myself thanks. Besides, I need my car for work tomorrow. Erick, would you mind helping me off the couch, so I can get up, please?"

Cassandra's huff went unnoticed. I really couldn't deal with her competitiveness right now.

"Are you sure you don't want to rest for just a little while longer?"

Not on your life. Next thing you know, dipshit will come over for a gander. I won't be vulnerable in front of Desmond.

"I'll be all right," I reassured Erick, and I swung my legs off the couch.

Erick stood with a grace and elegance I'd have never thought humanly possible, let alone for a man at least 6'1". His hands extended towards me and I had no choice but to accept them unless I wanted to appear rude.

Clasping his hands, surprise zinged through me at just how cool they were to the touch. They were smooth and defined, with not a scar in sight.

Beautiful.

With him helping me off the couch, I didn't have to exert myself. The man lifted me with little to no effort on his part. I had a feeling if he had used any energy I'd have ended up on the grass outside the gazebo.

"Thank you," I whispered thickly.

Erick nodded, his hands remaining in mine. To be honest, I was reluctant to let them go.

The sudden pulsing of my birthmark startled me. My eyes widened with fear as the pulses gained strength the longer I held on to Erick's hands. The fear was replaced with curiosity when the pulses made their way towards my abdomen, travelling slowly south towards my core.

What the hell?

Surprise and heat warred with each other, a slight crease forming at the bridge of Erick's nose.

Good to know I'm not the only one feeling strange and wonderful things. Disturbing, but wonderful all the same.

We'd only been holding hands for thirty seconds. I could only imagine what would happen if we continued, I wasn't so sure I wanted to find out right now. Letting go, I backed away on unsteady legs, my stilettos not helping.

Noticing my wobble, Erick moved closer, placing his arm around my waist, securing me to his side.

Warmth shoot through my body and the world and its people stopped. The very earth held her breath, before releasing it in an explosion of colour and sparks. My gaze darted to Erick, and I stared into his eyes, captivated by a soft light shining from within them, enhancing the emerald within. Flecks of red danced dizzyingly around his irises, swirling in time to pulses radiating from my birthmark.

He was breathtaking right here in this moment. A bomb could have gone off inside the house and I'd have been oblivious to it. Erick, it appeared, felt the same way, as he stared right back with a look of wonder softening his gorgeous features.

All too soon the moment ended, shattering the cocoon of intimacy that had embraced us seconds ago.

Releasing a shuddering breath, I was grateful for its end. I feared the intimacy we'd just shared; I feared where it might lead. Relationships were one thing I didn't do, not anymore, not since that night in the hospital car park all those years ago.

A slight movement in my peripheral vision caught my attention, and I turned to the right.

I stared straight into the face of a hulk of a man. He stood, staring up at me speculatively. His raven hair pulled back into a tight ponytail. His arms were loose at his side, yet ready for action.

This must be the Jordan that Erick spoke to during my 'episode'.

Gazing at the man with a beautiful russet skin-tone, he smiled at me before doing the most bizarre thing. He placed his right palm flat to his heart and inclined his head at me ever so slightly.

Erick's head swivelled towards Jordan, his expression stone. His gaze drifted between Jordan and I, before pulling me closer towards him.

The big guy met Erick's frosty gaze, and the smile I'd been admiring vanished. With a curt nod, Jordan turned to face back out towards the crowd.

Clearing my throat, I asked, "I'm guessing that's the Jordan you were barking orders at while I had my 'episode'?"

"I don't bark orders, I instruct. And yes, that's him. So, you remember our conversation?" Erick's mirth had me frowning.

"Oh, I remember all right. Speaking of which, that reminds me of the promise I made."

Stepping back, my hand formed a fist, thumb on the outside before I raised my arm and swung. It connected with his shoulder with a loud thump.

Silence descended around us. Cassandra gasped in shock. From the corner of my eye, I could see Jordan turn towards the gazebo, while the man named Tristan jumped to his feet, a thunderous look overtaking his Elven features.

Guess I'll be referring to him as elf boy.

Ellie raised her eyebrow and winced. Erick, on the other hand, barely even moved. I may have held back on how hard I hit him, but I'd still hit hard enough to warrant some kind of movement from him. Yet, there he stood as if I'd merely caressed his cheek instead.

I cradled my fist. I'd be regretting that little tantrum in the morning.

Damit.

"Evanee, what the hell is wrong with you? Why the hell would you do that?" Cassandra's screeched.

If the gazebo's glass hadn't already shattered, her screech would have done the job.

"When I promise something, I always deliver. I warned you what would happen if I woke up and was in pain. You agreed to the terms." I muttered, flexing my hand before I massaged the cramps from my fingers.

Elf Boy looked as though he'd just swallowed something vile.

"Ah yes, I recall that conversation, now that you mention it." Erick agreed, moving his arm exaggeratedly.

Oh please, like you felt that. You barely even flinched.

"Yes well, I woke up hurting. Don't say I never gave you fair warning. Now if you will all excuse me, I'm going home before Desmond comes up with some creative way to make me pay for all the damage." I huffed.

My legs were only slightly stronger than they'd been a moment ago, but I was determined not to fall arse overhead in front of one of the hottest men I'd ever met in my life. I bent and scooped up my clutch, momentarily forgetting my dress was low cut. When I eventually rose, pure carnal lust blazed in the emerald depths of Erick's eyes.

Clicking my fingers in front of his face, I grabbed his attention. "Up here, sonny boy, my eyes are up here."

"Um, what? Oh yes, yes, sorry." His cocky grin was anything but sorry.

"Yeah, sure you are." I shook my head and my eyes rolled upwards.

I made to move around the scrumptious specimen before me only to halt at his side when his arm snaked around me and settle on my hips.

"Let me help you to your car. You're still not one hundred percent. Don't bother arguing, because you won't win this one," he admonished when I opened my mouth to decline his offer.

That bossy attitude chafed at my stubbornness and independence; although, just this once, I'd let him win, I decided. I still had to make it across the yard, through the crowded house, and down the front steps. Judging by my roiling stomach and the blossoming headache coming to life at the back of my head, I wasn't going to manage that trip without falling flat on my backside at least once.

"Okay. Ellie, you good to move or do you need more time?" I called out to Ellie.

Ellie had already risen and was being supported by the Elf Boy, sorry, Tristan.

"I'm good, Evie. Luckily Brad is the sober driver tonight. We'll follow you." She whispered with tiredness.

Poor Ellie, she was whiter than a ghost, her blanched complexion almost the same colour as Tristan's pale skin. Brad had her purse in hand and was watching the two of us carefully.

"Well let's hit the road, people. Cassandra can't say the party was a pleasure. I knew I should have stayed home," I bitched.

Not waiting for her response, I took the first of two steps at the gazebo's entrance on wobbly legs.

My heavy pants by the time I reached the bottom would have outdone any asthmatic. Head thumping with an impending migraine, my already sensitive stomach churned just that bit more.

Yep, this is going to suck.

"I should have stayed home with Dean and Sam," I groaned with regret.

Erick looked down at me speculatively, before he asked, "Who are Sam and Dean, and why didn't they come with you to the party?"

I didn't bother turning my head to reply, because if I did, I was sure I'd throw up, which would be beyond mortifying.

"Dean and Sam Winchester happen to be two of the hottest brothers known to womankind. They save people from the things that go bump in the night. It's the family business." I spoke through my clenched jaw.

If he didn't know who the Winchesters were, I might consider hitting him again.

"I don't know who the Winchesters are. What exactly do they save people from, and how do you know they're the hottest brothers known to womankind?" he frowned.

Oh my word, I can't, I just can't. How does he not know Supernatural? Was he born under a damn rock?

"Look, they are fictional characters in the show Supernatural, and I swear if you ask me what Supernatural is I'll hit you again just on principle," I growled.

The vibration from his chuckle radiated through my sensitive body, tightening things below.

"Okay, I won't ask. Are you ready to keep going?"

Nodding, I focused on my breathing as the slow and arduous journey began.

It took what felt like forever to reach the back door, and I could feel everyone's eyes following our progress.

My night went from bad to worse the closer we got to the back sliding door. There, framed by the light from the kitchen, stood Desmond and Jared.

Desmond's sneer at Erick's hand on my hip creased his boy-next-door features; while Jared looked on, his cynical eyes assessing the scene before him. His stocky silhouette was slightly shorter than Desmond's, yet his stance gave the illusion that he was Desmond's height.

My hand tightened on my clutch the closer we got to the two men and my stomach churned just a little more, my heart beating a little faster.

Erick's hand tightened where it lay on my hip, making me wonder if my uneasiness had shown.

A whiff of Chanel slapped my nose as Cassandra breezed past to get to Jared before we did.

"Everything okay, Princess?" If you looked close enough, I was sure you'd have seen the honey dripping from Jared's voice.

It took all my will power to not roll my eyes.

"Of course, baby. Everything's great. Eve just had a clumsy moment. She and that friend of hers smashed all the glass in gazebo somehow," She crooned, her nails digging into his upper arm and hand while she smiled ever so sweetly at him.

Oh, sweetheart, you don't need to worry about any of us trying to steal him away from you. He is so far from my type, he may as well be from another planet.

It pissed me off that she couldn't even show Ellie and Brad the respect they deserved.

Looking between Cassandra, Jared, and Desmond, I realized this moment right here, this was where I'd be getting off the friendship train. Sadness gripped my heart. My sorrow not for the friendship that had ended, rather for the wonderful memories I had of us in high school before she'd become obsessed with popularity.

A weight I hadn't known existed lifted, the relief physical and emotional. My weak body sagged a bit more, as the cool night air caressed the path a single tear tracked.

Righto, time for me to go to bed. Since when do I cry in public?

Never.

Exactly. This is simply a physical response to the trauma my body has experienced. Now suck it up, princess, and get moving.

I looked up at Erick and I leaned in a little, catching his attention. He turned his head ever so slightly, acknowledging me whilst still keeping a close eye on the three before us.

"If you could help me up the stairs and through to the front, I'd appreciate it. I need to leave now," I mumbled my plea, anger at my vulnerability crackling throughout my body.

Would this evening and its humiliations never end?

"Sorry, I assumed these were more friends of yours," Erick apologised.

He gently eased the trembling thing that was now my body forward. I wasn't so sure I'd make it to my car. My was body growing weaker by the minute and my insides were trembling worse than a sinner on his death bed, facing the unknown abyss.

"No, they are not friends of mine. Not anymore."

"Don't sulk Evanee, it's not an attractive trait," Desmond slurred.

It was the last nail in the coffin. After months of putting up with his endless flirting and unwanted advances, I'd had enough. My gut may have been churning, but I wouldn't be dictated to by the likes of him.

"Know what, Desmond? If I hadn't already decked Erick here, you'd be next. Do you think I haven't seen you sitting in your car at work, stalking me like some kind of psychotic freak. You think I haven't noticed all the times you've made up some lame-ass excuse to stay late at work. When are you going to get it through that thick skull of yours that I'm not interested?" The longer I spoke, the louder my voice grew.

I doubted I would've said any of it had I been alone at work with him, out of fear of the consequences both professionally and personally. Having so many people around me, my friends around me, gave me the illusion of safety.

"Sheesh, Evanee, calm down. Drama queen, much. Give poor Desmond a chance. He's tried so hard to get you to notice him," Cassandra's sighed with exasperation.

She was not helping the anger that had replaced the churning within me.

"Stick it up your ass, Cassandra. I'm done with your self-centred crap and your utter lack of respect for anyone other than yourself," I seethed, my body shaking with a mixture of rage and adrenaline. It spurred me on through my tiredness.

"Evanee, that's enough! You'll apologise to Cassandra right now. Just because you're angry at the hurdles we need to overcome in our relationship, doesn't mean you need to take it out on everyone else. We can talk about this in private. Now come with me before you make an even bigger fool of yourself than you already have," Desmond admonished.

Are you kidding me? Hurdles in our relationship? What the hell is he even talking about? He's bloody delusional. I ranted internally.

And just like that, all semblance of control I possessed obliterated under the roiling rage within.

Before I could vent that pent up anger, Brad's deep, loud voice penetrated the murmurs now circulating us, "Desmond, dude, enough is enough. You need to get yourself some help. How many times does Evanee have to tell you she's not interested before you take a hint?"

His face red with rage, Desmond hissed, "Get bent, Brad. We all know you've never approved of Evanee and I. You think no one's noticed your little crush on her? Do you realise how pathetic you look, 'hanging' with two chicks? What, you can't bone one, so you hang with them both in the hopes you'll score from at least one of them?"

This sounded more and more like a high school drama, with an audience to go with it. Around us, people had now stopped talking and were inching closer to hear what was being said.

"You want to stop and consider your next words carefully, Desmond," Brad warned quietly, each syllable pronounced slowly, a sure sign Brad had reached the limit of his patience.

"Ooh, what you gonna do, bitch slap me?" Scoffing, Desmond finished digging his grave with his next words, "I mean come on, look at the two of them. They're just begging to be fucked. I bet any guy here could bend them over the nearest surface, and they'd love every minute."

42

His crude speech would've sickened me if I hadn't already been fuming.

Astounded silence descended for a second before all hell broke loose. Together, Brad and I descended upon Desmond, as a petrified Cassandra yelped, ducking behind Jared for protection. We made it as far as the second step, before Desmond's arm was yanked behind his back and into the air. His cheek came down hard on the balustrade and an imposing Erick stood calmly behind him. Brad and I stopped short, staring up at the two of them, tight-lipped and seething.

"You will apologise to the three people you just insulted." Erick's hiss was only a whisper.

"Fuck you, asshole!" Spittle dripped from Desmond's mouth, his manic eyes bloodshot.

Erick lifted Desmond's arm a little higher, forcing a pained moan from Desmond.

"I'd do what he says, Desmond. Judging from the position he has your arm in, it wouldn't take much more to dislocate that shoulder," Brad chuckled, his joy in seeing Desmond at a disadvantage clear.

When Desmond remained silent, I continued up the steps, gripping the railing tightly for support. Standing beside Erick, I leaned forward slightly.

Time for a little heart-to-heart, you sick freak.

"Now who's bent over, Desmond?" I baited. His spluttered reply silenced as I shushed him, "Shhh, don't speak, just listen. This is how things will play out. You will apologise to me and my friends for that disgusting and quite frankly disturbing little speech, then you're going to forget about any relationship you *think* we might have. I ever see you in the same vicinity as me outside of work and you won't like what comes next," I warned him.

Okay, that last part was ambiguous, but he didn't need to know I planned to go to the police if he didn't stop.

Straightening up, adrenaline flowed through my veins as I stood beside Erick, waiting for Desmond to decide his fate. I tapped my foot impatiently, waiting for him to respond.

"Tick-Tock Desmond, we don't have all night." I knew I shouldn't antagonise him, but it felt so good to have him at a disadvantage for once.

"Fine, fine! I'm sorry. There, are you happy?" He spat.

I shrugged at Erick and he released his captive.

Cradling his arm, Desmond turned, his red face marred by a bruise that was surfacing across his right cheek.

Mouth opening and closing, he looked between Erick and me before shoving between us to disappear inside. Cassandra and Jared followed not far behind him.

The adrenaline I'd had before disintegrated, leaving me shaky and nauseous once again.

"I think it's time to go." The loud grumble from my stomach emphasised my urgency to get to my car and back home.

Not needing further instruction, Erick secured me to his side and we once again made our way towards the kitchen.

Checking behind me for Ellie and Brad, I saw that Ellie looked no better than I felt.

I stumbled slightly and Erick held on just a little tighter.

For crying out loud, why am I this weak?

"Put your arm around my waist and hold on as best you can, okay?" His lips caressed my ear, sending shivers throughout my body.

He secured my arm around his back and my numb fingers gripped his hip. The man had no fat whatsoever beneath his shirt. I'd bet my house his stomach and arse were in the same condition as his hips. The thought helped focus my attention on something other than the wave of nausea I was riding.

Ambling, I looked down at my feet, forced to trust my rescuer to get me through the next couple of minutes. I had no idea how the hell I'd make it home, but I'd cross that bridge when I got to it.

A figure stepped to my left, as black boots appeared in my narrowed vision. They could have belonged to a giant from the size of them, yet they were a dead giveaway to the person standing beside me. Head rising ever so slightly, I offered Jordan a small pathetic smile. He smiled reassuringly in return, before extricating my clutch from my grip.

"Here, let me take that for you. It'll be easier to hold on to Erick without it." He spoke loud enough so he was heard over the blaring music.

Nodding, I speculated over the instant connection I shared with this giant of a man. It should have felt strange, yet I couldn't help feeling as if we had known each other in a past life. The connection I felt wasn't romantic, rather one of a kindred spirit.

Dismissing it, for now, I looked back down at my feet, focusing on breathing in and out. Yoga breathing helped until I got to the crowded dance floor, where the assault on my senses was just too much. Sweat, spilt beer, pot and vomit all mixed to form a pungent perfume. Combined with the constant beat of the music, I knew I was done.

The floor rose to greet me. Before my poor brain could register just what that meant, the world spun and I was suddenly staring up at the white ceiling, cradled against Erick's chest.

The grinding bodies barely noticed as they continued to make love to one another. It was beyond embarrassing that I was being carried out by a stranger and I was sure that any minute now I would throw up all over him, or whoever was closest, just to complete my night.

Being this close to Erick had its perks, though; one of which was the fact that I became very well acquainted with the wall that was his chest. The other was I got a better smell of whatever cologne or deodorant he used. It was better than any wildflower.

That I wasn't freaking out at this point spoke of just how down and out I was.

Every muscle within my body tensed when a prickling sensation started up at the back of my mind.

"Do you feel that?" I breathed.

Erick stopped, frowning down at me. "Feel what?"

The sensation came again. Studying the white door beside the kitchen, I'd have thought it was a guest room, yet something felt off. The closer we got, the stiffer my muscles became. The prickling at the back of my mind turned to needles piercing my brain.

Closing my eyes against the agony, an equally pained moan sounded from behind Erick's solid shoulders. Ellie's distress heightened the closer Tristan brought her to the door, her body drawn tighter than an archer's bow.

She feels it too. How? What's behind that door?

"Never mind. I'm going to throw up, you need to put me down, now," I gasped.

Sealing my mouth shut, I had no strength to pull my arm up to try to place my hand over my mouth.

Turning from the white door, the world blurred.

"We are nearly down the steps. Just two more to go." The rumble in his chest felt so good against my clammy face.

Seconds later my feet touched the ground, and I was helped to my knees, only to lose it in spectacular fashion.

CHAPTER 4

Now anyone who's ever thrown up knows there's no elegant way to do it. It doesn't look elegant; it doesn't sound elegant and it most certainly doesn't smell or taste at all pleasant.

Yet, here I knelt in all my glory, puking my guts up with Erick's muscular forearm gripping my waist, ensuring I didn't end up face-first in the ever-increasing puddle in front of me. Just when I thought I was done, my stomach found more liquid to bring up, until there was nothing left but to dry heave.

"Please, someone, just knock me out. Please!" I begged.

If I hadn't been careful with my drink, I'd have sworn someone had roofied me. There was no way my passing out could have caused this kind of reaction.

A warning buzz resumed in my head and my body once again felt as though it were being pulled in two different directions. As though he sensed something was happening, Erick drew me back against him, as though he were shielding me. Thankfully Erick's body was not as hot as Brad's, as I had a sneaking suspicion my situation would've been a lot worse.

I studied the ground around me, trying to distract myself from the pain and nausea, and recognised the roots of what could only have been the poinciana tree that sat at the side of Desmond's house. Brittle sticks and dried leaves lay forlornly on the surrounding ground.

"Feel better?" Erick's deep voice caressed my neck.

Nodding my response, I wasn't up for answering him just yet.

"Evanee, can you tell me what you meant when you asked if I felt anything inside?" he spoke against my neck once more.

Shit! How am I supposed to answer that without sounding delusional?

Deciding to through caution to the wind, my ragged whisper aggravated my already raw throat. "I don't know, but something felt completely off about the room behind that white door. I don't know how to explain it. Right now I just want to go home."

Exhaustion beat at me with a solid wooden bat. I finsihed, I couldn't take anymore tonight. All I wanted was my bed, so I could pass out in safety.

"Evanee, where's your car parked?" Brad's question took a while to register and the poor guy had to repeat the question once more before I understood what he was talking about.

Dehydration and exhaustion must be catching up with me.

"Near yours. My keys are in my clutch, but I don't think I'll be able to drive." A hoarse whisper was all I was managing right now until I got some water into me. Thank goodness I still had a bottle in my car from yesterday's gym session.

"It's okay, sweetheart, Erick has offered to drive you home. I will follow until I am sure you are home safely, then I'll take Ellie home."

Knowing what he said made sense, I nodded.

Brad didn't know exactly why I was skittish with strangers, but he was observant and protective enough to respect my need for safety. Being attacked in a carpark would do that to a girl.

"Okay. But if I pass out before I get home, only you can put me to bed, okay? Sorry Erick, I just don't know you well enough to trust you with something like that."

At least I was honest. I could be faulted for many things, but honesty was not one of them.

"That's okay, *mic lupt*ător. You should never apologise when it comes to matters of your safety." Erick's chest rumbled against my back.

Mic what now? What does that even mean?

Before I could ask, he scooped me back into his arms as if I weighed little more than a feather.

My head dropped to Erick's shoulder, and I chuckled, "Well Brad, on the plus side I can live up to the town's name for me — in looks, that is."

My smile must have looked like a grimace because Erick held me tighter.

"Which name's that, Evie?"

"Doctor Death, weirdo. I'm betting I look like one of my lovely corpses warmed up." Tiredness tugged at my consciousness, my words slurring together at the end.

"The town nicknamed you Doctor Death? Ouch, what did you do to earn that name?" Erick's amusement would have made me smile if the reason for my nickname had been a fond one.

"I existed. Oh, and I'm also a Forensic Pathologist." I tried to shrug, but my shoulder refused to move. "I mostly just ignore the locals who use it. Some of them will probably end up on my table at some point in time and apparently, the idea of being under my scalpel or bone saw is a little on the frightening side."

Doctor Death was a nickname I'd inherited at the morgue in my teen years as a joke between Steve, Uncle Bob, his forensic examiner and myself. I'd accidentally blurted out the body's cause of death as they had wheeled it in the door. After that, a running bet had started up each time a body was bought in.

But perhaps it was for another reason, too. My ability to sense souls trapped within corpses had developed not long after my father died while I was in high school. It had gradually heightened during my years at university, after having spent countless hours with the dead. No one other than my mother knew I could sense trapped souls and even then, we never talked about it. As for some of my colleagues at the morgue, they assumed I was a psychic of some kind, or having a laugh at their expense. It only helped draw attention to myself; a fact I resented.

Upon returning to Acrasin General, my nickname had re-emerged courtesy of Steve, as had the running bet. Ellie and Brad thought this was cool and usually tried to be in on the bets if they weren't on a crazy bender in Aeternum's lab.

It irritated the hell out of me that my high school peers had found out about my nickname. They'd turned something that was an in-house joke into a sneer whenever I was around town.

I took comfort because at least a small percentage of them would end up on one of my slabs at some point in time. Don't get me wrong, I didn't wish them any harm — quite the contrary — but there would come a day where they would be bare before me. I could decipher people's vices by looking at the condition of their bodies both inside and out.

Secrets had a way of revealing themselves after you died.

"I see. Well, at least you have a philosophical outlook on the matter." Erick's beautiful green eyes stared straight into mine.

Oh my! He's good looking and knows how to use big words. Makes the man even hotter. Ah crap! I've been in this town too long if a pair of beautiful eyes and carefully placed words has me drooling.

"It is what it is." My defences rose, and I brushed it off as best I could. I wasn't in the mood to talk about the topic.

"That's an interesting pendant you have there. It kinda looks like one of those old balance scales." The deep growl of Jordan's voice sounded from somewhere behind Erick's shoulder. Touching my pendant gently, I smiled at the memory of the day I'd received it.

"It *is* an old balance scale. It's the coat of arms for my mother's family. Each descendant is given one on their eighteenth birthday. It never leaves my neck."

"I saw a woman with that same pendant once. She had the most beautiful white hair, with pale blue eyes very similar to your own. She was pure grace, yet stronger than any fighter I've come up against in battle," Jordan reminisced.

Looking over Erick's broad shoulder, the gentle giant that was Jordan smiled at me with what must have been fond memories of his own.

"Really? That sounds just like my mother. She has long, silky white hair and her eyes are the same colour as mine. She's the strongest woman I know, and her grace is something I've always wished I'd inherited. Sadly, I got my clumsiness from my father's side. Where did you see her?" My inquisitiveness would not be suppressed.

"In Paris, I think. It was quite some time ago, however. I believe her name may have been Reagan, but my memory isn't that fantastic when it gets to names."

A distant look came over his handsome features as if he was remembering back to when he had seen her. Erick snorted as if whatever Jordan had just said was a total crock of shit.

"That's my mother's name, but it's unlikely you would have seen her in Paris. You look far too young to

54

have seen her in Paris when she lived there. My mother left France over 27 years ago."

I tried puzzling over what Jordan had just said, but my brain refused to compute the conversation.

"Perhaps it was one of your family members then." This came from Erick, who gently bounced his arm to get my head back to rest against his chest.

"Yeah, could have been. Who knows? I've never met them. I might once my mother smooths things over with them." The conversation was getting too heavy for my poor fatigued brain.

"Rest for now, you've had a big evening," Erick soothed.

We were nearly at my car.

I began looking around for Jordan — I needed my clutch to retrieve my car keys. Brad was suddenly there, clutch in hand.

"Hey, where is Ellie?" Guilt bubbled up my throat as I realised I hadn't heard or seen her since exiting the house.

"She's in my car with Tristan. She fainted before we made it to the front door, but she's awake now and resting in the ute," Brad reassured me.

A flash of orange light distracted me momentarily.

"Tristan… wait, is he the guy that looks like an elf out of *Lord of the Rings*?" The words were out of my mouth before I could filter what I was saying.

There was a second of silence, then hysterical laughter burst into the night. The chest beneath my cheek rumbled as if thunder were somehow bottled just beneath the skin. It turned out Erick's laugh was just as gorgeous as his looks.

Next to me, Jordan's laughter winged its way into the night, and Brad's laugh joined the two men.

"Did… did you just call Tristan an elf?" Erick's words were interrupted by bouts of laughter.

"Well, he looks like one! Come on, has no one seen the resemblance? The shoulder-length white hair, delicate jawline, plus the fact that he looks as if he has a stick up his ass or is constantly smelling something foul. Tell me I'm wrong." I pointed out.

Yep, it's official. My brain has malfunctioned. I'm so going to regret saying that tomorrow.

To my right Jordan leaned on my car, holding his belly from the raucous laughter. If Erick hadn't been cradling me, I suspected he would have been in the same position.

"What, no filter tonight, Evie?" Brad grinned, shaking his head as he tried to contain the rest of his laughter.

"Yeah..." I blushed. "He wasn't close enough to hear me, was he?" I was an honest person, I was, but even

I knew tact was important when it came to dealing with live human beings.

"He may have heard you, but I wouldn't worry too much about it. That's probably the nicest thing anyone's ever said about him when he's not around." Laughter danced in the depths of Erick's eyes as he grinned at me.

"Ha! I'd say it's the nicest thing anyone's ever said about him even when he is around. An elf, I never considered that, but I sure as hell like it." Jordan continued to hold on to the car in his state of hysterics.

"Would you two grow up? You have more important issues to deal with than whether I look like a fucking elf." Tristan's reprimand came from nowhere.

Oh, he sounds pissed. Bugger!

"TRISTAN! You will watch your tone, I'm well aware that there are other issues to deal with." The bite in Erick's voice lashed across the night, seeking a target.

Brad's body jolted, letting me know I wasn't the only one to feel the peculiarity in both his and Tristan's tones. There was no response from Tristan, yet there was tension in the air. Jordan was no longer laughing but had moved to stand just slightly off to my right, blocking my head with his enormous body.

Ah, crap. Me and my enormous mouth.

"Okay boys, let's just calm down. Erick, you can't fault Tristan for being pissed. I mean really, I did insult the poor guy by calling him an elf. Now if you could pop me in my car, I'd appreciate it. I'm extremely tired and just want to go home," I reasoned.

"Sorry Evie, let's get you and Ellie home to rest," Brad apologised.

The passenger door clicked open and Brad stepped aside, giving Erick enough room to place me in the loving embrace of soft leather seats. The coolness of the leather against my bared flesh was a slight relief, but the hushed interior of the car was not. Silence rang louder than church bells on a Sunday morning.

My eyes drifted shut, and I listened for the driver's door to open. The click and rush of chilly air signalled my rescuer's entrance. The car dipped ever so slightly on his side. Mechanics whirred as he adjusted my driver's seat to accommodate his long, denim-clad legs.

I bet his arse looks like candy in those jeans. Note to self must check his arse when he's not looking.

Music blasted through the sound system when the engine came to life. Eyes snapping open, I launched for the dashboard, turning the volume down. My head could not handle screamo right now, so instead, I switched over to the local radio channel. It usually played lousy music; but hey, I wouldn't be listening to it.

"Thanks again for all your help tonight. I'm sorry to be taking you from the party," I murmured.

My head rested peacefully against the headrest. I was tempted to put my seat back, but I didn't want to fall asleep.

"That's okay, I was about to leave when you turned up. I merely wanted to reacquaint myself with the locals." His smooth reply washed over me.

Hang on, reacquaint? That must be why he looks so familiar.

"So, you've been to Murder Point Bay before then?"

"I'm returning. My family's lived in this town since it was founded," he confessed.

He'd lived here before? Okay, this was news to me. My memory must be shot, that, or I was just useless at remembering the living.

I turned slightly to look at Erick's profile in the car's darkness. The glow radiating from the dashboard only partially illuminated his face, but I could see him clearly enough. My night vision had always been exceptional.

A memory of a man coming into the morgue a few times and leaving with a white Styrofoam box of something resurfaced. I'd been seventeen and on my work experience. Bob had never explained what was in the box, so I'd never asked. It wasn't my business. It didn't mean that I wasn't curious and itching to discover the contents of the box, but I knew the trouble Pandora had gotten herself into, and like hell was I going to join her little club.

As the memory surfaced, so did a name and the philosophical conversations we'd had a couple of times while we'd waited for Bob to return from an errand.

"Mr Tenebris. You're Erick Tenebris who up and left mysteriously, what, twelve years ago?" My voice was a tad bit on the shrill side as I realised that I was sitting in the car with my teenage crush. It was a good thing the car was dark; it saved me the humiliation of him seeing me blush.

I punched my teenage crush. Great. Real classy, Evanee.

"We've met before?" Taking his eyes off the road for a second, Erick looked me up and down before returning his concentration to the road ahead.

Well, that isn't the least bit insulting. Nothing like a hot guy not remembering he's met you. Then again, he probably had crazy hot women in his bed every night. A pimpled, wild-haired teenager who dressed like she was going to a funeral wouldn't have even been worth recalling.

"You could say we've met. You used to come into the mortuary facility at least once a week to see Bob. I did my work experience with him during high school." I didn't let on any more, I didn't want him remembering the awkward teenager I was back then.

It'd been a hard time. My dad had died not long before, and things had gotten a little weird around that time for me. The change had been difficult, to say the least.

"I remember you now. Bob used to rave about how much of a hard worker you were and how you had an affinity with the dead. We used to have conversations from time to time when Bob wasn't in the office, didn't we? Wow, you've changed since then."

My eyes remained focused on the road ahead. I could feel his eyes running up and down my body once again.

And cue the blush. Yep, never fails to make an appearance, even after all these years. One day I will conquer you, one day.

"Yeah, it's amazing what leaving puberty behind can do for a girl. I'm impressed that you remember," I drawled, miffed at his previous comment.

"Of course I remember. I have an excellent memory, not to mention it's not every day you come across a teenager who can name body parts in fluent Latin. So, I'm guessing you're the new forensic pathologist who took Bob's place at the morgue?" He sounded impressed.

"No one can take Bob's place. He's a bit of a legend, but yes, I'm one of the forensic pathologists at the morgue now. Desmond is the other examiner."

"I see. So that's how the two of you met."

"Yes." I left it at that. This wasn't a discussion I was up for right now.

Silence descended within the small interior of the car, music playing softly in the background, leaving me with thoughts of my colleague.

I woke to a gentle shake of my shoulders. Lifting heavy eyelids, the realisation I'd fallen asleep sent panic throughout my reclined body, before I noticed we had arrived at my house.

Brad came up alongside the passenger door, opening it while Erick climbed out of the driver's seat.

Brad helped me to stand.

I was feeling stronger than I had at the party. Some water and a good night's rest would do me a world of good and have me feeling close to my old self.

My gaze jumped to Steve's house across the road and I hoped we didn't disrupt him too much. He was a light sleeper and had the night off from security at the hospital. Our shifts tended to overlap, with him either starting earlier than me or finishing later.

I breathed a sigh of relief when his windows remained dark.

Shuffling towards my illuminated front veranda, the three of us came to a halt at my front door. Brad retrieved my keys.

I faced Erick, a blush creeping into my cheeks.

"Thank you for helping me tonight, Erick. I appreciate it. Hopefully the next time we meet you won't need to rescue me or subdue jealous colleagues." I hoped my smile would show him how grateful I was for his help.

"It was my pleasure, Evanee. I'm sure we'll bump into each other again. As for jealous colleagues, I just hope tonight didn't make things worse for you at work." His smile was slight, yet genuine.

Erick bent slightly at the waist and placed a gentle peck against my cheek, before exiting my veranda.

I watched his broad shoulders retreat towards the dark ute parked out front.

My eyes travelled down to his jean-clad arse, a small smile tugging at my lips.

Hot damn, I was right. That man has an arse as sweet as lollies. Delectable and bloody irresistible.

Erick stumbled, and his head snapped to where I stood. His lush lips tugged into a smirk as though he'd just heard what I'd said.

Frowning, I shook my head to clear the thought and turned to follow Brad into the house.

CHAPTER 5

Damit, I'm late.

The stupid tree just had to fall across the road on today of all days.

If I was being honest, my frustration wasn't really at Mother Nature, but more at myself for running late and feeling dreadful.

I slapped my identification card against the security panel and yanked the door open as soon as it buzzed.

Steve was leaning against the wall at the top of the railing above the loading bay and I could see him looking for our customary dinner I usually bought in on a Sunday evening shift. I didn't have any this evening, and I felt terrible about it.

"Sorry Steve, nothing tonight. Has Desmond left yet?" I puffed, making it to the top of the stairs.

"Yeah, he left on time." Steve nodded.

"Okay, thanks. I'll talk to you later, okay?" I called as I rushed towards the staff locker room, my thoughts turning to the last week.

Not only had I been having trouble sleeping, but I wasn't able to keep anything aside from biscuits and chips down. I still had a slight headache, which was nowhere near as bad as it had been last Saturday and

Sunday after my 'episode'. Any attempt or thought of cooking had me dry heaving over my kitchen sink.

I'd shout Steve to some takeaway to make up for the lack of dinner tonight. I'd even try to order something for myself if I felt up to it.

My shared office sat midway between a set of double doors leading out towards the hospital and the morgue. Our facility was nowhere near as big as the ones you got in cities such as Brisbane, Sydney, or Perth, but it did what it was meant to do.

Entering my office, I breezed straight over to the computer terminal, logging in.

Flopping into my black leather chair with a huff, I studied the room waiting for my login to authenticate.

There was no room for personal touches in the office, as it was shared by Desmond and I. In all honesty, it was a relief; I didn't feel like looking at a picture of my friends and family as I summarised my findings of the dead person I'd just cut open.

There were no planned autopsies for this evening, which was probably a good thing, as I had paperwork to complete for myself and Desmond's to check over.

Logged in, I began the tedious chore. Normally I hated doing the stuff, but tonight I was grateful to be sitting down and not staring into the bloody remains of the recently deceased.

~

"Everything alright this evenin, Doc?" Steve's cheerful voice broke my concentration from the data entry I was working on.

I looked up and realised I'd been at it for nearly two hours.

Normally I'd be counting down the minutes before I was done. I guess I'd needed the distraction from the events of late more than I realised.

"Hey Steve, how are you this evening? Did you remember to make it to your doctor's appointment on Friday?" I asked mid-stretch.

This was something I had to remind him of. Funnily though, I never had to remind him when a Rugby League game was on.

"Yes, I went. The quack says I'm as healthy as a horse and ta keep doin' whatever it is I'm doin'. My cholesterol's down, so's my blood pressure." His Queensland accent stressed his exasperation.

I beamed my pleasure up at him and ignored his dramatic eye-roll.

"Oh, Steve, that's the best news I've had all week. We'll have to keep up the healthy eating and don't think I don't know about those beers you sneak or the burgers you try to hide from me on my days off." Winking at him, I stretched my wrists.

"I don't know what you're talkin' bout. I'd never hide somethink like that from you." His attempt at an innocent face was terrible.

"Uh-huh." Standing, I stretched cramped legs.

"You never told me how your day off last week was? Get up to mischief?"

"I was enjoying a quiet night in with the TV before Cassandra decided it would be a smart idea to drag me to Jared and Desmond's house party. Let's just say the evening was a complete and utter disaster that had me puking my guts up on the front lawn, while a person I thought was a stranger, but turned out to be an old acquaintance, held my hair back," I shuddered.

It was not a moment I wanted to remember.

"What are we discussing?" The smokey voice of preceded a tall silhouette behind Steve.

"Evening, Mel. We were just discussing my disastrous night off last Saturday," I greeted.

Steve made way for Mel, who found a seat at the guest chair in front of my desk.

Mel, our resident live mummy as she liked to call herself — she was only fifty — was one of four forensic assistants and personally one of my favourites. Before transferring to our department, she'd been an ED Nurse. Her reason for the transfer was simple — less drama, angry drunks, or druggies coming in out of their minds. Plus, she didn't need to listen to the perpetual whinging of disgruntled patients complaining about the service or lack thereof.

Her tall, willowy frame was accentuated by a shock of short auburn hair that had only just started greying. Her frank and to the point attitude rubbed a lot of the staff up the wrong way, but I found it endearing.

Steve shook his head. "Did you drink too much? Cause you know you can't hold your liquor, girly."

"I hadn't even made it through one drink before I passed out," I muttered, massaging my temples.

I left the rest of the evening's events out, as I still hadn't dissected and examined them.

"You think someone drugged you? Because I hear that's happening a bit around here. Do you remember everything that happened before and after the party?" Mel's concern was echoed in Steve's now stiff posture.

"No, I don't think someone drugged me. Ellie had the same reaction I did and Brad was with us the entire time. The old acquaintance happened to be at the same party at the right time. Truth be told, I still feel off and haven't been able to keep anything substantial down all week, not to mention the lack of sleep. Hence, the lack of dinner this evening. I couldn't get past the smell of the raw food to even start cooking the stuff," I groaned.

"Bugger the food, you should probably go on up to the Emergency Department and get yourself checked out in case it's somethink serious. How's Ellie doin?" Ducking his head out as he spoke, Steve checked that the hallway and entry were still empty.

"Ellie seems to be faring better than I am. But she holed herself up in bed with a migraine on Sunday. I'll get myself checked out if I'm still the same tomorrow. Now go finish your rounds before we both get into trouble. Oh, and what did you feel like for dinner tonight, my shout?"

Sitting back down at the desk, I made myself comfortable once again.

"Don't be silly. We can chip in. How about we order something from that Asian place you like? They use fresh ingredients, don't they? It might be easier on your stomach," Mel suggested.

"That's a superb idea; I'll order now."

Nodding, Steve said his goodbyes and left Mel and I to start our debrief on what had and hadn't been done during Desmond's shift.

Order completed, Mel and I were 10 minutes into our meeting when the phone rang. The light indicated it was an internal call.

I snatched at the phone and my greeting brisk. "Doctor Sheperd, how can I help?"

"Doctor Sheperd, you have incoming. Dan just pulled up at gates." One of the female security guards answered.

If Dan was here, that meant it was a Dead On Arrival. I wondered who the Detective or Officer in Charge on duty was.

I hung up. "We have incoming, Mel."

Mel rose swiftly and exited the office heading towards the loading bay, ready to buzz Dan and the officers into the secure loading bay.

An email alert popped up on my computer, the coroner's name in bold. I clicked on it and read the instructions to perform a full autopsy on the body being handed over this evening.

Mmm, that was quick and a full autopsy to boot. A suspected homicide it is then.

Exiting my office, I headed for the change rooms. I made quick work of swapping over to scrubs and entered the mortuary, ready for handover.

By the time I arrived the stretcher was already in the fridge, waiting to be pushed into the morgue. The body lay hidden beneath a standard blue zip-up body bag.

Noting my entry, Dan and his newest assistant heaved the trolley into the morgue.

Unease hit me, my stomach churning at what lay beneath the bag. Something was very wrong with the body hidden beneath that blue plastic. I'd never had this kind of reaction to a body before.

It hit me then that this wasn't your average death; something violent and unnatural had happened to this man before he died. From where I stood I could feel he was a young male, but other than that, I couldn't tell much else.

The good thing was that the soul was no longer in the body, I realised with relief.

Mel wasn't far behind the men and within a minute of my arrival, she was at my elbow, paperwork in hand. Behind her followed Detective Bernard and some new detective, I didn't recognise.

"Hey Doc, got some work for you. You wanna do the honours before we do our handover?" Dan called out cheerfully as he wiggled his eyebrows at me, completely at odds with the setting.

For a funeral director, he always seemed to be in a pleasant mood. He'd been that way since the first time I'd met him at seventeen.

Detective Bernard nodded his hello, as everyone waited for my okay.

I threw my arms into the air in pretend exasperation and Mel sniggered in anticipation. "Oh fine! Put the body on the table and let's get on with it."

It didn't worry me that much doing something that made their night a little more interesting and light-hearted. I wasn't sure how both the newbies would handle it, though. Most thought I was full of it.

"We'll be in the viewing room, Doc. You know it freaks me out when you do that shit," Detective Bernard shuddered before leaving the room with his offsider in tow.

Plastic creasing and slithering echoed around the empty room and the thud of the body hitting the autopsy table resounded off the icy grey walls. Dan and his young male assistant stepped back from the body, waiting by the now-empty stretcher. Mel continued to fill out the paperwork required for the chain of custody hand over, while Detective Bernard and the new detective stood at the viewing window.

Clapping my hands together for show, I placed them over the top of the closed bag. Shutting my eyes, I drifted upwards towards that place within my mind that housed my memories in my mind's eye.

A wall with a window in the centre of it greeted me. Looking through the glass, a body floated in the centre of the room beyond.

There was a black door to my left, but I avoided looking at it — even as the doorknob rattled ominously.

I'd only ever opened that door once, and even then, it was only a crack. That night in the hospital carpark three and a half years ago had taught me to put extra locks on the door and to never approach it unless I was dying.

I drew my attention back to the body behind the window; the many doors in various colours and size within the circular room now forgotten.

The body was in early decomposition, with the abdomen deflated.

I frowned and mentally pulled the body upright as if it were a puppet on invisible strings. The body was that of a biracial male in his early twenties with a height of approximately 5'7".

The translucent image hovering over the length of the body allowed me to glimpse what he would have looked like before death.

Plus, markers such as the low root and large width of the nasal cavity, and the hyperbolic palate, showcased his African ancestry; while his angular eye orbits with a straight profile hinted at some form of Caucasian in his family.

His umber hair was shaved into a fade so you only caught a glimpse of its colour. His once brown eyes had since clouded over in death. I turned the mental image of him around so I could see the back of him.

A gasp stalled the air in my lungs and a chill shot down my spine.

My eyes took precious seconds to make sense of the mess that was now his back. Most of his thoracic vertebrae were exposed as if something had forced his skin to explode outwards. His rib cage gleamed white amongst the dried blood and tissue.

I flipped him back around to check his chest for an entry wound.

Strange, there's none. Where the hell is it? That's an exit wound, I'm sure of it.

Mel called out to me from a distance, her voice echoing in my mind.

It was time to head back. I'd seen enough — for now.

I allowed the room within my mind to fade and returned to the glare of reality. Breathing in deeply, the familiar soothing scent of antiseptic filled my lungs.

Eyes still shut, I recited my findings, starting with the appearance of the unidentified male.

Reaching the cause of death, I paused for a second before announcing, "Cause of death undeterminable until an internal examination is completed. There's sixteen-millimetre wound along his thoracic vertebrae, all signs suggest it's an exit wound. There's no entry wound at the front, so further examination is needed. Time of death could be roughly six to nine days ago, but further information and examination will be needed."

Shaking my head, I reached out for the bottle of chilled water I knew Mel had waiting for me. I still hadn't opened my eyes — I wouldn't, not until my heart had steadied and I'd had a long sip of water.

After a couple of more seconds and one more sip, I opened my eyes to see Detective Bernard and Steve standing beside Mel and Dan. I frowned at their solemn expressions.

"What? What's wrong?" I cleared my throat, hoping it would get rid of the tremor in it.

"Nothin', Doc, you got it right. It's just that… well, you went awfully pale and deathly still. We thought we might have to put you on a stretcher or something," Steve fussed.

Mel shuddered.

Steve continued speaking, his voice gruff with worry, "I yelled, clapped; heck, I even shouted into your ear and couldn't get you to come out of wherever you went. Even Detective Bernard tried yelling. Nothing seemed to work. You scared the hell out of us."

Mel knelt beside me, her hand finding my arm. "I'd like to check your pulse and do a quick examination if you're okay with it?"

She spoke as if I were a wounded deer who might bolt at any second, which was probably true considering my hatred for being examined. The incessant beeping and whirring of cardiac and blood pressure monitors never failed to transport me to the night I'd said goodbye to my father.

I still had nightmares of an ominous shadow tugging at the steering wheel of my father's car, forcing it to veer off the road and over the edge of the cliff. The crunch of metal and the shattering of glass pierces my ears, as my Dad's hoarse screams shred my heart.

The dream felt more like flashbacks than nightmares most nights, which wasn't possible, as my Dad had been alone in the car that night, while I'd been at home.

A cold sweat broke across my brow, panic creeping in just a little.

"I'm fine, guys. Really, I am." Seeing their mouth open in unison, I interrupted Mel, Steve and Detective Bernard before they could say object. "But Mel, if you'd like to do a quick examination, that's fine. This doesn't get filed, and it doesn't leave this room."

I looked at everyone present as I spoke, including the newbies.

"That's fine, sweetie, just let Mel do a quick examination. You're pale and cool to the touch." Steve really must be worried. He was calling me sweetie in front of everyone.

"Evanee, why don't we head to your office, so you can take a seat?" Mel rubbed my shoulder, motioning towards the doors with her other.

"We might grab a coffee until you're all good to go. There still a stash of biscuits in the staff room?" Detective Bernard rocked back on his heels slightly.

Mel nodded and Bernard signalled for the other detective to meet him in the hall.

We made our way back towards my office. The detective and recruit ducked into the staff room and Steve, Mel, and I kept going down the hall.

Doing an internal assessment of how my body felt, nothing seemed to have changed. I'd sit and let Mel fuss over me though, just because I liked her and loved Steve. Besides, they always bought a smile to the morgue when they were on shift.

As I sat down in my office chair, Mel proceeded with a basic check-up, utilising what she had on hand.

I remained silent as she checked my pulse, temperature, and glands.

"You seem to be fine. Your pulse is a bit on the low side, but nothing to worry about. You don't have a fever, but your temperature is on the cool side," Mel's matter-of-fact tone confirmed what I already knew.

"I'm fine. Other than a slight headache and some queasiness, I'm all good." I tried for a reassuring smile. It must have worked because Mel and Steve nodded.

"We'll monitor you this evening just to be safe. We'll be takin our break in about fifteen minutes, anyway. Just waitin on the food delivery. You guys go on ahead and start the preliminaries and I'll let you know when the food arrives." Steve left with a slight wave.

I left my chair and followed Mel out.

The detectives were already in the viewing room, hot coffees in hand.

Studying the body bag, I noticed they had double-bagged the body. Double bags meant liquids.

Never a good sign.

I stopped in front of the instrument table and checked that all the equipment I'd need was present.

I reached for two industrial masks with the two charcoal filters on either side, propping them on the bench near the door. Judging by the double bag, we would need them.

My gut told me this body would keep me busy well into the early hours of the morning, I'd likely not be getting out before Desmond showed up for work.

I was seriously hoping no other bodies dropped tonight; if there were, they would be waiting for Desmond tomorrow morning. My gift to the lazy bastard.

Mel rushed around, setting aside Kevlar gloves; nitrile gloves; sleeve protectors and face visors, while I collected two plastic aprons.

Gear at the ready, I was selecting a body chart ready for the notes when Steve knocked at the locker room door.

He wagged a finger at me before loudly admonishing me, "Hey Doc, no slicing until you've eaten something. I don't want to have to come in there and pick you up off the floor when you're covered in dead people juices."

Yeah, like that's going to happen. I've never fainted a day in my life. Okay, except for the other night, but you can't even call that fainting because I was semi-aware of what was going on around me. Damit all to hell!

"It's all good, I would never do that to you. I love you too much." I winked at Steve before I blew him a sly kiss.

Nodding at the Forensic photographer and her assistant, who'd just entered, I stepped aside allowing them better access to the body.

"Will you all be okay for 30 minutes? I just need a quick bite before starting on the body," I checked.

"You're all good, Doc," She confirmed as she unzipped her camera bag.

Mel and I exited the morgue, silently removing our gumboots in favour of something more comfortable.

Inside the staff room, I pulled three bottles of water from the fridge while Mel and Steve deposited plastic cutlery and containers full of the world's best-smelling food onto the little round table.

Steve beamed when he came across the Mustard Leaf Rolls I'd ordered.

My thoughts returned to the events of the previous Saturday and tonight's drama. I still didn't understand why I'd passed out as I had. There was nothing medically wrong with me — was there?

The feeling I'd gotten just before my episode, as if my body were trying to separate in two different directions, still had me perplexed. I understood the darkness of the oblivion was my body's way of dealing with the pain I'd been experiencing, but the other direction was a little harder to decipher.

Before departing my mind's round room, I'd noticed a golden coloured line with hues of pink strands interwoven between the gold at the centre of the room. I appeared to extend up through the mirrored roof.

My room was astonishing, even to me. There were hundreds of doors, yet they all seemed to fit within the round room. As I made fresh memories or nightmares, a new door appeared, usually reflecting the memory.

For instance, memories of my father and his death were sealed behind a beautifully crafted Tulip Oak door with an antique brass door handle, sturdy yet warm — just as my father had been in life. A wall of water guarded the door, the water in perpetual motion and the door never tarnishing or degrading.

Reaching into the memories didn't hurt; they felt beautiful and soothing, just as water could feel soothing against aching muscles.

There were only two doors that were barred in my mind — the black door that had the silver line emitting from the centre, and the one beside it that housed the nightmare from so many years ago.

The black door had an ancient feeling to it, as if it'd existed well before my time and would continue to exist long after I died. An antique copper handle with delicate swirls etched into it. The swirls reminded me of fog stirred by a gentle breeze, so delicate yet always falling back into place when the wind left.

The door to the left of it was the opposite in every way. Where most of the doors in my mind were beautiful wooden creations, the wood of this door was swollen and rotted. There was no beautiful handle; instead, a piece of string looped around a rusted hook just to the side of the frame held the door in place. It was the most unstable door in my mind — a thing of nightmares — and that string securing the door often snapped, allowing the horrors to escape and torment me until I could repair the damage.

"What are you thinkin bout, sweetie?" Looking up, I found Steve searching my face, a slight frown in place.

He looked like a father might when he knew something was wrong but wasn't sure how to fix it.

"Old horrors," I murmured. "You ever wish you could wave a magic wand and make some memories or events disappear?" I sighed, tired of carrying my burden and the guilt on my own, never being able to trust those I held so dear to me with my past.

The thought that I may never share that dreadful night with anyone made my heartache. How could I share it with someone I loved when more than half of what happened was beyond what science could explain? How could I expect anyone to forgive me when the guilt ate at my very soul?

Steve sat a little straighter, his eyes catching and holding mine. "Evanee, listen to me. Sometimes the worst events in our lives happen not ta cripple us, but ta strengthen what's already inside us. We can't always see it cause we're too busy tryin' to survive."

When he put it like that, I saw the logic in what he was saying.

"Are you talking about the old saying '*what doesn't kill me, only makes me stronger*'?" I cringed.

I detested the proverb. Not all horrors in our lives made us stronger, sometimes they crippled us for a time, only for us to heal to exactly the way we were before. Yeah, okay, we may be wiser, but that doesn't necessarily always mean stronger.

"Yes and no. We don't always become stronger, but we learn from the experiences and it teaches us somethin' new bout ourselves." Steve tapped the fork in his hand to his head.

This man had watched me grow from a shy, smart-arse teenage girl into a jaded, angry and sometimes sad woman.

I had a snarky comment ready to go but decided that keeping my mouth shut was the best option.

"One day, when you're ready and feel safe, you and I will sit down for a drink and you can tell me what happened to you on the Gold Coast. You came back a shell of the young women I used ta know. Now and again I see her peeking through, and it makes me laugh. I miss her and hope you let her come back when you're ready." Hurt laced his blue eyes, and I clenched my jaw against the pain lacing through my heart.

Enough, you are stronger than this. Get your shit together, girl! No one wants to see you cry.

"I miss her too," I murmured. "Maybe one day she won't feel so scared to come out. I'll think about that offer, Steve. Thanks for that."

Swiping at my cheeks with my right hand, I stood, glancing at the digital clock above the couch.

"But until then, Mel and I have a body to autopsy."

CHAPTER 6

It was days like today I was grateful for my brief training in Forensic Anthropology.

I stood suited up, industrial-grade mask and protective goggles hiding my features. Looking at the gaping wound in my patient's back, I knew there would be more than just flesh and organs for this autopsy. These bones held a story of their own and would need further in-depth investigation.

The decayed flesh surrounding the wound indicated the wound was indeed an exit point and not the point of entry, which made no sense, considering there was no entry wound anywhere on the sternum. I'd gone over it with a fine-tooth comb before I'd flipped the body over.

Staring closely at the exit wound, I searched for any microscopic trace evidence that would give me some sort of clue as to what might have exited the wound.

Mel stood beside me, waiting to take the notes. Both detectives remained silent in the viewing room, their expressions of horror and disgust speaking for themselves.

Staring down at the body, I began the rundown.

"Unidentified male, approximately twenty-two years of age. Appears to be biracial. Height 5'7"." Mel jotted down notes as I spoke, making it a little easier for me to concentrate solely on what I was doing.

I'd be doing up my notes after I'd completed the examination.

Frown deepening, I continued to examine the wound, talking aloud as I did. "There's some kind of translucent gelatinous substance coating the exit wound, muscle tissue and visible thoracic vertebras."

I reached for a swab on the tray closest to me and gently ran the white tip along the decayed flesh, before proceeding to swab both muscle tissue and bone. Sealing them, Mel noted the areas I took them from and set them aside for analysis.

I skimmed my gloved finger along the side of the wound, gathering some of the substance. Rubbing my index finger and thumb together, I looked closely at what was now coating my Kevlar glove.

A primal part of me sensed something that had every fibre within me wanting to shrink away from the body on my table.

My birthmark flared sharp and hot, my stomach churned, warning me that whatever I'd stumbled upon was not natural.

I looked on, incredulous when the substance created a small hole at the tip of my finger, the gelatinous substance sizzling its way through the top layer of my Kevlar glove.

"Shit!" Stripping it off, I dumped the glove onto the tray, my nitrile glove not far behind.

"What in the world? I've never seen anything do that to a Kevlar glove, have you?" Mel watched on as the hole in my glove slowly grew wider.

Striding toward the storage cupboard, I grabbed a fresh pair out, quickly making my way back. Slowly re-gloving, four sets of eyes focused on the body.

Then I remembered the swabs.

"Shit. The swabs, Mel."

Staring down at the swabs in question, her raised eyebrows confirmed what I already knew.

They were destroyed.

I think perhaps this might be something for Bob to assist with. Something's not right here.

I made a mental note to email Bob and ask for his assistance. I'd do the initial workup, but I'd wait on Bob to do the full autopsy. He was due to make an appearance in the next day or so.

In the meantime, I'd examine the blood, tissue, and the unidentified substance samples, or what was left of them, while further blood samples could be sent to Brisbane for toxicology.

"Right, Mel, let's get all the samples ready for analysis, and delivery for toxicology. I'll be requesting Bob's help on this one. He is due here within the next day or so, Detectives," I directed at the viewing window. "I'd like another set of eyes in case there's something I'm missing."

Surprised, Mel's eyebrows rose, but she kept quiet.

This was possibly the first time I'd ever admitted I wasn't one hundred percent confident in performing an autopsy without consulting my superior.

There's a first for everything, I guess.

"No worries, Doc," the Detective's voice buzzed through the intercom. "We'll leave you to it. I'll keep an eye out for updates. Night ladies."

The detectives made a quick exit and Mel busied herself labelling and bagging samples, as I continued my external examination.

We'd need to find a metal container of some sort to contain the Kevlar glove and ruined swabs. Plastic would not contain whatever had eaten through that glove.

~

My concentration was complete. World War III could have started around me and I wouldn't have noticed — it was always this way. My concentration on the task at hand overrode all sense of time and bodily functions, which was why it was entirely weird when the tingling warmth of my birthmark shattered the sanctity that was my escape from the real world.

Straightening my shoulders, I rolled my neck, gently arching my back and looking around the room wearily.

Mel stood beside the table, absorbed in her task at hand. Her concentration was still intact.

A movement in the viewing window drew my attention. Steve appeared at the edge of the window, talking animatedly to someone standing behind him. The mystery person glided into view, and my eyebrows rose.

"Hey Doc," Steve chuckled over the intercom, "I found this stray wandering round out the front, looking for someone called Doctor Death."

Mel looked towards the window, then back at me, eyebrows just as high as mine had been. The cheeky grin radiating from Steve's friendly face was a dead giveaway that he was up to no good. We were in the midst of an autopsy, and Steve knew only authorised personal were allowed back here, during an autopsy.

What is he up to?

"Hmm, Doctor Death, you say? Well, he certainly came to the right place. You tell him what happens to strays who wander into my parlour?"

"Yeah Doc, I warned him you liked to have a bit of fun with your patients before you sent them on their way. Tough man here reckons he could handle anything you throw at him," Steve baited.

"Ooh, tough man. Perhaps we should tell him what happened to the last two guests who came looking for Doctor Death, hey Mel?" I smirked beneath my mask.

Gently draping a cloth over the instruments on the tray, Mel shook her head at our foolhardiness.

Chuckling, I looked towards our guest. "Erick, you shouldn't listen to everything Steve tells you. If he had it his way every visitor, staff or not, would think I was

Death re-incarnate." Looking at Mel I continued, "I think we've gotten all we can off of him for now, Mel. Could you please place this gentleman in the cold-room?"

"Yes, Doctor Sheperd." She seemed glad to leave our interactions behind and quickly did as asked.

Disposing of my gloves, I clomped towards the change room doors, removing my gumboots at the door.

"Steve, could you please show Erick to my office? I'll be with you shortly," I called out not waiting to see if he did as I asked.

My protective gear and scrubs would need to be removed before I trekked through to the office. I didn't want to see him while smelling of dead people.

Entering the change rooms, I pulled my mask off and hung it beside the door for later use. Slipping into my comfortable shoes, I shuffled out.

"Erick," I greeted as I entered my office and saw the two men sitting in front of my desk. "What's brought you to my neck of the woods?"

I stood at the doorway and breathed deeply to calm my racing heart. The man had that effect on me. And I'd be damned if I'd let him see it.

"Is this how you guys keep yourselves occupied on quiet nights then, murdering innocent visitors and dissecting them?" He greeted back, a slight twinkle lighting his gorgeous green eyes.

"Oh yes. If you're lucky we kill you first," I smirked, leaning against the door frame.

The corner of his delectable mouth lifted ever so slightly.

Mmm, I bet he'd taste better than spiced rum. That delectable hint of vanilla and spices. Okay, this train of thought is not getting me anywhere. I need to stop eye shagging the poor man's mouth before he notices.

"So, Erick, what can I really help you with?"

I scooted around the desk and dropped into my swivel chair. My feet ached, courtesy of the four hours I'd just spent on them.

"How are you doing? Are you and Ellie feeling better since last Saturday? You seem to have recovered," Erick observed politely.

He seemed to live in a constant state of politeness.

Steve stood quietly, muttering about continuing his rounds and that he'd check on me later before he left the office.

I waived Steve off before addressing Erick's questions. "Ellie has recovered, I believe. She was slightly off-kilter for a day or two, as you can imagine. I've recovered just fine, thank you."

Liar, liar, pants on fire. Yay, seventeen-year-old me, had come out of her room.

Oh, shut it, he doesn't need to know that I've felt as if I've drunk the local pub's entire stock of booze and then run a marathon.

The snooty little cow always found the most inappropriate moment to pop her nosy head up.

"Good, that's good," Erick agreed amicably.

After a moment of silence, he shifted slightly in the chair. "I came here for two reasons, to be honest. I was hoping you might help me figure out a few incidents that were reported to me and perhaps provide me with some information on your friend Ellie?"

"Okay, what sort of help are you after? I must tell you though, with Ellie, if it's something she wouldn't tell you herself, I won't be telling you. Privacy and all," I said with forced calm.

I prayed my features were as neutral as I imagined them to be. I didn't want him knowing how much it hurt, feeling overlooked, even if that's exactly what I believed I wanted.

"You're a loyal friend, I like that," He smiled.

Why do I care so much about what he thinks of me? I berated myself.

I returned his smile, before politely saying, "Thanks. Now let's get to the questions you want answering, that way we can both get on with our night." My impatience was obvious, and I winced a little.

"I've had a few members of my entourage die under mysterious circumstances. They were reported missing to me by their partners or superiors before we found them dead. Even with my extensive knowledge of weapons and their impact on the body, I can't determine what has caused their deaths or left their bodies the way they were left. My on-board doctor is also stumped, and that's saying something. I've also been unable to determine where they were prior to their deaths."

"Why not go through the proper authorities? It's not as if I can perform an autopsy on any of your entourage within this facility," I pointed out.

"The local authorities won't be able to assist with this matter, as not all of the deceased are Australian citizens," Erick enlightened me.

"Well that is fair enough, why not report it to the relevant consulates?"

"That's where it becomes tricky." He didn't offer any further information, and I assumed he wouldn't no matter how hard I pressed.

"Well, as I said, there's not much I can do for you here. Bob would have a heart attack, not to mention the hospital's management."

Erick nodded. "I still retain the clearance Bob attained for me during his time here. You might not know this, but I helped him with cases from time to time, so I doubt he'd mind me asking for your help too much. As for the hospital's management, I can see how they might be an issue. I'd prefer if this issue was dealt with by as few people as possible." He fell silent, and I waited patiently for him to suggest how he'd like to proceed. "Let me think about the issue, and I'll get back to you."

"That's fine with me. You also mentioned wanting to know a little more about Ellie?" I prompted.

"Ah yes, I did too. How much do you know much about Miss Anam and her family and where they come from?" His question took me by surprise for a second.

Why on earth would he want to know about Ellie and her family?

"I'm afraid I don't know much. Ellie doesn't like to talk about her family a lot. The only thing I can tell you is that all of her family has some sort of military background. I believe she mentioned that her family's roots trace back to Ireland. Otherwise, that's all I can help you with, I'm afraid. You'd need to ask her yourself, but I will warn you she not inclined to talk about her immediate family." I shrugged.

Ellie had told me a little more about her family one drunken evening. They hadn't been thrilled with the fact that she'd had no inclination to work with the military. They were even more disappointed at the fact that she preferred to develop anti-viruses for private corporations than create viruses.

Truth be told, it wasn't that she couldn't develop viruses, she simply preferred the challenge that came with developing a cure to them. She'd heartbreakingly confessed how they'd accused her of going against her very nature; which I found completely odd, as she was the kindest and most genuine person I knew aside from Brad.

Erick nodded as though he understood. "I see. How long have the two of you been friends?"

Why couldn't he just ask her these questions?

I sighed. "We've been friends for around two years now. We met when we both came to work here. It's how I met Brad, too. We've been best friends since. Why do you want to know?"

There goes that damn curiosity again.

"No specific reason, I was simply hoping to get to know you all a little better." His hesitation had me wondering what it was he wasn't asking or telling me.

"Oh, really. Well, no offence, but I call bull. There's something else you're after, so out with it." Crossing my arms over my chest, I inspected the beautiful man sitting so elegantly across from me.

"Maybe another time." He avoided meeting my eyes, and I frowned. "I think I should head off. Thank you for the help, and I hope we can arrange for you to inspect my colleagues soon."

I nodded. "Sounds like a plan to me."

CHAPTER 7

Walking into work late Monday afternoon, the tantalising scent of fresh-baked lasagne and caramel topped vanilla cheesecake surrounded me, smelling better than any expensive perfume ever could.

I'd brought it in for Steve, myself and Bob this evening after I'd received a text from Bob on Sunday indicating he'd be up today to assist with the autopsy, and chat with Desmond about the issues I'd been experiencing.

Frankly, I was happy to hand this autopsy over to him. I'd scoured every one of my medical textbooks and my limited supply of Forensic Anthropology textbooks, hoping I'd forgotten something. Searching the net and pouring through medical and forensic journals had gotten me no closer to finding an answer.

I had no idea what sort of weapon might cause the damage to my charges back without some kind of entry wound. Then there was the acidic residue that'd eaten its way through my Kevlar glove and the swabs we'd taken. To say I was peeved was an understatement.

Juggling the armful of goodies through the double doors, Steve stood on the other side, a grin lighting his full-face when he caught sight of the goodies I was carrying.

"Evening Doc, what ya got there?" Sniffing the air, he tried to identify this evening's dinner.

"Dinner and dessert. Nuh-uh, Steve, I don't think so," I admonished, shifting the lasagne out of his reach and turning to give him the cooler bag I had looped over my left arm instead. "If you want to take something off my hands, I suggest you start with this. Less temptation for you."

His deep bellied laughter echoed through the hall and he relieved me of the cooler bag.

Reaching the staff room doors, Steve reached across and depressed the handle.

Time slowed seemed to slow, Steve's hand moving in slow motion as my birthmark tingled to life.

My head turned, and I stared down the hall towards the morgue, pins piercing at my lower back. Waves of pain, anger, and torment slammed into me, pushing me back a step before I realised I'd even moved.

Thinking of a steel wall, I slammed it in place and came back to myself. It'd taken years to practice this technique, yet I was finding it more and more difficult to do since the party last Saturday. Something had changed since then.

"Did we get any new bodies in today, Steve?" My body weighed down by some unseen force.

Steve frowned at me. "Yeah, actually we did."

Nodding at him, I withdrew into myself, leaving my body on autopilot, Knowing

I approached my mind's viewing window and studied the corpse floating before me. A thin layer of mist covered the body, obscuring it.

Weird.

Envisioning the glass gone, I pursed my lips and blew gently to disperse the mist. When it'd slowly trickled into nothingness, my breath caught at the sight of the decomposed body hovering before me.

I studied the cocoa brown withered membrane that'd replaced the once youthful fair skin. My gaze travelled south, noting the chest and pubic bone that confirmed the woman's sex. Gaze travelling back up, horror dawned and my breath hitched when I noticed a slight glimmer from within the decayed form.

Holy crap, her soul! It's still trapped!

How the hell was her soul still trapped in there? It should have released the minute, if not long after she had died. Judging by the state of decomposition, she'd been dead for at least six days, or possibly longer!

The glimmering soul was no bigger than a fifty-cent piece.

A soul's colour depended on what type of person they'd been in life. If you were a saint, your soul took on an almost luminescent pearl colour; if you were evil, then it was likely to take on the colour of blood. Not the stuff where it's a lovely bright red from all the oxygen, but that dark blood you get once it's done a circulation around your body and all the good stuff has been sucked from it.

It was rare to have a soul still a sold pearl colour, unless it was an infant who was yet to make decisions that would affect it.

Looking at this poor women's soul trapped within that decaying structure, I knew instinctively there was something very wrong with this soul.

Until I got closer to the body, in reality, I wouldn't be able to tell exactly what was wrong.

The hairs at the base of my skull stood at attention.

Raising my hands, palms up, the corpse rose further into the air. I turned my palms forward and as I rotated my wrists, the body turned in the air before me. Knowing what I would find at her back, there was no shock or horror when the wound finally come into view.

Lowering my fingers on both hands, the body returned to its horizontal position.

What are the odds of having two bodies with the same wounds within a week of each other?

A boom resonated through the viewing room, followed by a burning sensation along the side of my cheek.

Ouch, what the hell!

The booming noise came again, as the burning sensation in my right cheek blossomed again. I could hear Steve's voice yelling from somewhere outside my trance. Stepping back from where the viewing window had been, I let go of my connection with the room in my mind.

I came back to myself to find I was sitting in one of the lounge chairs in the staff room, with Steve kneeling before me, a look of concern causing the wrinkles around his eyes to deepen. Bob paced behind him, his eyes never leaving my face.

"Ouch! Please don't hit me again," I winced.

I rubbed at the hot spot on my rosy cheek, kicking myself for not realising how long I'd spent within my mind.

"I won't slap you if you don't do that again. What the hell happened, Doc? One minute you were there, the next you were gone. Your skin's like ice again," Steve growled, his fingers digging into my upper arms.

Oddly enough, his body heat didn't faze me as much as Brad's had the other night.

"You still playing that guessing game, Evie? I thought we decided you wouldn't do that when I wasn't around?" Bob groused, his worry washing over me.

"Good to see you too, boss. Sorry," I muttered ruefully, still rubbing at my cheek. "I didn't mean to check out on you guys. I'm fine now, I promise. We got a fresh homicide, didn't we?" My hands slid up to my temples, and I massaged them in slow circles.

"In a manner of speaking, yeah, we did. I won't bother asking how you know; although, one day you will have to explain exactly how your little psychic trick works, cause it's one hell of a party trick." Bob removed his newest pair of glasses from his oval face and began compulsively cleaning them.

"Yeah, let's not go there. If I knew how I did it, I'd start peddling it to make extra cash to pay for the many renovations my poor little house needs. So, have you examined the body yet?" I looked expectantly at Bob, and he didn't keep me waiting long.

"Not yet, no. We got the body in about an hour ago. We held off until you got in. I know how you love the weird and wacky cases." Bob replaced his glasses and attempted what I assumed was his best attempt at a stern look.

He failed and instead opened his arms, stepping towards me and bending slightly at the waist to give me my customary greeting.

I hugged him tightly, never wanting to let go. He was the closest thing I had to father, and I'd missed him. I'd been too ashamed to be in his presence for too long, the shame and guilt eating at me.

"It's good to see you again, baby girl," Bob gave up on trying for a stern appearance. "You're looking a little on the tired side, you been getting enough rest?" Good old Uncle Bob, always looking out for me.

My heart thawed just a little at his affection.

"Good to see you too, Uncle Bob. Work's been a bit on the hectic side lately. I need to talk to you about a few issues that have been cropping up all over the place here. There are a few dealings that I'm concerned about." My hand patted his back as I spoke quietly.

Pulling back, Bob looked me in the eyes; whatever he saw there had his forehead crinkling, adding at least five years to his handsome face.

"Sure, baby girl, we'll have a chat about it after we're done having a look at your mystery body and this new one," he agreed, his smile not reaching his eyes.

He was worried about what I had to talk to him about. I never rocked the boat at work. I came in, did my job and then left.

"Great. Now on a positive note, I brought in dinner and dessert for us tonight. Do you have somewhere to stay after your shift, or do you need the spare room at my place again?" Standing, I made my way towards the food, unloading the cheesecake and salad into the mini-fridge as I spoke.

"That's okay, Marg is coming to pick me up. She's visiting with some friends in the city while I'm up here. Thanks for the offer, though. She sends her love by the way and wants to know when you'll be coming to visit us, or when we can come and visit you?" Bob stood aside, before following me as I finished my pre-shift ritual.

Place food away, put my lab coat on, net my hair and do stretches to limber up. I'd skipped the stretches the other evening and regretted it the next day.

"I'll be sure to take a weekend off to come and see you guys. I've missed seeing Aunty Marg. I'd love for you both to come and see my house. I've finished the inside at last. I'm actually thinking of tackling the back yard now."

"I'm plannin on being outta town for this particular DIY project, Bob. It's a bloody death trap. There are wild animals livin back there, I swear," Steve said wryly and I stuck my tongue out at him.

Despite his words, Steve would be there. He couldn't help himself.

"Don't you start, Steve," I giggled. Finally limbered up, I looked to Bob. "Well, shall we go and see the bodies? I'm keen to see what you have to say about the initial body, Bob."

"Andrea is prepping the room for us. I'm quite intrigued by this body that has you so stumped. You've not been wrong about a cause of death since the day Old Man Hughes came in. Oh, those were the days, when the teacher actually had something to teach the student," Bob sighed happily.

I rolled my eyes towards the ceiling and plucked my gumboots from my locker, kicking off my black and silver joggers before slipping a foot into each boot.

"Hey! I didn't get his death wrong. I just didn't take into account the fact that he'd hit his head on the way down. The heart attack was still fatal," I objected snootily.

I smiled to myself, knowing he was never going to let me live that one down.

"Yeah, yeah. I'm still counting it as a win," his laughter bounced merrily off the cool walls of the change rooms.

Entering the morgue, I was grateful Andrea had already set aside the gear we would need to perform the examination.

"Fine, you can have it. Now, wait here while I help Andrea get the first body out *old man*." I just couldn't resist baiting him.

"Hey! Who you calling old, missy?" Chuckling at his indignation, I continued my path towards the freezer.

Sliding the door open, I stood aside as a gush of chilled air barrelled out faster than a bull at the Festival San Fermin.

"Evening, Andrea. How are you?" I smiled as my second favourite forensic assistant re-entered the morgue and came to stand beside me.

"Really good, Dr Sheperd," She grinned.

Stepping into the two-way freezer, we extracted the body from his resting place, the hushed crinkling of the plastic filling the still air. Tugging at the blue plastic, we slid the tray holding the weighted body onto the steel trolley.

Damn, this sucker's heavy. Frustration had me puffing my breath out harshly. *This is nonsense. No way am I this stuffed after hauling one damned corpse. Must be from my space out.*

"So, let's see what this gentleman has to say. I only managed to get a glance at the other body as it came in late this afternoon. Let's just say fluids are not going to be an issue, but we'll deal with that when we get to the new body," Bob huffed as we pulled the trolley to a stop, reaching our designated bay.

I opted to use double Nitrile gloves on each hand as opposed to just my left this time. Slipping the Kevlar gloves over the top, I looked up to find Bob staring at me oddly.

"You're going to want to double glove for this one. There was an acidic residue at the exit wound. It burned through my Kevlar glove before I got it off," I warned him.

Eyebrows shooting towards his hairline, he didn't argue. Instead, Bob tugged on two Nitrile gloves before popping on his Kevlar.

I grabbed ahold of the corner of the blue plastic firmly, the familiar whizzing of the zip releasing each metal tooth echoing throughout the room.

Beside us, Andrea stood at the ready.

I took a deep breath before I said, "Righto. Here we go. Andrea, could you read out my findings, please?"

Andrea nodded and began the run-through of the basic information as Bob inspected the front of the body, identifying any marks Andrea referred to.

When he finished, Bob nodded, standing back as Andrea and I flipped the male over onto his front. We wedged rolled towels beneath his neck and forehead and stood back to look at the wound that had left me so perplexed. What I saw had me cursing five ways to Sunday.

"What the hell! The wound… it's doubled in size, but that's not possible. The body's been refrigerated since Saturday night," I fumed.

"Are you sure, Evanee? What were the last measurements you took?" Bob queried as I reached for the measuring tape on the metal bench-top and quickly took new measurements.

Exasperated, I bent over the wound to measure it.

"Bob, the damned hole measured sixteen centimetres on Saturday. What's it now... thirty, maybe thirty-one centimetre," I seethed.

I looked up at my mentor, clenching my teeth against my frustration, praying he had some idea what was going on.

I could feel the beginnings of a headache starting to set in at the base of my skull.

"Don't look at me, Evie. Your guess is as good as mine. You said the substance was acidic, so did you try neutralising the acid before replacing the body in the freezer?" Staring at me over the body, Bob was a picture of calm and collected.

I frowned for a second. "No, I didn't think I would need to. I thought the cold temperatures of the freezer 'd neutralise it. Hold on, let me see what we have lying around that might help stop the spread."

Racing to the chemical cupboard, I searched for some Sodium Hydroxide.

Shit, there's nothing here. How is there no freaking Sodium Hydroxide? Think, Evanee, what else neutralises acids?

I turned and looked around the morgue.

A thought struck me after a moment and I jogged towards the change room door, dumping my Kevlar gloves onto the bench-top near the door, not bothering to remove my boots. It wasn't like we'd started cutting or anything.

Finally clunking into the staff room, I pulled open the little cupboards beneath the sink.

There, straight in front of me, was my saving grace. I snatched up the cardboard box and raced back into the morgue, lifting the small blue and white cardboard box into the air as if it were the key to world peace.

"Got it! Baking Soda; it should hopefully slow the corrosion — if not stop it."

Shaking some white powder into my nitrile gloved palm, I placed the box on the instrument trolley.

Bob and Andrea looked on sceptically as I sprinkled the baking soda over the area. Bubbles burst to life wherever the powder touched, hissing and foaming as if it were a rabid mutt.

"I think we can re-bag this body and get it ready for shipping," Bob said, with an odd note to his voice.

He wasn't so unaffected as I'd thought.

"I'll be taking it down to Brisbane with me. I don't know what that substance is and I'm not willing to expose any of you to it any further. Let's triple bag this body just in case," Bob ordered.

Together we replaced the body into his original body bag, noting that there was indeed a hole at the bottom where the acid had eaten through. Securing an additional two bags in place, we replaced the corpse in the fridge.

Bob and Andrea meandered over to the unidentified female's body still housed in her blue bag. Together they hauled her onto a gurney and wheeled her towards the table.

"You ready for this one?" Looking over his shoulder at me, light shone in the depths of Bob's eyes.

He was excited about this one. Hell, I think he was excited about the whole damn evening working on corpses, who by the looks of things, had a rather exciting story to tell. Truth be told, I was a bit excited as well. I didn't get to exercise my skills beyond the usual heart attack, poisoning, and maybe a homicide or two.

I approached the steel table, my stomach beginning to churn. My birthmark flared painfully to life and I winced behind my facemask.

So, you're the one who set me off earlier.

A low buzzing sensation crept its way up my neck to sit heavily at the base of my skull. Nose tingling, my eyes blurred ever so slightly.

Oh, hell no, it can't be? Surely not?

Allowing my eyes to blur fully, a second vision of sorts popped up. It allowed me to see into the body to the spirit was still trapped within.

Looking closely, I could see that my field trip into my mind's room hadn't been wrong. The soul of this poor woman was still trapped within this rotting corpse. Unlike in my mind though, I could now see its true colours.

There was something very wrong with this soul.

It was the usual pearl colour most souls were, with slight flecks of pink for the sins she'd committed in her life. Peering closer, I caught sight of the obsidian cracks, like lightning forks. encasing the outside of the orb. It was as if something had latched onto the soul and begun sucking the energy from it. The wretched thing pulsed, much as you might expect a wound to throb.

I slammed back into reality and retched heavily, horror and disgust overtaking any rational thinking. I made it to the wash-up bays, only just ripping my mask off before I lost it spectacularly.

There goes my chocolate cake from lunch.

"Evanee, are you okay? Sweetie, what is it?" Bob's sturdy grip held me together as my body tried its best to fly apart.

I focused on his hands warming the cold that had snuck around my mental shields, breathing in and out steadily.

I turned my head to the side, whispering so Andrea wouldn't hear what I'd just found. "Bob, there's something very wrong with this female cadaver. Her soul, shit me, her soul... it's... it's as if it was shredded, or something has tried to drain it. It's still trapped in her body and she's in so much pain the thing is throbbing from it. We can't cut her open yet or re-bag her."

"What do you mean her soul's still in there? How do you know?" Bob whispered back.

"I can't explain it right now, but I will explain it all later. It has to do with how I can guess patients' deaths. For now, though, you need to let me help her. She has to let go. Bob, do you have any idea how screwed up that soul is? I've seen nothing like it in my life," I whispered through the tears stinging my eyes.

I bent and rinsed my mouth under the tap, uncaring that it was where we washed our hands post autopsy. Hey, the tubs were probably cleaner than the plates I ate off at home. We disinfected them after every use.

"Okay, but Evanee, you need to explain just what the hell is going on with you once you've finished," he quietly demanded. "I'll be right by your side in case you need me. Although I think this time, we get you a chair, so you won't fall and hurt yourself," he reassured me.

He knew there was no use in arguing with me. I was too damned stubborn for my good.

"Thanks, Boss. Andrea, you're welcome to take your break now if you like. It might take me a little while to recover," I called over my shoulder.

Andrea passed behind us, heading into the staff change rooms.

I replaced my industrial mask and together we approached our newest charge.

I nodded to Bob to unzip the bag, bracing myself for what lay beneath.

The sight was grizzly, even for someone as used to death as I was. Looking at this poor woman's decayed shell and the liquids that were oozing slowly from every orifice, I observed body fluids sitting in the bottom of the bag and I was glad my stomach was empty.

I frowned in confusion. Why had her body appeared differently in my mind to what I was seeing before me? I'd never experienced this issue before. She was far more decayed than I'd first seen.

"Good grief, what the hell is going on with this body? Judging from the decomposition, I'd have said she died quite some time ago, as in weeks. So how are her organs still liquifying?" Bob asked, just as mystified as I was.

I had nothing for him, the only thing I could focus on was that battered soul and the need to help this woman find peace.

I braced myself against the icy steel table, mentally lashing my legs for being a bunch of sissies. Taking a deep breath, I grabbed a hold of the woman's legs while Bob grabbed the upper torso.

"On three?" Bob confirmed.

I nodded my affirmation.

"One, two, three, flip," Bob ordered.

The gaping wound burst into focus before she'd fully touched the surface of the table.

"Look at the size of this wound!" Blood drained from Bob's face and sweat beaded on his forehead.

The wound was worse than the male's, with the patterning around the rib cage almost identical to the wound on the other body.

"Looking at the wound and the bruising, she was very much alive when whatever was in her back expelled," I observed, trying and failing to repress the shiver running up my spine.

There was something different about the rib cage, though; I couldn't be sure, but the markings on the ribs seemed to be positioned differently. I'd look after I had coaxed the soul out.

"Right, you ready for this?" Bob queried wearily.

Not waiting for his response, I shut my eyes and drifted upwards to my round room of doors.

CHAPTER 8

I stood at the centre of my minds' round room, the doors of varying colour and wood surrounding me. Gliding across the carpeted floor towards the wall that held the viewing window, I stopped just shy of it.

Today the viewing window was smaller than usual, with a crisp white door off to the right. Depressing its silver handle, I entered the viewing room with trepidation. I didn't like to come in here unless I had to deal with a trapped soul. The power vibrating within the room scared me.

A radio morphed into being in the top left corner of the room.

Looks like I'll be able to communicate with Bob after all.

"Bob, you there?" My whisper fluttered from my lips quietly, as though I was trying not to disturb the dead woman in front of me from her eternal slumber.

"I'm right here, sweetie. I'm not going anywhere." His voice boomed over an old-fashioned speaker near the window and I cringed.

"Can you lower your voice for me? Everything's amplified in here," I whispered.

Closing the door, I drifted towards the woman's body on the stainless-steel bench. Her body now looked identical to the one inhabiting the morgue, apart from the translucent image encasing the corpse, giving me a glimpse at how the red-haired beauty had looked before her death.

"Will do," Bob's voice came over the radio, quieter this time.

"We have a Caucasian female. She's approximately nineteen years of age, with strawberry blond hair. Height approximately 5' 2". Right, let's see if I can coax her to let go," I muttered distractedly.

I exhaled loudly before gently pushing my cupped hands into the woman's shrivelled chest cavity. There was no physical sensation like you would normally get when you dug into a chest cavity. No suction or wet sounds, just a light tingle similar to the warning you get just before your limb is about to fall asleep.

I cupped the damaged soul tenderly, my fingers barely moving. Images of a petite freckled strawberry blonde child lit the blank wall in front of me, followed by images of a pubescent girl riding her bike. Unfamiliar adult faces appeared, then disappeared just as quickly. These were the positive moments and people within her life. If I didn't hurry, the awful memories would soon follow. It never ended well for me if I experienced a soul's death.

Raising my hands centimetre by centimetre, I pulled them towards the surface of the cavity. The fragile thing in my hands shuddered, warning me it would disintegrate if I tried to pull any further.

My breath stuck in my chest and I stopped dead.

Shit! This isn't working. Plan B it is.

"Hey, it's okay, I won't hurt you. If you'll let me, I'd like to help you find peace. You don't belong here anymore, there's nothing but pain and suffering for you here." My voice echoed within my mind and the morgue.

The orb pulsed hard before going quiet, giving me the impression she wasn't ready to leave yet.

The soul pulsed again in what looked like an attempt to communicate something to me; I just couldn't understand what it was trying to say.

"Look, I can't understand what you are trying to tell me. But if it has anything to do with your death, I can assure you I will try to find out what happened. We'll find out who you are, and I'll find your loved ones to give them closure. I rarely make promises unless I intend to keep them," I crooned at the delicate thing nestled in my fingers, praying it would let me extract it from the shell it was trapped in.

When the orb remained still, I once again tried to extract the soul. This time there wasn't as much resistance.

The soul breached the cavity of the chest before pulsing, halting me once again. An image of something I couldn't quite make sense of slammed into me. Its shape was blurry, yet from what I could make out, resembled something that belonged in a science fiction or horror movie.

What in the hell is that thing?

Pain slammed through my body — her pain. Acid dripped down my spine, my heart seizing from an invisible pressure. Gasping, my body went rigid, and I tried to draw air into tight lungs, all the while gently clutching the orb.

When the pain receded, at last, I gasped, "If that was a part of your death, I'm so, so sorry. I can't begin to fathom the amount of pain you were in. There's a good team of professionals on your case. We'll solve this, you have my word. We won't rest until we've found who or what killed you."

Tears of sorrow and pain trailed down my cheeks. As though satisfied with my promise, the female's soul rose. Reaching the roof of my mind, it paused before bursting into a shower of sparks, like floating embers from a firecracker. Each speck rocketed in a different direction, to what I could only assume were her loved ones. It was beautiful and heartbreaking all at once.

Chest heaving, I sobbed for the young woman taken too soon; for the pain she'd felt and the pain her family would feel.

I dashed my tears away, and I looked back at the body, rage replacing the sadness as I inspected the wound closer this time.

This wasn't done by any weapon I knew, but it certainly felt manmade. The human essence was there, almost as if it were a fingerprint. Yet, there was something else, something not human at all. The peculiar residue it left was unlike anything I'd seen or felt before.

Not only was her body drained of vitality, but whatever did this to her had tried to drain her soul as well. Judging by the state of her body, she'd been a fighter in life — her soul evidence of it. It'd held out where her physical body couldn't.

114

A thought so horrifying it made me shudder occurred to me. If her soul looked like this, what had happened to the young man's soul? All the evidence so far suggested they'd been killed by the same thing.

My voice shaking with anger, I called out, "Bob, can you still hear me?"

I would get these bodies the justice they deserved, come hell or high water.

Bob's disembodied voice crackled through the radio. "Yeah Evie, I can still hear you. Did the soul leave?"

"Yeah, it did. But whatever did this was the same thing that killed the other unidentified. It's not a weapon we've seen. Jane imprinted an image before leaving, but it was fuzzy; at least I hope it was. From what I felt, this weapon or thing it enters through the back attaches to the spine while latching onto the ribs. It somehow impacts the heart, making it feel as if there is an intense pressure that could perforate the organ at any moment. Hell, Bob, I've never felt anything so intense or painful. I'll take a closer look at the spine and rib cage. There was something different from John's rib cage," I puzzled.

Not waiting for his response, I touched the girl's shoulder and stepped back, motioning for the body to rise. As it rose, my hands mimicked a crab's claw rotating at my wrists and hands, flipping the body so that the back was to me.

Motioning for the body to stop, I stepped closer.

I loved examining bodies in my mind. I never needed magnification implements, or any other implement for that matter. It was amazing, almost as if I had access to undeveloped imaging technology. I could separate tissue from organs with a thought, remove layer by layer of skin until I had what I needed. I could strip a body to the bone in seconds. It was phenomenal.

Looking towards the back of the room, I noticed the gurney that held the unidentified male's body. I hadn't yet released him from my mind; instead, I'd stored him in the room, knowing his image wouldn't decompose here if I didn't want it too. The only thing that had changed was the wound's radius.

I suspected it wasn't my mind updating it, but his actual body changing in reality that had a flow-on effect in my mind. If I'd looked at his body before I came in for my shift, I'd have seen the wound had widened.

Each body I committed to this room to inspect left behind a single thread leading to the body in reality. I'd learned I needed to sever that thread once I'd finished with my charges, or things got interesting. What happened to them in reality, could effectively happen to them in my mind, maggots and all.

With a single thought, the mans' body materialised beside my newest charge, back facing me so I could compare both wounds.

The patterning around the rib cage was definitely the same. There was a small puncture mark in four of the ribs descending from the bottom of each scapula. The difference between Jane and John was where the puncture wounds sat in proximity to the spine. Where the punctures were closer towards the spine on the male, the woman's were further from her spine towards the sides, closer to

116

the underside of her breasts. I couldn't determine if this was because she was slighter than our male, or because whatever had lodged in her was bigger than whatever had attached itself in the other body.

I was missing something.

Stepping forward, I inspected the woman's vertebrae, then moving on to her shrivelled spinal cord. With a thought the woman's body stripped to the bone, her shrivelled skin and muscle tissue flaking away into non-existence.

"Bob, both the bodies have the same puncture wounds on four of their ribs, starting from just below each scapula. The only difference is the diameter. I'm not sure if it's because of their stature or if whatever made the marks are different in size." Huffing with frustration at what I was missing, I waited on Bob's response.

"Noted. Now I think it may be time for you to come on back to me. Your breathing is getting shallower and your hair looks as if it is going white at the roots. Judging by the paleness of your skin, I'll hazard a guess that your core temperature has dropped too," came his cautious response.

Worry crossed the divide between reality and my mind, but here in my mind things outside didn't seem as important. I had a promise to keep and damn it, I would keep it.

"Okay Bob, I hear you. Just a little longer, okay? I want to check one or two things. Oh, and we're about to have company. They've just stepped up to the guest's doors at the front," I warned.

The warm tingling at my lower back had only happened once before.

Erick. His name whispered through my autopsy room, snuck under the door, before flinging itself at the mirrored ceiling and escaping into reality.

He was talking to Steve. Tristan was once again at his side, while Jordan stood behind him. I watched the one-way mirror on my left, which was now a screen, as my whisper reached him. Erick halted his conversation for a second and turned to look towards the morgue. Closing his eyes, he paused for a moment before opening them again, locking his gaze with mine. A smile quirked the side of his lips, while laughter shone in the depths of his green eyes. They glittered like emeralds caught in the sun, with flecks of red scattered through the brilliant green.

I watched, a moth drawn to the light, as an obsidian flame swayed hypnotically in their depths. It felt oddly cold, but no less intense than a flame might feel if you held your hand over it.

How is he doing that?

Dismissing the question, for now, I turned away from the viewing window, dismissing the image altogether. I had work to do.

Bob's voice boomed over the radio again and my hands shot to my ears as he spoke.

"How in the hell can you tell someone is here to see us? Hold on, I'll go look," he huffed.

I didn't bother waiting for his confirmation; instead, I got back to the skeletons floating before me. All thoughts of our visitors and my new abilities were forgotten.

Slowly, I replaced the central nervous system, my focus on the portion located within the vertebral canal. There between Thoracic two and three sat two minute puncture wounds.

Interesting.

I called the internal organs forward, before returning the organs one by one, checking each as I did. Arriving at the glands, I spotted what I'd been looking for since I'd seen that grainy image. Every single one of the girl's glands had been larger than normal, as if her body had been fighting off an infection.

I looked closer at each gland, turning towards the male as I finished. His glands appeared, with the same symptoms as the females. I was guessing that once I inspected the lymphoid organs, I'd see signs of severe degeneration.

Their bodies had been fighting back before they'd died, or at least they'd tried.

"Bob, we need a white blood cell count. It looks as if their bodies were fighting an infection," I said excitedly. "In fact, it might be worthwhile chatting to Brad and Ellie regarding any possible viral outbreaks they might be aware of. They both have connections within the CDC and WHO. I don't think I've ever heard of an infection or virus being so specific in its selection of where it attacks. But who knows what could be out there."

There was no response, and looking towards where the speaker sat, I frowned at its absence for a second.

With a shrug, I continued to talk, hoping I was verbalising what I was thinking to my audience in the morgue.

"I'm going to glance over both their hearts now. Then I'd like to check both brains. Something doesn't add up with the puncture wounds at T2 and T3." My sentence was no sooner finished when a knock sounded from somewhere inside my mirrored room.

Odd. That's never happened before.

When the knock came again, I opened the door and stepped out into my mirrored room. Looking around for where the knocking had come, I found nothing. Shrugged I turned when the knock came again, much louder and clearer this time—and more insistent. The sound seemed to come from above me and not from one of the doors surrounding me, as I had initially thought.

Looking up, brilliant green eyes were the first thing I noticed. followed by the shirtless male hovering above me.

Erick?

I looked closer at the glass and it finally registered that Erick was floating above the glass in the centre of the room in nothing but a pair of jeans.

"Well hell, you don't see that every day. Should I let him in?"

A translucent image of me materialised across the room as I asked the question. She was the teenage version of me and was as wary as a stray cat being tempted with fresh fish by a human.

Her right shoulder rose, then fell in answer. *"You may as well. It's not like he hasn't been in here before."*

She had a point. He'd crept into my head the night of the party. I still wasn't sure how he'd even gotten in.

"I was vulnerable then. If I let him in now, I have a feeling he will always be able to get in. Do I really want him wandering around my mind, where there are doors that should not be opened?"

"Hey, he's helped us before and he didn't take advantage of you then. Besides, he looks like he could handle anything you throw his way. Now hurry and let the man in before he decides to leave," She urged me excitedly.

Another body materialised beside the teenager and I sighed wearily. This was the fun me, the carefree me, who I usually banished to the very back of my mind. The bimbo was full of laughter and mischievousness. She wore a burgundy bandage dress, matching strappy stilettos and was balancing a coffee and caramel martini in her right hand.

Pursing her lips, she purred, *"Darling, let the guy in. Goodness knows we could do with a bit of livening up around this place."*

"Oh, for goodness' sake. You know something's up when you two agree with each other. Fine, but if this ends badly I'm blaming the two of you," I groused.

They shrugged before drifting their separate ways.

"Enter," I commanded quietly.

The glass panel he was floating over shattered, a shower of green, red, and blue raining down to dissipate on the carpeted floor. A hum filled my mind and a wave of power rolled out gently from where he touched down on a bent knee, gently swaying me as it reached my feet.

"That was one hell of an entrance. You do weddings and birthdays too?" Hands at my hips, I tried for my best Miss Tough Lady persona. He was in my mind and needed to know who was boss around here.

"Ah, so this is where you come to think? I must say it's not what I expected."

Looking down at his body, he grinned as if he were the cat that'd gotten the cream, before looking back at me with a smirk.

"Is this how you see me? Semi-naked?"

"What are you on about?" I dismissed.

Okay, so I may have been perving just a little. Hey, I was only human; besides, he wasn't meant to know I'd been thinking of him in that way.

"I'm fully clothed in reality," he pointed out.

"Are you suggesting your current state of dress is thanks to my overactive imagination?" I feigned outrage.

"Hey, if the shoe fits," Erick chuckled, his eyes drifting up and down my body.

Clad in soft black jeans, Erick sauntered over to where I stood, his bare feet treading lightly over the lush carpet. Goosebumps shivered across my bare arms and I crossed them reflexively over my chest, trying my best to give him my sternest look.

Erick got straight to the point. *"Bob's concerned, and I must admit so am I. Your body temperature has dropped dangerously. Your hair is that white from the roots to your ears, it's practically glowing in the dark."*

He held himself loosely as if he was waiting for an imminent attack.

I rolled my eyes at him, huffing with exasperation. *"Erick, relax, nothing in my mind will hurt you unless you open doors you're not meant to. Look, come in here for a moment and see what I'm seeing. I have one or two more things to look at then I'll leave, okay?"*

Not waiting for his response, I turned and opened the door to the autopsy room before walking through. When he followed, I smiled to myself, closing the door behind him.

Erick's eyes darted around the room with curiosity and he murmured, *"What is this room?"*

Erick gave himself over to his curiosity, prowling around the edge of the room. He inspected every corner as though he were a caged animal looking for weaknesses in the fence line.

I shook my head at his behaviour, then shrugged my shoulder. *"This is where I come to dissect corpses or release souls that are trapped in their physical forms. I try not to come in here too often. Usually, I stand behind the window near the door there. I find it doesn't take as much of a toll on me physically if I'm observing from the window; however, sometimes I need to get up close and personal with a body, and in those cases, I come in here."* Pointing towards the bodies, I explained, *"These are the two unidentified bodies that we have in the morgue at the moment. I've been working backwards trying to spot differences and any evidence I need to pay attention to when I perform the autopsies in reality."*

I was already walking over to where the woman's naked body floated mid-air.

"So, what are you looking for?" Erick's deep voice rumbled from beside me.

Having fully inspected the room, he circled the bodies, studying the skeletal remains.

"The same thing killed both these people. I don't know what it is, but before this female's soul departed, she shared an image of something and the pain it inflicted on her," I shuddered at the memory. *"Erick, I've never felt anything as painful as what she experienced before she died."*

I cleared my throat, blinking tears of sorrow back. Looking up at the blank wall in front of us, an image flashed up. It was nothing more than a blurry, rough silhouette of whatever had attacked the young woman.

"What the hell is that thing?" Mostly, he sounded curious, rather than horrified. He got brownie points for not freaking out.

"I have no clue. I thought perhaps it might be some sort of magnification of a virus. Have you ever seen anything like that? I remember you telling me as a teenager you'd kept up to date with the latest scientific and biological studies."

He studied the thing on the wall, shaking his head. *"I can't say I've ever seen anything like that. I have to agree with you though; it resembles a virus in structure."*

"It's the only logical conclusion I can come to. I discovered unusual puncture wounds between T2 and T3. I was inspecting the spinal cord and brain stem before you popped in. Something tells me that the brain was compromised, but I don't see any external signs of infection or tissue damage. Do you see anything?"

Stepping up to the female's back, Erick inspected the outer layers of her brain, before agreeing with my findings.

Erick's gaze caught mine as he asked, *"How are you doing this, Evanee? These bodies are as real as the ones lying in the morgue."*

"I don't know," I shrugged.

That raised eyebrow of his spoke volumes about just how little he believed me.

125

"Seriously, I discovered I had a knack for predicting the cause of death when I was in high school and it's gradually amplified over time. I've always been able to sense basic information such as age and general cause of death, but it heightened during my residency and my continuous interaction with cadavers. The more I come in here, the better I get at viewing and dissecting cadavers in my mind. I could ask you the same question. How are you able to communicate with me, here in my mind?"

Silence descended as Erick studied me. Realising he had no intention of answering me, I shrugged and returned my attention to the body, continuing my search.

"There! Do you see it?" I exclaimed. *"There, at the base of the brain. There are two more punctures."*

"What the hell could do that and still leave the body functioning? There's no way this was done post mortem. Can you see whether the puncture wounds go any deeper than just the base?" Erick enquired with excitement and curiosity.

"I can layer the brain and magnify it."

The words had no sooner left my mouth when the brain expanded and separated into multiple layers. Focusing on the puncture wounds, I thought of blue dye injecting into each hole. Liquid sluggishly moved through the medulla oblongata, branching into the pons and cerebellum as if transparent tubes connected them. The pathways thinned out so that the liquid was no thicker than a pin. They branched throughout the brain, targeting specific regions of both the forebrain and hindbrain, yet the midbrain stood unaffected.

126

Floating around the brain, I looked at it from every angle. Erick said nothing; instead, he focused on the areas of the brain that were affected.

His body stiffened suddenly.

He nodded once as if he were listening to an invisible voice, before saying, *"Evanee, we need to leave now! We've spent too long in here. Your body isn't coping well."*

"Just a bit longer, please?" I didn't look at him as I spoke; instead, my focus was on the brain continually turning it.

If I left now, I wouldn't have the time to inspect the bodies again before they started decaying.

Erick appeared in front of me, his firm hands cupping my face, forcing my attention to him.

Speaking quickly and gently, Erick's tried his best to reason with me. *"You have no more time. Do what you need to do to put these bodies away and then we need to leave. Do you hear me? You're fading in reality; your body will shut down if you don't leave."*

"Fine. Give me a second," I sighed grumpily.

I shut my eyes, picturing the bodies as they had been when I last saw them in the morgue, with the exception of the sutured wounds on the male's back. Opening my eyes, I looked at each body and pursed my lips before I gently blew, releasing the bodies from my mind. They dissipated with little effort. They'd served their purpose, and I was grateful to them.

Approaching the door, Erick gripped my hand, practically dragging me. Turning as we exited, I watched the door brick up, the window disappearing with it to become a solid wall once again.

"How do you normally get out?" His head snapped in every direction around room.

I fought the urge to giggle at him. It was as though he was hoping for a door marked Exit.

"I usually just close my eyes and sink down. How the hell are you going to get out? No one's ever been in here," I frowned.

He smiled warmly, before letting my hand drop gently back to my side. *"I'll leave the same way I came in — through the roof. I can see a glass patch there. And don't worry; I'm sure I'm the only one who can see it,"* he reassured me. *"Now listen, I need to leave first, but as soon as I've passed through the glass barrier you leave. Do you hear me?"* He ordered.

Rolling my eyes at his bossiness, I nodded. I looked on as he padded barefoot towards the centre of the room. He looked back at me before bending slightly, then pushing off. There was no resistance; he simply vanished as he hit the glass.

Doing as he'd asked, or rather demanded, I shut my eyes and I allowed myself to sink as if I were a weight, back into the rest of my body. It was harder than usual, as if there were an invisible string attached to my wrist, tethering me to my mind. For a second, I dangled between my subconscious and my conscious, not knowing what to do. It was then that I heard Erick's booming voice as if he were right up in my face yelling at me.

Erick's concern washed over me, as he commanded, "Damit Evanee, return now, do you hear me? Let go, right now. You're out of time."

I flinched, yanking my right arm down, so that the string attached to my wrist severed. Plummeting, I braced myself for the impact. It had never been this hard before.

Yeah, this is going to hurt.

CHAPTER 9

I slammed back into reality with a pained whimper—it was all my poor body could manage, courtesy of the excruciating pain stampeding through it.

Shock set in and my body shuddered, jerked and twitched, while tears blazed fiery trails down my cheeks. I whimpered again, still twitching worse than a decapitated snake.

Erick's chest vibrated as he soothed me, "It's okay, *mic lupt*ätor, slow shallow breaths. Follow the rhythm of my chest. In and out. Feel how the pain is already receding? Squeeze my hand until the worst of the pain has dissipated."

Inhaling a shallow breath in time with his, I tried to relax my body as much as it would allow me. I gripped his hand tightly, holding on for dear life, while I hoped my body wouldn't fly apart.

"Tight... tighter. Ho... ho... hold me tight... er," I stuttered.

Speaking through chattering teeth proved difficult, but he seemed to understand what I needed.

Erick pressed me closer to his chest, his arms squeezing just that bit more. Together we sat on the sterilised floor, the chair beside us long forgotten as he held me together.

"I think perhaps we should take her into the office or staff room. It may be warmer in there. Perhaps someone could grab a blanket?" Erick suggested.

Erick rose, cradling my pain riddled body as gently as he could, almost as if it were a delicate piece of crystal.

"We… we real... ly need to st… stop meeting li... ke this," I chattered.

Burrowing deeper into his chest, I tried to extract every ounce of warmth he offered. My body was freezing, and I had a sneaking suspicion it would hurt beyond words if Bob touched me, just as it had hurt when Brad had touched me the night of the party.

Erick's chest rumbled beneath my check. "You think so? And here I was thinking this was our own special greeting. You try to die, and I come in and keep you tied to this earth. I must say, it's a unique way of greeting each other, but hey, whatever floats your boat."

We reached the staff room and Erick made a B-Line for the two-seater lounge at the back of the room. Lowering himself carefully onto the lounge, Erick cradled me to his chest, reminding me of the times I'd spent cradled in my father's arms after a rough day at school.

The shock must have slowly been wearing off as my teeth finally stopped chattering; although, I wouldn't have counted on me being able to walk anytime soon.

My hand drifted up to my hair, and I patted it, muttering, "Is my hair still white or has it returned to normal?"

I really hoped it'd returned to normal. I didn't quite think the hairdressers could fix it if it hadn't.

"Ahh, well umm, mostly, it has, except well, a handful of strands, which are only white three-quarters of the way down from your roots. It's odd though, they're not greying old white, more like fresh snow where the sun touches it and it shines, but that could just be the lighting," Bob answered slowly, unsure of how I'd react.

"Ah, crap. My hairdresser's going to crack. She has to work around my other white streak, and she hates it. She'll probably drop me as a client when she sees my hair now. Hair dyes won't latch properly to the white bits and getting the same colour is near on impossible," I groaned.

But it was worth it if we get justice for that poor girl lying on the table.

I didn't want to say this out loud, I had a feeling Bob was a bit of a nervous wreck at the moment.

The musky aroma of a familiar aftershave teased my nose, making me smile.

"Hey, Steve. What are you doing here? Is it rounds' time already?" I greeted.

A blanket was draped over Erick and I. And grabbing a fist-full, I tugged it up to my chin. I was trying hard to not think about who was holding me. It wasn't often I let people touch me.

"Um sweetie, I hate to break it to you, but it's already ten. You were off in la-la land for quite some time. Scarred the living shit outta Bob and me. Bob worried you weren't hearing his warnings, so he called me to come in. When you didn't respond to me, I knew you couldn't hear me. Luckily, Erick here stopped by when he did, or I'd have had to take some drastic measures to get you back." The graveness in his voice tugged at my heart.

Poor Steve. Note to self, bake him something yummy for the next shift. Wait… did he just say it was ten?

I tried to sit up more, but Erick's arm clamped down, stilling me.

"Erick, I need to get up, I need to heat our dinner, plus the food will help me recover quicker. Sustenance and all that nonsense," I babbled, flustered by his proximity and the heavyweight of his arms around me.

I could feel people's eyes on me and I didn't like it.

"You're not ready to stand yet. Your body hasn't yet reached a safe temperature and your lungs are still trying to recover. If you try to run before you can walk, you'll end up causing yourself more harm. Besides, I'm sure Bob or Steve can warm the food up, can't you, gentlemen?" And there was that authoritative voice that irked me so much.

Bob hurried toward the mini-fridge and pulled the door open, withdrawing the covered oven dish as spoke. "Of course we can. Now Evanee, what delicious treat have you cooked up for us this evening, and what do I need to do?"

"I'm not sure there'll be enough for everyone; although, if we work it right, there might be." I looked up at Erick, waiting to see if he or any of the others were hungry.

"Thanks, but we ate before we left home. You three go ahead though," Erick smiled down at me.

Nodding quickly, I replaced my head against his chest, frowning when I couldn't hear a heartbeat.

What the hell? My hearing must have been affected during my excursion.

Frowning, I lifted my head, readjusting it before replacing it. Still not hearing any rhythmic beat, I made to lift my head once again only to stop when Steve waved his hand in front of my frowning face.

"Earth to Doc. Hello, what did ya end up making for us this evening?" Steve called softly, his eyes narrowing slightly and his lips thinning.

He concerned I might slip from consciousness again, I could see it in his eyes.

"Sorry. Hmm, I made Bob's favourite, lasagne, and salad; and for you, I made a caramel topped French vanilla cheesecake. Not baked, just the way you like it." Sighs of bliss filled the staff room.

Together the two men worked in harmony prepping the dinner and setting the small table. It was a sight to behold.

I need to pull a sickie more often.

"See, they're just fine. Now, do you want a big piece or a small piece of lasagne?" Erick's chest rumbled, once again distracting me for a second.

Gathering my wits, I responded with the only rational answer when asked about food.

"There's only one size with something like lasagne and cheesecake and that's large. You know how women tell men size doesn't matter, well in this case, size matters and don't let any women tell you differently, cause she's talking rubbish if she does," I said matter-of-factly.

Four male heads focused on me for a second before laughter erupted around the room. Erick stared open-mouthed for a split second before his head fell back, his laughter joining the rest.

"I knew you were special the moment I laid eyes on you, Evanee. Tell me you're not taken?" Jordan sat down opposite the couch, his smile bigger than a Cheshire Cat's grin lighting up those puppy eyes of his.

"Jordan! I thought I saw you earlier. The answer to your question would be no, I'm not taken. Why, you planning on asking me out on a date? If you are, I have to say we may need to take your car—I don't think you'll fit in mine unless you practice yoga," I winked at him.

Erick tensed beneath me, his arms constricting me as a Boa python might when embracing its prey.

Gently patting his chest, I tried to get him to ease up.

Dude, you seriously need to let go a little, I think you may break me.

'*Sorry. I didn't like the way he was talking to you.*' Erick apologised telepathically.

Holy crap, he heard me!

'*I could hear and communicate with you during the party, but only because your defences were weak. Now, however, I believe I have a permanent link to your mind. Telepathy with one such as yourself is unique, but I can feel how uneasy this is making you, so I'll try to keep out of your mind as much as possible. It's hard though, as you have the most fascinating mind. All those doors. What could be behind them all?*' he teased.

'*Yeah, you can stay out of those, thank you very much.*' I warned, primly.

Erick didn't respond, as Bob appeared before me. He placed the steaming plate of food on the coffee table followed by some cutlery and a bottle of chilled water.

My mouth watered at the sight of food in front of me, and I breathed deeply before groaning, "Mmm, that looks good and smells even better. All that melted cheese. Heaven, pure heaven. Erick, could you please let me go so I can sit on the couch, or are you intending on feeding me?"

Okay, I hadn't thought that through. Stupid verbal diarrhoea, it'd be the death of me one day I swear.

"I'd be more than happy to feed you, *mic lupt*ător. Give me a second to rearrange you," Erick teased.

Cheeky bugger. I needed to understand what *mic luptător* meant. He'd called me that a few times, but I kept forgetting to ask him about it.

"For goodness' sake put me on the couch, Erick," I growled, smacking his chest lightly before he could respond with what I suspected would be a smart-arse comment.

He didn't argue, thankfully, as though sensing my increasing embarrassment. He maneuvered me to the spot on the couch beside him, before handing me my steaming plate of food.

Silence settled over the room and I chewed on my first mouthful of lasagne, closing my eyes in appreciation.

"Mmm. Oh yes, now that's good stuff," I moaned.

Opening my eyes, I looked around the room to see Steve and Bob tucking into their food, while our three guests watched unphased.

I frowned, swallowing my mouthfull before I said, "You guys run out of conversation or something? What's with the silence, guys?"

Grunts around mouths full of food were the only response I got, while Erick and Jordan looked on, smiles tugging at their lips.

"Fine, I'll start.," I muttered. "Erick, what does *mic luptător* mean?"

"It's Romanian. Roughly translated, it means little fighter," he explained reluctantly.

"Oh, that definitely sounds like Evanee," Steve laughed around a mouth full of food.

Never one to beat around the bush, Bob jumped right to the point as he speared more food onto his fork.

"So, Erick, what's bought you this evening? I didn't know you had returned to Murder Point Bay?" He tried to sound friendly, but I was sure I detected a note of firmness.

He watched Erick carefully and I could see him assessing how close Erick sat beside me. He was now in over-protective father mode something he'd done before my father died.

It was pointless — I could have told him it wasn't me Erick was interested in, he was just being ultra-nice to me for old times' sake. Not to mention I had no intention of acting on the attraction I felt towards him.

"I came to see Evanee about an issue we discussed during my last visit. Seeing as you're here, though, it might be good to get a third opinion on the matter." He sounded casual, yet somehow, I could feel his amusement.

Must be the mind thing.

"When did you and Evanee get reacquainted? I get the feeling your visit last week wasn't the first time you've seen each other since you arrived back in town," Bob said pointedly.

Yep, he was definitely doing the overprotective thing.

"Actually, Erick here was at a party I attended the other week," I smiled politely.

I left out the part with me passing out and Erick coming to my rescue. There was no need to stress him out.

"I didn't recognise Evanee here at first, and I don't believe she recognised me either," Erick shrugged. "Long story short, we became reacquainted after we noticed her and her friend Ellie having a rough time. When we finally got to them, they had both passed out."

'Are you freaking serious, Erick? Do you have any idea the amount of trouble you've just landed me in?" I protested. *"Of course, you don't. I could kick you,'* I fumed.

Beside me, Erick's eyebrows drifted up before a smirk settled over his delectable lips.

"You what! Evanee Sheperd, I could throttle you. Why the hell didn't you tell me this before you went off exploring in there?"

Ah man, now he's done it.

Bob's pissed at me right now and there would be no trying to talk my way out of it. That didn't mean I wouldn't try though.

"I'm okay, Bob. I have no clue why I fainted, but I'm all good. See, I'm eating food. A sure sign all is right in the universe." To emphasise my point, I shovelled another mouthful in.

"Oh, sure you're fine, that's why you nearly passed out on Saturday too." And cue Steve and his enormous mouth.

I looked over wincing at the vein bulging slightly on the side of Bob's neck. He would likely have a heart attack at this point.

"You What?" Bob bellowed. "Why the hell wasn't I told about this when I got in? Steve, you let her go in tonight without telling me what's happened over the last nine days?"

Ha! Take that, Steve, you can share in the yelling. That's what you get for dobbing me in.

"And you," he looked back at me, eyes blazing, "that was extremely irresponsible of you; you know better, young lady," he berated me, and I cringed.

Looking at Bob, I couldn't help but think he might need a hug.

That or he needs a straitjacket before he walks over here and throttles me to death.

'He's only looking after you. He's very worried about you. I'm seeing what he sees through his eyes and even I must admit that he's right. You've pushed yourself too far this evening. Your colour has not yet returned. I have to agree with him; it was irresponsible of you to do what you did tonight,' Erick reproved.

'I'm the only one who can do what I do,' I declared with exasperation. *'Those two bodies out there deserve justice. If I can give them that, give their families some peace, I damn well will. Don't you dare sit there*

and lecture me on how I choose to use my talent. I'm a big girl, I can do what I want,' I seethed.

'You're a stubborn and ungrateful girl who'll end up killing herself because of some misguided need to save what is already dead,' Erick hissed with frustration.

"Screw you, jackass! You do not understand who I am or what makes me tick. You can jump off that damn high horse of yours, or better yet remove that stick from up your arse, Mr my-way-or-the-highway!" My insides quivered with anger as our thunderous expression met.

Anger ran off him in waves, my skin tingling where those waves crashed against sensitized skin.

You could have dropped a pin in the morgue and heard it from the office. No one moved.

"One would think someone knocking on Death's door would be a little more grateful to the person who has not only saved her once but twice. Or are you just another spoilt brat like your friend Cassandra?" He held himself still—too still.

Oh, he's pissed. Well screw him, where does he come off telling me what to do?

"I'm not and never will be anything like Cassandra. I'm grateful for any help I receive, but don't confuse that with weak. Bob and Steve are the only men in my life who get to lecture me and get away with it. You," I pointed at him, finger shaking. "Do not get to breeze into my life after twelve years and start berating me as if I'm some child."

Nobody dared say a word. They sat staring open-mouthed, but I didn't care. My attention focused on the seething man beside me.

"You want some star dazed woman who'll preen and tell you how good looking you are? Or is that you want her to tell you what a man you are, maybe even kiss the ground you walk on? If that's what you're after, then I strongly suggest you walk back out that damn door and don't let it hit your arse on the way out," I challenged.

My hands were trembling, and I could feel my face burning.

I'm going too far, aren't I?

Rage flashed across Erick's eye, but I didn't care. I had a point to make.

"Oh and don't think Ellie will put up with your shit either because I guarantee you she'll take your arse to school and walk away still looking as fresh as a daisy. Lecture me, my arse," I scoffed.

Confusion replaced the anger in Erick's eyes, but I couldn't say anymore. Frustration and jealousy warred within me, adding to my fatigue, depleting me even further.

I muttered an apology before I fled the room to cool down.

Entering my office, I slammed the door.

~

Pacing the carpeted floor of my office, anger sizzled through my veins, heating my chilled body. Bob watched with consternation.

It hadn't been long before he'd sought me out. Slipping into the room, he'd wisely chosen not to comment on my outburst in the staff room; instead, he'd gingerly closed the door and stood patiently waiting for me to speak.

"There's something seriously off with those two bodies. Something's happening here and I'm not seeing it. What if we have a serial killer or worse, a potential viral outbreak, and I've missed something because I couldn't use all my skills?" my hands gesturing wildly, as I peppered him with my thoughts on the autopsies, avoiding talking about my outburst.

"We both know how you get, Evie. I'm worried you're pushing yourself too hard. I've been checking your logs lately. Don't think I haven't noticed you amending Desmond's reports; I could spot your work from a mile off. I get the impression you've been doing your job plus everyone else's around here since I left. You're spreading yourself too thin, my girl, and you'll break if you don't take it easy. That outburst in the staff room tells me just how stressed out and overworked you are," Bob warned, his voice soft.

I remained silent as he spoke—after all, how could I argue? He wasn't wrong.

"I'll address the mistakes that are being made by the staff here. And, yes, I'm aware of the missing or misplaced bodies. The hospital has passed their concerns onto me directly, and I'm working on it," he assured me.

"I issued Desmond with a warning over his conduct with you and I'll be issuing a second warning to him for his piss poor efforts with quite a few autopsies." Bob gripped my shoulders, looking me in my eyes. "You don't have to do everything around here, sweetie. I know how much you've tried to keep things going just the way I like them, but you don't have to. If you don't ease up, I'll be forced to make you take leave. Don't make me do it, because you know I will," he warned me, his voice husky from worry.

Looking at his warm smile, it reminded me of the same gentle smile my father had always reserved just for me.

I blinked rapidly and breathed through the pain as I realised Bob had known all along that I'd been trying to fix the problems happening around here without getting him involved. I thought I'd been doing a suitable job keeping things afloat, yet he'd known what I was doing the whole time.

The weight of the last few months lifted, and it was a relief to not have to worry about it anymore. Teeth clenching, I blinked hard again, attempting to control the tears that threatened to spill.

"Okay, Bob." It was all I could get past my clenched teeth, while I plastered a smile on my face that was faker than half the strippers' chests in Hollywood.

"I also want an explanation as to what is going on with you. When I left all you were doing was guessing the cause of death, now you're releasing souls and nearly dying in front of me." He searched my face, waiting for me to give him an explanation.

"I'll tell you everything, but not here, not like this. It's too complex. I don't think I'd survive it tonight," I said with a strangled whisper.

Never one to push me past what he thought I could endure, Bob nodded. "Okay, that's fair enough. Now, do you think we could join the others and maybe take a crack at dessert?"

Nodding, I hesitated by the door, my hand on the door handle. "Would you give me a minute? I won't be long. You can dish me up some cheesecake."

"Big or small slice?" He winked cheekily at me before turning and exiting the office.

He already knew what the answer would be.

I closed the door carefully behind him, finally allowing my first tear to fall.

Tears of frustration, pain, and sadness mingled with those of relief coursed down my cheeks. Relief that I had someone on my side, yet the loneliness and guilt I'd felt all these years still pierced my heart.

The last nine days caught up with me and I collapsed brokenly onto the guest chair. Head in my hands, I stared blindly at my sock-clad feet, only just noticing I no longer had my gumboots on.

A soft tingle at the back of my neck was the only warning I got before a powerful pair of arms embraced me from behind. Jerking upright, my head swivelled to look behind me. No one was there, yet I could have sworn I recognised the strength of those arms and the unique signature moving through my mind.

'Erick?'

'I'm here, Evanee. Don't worry, I wasn't wandering around your mind unescorted, I promise. I felt your sadness and thought I might offer you some comfort,' he reassured me.

That was sweet of him considering I'd just shat all over him. Great! Now I felt like a bitch.

'Thank you. No one else knows, do they?' I asked, horrified at the thought they might know I was crying in my office.

'No, they don't. I feel your emotions through our link. You can do the same if you want to; although, I'd advise caution when entering my mind without me knowing. Now you probably should come back, Steve and Bob are beginning to suspect something isn't right,' Erick warned.

'I'll be there in a second. I just need to freshen up and put some shoes on; mine seem to be missing in action. If you could please get out of my head, I'd appreciate it.'

The cheeky bugger was laughing at me, I could feel it.

I conjured an image of me sticking my tongue out. He always made me feel so many extremes—from rage to banishing my tears in a moment. It was baffling and frightening at the same time.

'Before you go Erick, I'm sorry for snapping at you earlier. I try not to bite people's heads off trying to help me,' I acknowledged miserably.

An impression of him nodding popped into my head. *'It's okay, Evanee. I should probably apologise for snapping at you the way I did. In my defense, Bob wasn't the only person you scared tonight. Nevertheless, I'm sorry. Now hurry up, before Bob sends out a search party,'* Erick chided before his presence left my mind, leaving me oddly empty and once again alone.

Sighing, I trudged towards the change rooms and cleaned myself up, replacing my shoes before making my way back to the staff room.

Erick's eyes found mine, and he tracked my approach towards the lounge where he sat.

Stopping mid-conversation, Bob studied my posture, which I was sure reeked of defeat. I wasn't worried though, I'd pick myself back up—I always did.

In many way's Erick's nickname had been spot on—I was a fighter. I'd had to be a fighter from the time my father had died, to the bullying and name-calling at high school and then again during and after that night during my last year of placement. Yet I wondered how much more I could withstand before the fighter within me grew too tired to fight anymore.

I focused on the two men who meant the world to me, my smile genuine this time. I filled it with the love and warmth I felt for them.

The three of us enjoyed our slices of cheesecake, the past moments forgotten as we laughed and joked with our guests.

Reluctantly, I approached the issue, pressing on my mind again. "So, what's next, Boss? Do you want me to perform the autopsies on the unidentified bodies?"

Work-related topics were safe, and I needed safe right now with all my weepiness. I leaned back and crossed my legs, warmth finally setting in followed closely by fatigue from the mental and physical exhaustion. If I didn't get up soon, I'd end up curling into a ball and falling asleep on the couch; or my head would just drop back and I'd pass out sitting as I was—whichever came first.

"I'll be taking the lead on both the bodies if you don't mind, Evie. I'll have them transported to Brisbane where I can ensure better safety measures are in place. Oh, and I'll be sure to put in a request to have you copied in all the results. For tonight, however, I want you to go home and get some rest. I also want you to take the next two days off—and by days, I mean the entire day. Don't think you can get around me by coming in at night." Bob's stern look had my mouth shut before my protest made it past my lips.

Damit, he knows me too well.

Nodding, I beseeched, "fine, but only because you're the boss. But I want updates, don't shut me out, please. I made a promise and I need to keep it. Did you hear what I found while I was off in la-la land?"

This was important to me. I'd made a promise to that young woman.

"You know I wouldn't do that to you Evie, and yes you were whispering quite a bit. I recorded it with my phone, I'll play it back before I delete it. Now will you be

148

okay to drive home, or do you need to stay in town for the night?" He switched topics.

He was so caring and thoughtful, always looking out for me, and I knew no matter what he would always be there for me.

Cringng inwardly, it occurred to me I hadn't yet told him about what had happened while I was away at University.

I didn't know why I hadn't. Maybe it was the shame that I hadn't been more careful with whom I dated. Or maybe it was the fact that I feared what he'd think of me after I told him what I'd done to the guy.

Perhaps it was time to tell someone; to return the trust he so obviously had in me. I said I'd tell him about these new powers I'd developed. Perhaps starting from that dreadful night might help explain how things had progressed to where I was now, even though I had no clue what was happening to me.

Before I could respond to his question about transportation, Erick volunteered. "Bob, I'd be happy to drive Evanee home. I know where she lives, and I've driven her car before."

Two sets of eyes studied Erick and me, waiting for an explanation for Erick's statement.

"Did I forget to mention Erick drove me home after I blacked out at the party?" I explained weakly.

The men's 'you know you didn't' expression spoke volumes.

My shoulders sagged in defeat and I sighed, "the pain I felt was so excruciating that I blacked out. It left me feeling sick after I came too. To be honest, the pain came from around the vicinity of my birthmark. I've been thinking that maybe I should get it checked for cancer or something. It's been flaring up alot lately."

I looked to Bob for his opinion on the matter.

"You could do, although I doubt it'd be cancer. Would you like me to take a quick look at it to see if it has any discolouration or has changed shape in any way?" Bob offered.

I nodded and stood. My birthmark wasn't exactly in a place where I could get up close and personal with it, not unless I intended to become a human pretzel and kiss my arse.

I lifted my shirt just over my hips, and Bob looked at my lower back, his warm fingers poking gently at the area.

"It looks normal to me, sweetie. You aren't experiencing any pain when I touch the area and I don't think it's changed, but then again, the last time I saw it was when you were in your teens. If you're really worried, then perhaps go see your GP. What do you think, Erick? Your eyes are better than mine," Bob deferred to Erick.

"Would you mind turning your back to face me, please Evanee?" Erick asked, and I complied.

His firm hands gripped my hips and supple fingertips dug in ever so slightly to hold me in place. The feeling was intensely erotic and goosebumps broke out over my flesh.

Working overtime to erect a wall, I prayed my oh-so-naughty thoughts wouldn't slam into him.

His hand dropped from my right hip to trace across my birthmark, and the breathe stalled in my lungs.

My thoughts of how mesmersing his fingers were against my flesh stalled when the room blurred and tilted.

The sudden image of Erick standing naked behind an equally naked woman flashed behind my eyes, and I blinked rapidly. His long fingers gripped her hips much as they'd gripped mine, leaving slight indents around each fingertip. The woman was bent over a beautiful teal antique lounge, their bodies joined at the waist. The flickering light of the fire behind her shone through the strands of shoulder-blade length white hair that'd fallen across her face. Gripping the back of the lounge with one hand and the arm of the chair with the other, the woman's knuckles strained from the intensity of her grip.

The image bled into a fresh scene and I fought the shiver sitting at the base of my spine. Erick's toned body stood facing away from me at the foot of a giant king-sized bed; his hands gripped the pale thighs of what I assumed was the woman he'd had bent over the teal chase moments before. The muscles at his shoulders bunched and rippled seductively as he gripped her thighs tighter. I surveyed the scene, mesmerised by his tight arse and his gentle thrusts into her. The delicate arms of the woman fisted the blankets beneath her, dragging them closer towards her with each thrust.

Erick's head tilted back and the fire's light was caught and trapped in the burnette strands of his hair. His hands tightened against the woman's thighs. His back, glute and thigh muscles visibly tightening as a long, low groan exploded from his parted lips, caressing its way down my now thrumming body.

The scene changed once more, and I wondered if I was panting as hard in reality as I was now.

Erick now sat amongst the bunched blankets, the white-haired woman straddling his waist, while her hips ground against where they joined. Erick's held the woman close to him, one hand caressing the roundness of her arse, while the other hand reached across her back to caress the slight swell of the underside of her breast.

Erick trailed his fingers lovingly across her shoulder toward the back of her scalp. His fingers pressed lightly against the woman's head, and she obliged, tilting it to the side. Erick pressed tender kisses across the taught skin of her exposed neck. Lifting his head, Erick's mouth opened to reveal sharp elongated canines.

The vision was so intense I forgot my body was standing in the staff room. My eyes darted to his hand cradling the woman's glittering white hair, the soft firelight reflecting off the individual strands caressing her pale flesh. The effect was spectacular as though diamonds were trapped in each thin strand of hair.

Mouth gaping, my eyes widened in horror and morbid fascination when Erick bent forward and placed those sharpened canines at her neck. Trailing them across her exposed skin, Erick bit down, thrusting fiercely into her at the same time.

Just as suddenly as the vision appeared, it disappeared, leaving me panting worse than a bitch on heat.

Eyes wide with shock, I looked around the room taking in the surrounding occupants. No one had moved.

Holy crap on toast! What the hell was that? I panted, bewildered by the intensity of the daydream.

Panties soaked, I fought the urge to cross my legs.

Erick's finger stilled on my birthmark, and the fingers on my hip tightened before he eased up. I fought the urge to turn my head to look at him over my shoulder.

This is so embarrassing. I seriously need to lay off the Paranormal books and TV shows.

'Ever think that perhaps someone's trying to tell you he doesn't belong to you?' Oh goody, seventeen-year-old me had joined the R18 viewing.

'Don't you have something else to do, or somewhere else to be?' I snapped at her.

'Nope. I'm a figment of your overactive imagination and judging by that scene, I'd say kinky imagination too.' She snorted.

'Will you shut up? You're such a snooty cow, you know that? And no, I didn't think someone might be trying to tell me something, considering it was just my mind malfunctioning. I'm overtired, that's all. Now go back to your room and stay put. If I wanted your damn opinion, I'd come knocking.' I retorted silently.

Fine. But don't say I didn't warn you. We all know you have a terrible track record with men, that's why I'm here after all. Someone has to balance this mess of yours. With that, the pessimistic little cow disappeared.

Caught up in my thoughts, I didn't notice Erick releasing my hips until Tristan hissed. He now stood beside the couch. Erick's head snapped to Tristan, seemingly unphased by the thoughts he'd been starring in. Tristan's gaze darted towards me before he looked back at my birthmark, his shoulders rigid.

I twisted slightly, trying and failing to see what Tristan had hissed at.

"What, is there something wrong with my birthmark? Do you see something?"

"No, everything looks fine, Evanee. Bob's correct in saying the colour doesn't appear off," Erick murmured. "Out of curiosity, how would you best describe your birthmark?" Erick enquired, his fingers trailing across my lower back as he continued to study my birthmark.

Well, that has to be the oddest question I've ever been asked. And If he doesn't stop touching me like that, things will get interesting.

"I'd say it reminds me of a Scythe, to be honest. My mother has something similar in the same spot. Why the weird question?" I frowned at him.

"We'll talk about it another time, but for now I think it might be a good idea to get you home. Are you ready to leave?" Erick checked, dismissing our previous conversation.

I stepped to one side so he could stand. Not satisfied with his answer, I'd decided grill him about it on the way home.

"Let me grab my things first, and then I should be all good to go."

I plucked my empty plate off the table before collecting Bob's and Steve's plate on my way through to the bin. I liked to clean the kitchenette after we ate, but fatigue had set in and I just didn't have the energy to stand much longer.

Bob's hand touched mine lightly. "It's okay, sweetie. You go on home and rest up. I meant it when I said you have the next two days off. I'll take care of things here."

I nodded, unable to speak past the lump in my throat. It felt as though I was being reprimanded for something, yet logically I knew I wasn't.

"Oh, and Evanee, no more playing your game without one of us here. We came dangerously close to losing you tonight." Bob stared at me with one eyebrow raised.

Again, I nodded without saying a word.

As though sensing how upset I was, Bob walked forward, his arms coming around me to form a cocoon of love and warmth.

My head dropped forward to rest on his shoulder, and he turned, whispering into my ear, "I can see what you're thinking princess. You're not in trouble. You've always cared for those around you, both the living and the dead. Tonight was too close of a call for my liking. Losing you would kill a part of me, not to mention Steve. So, take the next few days to relax and recharge, okay? You can come back to work on Monday."

Pulling back, he looked into my eyes.

"Okay, I will," I said with a strangled whisper.

I squeezed him one last time, and I stepped out of his embrace.

"Erick. It was good to see you again. Perhaps when there's not so much going on we could talk about that case you need another opinion on," Bob farewelled.

Erick reached past me to shake Bob's hand. "Sounds good, Bob. I'll give you call to dicuss the details and specifics. I'll talk to Evanee once she's feeling better."

Erick stood at my side ready to go, while Jordan and Tristan headed towards the back door.

"Hey, Bob, why don't you, Steve and Aunty Marg come by my place tomorrow? There are a few things I'd like to talk to you about," I asked nervously, looking to Steve as I finished.

"I'm sure we can manage that. How about we drop by your place tomorrow midday? Marg and I will bring lunch," Bob offered reassuringly.

With a quick nod, I left the staff room to collect my bag. Emerging from the changing rooms, Erick stood exactly where I'd left him. Together we made our way to Jordan and Tristan waiting beside the morgue doors.

Tristan rounded the corner first, with Erick and I in the middle and Jordan bringing up the rear. Together, the four of us made our way towards the loading bay. I stared hard at the ground in front of me and avoided looking at or talking to Erick.

I stumbled over my own feet, and Erick's hand shot out, shackling my waist to steady me.

"Thanks." I mumbled, a ferocious blush stinging my cheeks. It would have put any virgin bride on her wedding night to shame.

Erick's arm remained around my waist, branding me. The image of him bent over the woman as he thrust into her had been seared into at least half of my brain cells. The other half of my brain had short-circuited the minute I'd seen that body of his in all its glory—even if was just in my imagination.

Passing the security desk, I waved at Andrea, who's wide smile said she'd noticed Erick's arm. My blush continued to heat my cheeks, and I slapped my security card against the security panel, the door opening to give way to the salty air rushing forward to greet us as we stepped out. Looking up, I noticed Tristan continually searching the area as if someone might be about to jump us. I could have told him the hospital grounds weren't the issue, it was the carpark that could prove to be the danger area.

We arrived at my little hatchback, and I hit the button to open my car before handing Erick the keys. Opening the back door, I threw my bag onto the backseat.

Shutting the door, my hand reached for the door handle of the front passenger door only to encounter Erick's hand already gripping the handle.

I mumbled an apology and Erick smiled at me, "That's okay. No harm, no foul."

I slid onto the seat and clamped my legs together to stifle the ache. Need, unlike anything I'd ever experienced, gripped my over-sensitized body. My clothes scratched at sensitised skin and I was tempted to press my hand between my legs to ease the ache.

Erick slid into the driver's seat, once again readjusting it to fit his sizeable frame.

Erick stilled, his nostrils flaring for a brief second. His hands gripped my staring wheel, and my eyes darted to them noting the strain of his knuckles. It was same strained white-knuckled grip he'd used when gripping the legs of the woman he'd been making love to.

A fresh wave of moisture leaked from my core and I bit my tongue against my groan.

With a mumbled cursed, Erick started the engine and pulled away smoothly.

"What about Tristan and Jordan?" Looking back, both men in question had disappeared from view.

"They'll meet us at your house," Erick growled through clenched teeth.

I frowned at his tone but forgot about it when my eyes darted to his lap and I spied the bulge trapped beneath the zipper of his jeans.

My eye darted out the window and my lips pressed together in astonishment.

Wow! Now that's what I call a hard on. Oh shit! Please, please don't let him have heard or seen my horny thoughts.

My mind raced and I settled myself against the seat, sighing tiredly as I stared out at the passing street lamps. At some point my body relaxed and before we left the city, my eyes drifted shut, the world dropping away.

CHAPTER 10

Ding!

I nearly jumped out of my skin when the doorbell chimed. I'd been twitchy ever since Erick had dropped me home last night. The soft kiss to my cheek at the front door had been a pleasant distraction, but like all good things, it'd come to an end.

I'd woken at intervals, the enormity of what I was about to do today sending my heart into a frenzy each time.

My insides had been in a constant state of vibration since I'd woken, and my heart was attached to a horse that'd taken off from the gates at the Melbourne Cup.

The static buzzing around my head resembled the snow you used to get on the old television sets.

Today was the day I'd tell three of the most important people in my life the dirty secret and burden I'd been forced to bear in secrecy. I couldn't hide it any longer considering recent events. This moment would be crucial in determining if I'd ever share this dreaded secret with anyone else.

I tried to rise, but my legs refused to move as the chair I'd been using for support scooted back.

I'd been sitting at the dining table for what felt like the better part of the morning; staring at the door, willing Bob and Steve to forget about our appointment.

It hadn't worked.

The chime of the bell shredded my nerves just a little more, and I forced my legs to support my weight. Wobbling worse than a hen after her bachelorette party, I stumbled toward the front door. Bashing into the couch table, picture frames and ornaments trembled violently. Thankfully they didn't fall; I didn't think my legs would have allowed me to bend over and pick them up.

"Man, that will leave a bruise," I winced.

Sighing, I continued my journey towards the door, yanking it open to greet my guests.

There's no use trying to stall. I may as well rip the damned band-aid off.

Uncle Bob, Aunty Margaret, and Steve stood on the doorstep, holding various platters of food. If I hadn't been so nauseous from nerves, I'd have been salivating at all the goodies.

I'd secretly hoped Aunty Margaret wouldn't come; I wasn't sure how she was going to take my story — or its ending. I didn't want the relationship I had with her to change.

If Uncle Bob had been like a father to me, she'd been the fun aunt you wanted to hang around with all the time.

It didn't matter that I wasn't a blood relation, she'd taken me under her wing when my mother and I had been lost to grief. She was the one who'd taught me how to cook. My mother had always been a hopeless cook, with my father doing most of the cooking until he'd died.

I'd lost a lot of weight after he died, and it hadn't been all grief.

"Hi everyone. Come on in," I welcomed with fake brightness. Stepping to one side, I made room. "Sorry for taking so long, the table and I had a disagreement." I rubbed at my upper thigh.

"Oh yeah? I'm guessing you lost, considering the thing's still in one piece," Steve spoke up from the lounge room, where he'd already made himself at home.

He knew his way around. Uncle Bob and Aunty Margaret hadn't been here since I'd first brought the house and begun renovating it.

"Hello, beautiful girl. How have you been?" Aunty Marg opened her arms for our customary hug.

Returning her embrace, I soaked up every ounce of love she offered.

"I've been okay. I managed to finish the renovations. You should see my bedroom now," I mumbled into her shoulder.

She pulled back, her piercing eyes looking into mine. When a crease appeared in between her eyebrows, I tensed.

She knows something is wrong.

"Well, why don't you show me through to the kitchen, and we'll put these sandwiches down. Then you can tell me what's put that look in those beautiful eyes of yours? It's been too long since we last saw each other." Not waiting for my answer, she breezed down the hall towards the kitchen, leaving Uncle Bob standing at the entrance to the lounge room.

He was looking at the open-plan flow between the lounge room, dining room and kitchen.

"I love what you've done with the place, princess. I'm glad you removed that wall between the kitchen and dining room, it draws the eye to your beautiful kitchen and then on to your derelict back yard." A cheeky grin lit Uncle Bob's eyes as Steve snorted a laugh.

"Bob, don't you dare give Evanee grief. She will get to the jungle at the back when she isn't working so hard. Isn't that right, sweetheart?" Aunty Marg chastised.

Good old Aunty Marg always coming to my defence. Looking at her, I gave her a sweet smile and nod, then turned to poke a tongue at Uncle Bob.

Uncle Bob gave an indelicate snort and together we migrated to where Steve sat comfortably. Uncle Bob, Steve, and Aunty Marg had been the ones to help me select this house after I'd returned to Murder Point Bay.

Thinking of that day brought on another much older memory.

"Hey Uncle Bob, do you remember the day you told me I wasn't allowed to date until I was married?" I asked.

Aunty Margaret had made her way to the lounge and sat beside her husband.

I looked up in time to see Bob smiling fondly. "I do actually, and I still adhere to that rule I'll have you know, young lady. My word, it's been years since you called me Uncle Bob. You've now called me that at least twice in the past 24 hours. What's going on, sweetheart?"

Worry crept into his eyes. I sucked in a deep breath, pausing a moment before taking the plunge into the abyss.

"Looking back now, I wish I'd listened to you. It might have saved me from a world of hurt." Staring hard at my hands, I wondered, not for the first time, why I was doing.

"What's happened, Evanee? Why did you ask us to come over today?" Aunty Marg took hold of Bob's hand and sat slightly at the edge of the chair, waiting patiently for me to answer.

"Mmm... well, the thing is..." I huffed in frustration. "Shit, this is harder than I thought it would be."

I jumped from my chair to stand in front of the TV and started pacing, my hands twisting.

"Darling, it's okay. You just need to start at the beginning and then go from there. No one here will judge you. Am I right, gentlemen?" Aunty Marg soothed.

Right there, that was why I loved this woman so much. It was why the last few years had been so hard to bear. She was so much more than an aunt — she was my friend too. The men in question both nodded and sat forward, waiting for me to continue.

I need to open that forsaken door. It will take everything I have to go back in there and shut it. It always does. So easy to open, yet so hard to shut.

Breathing in deeply, I once again perused my hands. There was no way I could look at the people I loved and held so dear to me, while I relayed the series of events that took place all those years ago. Perhaps I'd start with my father's death and my abilities, then proceed to that dreadful night.

"As you all know, I seem to possess a certain affinity for dead. I've always been able to predict the cause of death without needing to do a physical examination on the body. The truth is, it goes beyond just being able to predict the cause of death. I can visualise what a person looked like before their death," I murmured.

I stopped and looked at the three faces staring back at me.

"This started not long after Dad died. It shocked the hell out of me to see him standing beside Mum in the hospital. He said nothing, he just smiled and blew me a kiss before walking out. I've not seen an apparition since that day, thank goodness. Dad's been the only spirit I've seen so far."

Pausing, I swallowed past the grief that still haunted me all these years later.

"After that day, well, things escalated from there. I could tell if someone was close to death, and how people had died. I kept it to myself as much as I could, but it kept overflowing. It was hard at university, especially when I had to work with cadavers. The more I worked with the dead, the further my gifts progressed, to the point I could see souls departing their bodies after they'd died. Sometimes a soul would linger, but eventually, it would depart. It wasn't until my residency that things changed exponentially."

I looked to where Steve sat at the edge of the lounge, his focus entirely on me and my tale.

My smile was slight. "Steve, you mentioned the other evening that I'd changed since coming back from the big smoke. The truth is you're right, I have changed. I'm sure you all noticed my lack of contact, starting about three and a half years ago. I want to reassure you it had nothing to do with anything any of you think you might have done. You see... Shit!" I sobbed, before biting my tongue.

The door was open the memories were flooding through me. I swam against the current, trying to stay afloat; trying to stay above the memories. My shaking hands gripped at my head, coming down to scrub at my face.

There'd been times when I'd thought seriously of trying to scratch my eyes out. Logic had always prevailed, no matter how deep in the abyss I was.

I sniffed indelicately. "Towards the end of my last year of prac, this guy from my class asked me out to dinner a few times. I won't say what his name is, as his family is fairly well-known in Brisbane, but I'm guessing that Uncle Bob will know who it is by the end. Please don't say his name and please don't say anything to anyone else."

I didn't wait for him to acknowledge what I'd said. I wanted this over, I wanted this off my chest.

"Anyway, this guy asked me out. The first two dates went okay; he came across well-mannered and articulate. I didn't get the butterflies I'd been hoping for during that first date, but I gave it another go and thought I'd see how I felt by the end of the third date. We agreed to meet at a restaurant on the Gold Coast and I caught a taxi just in case I had one or two drinks and couldn't drive."

I shuddered visibly at the memory.

"The minute I left home, something felt off. It was as if my gut was trying to tell me I shouldn't go. I put it down to fatigue after having pulled an extra-long shift the day before." My mouth was moving, yet my hands told a whole other story. They were flying everywhere as my words spilled forth. "I got to the restaurant early and waited outside until he arrived. He was very polite and a perfect gentleman like the previous dates. Dinner went okay, although something felt off about him that evening. He kept trying to touch me, and you know how much I hate being touched by people unless I've known them for a while."

My hands clenched into fists, as though I were sitting in the restaurant right at that moment.

"I ended up putting my hands on my lap just to avoid him touching me. By the end of the date, I knew he wasn't for me. The guy pissed me off halfway in when he yelled at the waiter for not bringing his water on time. Who does that?"

I looked at the anxious faces, all sitting at the end of their chairs waiting for me to get to the part I didn't want to get to.

"When dinner finished, I insisted on paying my way, as per normal. This seemed to piss him off. Looking back, I think it was probably because he thought I'd feel obligated to go home with him if he'd paid for such a lovely meal. We left the restaurant, and I ended things right there."

Memories pierced my brain, the mirrored ceiling within my room of doors projecting the horrors of that dreadful period within my life.

"That was a lovely dinner. Would you like to come over to my place for coffee and dessert? My penthouse has this brilliant view of the city. You know how my parents always want the best for me and all that," Brian smiled magnanimously.

He was as greasy as the amount of product he'd slathered in that coifed hair of his. I hated when men put that much gunk in their hair.

"That's okay Brian, I should get home. I have a shift tomorrow morning. These last six months are importantand I need to make them count if I want great references." My finger flew over the screen of my phone as I text my details to the taxi company before I'd even finished my sentence.

I wanted out of here. He was looking at me as if my clothes were already off.

Yeah, so not happening dude. Keep dreaming. The third date does not translate to sex, buddy.

"Are you sure? I have some great pastries I bought today. They're from the little deli around the corner from work. You know the one, right?" Brian persisted.

"Yeah, I'm full, but thank you."

I wasn't, but he didn't need to know that. The bloody portion sizes had been stupid for the price I'd paid.

"Are you sure? These pastries are superb. You won't be disappointed, I promise." His 'my shit don't stink' smile was getting on my nerves, as was his persistence.

I'd have said yes the first damn time you asked me if I wanted to leave with you, shit for brains.

"Yeah, I'm sure. Look, my taxi's arrived. Thanks for a great evening and all. I guess I'll see you around the hospital." I stuck my hand out, waiting to shake his hand, hoping he'd catch the hint that I was done.

It was purely out of politeness. I wanted nothing more than to be in the taxi, speeding towards my little apartment. The second he took my hand, I knew it'd been the wrong move.

He grabbed my hand and squeezed it hard, animosity shining in the depths of his small eyes.

Blinking back tears, I fumed silently. Yeah, he got the message, and he's pissed at me. Well, tough.

His hand tightened further, eliciting a cringe; this seemed to please him and a smile of satisfaction crossed his features.

"You're hurting me, Brian. You can let go of my hand now." My throbbing hand was released, and I opened and closed it, trying to get feeling back into it.

"Sorry, I didn't realise I'd squeezed so hard," He smirked.

"I'm sure you didn't."

Asshole.

My hand would be bruised tomorrow, I could feel it. I slid into the taxi, greeting the elderly driver before giving him my address as he crept away from the curb.

My fourteen-hour shift was a nightmare. Not only did Brian end up not showing up for his shift, but one other resident called in sick as well. My feet and shoulders ached, while my birthmark throbbed incessantly. I was sure I was seeing double.

Keys in hand, I made my way to the exit, heading for the parking lot. Finally reaching my little bomb, the key had only just made it into the keyhole before a searing pain lanced through my birthmark, stealing my breath with its ferocity.

Tears of pain streamed down my face and I tried desperately to retrain my lungs to breathe.

Finally, I drew in deep lungfuls of fresh air. My eyes still watering from the pain and effort.

A body slammed suddenly into my back and a large hand slapped over my mouth. Shocked, my body took precious seconds to tense to fight back, a muscular arm forming a chokehold across my neck before I was dragged backwards.

My oxygen-starved brain finally caught up, and I struggled, kicking my legs outwards. My handbag lay forgotten at the door of my car, leading me to conclude this wouldn't be a snatch and grab robbery, which left only one other option.

Hell no! This is not happening! *My mind screamed.*

Fighting with every ounce of energy I had in my already weary body, my fatigued fingers scratched at the arm around my waist, my nails cracking under the pressure. I attempted to bite down on the hand clasped over my mouth, only nipping a bit of buckled skin.

"Fuck! That hurt, you stupid slut. Now stop resisting before I knock you the fuck out," my abductor spat.

A musky cologne and rancid deodorant hit my nostrils, recognition creeping into my immobilised brain.

Brian?

The guy attacking me was Brian.

His hand dropped from my mouth to my throat, tightening his hold so that my airway blocked. All futile attempts to free myself diminished, as I struggled to draw my next breath. I couldn't believe I'd been stupid enough to say yes to this sadistic rapist.

Icy fury trickled through the fear and time slowed, as he dragged me further back towards the new ute the wanker had been bragging about only yesterday.

I recalled how he'd boasted, how much the thing had cost, and how he'd had a steel canopy specifically made for the back. Now I knew why the bastard wanted it windowless.

What had been a trickle of icy fury increased to a steady flow. It pounded at my fear riddled brain demanding access until it finally gave in allowing the fury to infiltrate it.

The trees dancing merely in the salty breeze ceased; the earth herself paused, and the people in the surrounding area came to a standstill with her.

A masculine energy, as old as the earth herself, turned in my direction, searching for me, before focusing on me.

The surrounding air vibrated with the sheer amount of energy and rage exuding from him. Next came a more feminine touch, and I sensed she was as old as the man.

Seconds later, I felt my mother stop where she was, my name falling from her lips.

Once again I felt the man's presence closer by this time. His loving smile imprinted on my mind, yet no face accompanied it.

"Trust your instincts, sweet child Open that door you fear so much in that brilliant mind of yours and let your true nature emerge. It'll protect you and guide you in times such as these. To ignore it is to ignore a crucial part of yourself," *He crooned.*

I remembered the exact day that door had shown up; it'd been the day of my father's death when I could have sworn I saw his ghost standing beside his own death bed looking between my grieving mother and I. He had smiled at my mother with so much love it'd hurt to look at. Turning to me, he winked, blowen me his usual kiss before he'd turned and left the room.

Until now, I'd stayed away from that door. Whatever was behind it was cold and had enormous strength, more than I felt I could handle.

"Do not be afraid, sweet child, it won't hurt you. Let go now. I can't help you, this is something that only you can do. Now hurry, unlock that door, sweetchild. NOW!" *he yelled, his rage and frustration odd considering I didn't know him.*

I listened to the man in my head because, well, what other choice did I have? Focusing on that blackened door I feared so much, I nudged it open. Bright white light flooded my mind, and with it, a cold rage and strength I'd never thought existed surged through my veins.

Still pacing in front of my television, I rasped, "it's here where things become a little foggy. It's as if the next part was a dream, it's never as clear as I want it to be as if I'm looking through a dust-covered window."

I looked up briefly to see if I still had the attention of my audience congregated in my lounge room. No one had moved a muscle the entire time I'd been speaking, so I continued my tale.

173

The world once again sped back up. Brian was too busy dragging me to notice any of the warnings. If he'd been looking he'd have noticed my hair whitening or the fact that my skin had gone ice cold. My eyes were now casting eerie shadows just in front of me.

I no longer fought for air, as an unnatural calm fell upon me and with it the realisation of what I needed to do.

Body going limp, I faked a faint.

"Oomph. What the hell? Oh, come on, don't tell me you passed out, are you serious?" Brian raged, his left arm dropping to compensate for my weight.

I came alive then.

My bent knees exploded upwards and my limp head snapped back, a crack winging its way into the night air. My heightened vision followed each crimson speck spraying through the night air. Brian's painful yelp preceded him cursing my very existence. I didn't care though, because I was free.

Losing his balance, we fell together, hitting the tar with a thud. Dropping off him, I rolled out of arm's reach and rose to my knees, my gaze snapping to his horizontal form.

A smile colder than the winds that touched the peaks in the Arctic tugged at my lips and my hair, which had come loose in the struggle, lifted, floating gently in an unearthly wind.

Raw energy bled off my crouched form, driving into the ground beneath my palms. Cracks forked across the tar.

Brian was trying to stem the flow of blood dribbling down the sides of his face from what was sure to be a broken nose.

"Fuck! You bitch, you're dead, do you hear me? Fucking Dead! After I'm done screwing you, I will watch the life bleed out your fucking ey...." His rant cut short when he finally looked up to where I crouched and into the very eyes he kept harping on about.

Whatever he saw in them had him launching to his knees, before scurrying sideways into the nearest car.

"Nothing to say, Brian?" I crooned. "Tell me, what is it you see that has you scrambling back like a frightened little puppy? What's elicited that delicious scent of fear I'm smelling?" I grinned savagely. "You chose the wrong girl to fuck with, mate."

Calmly rising, I stalked towards him as he cowered against the car. His fear heightened that coldness within me, excitement rising as my gaze zeroed in on the small orb at the centre of his chest.

A very faint speck of white surrounded by blood red, mustard and obsidian shone from within that small orb.

His soul.

All I'd have to do is bend down and place my hand over that little ball and it'd come to me. No one would ever know why he was comatose.

The power was exhilarating, riding me like the wild hunt, spurring my need for vengeance.

Gazing into that wretched soul of his, I caught glimpses of the women he had beaten, the women he'd tortured and raped. He'd been doing this since he was a teenager, and had no empathy for the women he'd hurt. He was a true sadist, thriving off the hurt and pain caused. It would be so easy to take from him what took from those women.

"Nothing to say, Brian? Tsk tsk. Mummy and Daddy won't be saving you from what's about to happen," I taunted. "Every action has a consequence. You took something from all those women you raped and tortured, something they may never regain. Now... well, now I'm here on their behalf. I'm here as their voice as well as my own. When a woman says no, you little prick, she means no," I growled. "And if she can't say no because you've drugged her, then keep that tiny dick of yours in your pants. Speaking of dicks, by the time I'm done with yours I'll be surprised if you're ever able to use the little fella again."

Horror and panic rolled off him, beating at me, fuelling the darkness within. It fuelled my need to inflict the pain he had wrought on so many.

Stepping forward, my body blurred. One moment I was in the middle of the road and the next I was at his side. What should have taken at least ten steps took only one. The speed was exhilarating.

Crouching down with a confidence I hadn't felt moments ago; a deathly pale claw shackled his left wrist — my hand, so changed.

"Brian, this will hurt. What was it you said to Stacey, again? Oh yes, that's right, if you scream I'll hurt you more? So Brian, here's the deal, if you scream I will hurt you more, so pretty please scream as loud as you can," I crooned with anticipation.

When he remained silent, I yanked his wrist upward before stretching the arm into the night air. Pushing up from my crouch, my knee bent at the last second, as I brought his elbow down over my knee. The bone obliterated with a satisfying crunch, his screams erupting loud on long.

"Oh, Brian." I shook my head, smiling in satisfaction.

The part of me that believed in peace and equality had long been locked away safely within my mind, where she wouldn't feel the backlash of guilt for the pain being inflicted.

"That has to be the most wonderful sound I've heard all day. Now next on my list would be that hand of yours. I think we should end your career as a doctor, don't you? I mean you just haven't quite grasped the point of the Hippocratic Oath," I pouted at him.

Grasping his left hand, I crushed it in my firm grip. The pop and crackle of bones snapping under my firm, relentless grip vibrated through my palm.

Not waiting for his screams to die down, I moved towards his bent legs. Looking down at the pathetic excuse for a human rocking from side to side grasping his arm, I stopped speaking. There was no point. It wasn't like he could hear me past the blood rushing in his ears, anyway.

177

Brian was looking rather pale, though. He'd likely to pass out after this next break.

Placing my foot on his right knee, I forced him to straighten it. I wasn't a big girl by any means, but thanks to the power riding me, I didn't have to exert too much pressure or wait too long before his knee shattered. He didn't scream this time, he simply passed out.

It was then that I heard my name being crooned.

"Evanee, baby girl, look at me. You need to stop, you need to look at me, my sweet angel. Come back to me, baby girl." Her sweet tone stalled my foot from coming down on Brian's opposite knee.

Recognition flickered somewhere at the back of my mind. I knew that voice, it'd sung to me as a little girl. It'd soothed me when I was hurt.

The pure rage and power riding me made it difficult to pull back.

The woman crooned gently once more, "come on, baby girl, you can do this. You need to take control of it."

"He hurt me," I snarled. "He's hurt so many women. He needs to pay for the hurt and damage he's caused," I raged.

"I know he does, baby. He deserves every bit of pain you've caused so far. I see what you see. But if you keep going, you'll end up killing him and I know the sweet girl I raised would never want that. Come back to me, sweet angel. Come back and we'll work on healing you. I'll make sure you and the women he's hurt will have justice," my mother swore.

Warmth tickled at my feet and legs, slowly ascending as my power gently released its hold on me.

"Very well, but there's one last thing I need to do," I murmured.

I moved then, gliding between Brian's legs. Bending over, I placed the tips of my skeletal fingers at his Khaki covered crotch. Thoughts of rotting fruit, of decayed flesh, flashed before my eyes.

Rising, the pong of rotting flesh left to decay in the sun for hours wafted into the salty night air.

"Now he'll no longer be able to cause pain or give pleasure to any woman," I purred with satisfaction.

The cold power retreated behind its blackened door, closing slowly, the vacuum sucking every bit of power back behind it. It shut with an echoing boom, and I dropped to my knees, spent physically, mentally and emotionally.

Looking up as my mother's arms came around me, she placed gentle kisses on my forehead, murmuring what a good girl I was and how proud of me she was.

I stared bleary-eyed at my mother, darkness encroaching on my vision. "Mummy?"

My world descended into darkness.

"I woke in the hospital eight hours later. The cops had been waiting to talk to me about what happened. Mum told them she found me passed out beside Brian. The last I heard he had to undergo an elbow, knee, and hand reconstruction. Doctors couldn't work out why his penis smelled and looked as if it were rotting, yet it never fell off," I winced. "His parents tried to sue me, claiming it was me who attacked their precious baby boy. That fell through when I gave the police names of every single one of the girls he had ever raped or tortured."

Scrubbing at my head, words kept spilling out, "Their names are still seared into my brain, and it's an extensive list, let me tell you. The cocky bastard kept souvenirs from each of the poor women. The police gathered enough evidence to lay charges against him. Mum pulled some serious strings to keep my name from being mentioned in the media. I still have no idea what she did," I confessed.

I slowly and carefully closed the rotted door within my mind. It was a lot easier this time; it didn't creak and groan as if it was about to shatter. There wasn't a crushing force behind it, not now that I'd given voice to what had happened.

Forcing myself to stop pacing, I turned hesitantly back to the three people I cared so much about, petrified of the disgust and fear I was so certain would be on their faces.

My eyes widened when I finally took in a heartbroken, Aunty Marg, who was now crying openly.

Steve was hunched over, his head clenched between fisted hands. He was muttering beneath his breath, his angry words unrecognisable.

Beside Aunty Marg, Uncle Bob removed his glasses and wiped his red-tinged eyes.

his facial features, watching the emotions chase each other across his face.

I watched hurt, anger and sorrow war with each other in his hooded eyes. Lumbering to his feet, he took one step at a time until he was past the coffee table. This was it. This was the moment where he would either acknowledge what I'd just told him, or he would walk past me and out the front door.

Steve rubbed at his stubbled head, hands rubbing back and forth as he battled with whatever emotions were raging within him.

His breath rushed out of him and he took one giant step, tugging me into his giant arms as he gritted out, "Shit, Evanee, I'm so mad right now. Not at you though, but at the arsehole who hurt you. I could kill him right now and sleep well tonight. From now on you'll not be walkin' to your car alone, do you hear me? If I'm not on, I'll make sure someone walks with you. This is not up for discussion." Putting me at arms' length, he searched my tear-filled eyes. "I'm sorry I couldn't be there to help you. But I'm so proud of you for telling us what happened. I'm also proud of you for not killing the guy. You did something better; you gave all those women a voice and the ability to get justice. I've got just one question though?"

Nodding, his lips tugged up into a half-smile. "Did you really make the guy's penis rot?"

I nodded at Steve, who winced in mock sympathy. "I can't say the bastard didn't deserve it."

Giggling, I looked between each of them. "So out of everything I just told all of you the only thing you guys are taking away from my story is me not killing the guy? None of you is going to mention how weird it is that I broke his bones with little effort or my transformation?"

Seriously, no one found that weird at all?

"Sweetheart, listen to me," Bob smiled, "You'll find that not everything can be explained by science in this life. There are events that happen or beings who exist, that are beyond the science of our time. I learned this a long time ago. I think I speak for everyone in this room when I say that no matter what happens we will always love and cherish you. If you keep true to who you are in here," Bob patted his chest. "That's all we could ever ask for."

Not knowing what to do next, I gave into the relief that'd been hovering just out of my reach for so long. Loud sobs wracked my body, and I allowed myself to break apart with the people that loved me so dearly. They would help put me back together.

They loved me unconditionally.

CHAPTER 11

With all the drama that had entered my life recently, I was feeling off-kilter.

Questions I'd ignored and put off about my psychic abilities were now rearing their ugly heads. I'd finally shared my darkest secret with the people I loved, and although emotionally spent; I felt one step closer to finally healing.

Despite taking such a monumental step in confessing what had happened with Brian, I was still on edge.

The arguments with Erick and my attempts to resist the pull I felt between the two of us were wearing me out. I didn't want to rely on him, yet he always seemed to be there when I was at my worst.

Standing at my kitchen sink, I dialed my mother number, praying she'd have words of wisdom for me in my hour of need. Staring out at my derelict backyard, I waited for her to answer.

"Hey, how's my baby girl going?" Reagan's soothing voice came through the speaker, and I smiled fondly.

"Hey, Mum. I'm okay. How are you going? How's life in Paris and your family?" I answered, avoiding her question for the moment.

"Life in Paris is just as fabulous as I remembered. The tension is still there with your grandfather, but it's nowhere near as bad as it was the day I left. The entire family is eager to meet you," she chuckled.

I snorted, "I bet they are."

I had no interest in meeting my mother's side of the family at this point in time. Maybe at a later stage, but right now they were the arses that had abandoned their flesh and blood.

"Evanee, don't be like that. They're trying." My mother's disapproving sigh plucked at my heart and I regretted my outburst.

This was important to her, and I respected that, even if I was likely to never respect her family.

"Now that you're making amends with them, does it mean that it's safe for me to ask why they had such a major objection to you marrying Dad?" I ventured cautiously.

I'd been wondering this for years. John Sheperd may not have come from a wealthy family, but he was educated and had loved my mother more than life itself.

"It was multiple reasons, but their main objection was that I broke off my engagement to Bastien to be with your father," she admitted.

Shocked by her confession, I was at a loss for words.

"Evanee, are you still there?"

"Yes Mum, I'm still here. Are you saying you had an affair with Dad?"

"Yes and no. Now before you go jumping to conclusions, let me explain. My engagement with Bastien was an arranged one. The family line was and is dying out. My generation has produced no heirs and we've lost far too many of my uncles, aunts and cousins to various accidents over the years," Reagan sighed on the other end of the line. "Bastien was at the top of his game, he'd branched away from his family and opened up his own company. They thought the two of us marrying might produce heirs and prolong the family bloodline. I only went along with arrangement out of duty to my family." Pausing briefly, I waited patiently for her to continue. "The week before I was due to get married I visited Louvre, and that's where I met John. My entire world shifted that day. It stood still. At that moment it was just the two of us and I knew then that he was special, that he was the one I was meant to be with."

It was rare for Mum to talk so freely about the past. I let her continue without a word of interruption, lest it halt the flow. But there was one thing I needed clarified.

"Did it felt as if the world stood still when you touched Dad?" I asked nervously.

My stomach clenched at the memory of the first time Erick and I had touched at the party. Pushing the memory away, I focused back on the conversation at hand.

"Yes, it was as if no one else existed around us. If I didn't know any better, I'd have sworn Fate herself had planned for us to meet that day," Mum sighed happily.

Contemplating this turn of events, Reagan's soft voice dragged me back to the present. "Evanee, you've gone silent again. Why did you call me? I can't imagine it was to hear about how your Dad and I met."

Damit. She knows me too well.

"I told Uncle Bob, Aunty Marg, and Steve about what happened that night outside the hospital," I blurted out before I could censor my words.

It was never easy keeping secrets from my mother.

Reagan's wariness trickled through the speaker. "Did you tell them everything that happened?"

"Yes, I did. It was time. I can't take the guilt anymore. The burden of carrying the secret, it's just too much for me." Emotion clogged my throat the longer I spoke and I sniffed indelicately.

"I thought we agreed that you would never speak about what truly happened that night to anyone other than me. You know how important it is to keep your gifts a secret. We agreed that if you told anyone, you would leave the part out about your gifts," Reagan reminded me.

Anger and frustration bubbled up at her reminder.

"You mean my *psychic ability,* the ones where you won't tell me where it came from and whether anyone else in the family has it?" I snapped.

My body quivered with hurt and frustration. "Well, mother, it's a little too late for that. That power you said was contained in my mind has gotten a hell of a lot stronger. Uncle Bob and Steve already knew I was psychic. They've known since my first day of work experience during High School."

"How did they find out?" Reagan whispered wretchedly.

"I blurted out the cause of death on the first body I came into contact with. It was an accident. I didn't realise a body was coming in and Uncle Bob didn't realise I'd left the pathology lab. I stumbled across them placing it in the freezer and asked why someone with an aneurism would need an autopsy. Since then it's become a bit of a guessing game."

Picking up my phone, I stomped towards my room, flopping down onto my bed.

Why couldn't my mother understand that I couldn't keep this secret anymore? Why was it so important to hide my psychic ability from the people I loved and trusted the most? If I hadn't, I might have been able to connect with others like myself—like Erick. I might not have felt so alone.

"Has anything else happened besides what you've just told me?" Reagan asked, her motherly instincts kicking in.

"Besides me leaving a man in a perpetual state of rot? … let me think… now that you mention it, I can see souls trapped in the dead. Oh, and I can interact telepathically with a man I haven't seen since my teenage years," I replied sarcastically.

I frowned at Reagan's silence. She was hiding something from me, every bone in my body could feel it.

"Just what the hell is going on with me, mother? There's something you're not telling me."

"Who is it? What's the guy's name, Evanee? This is important," she demanded.

Why the hell does it matter who I can talk to telepathically? Isn't it shocking enough that there's someone else out there with similar abilities to me?

"Evanee!" Reagan snapped. "Answer me right now. Who can talk to you telepathically?" Her authoritative tone startled me enough for me to push aside my petulance and answer her.

"Erick. Erick Tenebris. He's returned to Murder Point Bay after being away for nearly twelve years," I whispered in answer.

An image of piercing green eyes popped into my mind at the mention of his name.

"Tenebris, why does that surname sound so familiar? You said he was returning to Murder Point Bay? Did he say why he left, or how he's able to communicate with you mind to mind?" Reagan demanded.

"I have no clue where he went; I didn't feel it was necessary to ask. As to why he can communicate with me, I have no idea how he does it. All he said was that his abilities had been present since childhood. He's shocked about my abilities though, and seemed to think I wasn't fully human for some bizarre reason," I admitted reluctantly.

"Evanee, listen to me. I've only ever tried to do what was best for you. Yes, I will admit there are some

189

things I haven't told you about. There are things I'd hoped I'd never have to tell you about, but your abilities are escalating." Reagan's nervousness set me on edge. "This is something we need to discuss in person, not over the phone. Perhaps me rekindling my relationship with my family is a positive thing. It'll allow me to explain things about your ancestry, things that will answer all the questions you have about your abilities," She was murmuring now, suggesting she was likely out somewhere and didn't want to be overheard.

Exasperated, I pleaded, "Can't you just tell me now? I mean how am I'm meant to stop things from getting worse if I don't even understand what is going on with me?"

This phone call had been a disastrous idea; not only had it awoken my anger, but it had left me with far more questions than answers.

"Evanee, I have to go. I'm sorry, baby girl, but I promise I'll book a flight back home as soon as possible. I'll answer every single one of your questions when I return. In the meantime, stay away from Erick until I know more about him. I love you, my sweet angel."

The line went dead before I could protest. I didn't even have time to tell her I loved her too.

CHAPTER 12

My days off passed quicker than I'd expected, my mind continuously churning over what my mother had said.

I kept myself occupied doing laundry and housework, and could now officially say that my house now sparkled within an inch of its life. I even got a head start on my backyard.

Wednesday afternoon I'd gone around the yard collecting any scrap metal I came across. Staring at the pile in the corner of the yard, I made a mental note to ask Brad for his ute on the weekend so I could take it all to the dump.

I was excited about the prospect of finally having somewhere to entertain Brad and Ellie in the summer months. Plus, I'd be able to BBQ; I loved cooking outdoors when I got the chance.

The buzz of my phone on Thursday evening stalled my thoughts on just how close I wanted my new jacuzzi to the patio. Digging my phone out of my shorts' pocket, I smiled down at the name lighting up my screen.

"Evening, stranger. What mischief have you gotten yourself into?" I teased.

Striding back to the cover of the patio where a lonely camp chair sat, I plonked myself down and settled in for what no doubt would be a lengthy chat.

"I was about to ask you the same thing," Ellie chuckled. "The rumour mill has been in overdrive about a hot visitor, and you possibly getting the sack. You don't even want to know the rumours going around about you and said visitors," Ellie sang sweetly down the line.

She barely managed to pause for a second for dramatic effect, before she blurted, "Okay, so get this, apparently an intern upstairs has seen a man that sounds suspiciously like Erick coming to visit you, like a lot. Oh, and Bob caught the two of you at it in the staff room, which is why you are getting the sack and all," Ellie chattered excitedly.

Laughter burst from my compressed lips, stopping Ellie in her million miles an hour track. I kept on laughing until tears streamed unchecked down my cheeks. Ellie said nothing the entire time.

"Are… are you serious? People think Erick, as in the great and mighty Erick Tenebris, and I are sleeping together. You realise how stupid that sounds, right?" My poor stomach ached from laughing too hard and I rubbed it.

"What's so stupid about that, Ev? You're one beautiful woman on the inside and outside. He'd be damn lucky to even get your attention," Ellie exclaimed, outraged at the blatant dismissal of my self-worth.

Aww, she is such a sweetie. A terrible liar, but sweet none the less.

"That's lovely of you to say, Ellie, but let me put those little rumours to rest. No, Erick and I are not going at it like rabbits in the staff room. Also, I wasn't fired, Bob forced me to take until Monday off after I burnt

192

myself out." I rolled my eyes at the stupidity of the gossipers wandering the hospital grounds. "The only truth in all that gossip is that Erick has been coming to the office, and I can tell you it's not to play catch up with me. He's been asking after you, actually. Oh, and he wanted my help with some issues he's having with his entourage who've turned up dead."

Ellie stuttered in the background, and I raced ahead to ease any fears she might have about Erick's questions about her.

"Oh, but don't worry, I didn't give much away about you. I told him to get off his arse and ask you himself," I soothed.

Reclining back, I looked up at my roof.

I need to get up there with a ladder and get the cobwebs and mould off. Hell, I'll probably just repaint the damn thing while I'm at it.

"Uh, why the hell would Erick be asking about me? And what bodies are you talking about? Wouldn't they all end up coming through you anyway?" Ellie's curiosity was as bad as mine.

"I have no idea. He probably likes you and wants to ask you out. I'm not a hundred percent sure about what's happening with the bodies. We were supposed to talk about it the other evening. I must check with him the next time I see him. Thanks for reminding me. Hey, talking of Erick, I need to talk to you about something."

Changing subjects, I sat forward, focusing on the concrete under my feet.

"This sounds serious. What's on your mind?" Ellie answered distractedly.

I could hear what sounded like a packet rustling in the background.

"I need to talk to you about what happened at the party. About how the glass shattered, and why your scream might have triggered my blackout?" I responded with caution.

The rustling from Ellie's end suddenly stopped, before she cautiously replied. "I do not understand why the glass shattered. All I can think is that the glass was unstable before I screamed, and my high pitch must have somehow impacted a crack already in the glass. I have no clue."

Liar, liar, pants on fire.

"As for why you passed out while I was screaming, I thought you would know more about that than me? You've heard me scream before and you've not passed out then. Maybe it was something you ate, or maybe you're coming down with something." Her response was weak, and her deflection a dead giveaway she knew more than she was letting on.

The question was why she felt she couldn't tell me the entire truth?

"I'm feeling fine, maybe a little confused, but definitely fine. Ellie, you know you can trust me, right?" I reassured her. "You know you could tell me anything and I'd never judge you for it. I might joke around a little, but I'd never judge you."

I hoped that my encouragement might help her feel comfortable enough to tell me whatever it was she was hiding because she was hiding something. Her weariness said as much.

"I know I can trust you, silly." Ellie's nervous laughter wasn't very reassuring. "Maybe it was all the stress from Desmond hounding you, and too much work that made you blackout? Hey, you know what we need? We need another get-together. You, me, Brad and a shit load of alcohol."

Frustrated at the lies and lack of transparency surrounding my life, I let the conversation drop. I'd eventually find out, I just needed to practice a minor thing I wasn't very good at — patience.

With a lengthy sigh, I agreed, "Yeah, that sounds like a marvellous idea. Do you remember the big fella Jordan, who was at the party?"

"It's kind of hard to forget any of the people we met that night." Her relief at the change in topic was short-lived as a microwave pinged somewhere in the background, promptly eliciting a series of curses from Ellie.

I was guessing she'd made something explode in it.

"I was thinking of inviting him over on Saturday night. What do you think?"

I knew they'd all get along; it was just a matter of getting Ellie and Brad to allow someone new into our circle. Apparently we all had our own trust issues. Go figure.

"Maybe we should invite the others too? It'd be kind of rude not to, especially since they helped us out at the party," Ellie pointed out.

Damit, she's right.

"Plus, I wouldn't mind setting my eyes on Tristan again. I like Erick and all, but not in that way." She admitted.

I snickered at her confession.

"Yeah, okay, I'll ask Erick, but I wouldn't hold your breath waiting for Tristan to come. I get the impression I won't be on his Christmas card list this year," I grouched.

We hadn't connected. It was probably the slap I'd given his boss the first day I'd met him, or that I'd called him an elf.

"Fair enough. What time do you want us to come over?" Ellie muttered, as the crinkling of a packet sounded from her end.

And here came the bribery and corruption part of the conversation.

"I was hoping you and Brad might be up for a working bee," I said cheerfully.

I purposely didn't mention what I had planned, knowing full well that if I went in with what I was intending to do, she'd bolt quicker than a spooked horse.

"Ah yeah, okay cool, as long as there's food and alcohol you know I'm in. What are we tackling?"

Boom, she'd just locked herself in.

No backing out now Ellie, you're mine, biatch.

"The backyard." I announced with glee.

The profanities erupted on the other end, and I flopped backwards giggling, listening gleefully to Ellie using every swearword she could think of. Some of them in unfamiliar languages.

"Now Ellie, it's not that bad. Just some long grass and small animals." Stirring the pot was so much fun, especially if said pot was Ellie. Her temper could be worse than mine and that was saying something.

"Long grass, my backside. Evanee, you'd need to light the lot just to get to the tree in the middle! Why do you do this to me?" She wailed.

Laughing hysterically, I waited for her to finish huffing, dragging out the torture just a little longer. I knew Brad would say the same thing when I spoke to him, which reminded me.

"Hey is Brad home yet, or is he still at the gym?" I'd call him before Ellie let slip what I had planned.

"No, he's not home. I have half a mind to ring him now before you do and tell him your evil plans," she huffed sullenly.

"Yeah, yeah. You and I both know you won't be giving him a head's up, otherwise who else will suffer alongside you?" I stirred.

I still hadn't told her I'd cleared the backyard—I would soon. This was just too much fun.

"Damn straight. Why should he get to rest up at home while I have to slave away in a tetanus minefield?" Ellie grumped.

Holding my stomach, I marvelled at how good it felt to laugh, at how wonderful it felt to be happy again. It hadn't happened all that much in recent years, but I'd work on it.

I put her out of her misery; regaling the tale of my slaving away in the backyard and in the house on my days off. I was proud that it was nearly done. I really wanted to just have a hangout session.

She sighed with relief. "Thank goodness for that. I swear Evanee, that backyard of yours gives me nightmares, and I don't need anymore."

Ellie paused for a second.

"Hey, Brad just got back home I'll pop you on speaker. Oi Brad, Evie's on the phone! Get your backside to the kitchen!" Ellie bellowed.

Cringing, I pulled the phone from my ear.

Damn, that girl has a set of lungs on her.

"Is she? Hey weirdo, what's up?" Brad puffed.

"Hey, man. Good workout?"

"Yeah, I kicked arse. Nothing like a good sparring match to get the heart racing," Brad chuckled, his breathing slowly returning to normal.

I cringed, "that sounds painful to me, to be honest. Anyway, I was wondering if you'd be keen on doing a working bee this weekend? Food and drinks supplied, of course."

"Yeah, cool as. I'm always in, as long as it's not your backyard," he agreed.

Ha, sucker.

I chuckled evilly, "Funny you should say that; because there's only one area left to tackle."

"Oh hell no, Evie! You're not seriously thinking of doing the backyard? Ah man, come on Ev, no!" Brad groaned with despair.

"Would you relax? Between you and Ellie, I don't know which one of you is the bigger sook. Look, I've already cleared the debris that was lying around. I've also mowed the damn thing too. All we'll be doing is hopefully making a start on the fire pit and tiling the patio," I sighed with exasperation. "Although, I do need to borrow you ute, if that's okay?"

"Yeah, yeah, okay. And yes you can borrow the ute."

The sound of him sipping beer had my tastebuds tingling in envy.

Ah man, I want a beer now. I might pop down to the bottle shop and grab a six-pack, then I'll chill with a homemade burger.

Getting up, I laid out my plans for the weekend for Brad. I shut and locked the kitchen door before I

199

swiped my purse off the kitchen counter and made my way towards the front door, flicking the outside lights on as I breezed past. It'd be dark by the time I got home.

"You're a good man. Hang on a moment, will you?"

Climbing into my car, she revved to life. Sliding my gear shift into reverse, I waited patiently for the Bluetooth to take over.

"Brad, you there?" I checked.

"Yeah, I'm still here. Are you in your car?"

"Yes, I am. Hearing you drink your beer had me craving some. What alcohol do you want for this weekend?"

Exiting my driveway, I turned toward town, mentally taking notes of what alcohol to pick up. I was halfway to the bottle shop when I remembered that I needed to ask Brad and Ellie a few questions relating to the two bodies I'd examined.

"Oh, there's something I need to talk to you and Ellie about while I have you on the phone. But give me a second."

"No worries," Brad murmured distractedly.

I could hear them chatting about the exploded potatoes. Brad was telling Ellie to just clean the stuff up and he'd cook. She bitched that she didn't know how the damn things had exploded. Driving into the drive-thru, I secured my order before exiting. I waited until I was a safe distance away from listening ears before focusing back on Brad and Ellie who were still holding.

"Hey, you guys still there?" I checked.

"Yeah, we're here. What's going on?" Ellie asked.

"What I need to tell you was approved by Bob, but it's still confidential. This does not go beyond us three, okay?"

"That's fine. You know we can keep our mouths shut," Brad reassured me.

They had to, working for a private corporation such as Aeternum. The only thing they'd been able to tell me was that they both worked with viruses. They knew how to be discreet.

"Roughly a fortnight ago I received an unidentified male. Nothing seemed out of the ordinary until I flipped him over and noticed a large freaking hole in his back. And that's not the weird part, trust me. The weird part would be the fact that the wound was an exit wound with no point of entry. It had some sort of acidic residue on the flesh surrounding the wound."

I turned into my street, watching for any children playing nearby.

"This stuff was potent enough to continue eating away at the skin after being in storage until I took the body back out on Monday. Did I mention it ate through a pair of my Kevlar gloves as well?"

"Shit really? Did you identify what type of acid it was?" Brad sounded closer to the phone this time — I'd caught his attention.

"Nope, I sent what little of the swabs were left for testing. But guys, this thing is unlike anything I've ever seen. Initially, I thought it was some weapon, but after seeing the penetration holes in the spinal cord and brain, I began leaning towards a virus or bacteria."

Pulling into my driveway, I scooped up my phone and hit speaker. Turning my car off, I sat back.

"Fuck, Evie, I've not seen or heard of any virus or bacteria like this. Have you, Ellie?" Brad checked.

"No, I haven't heard of anything on that level, but that's not to say that the government has nothing in the wings. I could reach out to my brother, Ronan, maybe see if he's heard of any experiments being undertaken. I'll do it discreetly, don't want my mother finding out," Ellie volunteered.

Considering her mother was high up in the military, I wouldn't be surprised if she already knew.

"Thanks, Ellie, I appreciate it. I took double samples of John Doe hoping you guys would be able to take a look. I get the impression this isn't some run of the mill virus or bacteria. It feels different, more bio-weapon in nature. That's not all though!" I took a breath.

These two were the last of my close friends who didn't know, and technically they shouldn't, but they had access to high-level information. Even if they couldn't outright say anything, they might be able to hint.

"On Monday I went to show Bob the male, and an unidentified female turns up with the same wound pattern. Now the acid had stopped eating at her flesh by the time she got to us, but her wound was at least twice the size of the male's. I'm not sure if it was from the acid eating at the flesh or whether it was because whatever caused the wound was bigger. Now my gut's telling me there's more to this than just two random bodies. It won't surprise me if we get another one sometime soon."

The silence was deafening as I sat in the darkening interior of my car, contemplating the severity of the last bit of my statement.

"You thinking serial killer?" The graveness in Brad's tone echoed in the depths of my soul.

"I'm not sure. Other than the physical wounds, the two bodies have nothing in common. No physical similarities and no genetic connection that I know of. Detective Bernard is looking into it, but I doubt he'll find anything." Sighing, my thoughts centred on the bodies and what I'd found. "There were other things that struck me as odd, such as each body had an indentation on the heart and scratch marks on the four upper ribs. When results come back, I know they'll show an increase in leukocytes. I'll get an edited copy of my personal notes to you guys. Maybe you'll see something I'm missing. This doesn't feel personal. But guys, the injuries are unlike anything I've ever seen," I exhaled shakily.

No forensic pathologist wanted a serial killer on their hands. Serial killers meant longer hours and more pressure from above to discover some miracle piece of evidence that would help either bust the killer or add to the profile.

Brad and Ellie agreed to look; the seriousness of the conversation bringing down the collective mood.

If anyone knew of a biological weapon that could have caused this or could find out, it'd be them.

CHAPTER 13

With dinner finished and three beers into my six-pack, I decided to ignore my mother's warning about staying away from Erick. Part of it was me rebelling against my mother, the rest was plain curiosity. I'd finally met someone with abilities like mine.

It was time to experiment a little with the link I shared with Erick. I wasn't entirely sure it would work, but hey, what did I have to lose?

Grabbing another beer, I headed over to my favourite couch, sinking into soft cream cushions.

Ahh, bliss.

Popping my beer on a wooden coaster on the coffee table, I laid back. I had no clue where I would even start.

Well, considering he popped into your mind, that might be a good place to start, don't you think? Seventeen-year-old me had decided her expertise was needed because obviously, I was taking too long to come up with an idea.

I know. The thing is, he warned me about just popping into his mind. I still don't even know how everything works. What if I open that door again and something escapes? Mum isn't here to help reel me back in. I could hurt someone.

You could, darling, but it's time to live a little. And cue the bimbo, she just had to add her two cents' worth.

It's getting crowded in here. How about you both shut it and let me concentrate a little? I'll call you if I need you, okay. I could fairly see them shrugging as they faded away.

Eyes drifting shut, I breathed in deeply. Gently drifting around my round room, I arrived underneath the hole Erick had created.

I looked up at the glass panel and could see that there was darkness beyond it, yet there were flecks of green and red trapped within the glass as if it'd somehow captured Erick's essence.

I reached for those little flecks, my bare feet lifting off the floor, the pale blue dress I wore floating gently around my ankles. My fingers skimmed across those emerald and garnet flecks and golden veins appeared wherever my finger-tips touched.

Here goes nothing.

Focusing on how Erick had looked the last time he had appeared in my mind, in all his half-naked glory, I gently and cautiously whispered his name.

He'd warned me not to intrude into his mind, but I had no idea how to control what I was attempting, so I'd hold on for the ride and hope things didn't go to hell along the way.

The glass held in place, but the scenery beyond it changed. Swirls of emerald and garnet intertwined, while sparks of gold exploded at random intervals. It was magnificent, reminding me of the kaleidoscope I'd had as a child, and how much I'd loved the colours and beautiful patterns.

The scene halted, and I gazed into what I hoped was Erick's mind. Unlike my circular room, he housed a library and what looked to me like a medieval dungeon. There were thousands of books, with no labels on the spines. Doors were scattered between randomly aligned shelves. They were thick and solid with iron bars slid into place, locking in whatever memories stood behind them.

I was so caught up by what I saw I didn't think twice before my palm flattened against the glass panel before me. Searing pain shot through my hand and up my arm. My incorporeal body contorted in pain, while distantly I could feel that my physical body bow off the couch.

I couldn't remove my hand; the panel that'd been glass moments before, now gelatinous and pulling my hand inside. Blue and white flames licked at my arms, and I was burning from the intense heat.

I cried out again, tears trailing down my face. Why the hell had I thought this would be a good idea?

My hand wouldn't release and try as I might, I couldn't form a single coherent word. All I could do was sob from the pain.

In a panic I looked around me; I now hung mid-air within my circular room. Through tears of pain and anguish, I looked to that blackened door. Memories of the coolness; of the power it held becoming more appealing by the second.

I have no other choice.

Envisioning a door chain, I released the latch inch by inch until the chain was at its full length. Icy air swirled excitedly through the gap before a blinding white light burst through.

'Please help me! The pain... it's too much,' I begged that blinding white light.

Despite being kept behind lock and key, it didn't resist my plea, slithering across the carpeted floor; a cold mist arched up, tenderly caressing my feet.

The mist surged up to engulf my body, and the relief was instantaneous.

Staring daggers at the trap I'd set off, I ground out one word, *'enough!'*

The flames stuttered momentarily before they blazed hot once more, the glass continuing to hold me captive.

'Persistent, aren't you? Well, when I say enough, I... mean... enough,' I ground out between clenched teeth.

Conjuring the image of liquid nitrogen, I directed the mist down my arm, coating the flames and freezing them in place. Not stopping at my arm, I continued to the glass above my head.

Onyx sparks hissed when the liquid ice touched the panel.

Kneeling at the panel, I pulled my left arm back, throwing as much power as I could into it, I bought my fist down hard.

Nothing.

Staring hard at the untarnished panel, I finally noticed the multiple layers of traps Erick had set.

'Are you kidding me? How many traps does one bloody man need? Right, I'm done. I want out.'

Black flames blazed to life, licking at my left fist; I bought it down to fracture the square, obliterating it with my second punch.

Hurtling through the shattered glass, I had milliseconds to react before I landed face first. An age-old instinct I didn't realise I had kicked in, and I tucked into a ball a split seconds before I landed gently on silky oak flooring. Shoulders straightening, I knelt stairing at the floor, panting the last of the pain away, my foot at the ready to take a step if need be.

I lifted my head and scanned the room, waiting for another trap trigger. Holding my power close to my body, it swirled around me in lazy circles. Loose tendrils of hair framed my face, and the glimmering strands caught my attention briefly. They sparkled as snow might in dawn's first light.

'I wondered what my traps had caught.' Erick's growl reverberated around the room. *"Whoever you are, you shouldn't have come here.'*

He doesn't recognise me.

Between the mist and my snowy hair, I could understand his confusion. It didn't mean I wasn't any less pissed at the pain I'd gone through.

I rose from my crouch and I faced the direction of his voice. My fists clenched against the anger.

'Considering you invited me not even a week ago, and I adhered to your warning, I find it entirely rude that you'd still allow your little traps to go off.' I ground out.

'Holy shit! Evanee, is that you?' Erick's bewildered voice echoed through his mind, before he materialised in the room.

'Bingo! Must say it's a pleasant area you have here. Makes mine look positively sterile and cold.'

The mist, which had slowly seeped from around my body to cover the wooden floor beneath my bare feet, relayed information from every direction. It whispered of the books and shelving that went on and on, forming a kind of maze. None of the books held titles, which was probably a defence mechanism. Some barred doors rattled at the hinges yet held firm; whilst others glowed red at the hinges and handles.

All this was relayed to me in seconds. The mist and I were methodical in our search, touching nothing—only looking, mapping and remembering.

'We each have our preferences. You're clean, methodical, logical and reflective; thus, your mind reflects that. I, on the other hand, not so much.'

Mist lapped at his boot-clad feet, and with a thought it climbed his body, removing not only his heavy leather boots but the leather he wore as armour. If I was going to float around his mind in a dress, then damit, he could be a little less formal.

Once again, he stood before me dressed in jeans and barefooted. Apart from a black fitted t-shirt, he looked just as he had the day he'd crashed into my mind.

Holding his hands out, he gazed down before looking back up at me, his eyebrows raised in question.

'That's better, don't you think? We aren't at war. Yet.' I bared my teeth at him.

Crooning to the mist, it ceased swirling and retracted towards me.

'No, we aren't at war, mic luptător. Is there a particular reason you came to visit me or were you just testing my defences?' He asked pointedly.

The mist finally returned to me, and I allowed it to once again coat my skin. It compressed, creating a second layer of skin that glittered and swirled lazily, always in motion.

Beautiful.

'No, I didn't come here to test your defences.' I huffed. *'I remembered your warning about showing up, and I tried calling out to you, but you must not have heard me. As to the reason I'm here, I wanted to get in contact with you. I couldn't find you or anyone else on social media or in the phone directory, and I don't have any contact numbers for you, so I thought I'd give this a crack.'*

Gliding over to one of the leather couches, I dropped gracefully into the armchair. Where Erick had looked like a caged tiger in my mind, I resembled a panther lounging luxuriously.

'I see. Why didn't you just drive out to the manor?' Erick questioned wearily.

Still wary of the mist that circled my body, Erick placed himself in the winged leather chair opposite me.

Smart man.

'You're kidding, right?' I snorted. *'It's too far out and I ran out of time. Besides, I you haven't invited me and I have a list of things to do and only so many daylight hours to do them in. I've only ever driven past your estate or run along the boundary in the state forest. I'd probably get lost just driving up your driveway.'* Dismissing his suggestion with a wave, I looked around some more.

'Okay, that's fair enough. You have my undivided attention.'

Ah, now there was a look I was all too familiar with. After all, it mirrored mine, time and time again.

Curiosity, she was a bitch.

'I'd hoped to invite you, Jordan and Tristan to my place on Saturday evening. It would be my way of thanking you for all the help you've given me lately.' Looking distractedly around, my attention focused back on him. *'Do you have a pen and paper, or will you remember my number?'* I challenged him. *'I'd ask for yours, but I haven't mastered the whole doing things with my body in reality while I'm off gallivanting mentally.'*

'*Recite it for me. I'll remember it,*' he smirked.

He got me to repeat it twice more before we both stood.

'*Thanks for the hospitality, or lack of it. I won't be dropping in again if it's all the same to you.*' I grimaced.

Stepping around him, I glided towards the square that had now knitted itself together. Swirls of white, gold and onyx drifted lazily within the small square patch.

Erick glided to my side and lifted his head to inspect the new patchwork.

'*You are unique, Evanee. I don't think I've ever seen anything like what I'm looking at right now. Then again, I don't think I've ever had a woman barge through my defences as you did either. I have a question for you before you go, which I hope you'll answer for me?*' Erick waited for my go-ahead before continuing.

Transfixed by the beauty above me, I nodded distractedly.

'*What are you?*' At his question, my head and gaze dropped to his. '*The power clinging to you and around you is like nothing I've ever felt. It doesn't feel human, it feels more ancient somehow. How do you use it and where does it come from?*'

He gazed, intrigued, at the mist lazily swirling across my skin. It was therapeutic and felt as if someone were gently caressing me.

Thinking about what he'd just asked, I really couldn't answer any of his questions conclusively. How could I, when I was still trying to find those answers for myself?

With a shrug, I gave him the only answer that came to mind. *'I'm human just like you, and I don't know where my power comes from. I've only ever accessed the door it's kept behind once before tonight and let's just say it didn't end well for anyone then.'* Wincing at the thought of Brian, I soldiered on. *'Since the party though, I've needed to access that power alot more. I'm guessing it manifested because of either my father passing away, changing hormones or a combination of both. I was sixteen at the time my father died. How do you use your power?'*

Erick shrugged. *'It's something I've always had. Even as a child, I knew I had certain gifts. It wasn't until I hit puberty that they fully manifested. I'd thought perhaps you were psychic, but now I'm beginning to think differently.'* Erick stared at me thoughtfully. The feeling of being under a microscope now intense.

With increasing nerves, I prepared myself for a hasty exit. *'It's been a good chat, but I need to be going. I'm sorry if I hurt you it was purely in self-defence against your traps. Oh, and the invitation for Saturday still stands. Shoot me a text or call me and let me know if any of you are coming.'*

Smiling, I positioned myself in the middle of the square.

'I can understand that. I guess I'll be seeing you around?' Judging by that response, I was guessing he would not be coming on Saturday evening.

'Yeah, you might. Would you mind giving me a hand exiting? I'd like to leave more peacefully than I entered.'

Eyes twinkling, he obliged me with a smile. *'Think of how you would like to leave. Think of your room and the doors in it. Focus on that and allow yourself to drift.'*

I nodded and stretched my hand out before me. Staring at the mist still gently caressing my skin. Erick stood quietly watching, allowing me to focus wholly on what I was attempting.

Thinking back to how he'd bent and pushed off before exiting my mind, I tucked my elbows slightly at my waist before I closed my eyes, envisioning something denser than mist. I imagined fog racing through the valley to coat empty fields. Lazy tendrils swirling around gravestones like it always did in horror movies, as if it were alive.

Holding the images in my mind, my eyes flicked open, and I stared at the pane of glass I'd entered through, picturing myself gliding through those beautiful glistening veins of colour.

I was as light as a feather, floating up and out.

My eyes fell shut for not even a second before I opened them to find myself standing back in my round room.

It's good to be home.

Looking down at the power that still clung to me as if it were a child clinging to its mother, begging her not to leave it, I smiled affectionately.

'I know you don't want to let go, but it's time. I'm not as afraid of you as I was. There'll be other times where I'll need you, and those times I won't be so scared to call on you. Thank you for what you've done for me, but it's time to go back.'

Swirling impatiently and aggressively, it refused to leave.

'How about this? You go back behind your door and I'll leave the door unlocked this time?' I crooned.

I waited patiently for a response. The swirls slowed to a slow crawl — I had my answer. I removed the lock, showing that I intended to hold up my end of the bargain.

Extending my arm in the door's direction, the mist rolled gently from my body and back through the doorway before the door shut heavily behind it.

There was one last thing I needed to try before I left.

Focusing on the glass patch above my head, I envisioned it as a door instead. I would place the door amongst my others, near my father's door. Red cedar framed the thick heavy glass with flecks of emerald, garnet and gold winking from its depths. They were mercurial; never stopping, always intertwining. I didn't bother with a door handle or lock. Satisfied, I shut my eyes once again, descending back into my body.

I stared at the ceiling for a moment before giddy laughter erupted from my dry lips.

A *ting* from the coffee table beside me signalled a text message received. Rolling over, I attempted to reach for my phone.

"Argh!" My limbs flew flapped uselessly before I landed face-first on the floor. "I did not think that through," I groaned, rubbing at my nose.

Too tired from my explorations, I didn't bother trying to get off the floor; instead, I rolled to my back and reached up for my unfinished beer and took a sip. Cringing at the warm acrid flavour, I replaced it on the coffee table.

Retrieving my phone, I looked at the time and realised that nearly an hour had passed since I'd first tried to enter Erick's mind.

No wonder my beer's on the warm side. Yuck!

Swiping my thumb across my phone screen, I pulled up my messages.

```
That was incredible. One second you were
  standing there, the next you were mist
    floating through the tiny cracks.
```

Reading the message twice, I realised the message was from Erick. Yeah, I was feeling slow tonight.

> Really? That's awesome. It was kind of the effect I was going for. Can't let you be the only one with the grand entrances and exits.

Hitting send, I entered his name into my contact's list.

His name pinged across my screen with a new message a few seconds later.

> Mmm, after that performance I have some work to do, I think. I'll check my schedule for Saturday and get back to you tomorrow.

Ah, so he hadn't forgotten my invitation.

Rolling to my knees, I braced my hands against the couch and coffee table before hauling my lazy and rather cold backside off the ground.

I drifted through the empty house, dragging my tired body off to bed.

My phone vibrated with an incoming call, and I frowned at Erick's name before hitting answer.

"Hey, Erick. What's up?"

Bedroom light on, I flipped off the remaining lights, and my house plunged into darkness.

"I wanted to check whether you were okay. You traipsing through your mind never seems to end well." His husky voice sent shivers across my body.

Once, he'd only had to pull me from my mind once. He would never let me live that down.

Scrubbing at my face, I sighed heavily, "Thanks for the concern, but I'm all good. Admittedly I may have landed face-first on my carpet after I rolled off the couch, but I'm all good."

I winced at my foot in mouth comment, hoping he wouldn't think I was a total freak.

On the other hand, I didn't have to worry about sounding cool and classy with this man. He wasn't interested in me, and he had seen me throw up. There was no coming back from that. Ever!

"You fell off your couch?" Erick's warm chuckle slid across my body, as though he were standing in the room with me.

Blinking hard, I winced at the loneliness that crept over me, as it did some nights. Oddly, it never seemed to affect me during the day though.

"Yeah, I did. My shoulder took most of the brunt before my nose could, so no harm done. Anyway, I need to go. I still have to shower before I can pass out." I yawned with exaggeration.

"In that case, I'll let you go. I wanted to make sure I wouldn't have to pay you another visit just to revive you again. You and death seem to drawn to each other, and I'm not sure Ellie or Brad would appreciate you departing so soon," he pointed out.

Some days I highly doubt anyone would miss me at all.

Oh sure, initially they might miss me, but I knew they would move past it, eventually.

"Mic luptător, why so sad? What are you thinking of?"

"How do you know what I was feeling? You weren't running around my mind, were you?" I thought he hadn't been—I'd have felt it, surely?

Erick sighed. "No, but that doesn't mean I can't still feel some of your stronger emotions. Your sorrow was beating at my mind."

"It's nothing, Erick. All is good on this end. Thanks for the concern, though. I guess I'll see you around." Leaning against the door frame of my ensuite, my weary head followed, and I shut my eyes.

"Goodnight, mic luptător. I hope you have sweet dreams," he murmured.

"Goodnight, Erick. Don't let the bed bugs bite," I smiled softly, before I hung up.

CHAPTER 14

Nausea assaulted my stomach at the knowledge that I'd have to face Desmond without the protection of Bob today. It had me stressed, and I'd worried all weekend about going back to work on Monday.

I'd not seen or heard from him or Cassandra since Desmond and Jared's house party, and to be honest, I was grateful for the peace.

My nausea, with a side of panic attacks, had started on Sunday and by Monday I was a nervous wreck, constantly looking over my shoulder; convinced I'd see Desmond sneaking up on me.

Neither Jared nor Desmond had been around the hospital for the past two days, thankfully, but I couldn't shake the feeling that someone was watching me. It didn't help that the bodies sitting in the morgue's freezer had required only external examinations or at the most, a partial autopsy.

I'd spent most of my time catching up on paperwork, consulting on some cases interstate and re-examining my notes and secondary tissue samples I'd taken from the two unidentified bodies. I was yet to pass them on to Brad and Ellie, mainly because that would require me going to their labs, which was where Jared worked.

Lately, I'd received numerous text messages from Ellie and Brad complaining about the science division's staff room now being a gathering place for

Jared, Cassandra and Desmond. I'd sympathised but had been quietly grateful I wouldn't run into any of them.

It was both a blessing and a curse to have nothing to do.

~

Arriving early on Thursday evening, Ellie and Brad sat in the pathology lab for an hour taking turns staring through the microscope at my secondary samples. They'd departed with perplexed and somewhat excited looks on their faces, and assurances they would do further research.

A slight glimmer of hope emerged later that evening when Detective Bernard rang to notify me that he'd received the identities of both the unidentified bodies.

It turned out the male was an immigrant from somewhere in South Africa. His name was Jacob Ngwenya, and he'd been living and working in Acrasin for the past two years, poor bugger.

Lucy McMullen was an Australian born twenty-year-old nursing student. She'd been living in Murder Point Bay for the past year, completing her rural residency with the local hospital.

"I've already notified their families, and they'll be in touch with Bob to discuss viewing the bodies," Detective Bernard hastily notified me.

"Thank you, Detective. If you could shoot through those details and I'll amend our records to reflect it…" Detective Bernard's long tired sigh interrupted me.

"Already done, Doc. Ah, crap, I've got to go. I have another callout," he groaned, sounding harassed.

The phone went dead, and I frowned at it.

Fair enough.

Detective Bernard's wonderful news disappeared two hours later when my birthmark heated uncomfortably. I tried placing an ice pack on it, and numbing cream, but the darned thing continued to burn a hole through my lower back.

To distract myself, I re-read the email Bob had sent this morning. They had found no additional evidence on either of the bodies. I responded with an update on Brad and Ellie's help in assessing the secondary samples of my work.

With a long-suffering sigh, I checked my phone for messages to distract myself. Groaning at the blank screen, I cursed myself and my damned curiosity. I couldn't help by wonder why Erick, Jordan and Tristan had gone silent after Saturday night's fun.

Jordan had been the centre of attention; his antiques had had all of us in stitches, even a tense Tristan had laughed occasionally. I'd tried to fish for more information about the bodies Erick had wanted my opinion on during the evening, but he'd felt it better that we discuss the bodies at another time. After that, the evening had descended into mischief and laughter, with outrageous card games and shots featuring as the night's prime entertainment.

My curtains had remained tightly shut all of Sunday, with a bucket as my constant companion.

Another sharp stab to my lower back jolted me back to the present, all reminiscing forgotten. The stab was hard enough for me to scoot the chair back as I jumped from foot to foot, rubbing at the blasted thing.

"Look, if you don't stop this crap, I'll book an appointment with the GP on Monday and have you permanently removed. Do you understand me? I can't take the pain anymore, and you're just pissing me off now. I don't care how big the damn scar will be once you're removed, but it'll be worth it," I hissed in pain.

Stalking out of the office, I stomped into the staff room, yanking the fridge door open. It was clean and organised—just like the rest of the morgue. If someone wasn't murdered soon, I'd probably end up sorting out the linen closet down the hall or cleaning Brad and Ellie's lab, which would no doubt incite an all-out war between the three of us.

The next stab to my lower back buckled my knees, as unbidden tears spilled down my cheeks.

Something was very wrong.

The pain dragged memories of the pain I'd felt the night Brian had attacked me to the forefront. My body quivering, short pants puffed past my parted lips. My gut contracted painfully, warning me an attack was imminent, yet I couldn't tell who or where it was coming from.

Panic bubbled up within me, stalling when a warm breeze washed over my chilled body, the sensation unnerving and out of place, considering the room was air-conditioned. A shower of golden sparks brightened the dreary staff room seconds before I heard a merry whisper.

"You can't change what is coming, Evanee. You wont escape fate. No one can escape me. So many have tried and failed. Your Prince may have intervened the last two times, but he can't save you from what's destined to happen. Your rebirth will happen, for I have foretold it." Sighing softly, the mysterious feminine voice continued, *"You've been my favourite project, Evanee Messorem. Say hello to your great-grandfather for me."*

The lights flickered twice before I was once again alone in the staff room.

I dropped forward to grip the tiled floor with shaking hands. Drool dripped from numb lips, mingling with my cascading tears to form a small puddle between my white-knuckled hands. I couldn't move. My mind shredded, unable to form any kind of logical or clinical thought; it was no better than a hunk of meat on the butcher's table. What thoughts I had raced then faded, while I tried my best to catch at least one.

Finally calming enough, I registered the tenderness of my skin; of the biting cold beneath my knees and palms.

I blinked dazedly, struggling to bring the room back into focus. Crawling as quickly as I could, I escaped to the corner of the room between the couch and the wall, pulling the little side table away from the wall so it slid to the middle of the room.

I curled into a ball and gently rocked back and forth, trying and failing to soothe myself. My mind continued to race faster than a V8 supercar on the Bathurst track. Round and round it went.

It was all too much; the continuous pain, the fatigue, nausea and now I was hearing the voice I'd heard the night of my attack—the one I thought I'd imagined.

This is it. It's finally happened. I've lost my freaking mind. Is this how it feels to have a breakdown? Who the hell did I just hear and why'd she call me Evanee Messorem—that's not my surname! Should I call the Psych ward to come over and assess me?

Around and around thoughts and questions circled, seemingly never-ending. The searing pain continued to burn a hole through my lower back, while my poor womb seized around the red-hot poker twisting through my organs.

Time had no relevance as I huddled in the protective circle of my arms. Blood continued to pound a rhythm out that put even the loudest African drums to shame. I had no sense of smell or hearing, whilst sight was off the table, with my head buried against my legs.

Tingling at the back of my skull upped my anxiety, and I tensed, preparing for the next assault to come. When none came, I realized I wasn't under attack. Instead, the tingling heralded Erick's arrival within my psyche.

'Mic luptător, what's wrong? Your panic has my heart racing.'

'I don't know what's going on. I think I might be slowly losing my mind.' I shrilled, mentally.

There was no hesitation on Erick's part as he sent waves of reassurance and calm through my mind. *'Evanee, you need to calm down, you're on the verge of*

226

a panic attack. You need to slow your heart rate and breathing down.'

'I can't, it's happening again. The pain's back, just like that night with Brian. Something's coming for me.' I shrieked, my fear getting the better of me.

'Evanee, breathe slowly... concentrate on breathing, just for a moment.' Erick soothed.

Doing as he said, I slowed my breaths, while I worked on grounding myself. It was something the shrink had recommended after my attack. It would help to calm my mind and anxiety enough to deal with the situation at hand logically and methodically. Just the way I liked it.

Systematically, I dragged my freaked-out mind to my physical body, working from my toes through to my fingers; becoming *present* within myself again.

After a few minutes, I could straighten my legs, and my head came up to rest against the wall as my lungs expanded, circulating much-needed oxygen to cramped muscles.

'That's it, keep going... you're doing great. In and out.' I could hear Erick's calming voice in my mind.

After a few more minutes, I finally felt ready to open my eyes. I contemplated sitting there until one of the security guards came in to get me at the end of my shift, but considering I'd never been a quitter before now, I figured now really wasn't the time to start.

I stood gingerly, my legs tingling with that horrible numb tingle you get when you can't feel anything. Not quite pins and needles, but close enough to make you wince and rub at it like a mangy dog scratching at an already raw patch of skin.

Leaning against the smooth wall behind me, I used it to support my shaky frame. My pale hands gripped the couch, and I slid weakly over the arm of the couch. Tiny dots danced in front of my vision as if I'd just gazed at multiple mini suns.

"What the fuck just happened? It has to be my brain, right? Yeah, that's it…" I murmured to myself, or Erick, if he was still there. "My brain's finally showing signs of stress. I've been in my room of doors too many times over the last couple of weeks. This is my brain's way of telling me to slow down and take it easy," I reasoned with myself.

'Evanee, you need to tell me what happened. I can't help you unless you tell me.' Erick's frustration nipped at my fragile mind.

"Okay, so I'm going with brain malfunction. I can deal with that. I mean why else would I be hearing the same women's voice I heard the night of my attack?"

Erick's outrage lashed at my mind as he bit out, *'what attack, Evanee? Who the hell is Brian?'*

Ignoring him, I kept on muttering to myself. "Not to mention my damn surname isn't even bloody Messorem for crying out loud, and I don't have a great-grandfather. They're all dead!"

Hysteria set in, the manic high-pitched laugh coming out of my mouth proof enough.

Tension pummelled at my mind, Erick's weariness mixing with the panic racing around my mind.

'What did you just say? Evanee, this is important, who thought your surname was Messorem?'

My silence amped up his frustration and anger. I cringed in pain and sensed as Erick realised his mistake, quickly slamming a wall down to protect me.

'Hang on, I'm coming to you. Do me a damn favour, try to stay out of trouble, will you?' He ground out before he left, and I was once again alone with my broken mind.

"Fantastic. It's not like I go looking for trouble, or anything. Trouble seems to seek me out," I ground out petulantly.

The shrill of the work phone startled me, and I rolled off the couch Ace Ventura style, my limbs flying in every direction as I threw myself onto the floor, the thud jarring me.

Rising onto my hands and knees, I backed out from between the couch and coffee table. My hand slapped clumsily at the dining room table and with death grip fingers I hauled my backside off the dreary sterile floor. Pushing off towards the doorway, I sought the phone that continued to buzz annoyingly. Fumbling with the damned thing as I tried to bring it to my ear.

"Doctor Sheperd, are you there?" Mel's curious voice echoed from the receiver.

A squeak was all my fogged brain could manage.

Get a hold of yourself, Evanee. This is work. Pull yourself together.

I coughed to clear my throat before I tried again. "Sorry Mel, yes I'm here. What's going on?"

So I was still a little on the rattled side, but hey, at least it was better than the damn squeak.

"You okay, Doctor? Do you need help?" Mel checked, hearing the shake in my voice.

Clearing my throat, I tried again. "I'm okay, thank you, Mel. What's going on?"

That sounded better.

"We have incoming. DOA. 5 minutes out," she informed me with her usual briskness.

"Thanks, Mel. I'll get ready if you wouldn't mind dealing with the handover? They say anything else?"

"Nope."

"Okay, I'll see you in the morgue."

It took me a few tries, but by the time I heard the truck pull up, I was vertical and ready to go. My hands still shook, but at least the rest of me was cooperating.

I rushed towards my office, checking to see if the coroner had emailed regarding the DOA, noting I'd only received permission to perform a partial examination at this point. Hitting print, I grabbed a new folder, clipping the email to it before depositing it in the drawer.

I raced to the change rooms, pulled on my gumboots gingerly, slapped on gloves, sleeve covers and a mask before butting the adjoining door to the morgue open.

My internal alarm bells clanged loudly within my mind as soon as I entered the morgue and noticed the two new undertaker's assistants standing in the freezer beside the gurney, carrying a blue sealed body bag.

They're new. I frowned, pausing for a second.

Odd, Dan never mentioned any new employees starting with him, yet they must have had identification or Mel would have sent them packing.

"Gentleman, do you have the paperwork?" I finished placing the clear protection goggles on as I clomped towards the two-way freezer, the white mask strapped over my nose and mouth muffling my voice.

"Yes, Doctor," The taller of the two answered.

"Who are the Detectives in charge?" Watching them closely, I waited.

"We're here, Doctor Sheperd." Detective Bernard and another police officer in training for Detective rounded the corner.

Nodding, I signed the required chain of custody form, accepting the responsibility of my new charge. Mel would scan the barcode, creating a new file for my notes to attach to electronically.

"Thank you, gentlemen. You have a lovely evening," I dismissed them.

Waiting on them to exit the freezer, I held it together by the skin of my teeth. Scorching hot pain had resurfaced as I'd entered the morgue, and I knew before even examining the body that this would be a repeat of the previous two.

The one difference was that this body was fresh—rigor mortis hadn't even set in yet. I wasn't confident enough to enter my mind's round room, so I wasn't entirely sure what to expect under the blue plastic, but I prayed it wasn't like the last female victim, Lucy.

I retraced my steps back into the room and studied the two funeral director's assistants walking down the ramp towards the van, through one of the viewing windows that overlooked the loading bay.

The van appeared legitimate, with all the correct markings, yet something felt off with the two men, and I committed each to memory.

One was stocky and in his mid-40's, the other lanky in his mid-30's. I noted their facial features as they turned back to look around the parking bay, then up towards where I stood studying them in the morgue.

The enormous roller door squeaked open, and they slowly made their way out into the secured hospital parking bay. My eyes never left the van until the roller door clanged shut.

I called out to the three members still left in the freezer and loading bay beyond, "Anyone else have a bad feeling, or am I the only one?"

My head swivelled to acknowledge Mel and Detective Bernard's presence once more.

Oh yeah, they're both as tense as me. Looks like I haven't lost my mind after all.

"Those boys look familiar to you, ladies?" Bernard's concern only amped up my nerves.

The police officer beside him shifted uncomfortably.

"No Detective, they didn't." Mel crossed her arms over her chest. "I took copies of their identification tags, and we now have images of their faces from the CCTV footage. I'll chat with Steve and Dan tomorrow and see what they have to say."

There was a reason Mel was my favourite assistant. Her efficiency and intuition were exemplary.

"I'll run a few checks, just to be on the safe side. They arrived a little too quickly at the crime scene for my liking. But as you said Mel, they had all the correct identification documents." Detective Bernard shrugged and made his way to the viewing room.

Nodding, I re-entered the freezer to collect my newest charge.

The steel shelves were close to bare, with only two bodies ready for collection on Monday. I was glad I wasn't the only one feeling paranoid tonight, but something was coming. I couldn't tell what or when, but every fibre of my being screamed I was in trouble—I just couldn't tell where the danger was coming from.

Hauling the gurney out of the freezer, Mel followed beside me.

Detective Bernard came into view. He was on his phone, speaking quietly into it. The new officer sat in the chair, a concerned look on her face.

"All right, let's get this show on the road," I spoke loud enough for all to hear.

The large zip releasing its clasps echoed loudly throughout the now silent morgue.

CHAPTER 15

Scissors snipped at bright pink cotton, threads snapping as the blades moved upwards. The neon pink of the fabric was blinding, courtesy of the fluorescent light shining down overhead. I'd be glad once we removed the dress; the glare agitated the headache that had pulled up a seat at the back of my head.

Peeling the fabric back, the women's emaciated body was exposed. I looked down, and the young women's delicate features jumped at me as I studied her almond-shaped eyes accentuated by well-executed makeup. With the dress off, you could tell the true colour of her unblemished skin. It reminded me of the porcelain dolls I'd played with as a child, so smooth and pale.

She wore no bra, the dress too low cut to permit one. The G-string she'd carefully chosen hugged her slender hips, still intact; it was the same colour as the dress. She'd chosen her clothes with care, leading me to wonder if she'd been on a date or intending to pickup at whatever event she was attending.

The forensic photographer had finally left, leaving us free to begin our examination.

Clipboard in hand, Mel stood at the ready.

"Female 55-6969-785, twenty-two years of age, Caucasian. Hair is black, eyes were blue before changes of the vitreous humor. Dead on Arrival, no signs of trauma to the front of the body. Underwear and dress were intact, no signs of outward trauma around the thighs and vaginal area."

I carefully removed her underwear. "Initial examination suggests no trauma or recent sexual activity. Further examination will be needed. Rigor is setting in, suggesting the body is only recently deceased, yet as mentioned previously there are notable changes to the vitreous humor." I frowned beneath my mask.

So how the hell are her eyes clouded over, when her body is only just starting to show signs of early stages of death?

A knock at the window drew my attention away from my charge. At the window beside Detective Bernard stood Erick, Tristan, and Jordan.

I stiffened. "Who let you, gentlemen, in?"

"Steve. Gave him and Bob a call to let them know I was coming in," Erick explained, his green eyes drinking me in.

"You okay with this, Detective?" I checked with Bernard.

"Yeah, Doc. Bob's message just came through. They're good to be here," Bernard confirmed.

"Okay, well you guys know the drill. No talking about what's said or seen during the autopsy, and no photos," I ordered.

All three men nodded before Jordan waved goodbye and exited the room.

Now, where's he going?

My question was answered when he passed the window that overlooked the loading bay seconds later. He meandered down towards the door beside the massive roller door before I lost sight of him.

Shrugging, I focused my attention back on the body before me. I knew what needed to doing now that a visual examination had been conducted of the front of the body.

"All right, let's see whether anyone's home before we turn her over, Mel. Nobody speaks until I'm done," I warned.

With great care, my hands hovered over the young woman's sternum, not touching her. I didn't need to go into my round room this time, as I had no intention of examining her as I had Lucy.

My eyelids drifted shut as I focused, searching gently.

"Ah, there you are," I mumbled. "Why haven't you left yet? There's nothing for you here."

Hovering within her was the beautiful orb that was her soul. Her colours swirled intermingling, constantly in motion as pinks, pearl, yellow, with just a touch of red surfaced then disappeared once again.

She'd been good in her life, but like all people, she'd had her sins.

Smiling gently, I coaxed the soul with the part of me that intertwined with the dead so seamlessly.

Then my essence brushed softly against her soul, and I immediately knew it was a mistake. The excruciating pain she'd felt and still felt slammed into my mind, ripping tears of anguish and pain from me so they fogged my glasses and I sobbed.

Hesitating would only scare this poor girl's soul, and she was in enough pain.

Teeth grinding, I continued to coo and whisper words of encouragement, shoulders sagging just a little when the minute orb shifted, trying to surface.

All up it took no more than five minutes, yet felt like an eternity before the soul released itself. Emotions and impressions drifted into my mind as the soul imparted one last bit of knowledge to me before drifting lazily up and out of the building, leaving me in no doubt she had experienced the same fate as the two previous victims.

My body sagged slightly, and I caught at the table to brace myself.

"Evanee, are you okay?" Erick questioned with worry.

When I failed to answer straight away, Erick yelled a little louder, his voice booming over the intercom.

I raised my hand in acknowledgement. Stiffening my legs, I retreated towards the desk area, my fists now clenched against the shaking that had set in.

Thankfully, I'd pocketed my phone before leaving the office. Ripping at my Kevlar glove, I finally removed it, dumping it on the desk before I searched for my mentor's number. Bob answered on the second ring.

"Evanee, talk to me. Is everything okay?" Bob sounded concerned.

"Hey, Bob. I'm okay, but I thought you should know we have another one. Female, twenty-two, DOA."

"Fuck! Are you serious? What the hell is going on there, Evie? The labs still haven't come up with anything definitive, and the other two's white blood cell counts were through the roof like you said they would be," Bob huffed with frustration.

Did he just swear? Wow, he must be stressed if he's cursing.

Inside the viewing room, Bernard, Erick and Tristan stiffened. Surely they hadn't heard what I was saying. Mel was in the room with me and I could tell she hadn't.

"Yeah. I haven't turned her over yet, but I'm sure I know what I'll find once I do. Do you want me to proceed with general DNA collection and leave the full autopsy to you?"

"Yes, please. Photograph and collect evidence. I want the body shipped out tomorrow. I'll be in contact with Detective Bernard and the coroner to discuss each victim and the possibility of there being a serial killer." He didn't bother to hiding how harassed he was from me.

The idea of this being the work of a serial killer set my stomach in knots.

"Oh, and one other thing," I added, "Two new undertaker's assistants dropped the body off. Copies of their IDs were taken, and they were caught on CCTV. They had the correct paperwork, but none of us knew them and we know most of the recruits." Looking up at Erick as I relayed this, his eyes reflected my concern with a hint of anger and frustration.

I watched as he turned to Tristan and addressed him briefly before focusing on me once again.

Tristan turned slightly from Erick and pulled his phone from his pocket, speaking into it.

"Okay," Bob sighed, "have Mel send through copies of their IDs and the CCTV footage, I'll have someone follow it up here."

Bob never took chances with security.

"Will do. Bob, you and Aunty Marg know I love you both, right?" I felt the need to remind him I loved him and Aunty Marg.

"Right back at you, kiddo. Are you sure everything is okay?" My heart clenched at his concern and my stomach protested as my dread amped up that bit more.

"I'm okay. My birthmark's been burning a hole through my lower back lately, and I'm not sleeping all that well, but other than that I'm fine," I confessed.

The continuous nightmares were always the same. I always died in excruciating pain.

"Okay sweetheart, you make sure you let us know if you need us up there. Now get back to work and send the new body down to me ASAP." I grinned at the sternness he was using to try to conceal his affection.

"Yes, sir. Night night."

"Night night, kiddo," he murmured with tenderness.

Hanging up, I re-gloved, contemplating my next move.

Turning the body over would allow me to confirm the exit wound I knew would be there. With any luck, I might get an accurate measurement of the wound before the acid ate too much at the tissue. This woman was a breakthrough; she would allow us to establish a more realistic idea of the thing that had inflicted the wound.

Decided, I approached Mel. "Right Mel, time to flip her over. Let's grab some towels for the face."

Mel grabbed a couple of towels to help support the body's head and face while we examined the back. The towels would support her facial features, so they were not disturbed or contorted too much while she was on her stomach. Her family might choose to have an open-casket funeral.

Flipping her over, we adjusted her face to one side before strategically placing the towels at her neck. Task completed, we stepped back ready to examine her back. And that's when I noticed—there was no hole.

Mel plucked the camera from the steel bench and was already snapping while I continued to examine her back, perplexed why there wasn't a gaping wound.

She'd died with the same amount of pain as the female before her, so where was the damn hole?

Snap snap. Photo after photo appeared on the digital screen.

We started at her feet, marking any wounds on the body diagram form, before slowly working our way upwards towards the scapula, roughly where the wound should have been.

I noted a slight incision to the left of the spine. The wound appeared to be nothing more than a scratch and showed signs it had begun healing.

Concentrating on the small incision, I brought the tape to the tip of it when movement below the surface of the skin stopped me in my tracks. I looked up at Mel, but she was still snapping away, oblivious to what I thought I'd just seen.

Putting it down to an overactive imagination and fatigue, I shook my head before once again trying to measure the wound. The measuring tape had no sooner touched the skin before movement rippled the skin once again. It was only the slightest of twitches, not the spasms muscles might make after death.

Removing the tape, I slowly placed it back on the steel bench.

This time Mel had noticed the movement. She placed the camera on one of the trays and we focused on the area, horror and morbid fascination rooting us to the spot as the skin expanded ever so slightly before flattening again.

"Tell me I'm not the only one seeing this?" I muttered nauseously.

"What are you seeing, Doc?" In my peripheral vision, I could see Detective Bernard craning his neck.

Swallowing hard, I said, "I'm seeing movement beneath the skin located over the upper thoracic vertebrae, which could suggest insect activity. There's a wound beside her spine, but with a wound in this stage of healing I wouldn't expect insect activity." I reached for a scalpel from the bench beside me. "Making an incision to the right of the spine."

Gripping the scalpel, I touched the tip to the skin just beside the spine. The wet ripping of skin had my body jumping a mile high. Hand jerking back, my stomach tightened as translucent spikes shredded the women's porcelain skin.

Five spikes protruded from where her spine should have been, and the stench of burning flesh wafted into the air, sticking to the back of my throat.

Sizzling followed by an unfamiliar scent drifted up; the acid I'd found on the previous two victims now ate at flesh surrounding the spikes.

Speechless, I continued to stare at the horror unfolding before me, my hand gripping the scalpel even harder.

This was not like any insect I'd ever seen.

"Evanee, what are you seeing?" Erick's open palms hitting the viewing room window rattled the glass.

Ignoring him, I addressed Mel. She was my priority right now.

"Mel, I want you to leave right now. We have contamination, head to the change room immediately." When she went to grab the camera on the bench, I shook my head. "Leave it. Go, now!"

Not needing to be told twice, Mel turned and bolted as quickly as her gumboots would allow.

"For fuck's sake, answer me! What the hell are you seeing, Evanee?" Panic laced Erick's voice. And to be honest, he wasn't the only one feeling that way.

There was no time to answer. The door to the locker room had just shut when a fiery sensation spread across my lower back.

My pained scream echoed in the sterile room.

Shards of skin, muscle and sinew exploded up and outwards from Lucy's back. Flecks of blood and chunks of soft tissue splattered across my clear glasses, while the floor on the other side of the autopsy bench appeared to have had a paint balloon dropped on it.

Swiping viciously at my coated goggles with the underside of my sleeve protectors, my visibility went from speckled to smeared.

"Shit!" I bellowed.

My glasses clattered to the ground, while I focused on the carnage now lying on my autopsy table. Searching for the translucent spikes from before, I saw nothing.

Morgue once again deathly silent. The tick-tock of the clock above the viewing window boomed in the silence, offering little comfort.

The wet slurping of muscle and tissue separating filled the air as the movement started up again. Unable to comprehend the creature now rearing up from the spinal column, my mind hit a blank for a second, before thoughts of a mutated jellyfish or witchetty grub came to mind—and were just as quickly discarded.

The grotesque creature rearing from the cavity was not something Mother Nature had created; and if she had, I'd say she was seriously pissed at humans.

I stood stock-still and waited for the thing to make its next move.

I didn't have to wait long.

Pink tinged tendrils needle-thin withdrew from within the corpse's spinal cord and slithered back inside the creature.

Well, at least I know how the spinal cord and brain were infiltrated.

It occurred to me then that the thing had no visible eyes.

I need to get out of here. I wonder whether it'll notice if I move.

Not daring to speak out loud, I moved my left foot slowly behind me, leaning backwards.

The creature stilled and so did I, leaving me to wonder if it had stopped because its feelers had fully retracted or whether it had noticed my movement.

Throwing caution to the wind, my right foot left the ground. It was the wrong decision.

The creature reared higher, calcified limbs scraping along the exposed white bone, the retracted feelers flared out once more.

"Evanee, run!" Bernard bellowed his warning a second too late.

There was no time for screaming like in the movies, no time to turn and run. One second the creature was in the dead women's back, the next it was digging blood coated claws into my jugular.

My panicked eyes darted to where my audience stood, uncertain of what was happening. Detective Bernard slammed the window once more, his horrified expression transforming into one of fear.

Instinct warned me not to move, yet self-preservation demanded I rip the creature from my throat. The claws clung tight enough that any slight movement would draw blood.

A clear tail no thicker than a pen rose before my face. At the end sat a white barb, clear mucus seeping from its tip.

My petrified eyes tracked that barb as it crept over my shoulder.

Still clinging to the scalpel I'd picked up earlier, I debated whether to use it; opting out as the image of the acid the spikes had secreted popped into my mind.

I couldn't stop what was about to happen, losing control was more than my fragile body and mind could handle.

Breathing was becoming increasingly difficult; the creature's hold tightening further. Spots danced before my eyes, as darkness hovered at the edge of my vision.

The world stood still for a second and my gaze locked with Erick's bewildered one. I watched as my fear took a hold of him, and he punched at the thick glass.

The creature's tail reared up before striking down to pierce my back. There was nothing anybody could do to save me.

My scream remained trapped by the creature covering the lower half of my mask and my mouth.

In a moment of clarity, I remembered my round room. My soul fled upwards towards my room of doors, a barrier erecting as it entered.

Red bled down the walls, doors and along the roof. A sanguine mist slowly filling my mind. Across from me, that black door that housed my gift rattled violently, almost unhinging. Extending my arm towards it, I knew what needed to be done.

Flicking my wrist, the door blew off its hinges, finally freeing not only that cool mist I'd called upon the other evening but something deadly and dark, something ancient lying in wait within me.

White-hot pain seared every part of me, body and mind. I screamed over and over again, until the glass above me, and the door to Erick, shattered.

My knees hit the soft plush carpet within my mind and unyielding concrete outside, my internalised screams never faltering while that ancient power overtook me.

The skin at my jugular gave way easier than cling wrap over a bowl as the creature twitched and clenched down on my throat.

Just as suddenly as it had attacked, the attack stopped. Tail ejecting from the puncture wound at my back, the creature thrashed wildly before dropping to the ground dead. Smoke tendrils wafted from the hideous thing before it crumbled in on itself, dissolving into a fine ash.

Precious blood cascaded from the wounds at my throat, while a fine trickle made its way down along the side of my spine, soaking into my scrubs. The acid from the barb sizzling my flesh; I was pain's prisoner, unable to escape.

That ancient power that had gripped me so fiercely moments before settled to a vibration, the frigidness of that power simmering to a cool breeze that tugged at my hair, gently caressing my wounded body.

My screams finally died, my energy depleted at last. There was no fight left in me and my body knew it, the world tilting as I gave way to exhaustion.

The shattered glass of the viewing room, with its broken and crumbling wall behind it, disappeared from my view, as did the freezer door now bent in half hanging by a single hinge. Glass, concrete, and steel lay scattered around my spent form, the body of my deceased patient lying forgotten amongst the debris and gore near me.

My heartbeat slowed, and I closed my eyes, shutting my surroundings out and focusing wholly on my room of mirrors.

The bimbo and teenager stepped up beside me, their arms coming around me.

Together, we looked towards my father's door. That beautifully carved silky oak door with the antique doorknob. The door opened softly and memories flooded through, seeking a viewer.

Memories of dad taking me camping for the first time. The times we had snuck out for an ice-cream when we'd told my mother we were going to get bread and milk. She'd known what we were up to the . My father dancing me around the room on his feet. There were family trips when we were all so happy.

Memory after memory played out, warmth cocooning us.

An amber glow surrounding my kneeling form pulled my attention from those beautiful memories. Looking up, my swollen eyes met mercurial ones. Liquid amber intermingled with silver swirls, carmine specks appearing intermittently.

Jordan? Help me, please. Escaping on a whisper, my numb lips refused to utter anything else.

The images of my father faltered, spluttered, then flickered out.

Looking around, I found myself alone. The red that had been encroaching at the edges of the mirror finally consumed what little was left.

Darkness consumed me, swallowing me whole.

CHAPTER 16

Moribund — near death, to be in a dying state; or in my case, trapped in a black abyss. I'd heard that word before; used it, but never thought to apply it to myself.

I thought blacking out would bring peace or freedom from the pain my body was experiencing. I'd been wrong. Oh, how wrong I'd been.

My body may have been dying, but my mind felt every bit of pain my physical form was going through. The agony was my new unwanted companion, and there wasn't a damn thing I could do about it.

Voices drifted in and out of the darkness, most of whom I recognised.

"Evanee! Evanee, baby girl, listen to me, Mum's here. I need you to hang on just a bit longer, okay? You hang in there, baby girl, we're here with you," Reagan's soothing whispers permeated the darkness I was ensconced in.

"You?" Hang on, that was Jordan's voice I was hearing.

"Don't just stand there, Jordan! Save her, damit! I can't touch her in this form unless I plan to reap her. Please, please save my baby, I can't lose her too." My mother's voice broke, her heartbreak piercing me.

"Why do you think I'm hovering over her, Reagan? Tristan and Erick are replenishing. Her power blasted the three of them through the fucking wall, right through the damn change rooms and into the pathology laboratory. The only reason I'm standing is because I sensed her power releasing and ducked. How I have no clue. Vampires have no connection to Reapers, so I shouldn't have sensed her power," Jordan murmured, perplexed.

I could feel Jordan kneel beside me, his power circling my physical form, creating a barrier of some sort.

"Shit, she's lost too much blood and is haemorrhaging power at an accelerated rate. She won't make it to the ED, not in this state. She needs my blood if she even stands a chance of making it," Jordan growled.

"Do it, do what you need to do. Please Jordan, save her," Reagan begged with a sob.

Time had no meaning or relevance in the abyss. All I knew was the pain.

Is this what those poor people felt?

"You need to leave, Reagan. Erick is approaching and fast. I will protect her, I swear it. Now go!" Jordan's urgency clawed at the darkness.

"Okay, okay. Don't leave her side, Jordan, not under any circumstances. If anyone finds out she's part reaper, she'll never be safe. And if she's harmed in any way, I'll make it my mission to reap not only you but your master too," Reagan threatened menacingly. "Don't think I won't. There's nothing I won't do, no rule I won't break for my child. If anyone asks, you contacted me through her phone. I will re-emerge the day after tomorrow, which should be a sufficient time lapse to not make anyone suspicious. Hang on, my sweet angel, I'll be back. Jordan will take good care of you," Reagan whispered.

My mother's presence dissipated as the pain once again dragged me down into the darkness.

It poured over me, filling every part of me once more.

~

"She won't make it with modern medicine, Sire. My blood only just kept her heart beating; she needs more. The doctors have her hooked up to all these machines and yet no one can tell us why she won't wake or why she's deteriorating so quickly," Jordan's voice whispered in the darkness.

The pain had ebbed, reality once again reaching me.

"Don't tell me what I already know, Jordan. This needs to be thought over first, the ramifications could be disastrous. We're unsure just how powerful her psychic ability is, or what her heritage is. As it is, we won't know what effect your blood has had on her until she resurfaces." Erick was always methodical and logical. It could drive a person nuts.

"Forgive me Erick, but if you do not do this, I will. I made an oath and I will not break it. If this is what it takes to save her, consequences be damned," Jordan hissed.

The familiar beep of a monitor spiked in time with my increased heart rate, my frail wounded body struggling under an unseen pressure.

"Did you hear that? I think she can hear us, that or at the very least Jordan's rage is triggering her." Tristan's intrigue did not sit well with me. It felt out-of-place considering the circumstances.

"Calm the hell down, Jordan, before you kill her," Erick snarled threateningly. "There are rules that we need to follow if we are to avoid the council. The man in me wants nothing more than to save her, but as Prince, I need to approach this with caution and logic. I smell the decay that has set in, and no one knows what caused the damage to her neck."

"I'll do another sweep of her body now, Erick. See if there's anything I missed," Tristan soothed.

Darkness and pain once again crashed down on me, and I was lost There was no fighting it.

~

"The blood she lost has been lost and she was checked for any further trauma, but we can't seem to find what's causing her coma. We've also noticed an increase in white blood cell activity and are investigating what might cause that. We've started her on a course of broad-spectrum antibiotics, hoping it will counteract any infections she might have."

I didn't recognise the female speaking.

"Fine. Do what you need to do," Reagan snapped.

If I'd thought the woman was removed and sterile during her brief speech, my mother was positively arctic. She was angry.

"That bitch doesn't know her arse from her head. Where the hell did she even get her medical degree from, the back of a cereal box? I probably know more than that stupid cow," Reagan fumed.

Oh, Mum is pissed. I'm so glad I'm not on the receiving end of it.

"Reagan, they're doing their best. None of us has been able to reach her. I smell what you see. She's dying, and whatever attacked her in the morgue has done something to her—we just can't figure out what," Jordan reasoned. "Detective Bernard was the only one who glimpsed the thing. It was somehow cloaked. With all our combined years of knowledge, you would think one of us would know what attacked her. Erick is meeting with his family to discuss how to proceed." For a big guy, Jordan sure knew how to soothe a cranky woman.

Oh, he is my go-to man the next time mother dearest cracks it.

"Once they figure out she's part reaper, he'll kill her. You know our histories, you know how much our species despise each other. It's pure luck he doesn't know what I am." My mother was pacing, I didn't need eyes to know she was. I could feel her energy, even through the pain.

"I like to think of it as fate, and the only reason vampires hate reapers is because you remind us of our mortality. No one escapes death, not even the living dead. Now simmer down, Erick's here now," Jordan warned. "As far as anyone's aware, she's just another human with unusual psychic abilities. I never would have connected the dots had I not known who you were, to begin with," Jordan cautioned in a gruff whisper.

"If you know what I am, then why are you helping me?" I hadn't heard my mother's voice this tremulous since the day she'd delivered the eulogy at my father's funeral.

"You saved my life once in battle, not that I expect you to remember. I was a fledgling and you swooped in like some avenging angel. I owe you my life. As for wanting to see your daughter live, well that's a little harder to explain. And before you ask, because I can see it on your face, no, I'm not interested in a romantic relationship with Evanee. She's a special woman, but not the one for me. Now quiet, they're here."

I couldn't make sense of a thing they were saying.

What the hell are Reapers and did they say the living dead?

Erick's entrance distracted my bewildered mind momentarily.

He addressed the room abruptly, which surprised me. "Good evening, Reagan. Jordan, update."

"It's not good. They can't tell why she hasn't risen from her coma. They're saying her white blood cell count has risen, and that she's likely fighting an infection. But we already knew this." Jordan spoke stiltedly and to the point, leaving me to wonder what had caused so much tension between the two of them?

"I've spoken with my Aunt Paige and with your permission, Reagan, I would like for her to look over Evanee? Once she's satisfied, she's said she will indicate whether we should proceed with giving Evanee more of our blood."

The response never came, as I once again lost my struggle to resurface.

~

Soft golden tendrils of light nudged at my weary eyes, enticing them to open.

My body was heavy, and the strangeness of it made my eyes snap open. Reflected by the mirrored ceiling, my face was clouded with fatigue and pain beyond what any one person should or could suffer.

My eyes prickled with tears of relief at the realisation I was no longer in the black abyss but in my round room.

Utilising the mirrored ceiling, I noted the changes my body had undergone within my mind. My once ash-blonde waves were now a pure white, and where my luscious curves had once been, bones now jutted against deathly pale skin—almost translucent.

What the hell has happened to me?

A loud thud resounded through the room, the glass panels above me shaking ominously. It came again. It sounded suspiciously like fists pounding at a door for entry.

I feared the roof wouldn't survive another round.

Head rolling gingerly to the right, I searched for the source of the noise. When I couldn't spot anything unusual, my neck rotated centimetre by centimetre until it came to rest wearily on the left.

That's when I noticed Erick's door. The colours trapped within the repaired glass swirled viciously. Large garnet and gold swirls intermingled with each other before colliding with sparks of emerald, seemingly at random. It was far more chaotic than usual. The red cedar frame was splintering under the unseen impact, and I realised Erick was the one causing all the ruckus.

Slow on the uptake there, Evie. You must have left a good portion of your brain in the abyss.

Concern chased fear from me as I studied the cracks in the door's frame.

Much more of this and our connection will fragment, and I don't think I have the strength to fix it.

Concentrating, I gathered every drop of energy and power I possessed, focusing on the kaleidoscope glass. It liquified, and slowly the sharp rainbow of the colours dripped and melded.

Exhausted, I closed my eyes, my body going limp. Re-opening heavy eyelids was a challenge, but I needed to see him. I needed to see someone.

There, in all his glory, framed by that beautiful cracked cedar, stood Erick.

Tears of joy and relief sprung into my eyes.

A second, much larger shadow loomed behind him, signalling that he wasn't alone. I didn't need to guess who was behind him, after all, I now had a part of his power trapped in a small corner of the glass mirror above me. It waited patiently for me to accept or release it. It would stay where it was until I had made my decision.

As to why I now had a piece of Jordan's power within my mind, the only answer I could think of was it had something to do with the blood transfusion he'd mentioned giving me.

The two tall men glided in slowly. They looked the same as they had the last time I'd seen them both together. Both were clad in light denim jeans with a printed shirt; the details on their shirts blurring together, making it difficult to read.

Eyes drifting shut once again, I allowed my body to rest. I was safe, I was no longer in the abyss, and Erick and Jordan were here.

The tears that had pricked at my eyes before now trickled down the sides of my face and into my hairline. Once they started, they wouldn't stop. My nose ran, which was completely mortifying. Apparently just because I was in my mind's room didn't mean I wasn't still an ugly crier.

Shadows clouded my weak body as the two men knelt beside me, a gentle palm softly petting at my hair.

"Hey," I whispered raggedly.

Good grief, my voice is shredded.

"Hey yourself, princess." Despair rolled off Jordan.

I didn't need to see him to know he was having a rough time seeing me in this state.

Maybe I should have tried a little harder to freshen up before I let them in.

"What are you guys doing here? It's not every day a girl gets a visit from two fine-looking men," I teased lightly.

My eyes wouldn't open, so I couldn't tell whether I'd been able to make them smile or not.

"Mic luptător, can you open your eyes for us? I've missed seeing your beautiful blue gaze," Erick murmured huskily.

"Gee Erick, flattery will get you everywhere with a girl." I tried and failed to smile. "Okay, I'll try, but it's hard at the moment. I seem to be weak for some reason." The last part of my sentence was lost to the crackle of my cough.

When at last my coughing had stopped, I gingerly lifted my eyelids and I once again looked at the two men.

"Is that better?"

Water still leaked from my eyes, and snot still trailed from my nose. It was beyond mortifying now, but I didn't have the strength to lift my hand to wipe any of it.

"Much better. Do you know where you are and what happened?" A concerned wrinkle had formed between Erick's eyebrows and I wanted nothing more than to reach up and smooth it away.

Sadness emanated off him, and I didn't know why. Bending a white piece of material appeared in his long supple fingers, and he wiped at the liquid leaking from my eyes and nose.

"Yes, I'm in my room of mirrors. You may have to give me a minute. I'm feeling a bit on the foggy side," I said weakly.

"That's okay. Take all the time you need. Perhaps Jordan could fill you in. It might jog your memory a little. Mine's a little unreliable, as I wasn't conscious when he first reached your side," Erick smiled.

With an infinitesimal nod of my head, I gave Jordan the go-ahead.

"Wait! Before you start, could someone please straighten my head, that way I can see you both."

Erick shifted slightly, his careful hands cradling either side of my face. My head rotated, and I was once again starring up at the mirrored roof.

"Okay, go."

"Once upon a time..." Jordan's cheeky grin tugged at the corners of his full lips.

"Hilarious, smartarse," I snorted softly.

"It is, isn't it? It worked though, didn't it? I got a smile," he grinned.

"I'd throw you the finger, but that would require me to move."

"And there she is. Now shh, don't interrupt. Once upon a time, there was a sassy forensic pathologist. Now she was in the middle of an autopsy when something very bad happened," he sighed sadly. "Knowing she was in trouble, she escaped to her secret room of mirrors, where she hid until someone could come and rescue her. That courageous and selfless rescuer was me, by the way."

Oh, good grief. The man's ego is enormous.

Erick looked up at the mirrors, rolling his eyes as he huffed in exasperation. He obviously felt the same as me, but we stayed silent, waiting for Jordan to continue.

"Now, back in the real world, the brave hero raced into the morgue as fast as he could to save the said damsel in distress, only to find her lying on the floor covered in both her blood and some dead woman's fleshy bits. Upon first gazing at the mess before him, he thought his old friend Jackson Pollock had risen from the grave and tried to recreate his Free Form painting Jordan shook his head. "The brave hero raced to the side of the damsel, that's you by the way, and tried to wake her, but he couldn't," Jordan huffed exaggeratedly.

Wow. Remind me never to let the man reiterate a series of events.

His flair for the dramatics any other time would have been funny, but right now it was setting off flashes of red and black throughout the room.

The men looked around and then at each other, their expressions of concern not going unnoticed. The hairs on their arms rose, and in unison they moved to rise, searching the room for the cause.

What they didn't realise was the cause was laid out flat between them.

CHAPTER 17

The mirrored roof above us rippled and the soft glow throughout the room flickered once, twice before sputtering out, plunging the room into darkness.

Amber and carmine eyes glowed before Jordan's power slammed into place. It shimmered around him, mimicking a solid rock wall.

On the other side of me, Erick continued to search the room, a golden flame creeping from his hand up to his shoulder.

Power bowed the edges of the room, solidifying Erick's door.

Hissing, they stood by my side, moving to protect me.

My hands shot out to shackle their ankles, dousing their powers instantly. They stared down at me in shock, waiting to see what I did next.

"Lie down beside me," I commanded.

Quietly they obeyed my command, and as they did, my hands moved to their wrists, holding them at my sides.

Staring at my reflection, two white pearls with gold and onyx veins shone back at me; flashes of electric blue crackled through them intermittently.

Erick inhaled sharply when he noticed my eyes, but said nothing.

The mirror misted over and images raced across the screen; blurry and chaotic at first, they slowly solidified.

Breathing in deeply, I concentrated on slowing my racing thoughts. Power longed to flow through me, and I let it. It was familiar now and grounded me.

Mist coated the carpet, drifting around, between, and over the three of us.

The flurry of scenes in the mirror came to an abrupt stop as an image of the two funeral director's assistants came into focus. I replayed the handover of the body, their looks as they had left the morgue and my conversation with Detective Bernard and Mel about my bad feeling.

"What's happening, Evanee?" Erick whispered.

"Jordan triggered my memory. I'm not the only one doing this. My power is pushing for me to remember exactly what happened," I whispered back.

"Your power?"

"Yes, my power. Didn't you notice the massive hole behind you?" Arching his neck, Erick looked to where I was referring to. "That was where I kept my power contained before whatever happened. Now, well… now, who knows what it has planned for me."

The images continued to fast forward past Erick's entry, coming to a halt towards the end of my conversation with Bob.

"Right, Mel, time to flip her over. Let's grab some towels for the face."

Mel came into view, towels in hand. Together we flipped the body over, adjusting her face to one side before placing the towels at her neck.

Skipping the examination of the back of the lower half of her body, I moved ahead.

Smooth porcelain skin magnified to show the small incision I'd discovered.

Concentrating on the small incision, the tape came into view as I put the tip near the woman's skin. My hands stalled at the movement below the surface of the skin. Mel came into focus; she was still snapping away, oblivious to what I'd just seen. The measuring tape touched the skin again before movement rippled once again. It was only the slightest of twitches.

On the floor, I felt my body twitch, and I clutched tighter at the two solid wrists in my grip. The measuring tape disappeared from view as we stared at the skin expanding ever so slightly, then flattening again.

"I'm seeing movement beneath the skin located over the upper thoracic vertebrae, which could suggest insect activity. There's a wound beside her spine, but with a wound in this stage of healing I wouldn't expect insect activity."

My hand reached for a scalpel from the bench beside me.

"Making an incision to the right of the spine."

The tip of the blade touched the skin just beside the spine. The wet ripping of skin echoed through the room as my body jerked both on-screen and on the floor.

In the vision, I yanked my hand back as translucent spikes shredded the women's porcelain skin.

A horrified Mel and perplexed Erick flashed onto the mirror before my focus snapped back to the five translucent spikes protruding from where the spine had been.

You couldn't smell it now, but I knew the air had reeked of burned flesh. The sizzling that had emitted from the women's body now played in high definition, the mist swirling faster, becoming more agitated as the images progressed.

"Evanee, what are we seeing?" Erick asked with astonishment.

"Mel, I want you to leave right now. We have contamination, head to the change room right now." When she went to pick the camera off the bench, I shook my head.

"Leave it and go. Now!" Mel's figure disappeared from view as she turned and bolted from the room.

Bernard's yell of warning echoed throughout my mind and I noticed for the first time a fiery glow surrounding his body.

Strange, I don't recall seeing that in the morgue, or any other time I've seen Bernard.

The next images slowed to a crawl as shards of skin, sinew and muscle exploded upwards and outwards. The screen blurred with blood, which smeared as I wiped at my glasses.

Crying out in pain on screen, my lower back spasmed at the pain I'd felt at this moment.

The creature reared from my charge's back, and I gulped at the horrifying image that was the creature now in high definition in the mirrors above our heads.

I held on tightly, bile rising into my sore throat as my attack played out in slow motion.

Erick and Jordan flinched beside me when the creature lunged, their heavy swallows loud beside me.

~

"Evanee, what the fuck was that?" Erick's voice was strained.

Beside me, both men were as stiff as ironing boards.

"You really couldn't see it from the viewing room?"

"No, none of us could," he raged helplessly.

"Interesting. What about the glow around Detective Bernard, could you see that?"

"I can see it now, but only because you just mentioned it. What does it mean?" Erick frowned.

Shrugging at his question, I focused back on the scene unfolding before us.

I thought this was where the images would stop, as this was where I had blacked out, but they continued to play as a burst of what looked very much like my mist exploded outwards from my body.

The autopsy table in front of me buckled as the deceased woman's corpse catapulted into the freezer door, buckling it in half before thumping to the ground.

To the left, the viewing window imploded, shards of glass spraying the three men behind it. At some point, Bernard's partner must have left the room, as she didn't appear to be amongst the group shielding themselves from the glass.

My power didn't stop there; catapulting all three men through the wall behind them, and the one behind that before they finally came to a rest in the laboratory behind the change rooms.

To my right, the window where Jordan stood stricken shattered outwards.

The roller doors buckled and the small door beside it smashed open as my power found freedom, at last, winging its way into the starry night.

The creature that had clung to my throat now lay twitching on the ground before black and green flames engulfed it. In mere seconds the creature was nothing more than ashes.

The screen flickered, going black, and the lights came on once again.

The power rushed from my body, leaving it to twitch and writhe as pain once again slammed through my fragile body.

I released Erick and Jordan and my fingers clenched into fists. Had this been reality, blood would have dripped from the crescent wounds embedded within my palms.

The mist that had previously raced around the room crashed against the doors as waves might against rocks, begging to be let out of the room filled with so much pain.

Jordan sprang to his feet, pacing the room, a predator in a cage in need of freedom.

Erick rolled to his knees beside me.

"Evanee, Evanee. Look at me, mic luptător. Are you okay? Speak to me," he begged.

"I'm okay. I wouldn't touch me, or you may see the rest." My breath shuddered out between clenched teeth.

"What rest? What else happened?" His hands appeared on either side of my face.

"Erick, don't!" I groaned.

The room disappeared around us, as pitch-black that no night sky could compete with engulfed us. Pain slammed into Erick, my eyes wide with fright and the never-ending pain I still felt showing in their depths.

On and on it went in a vicious circle, his physical connection enabling him to feel what I felt. Snarling at the agony we felt, his lips drew back, and my heart skipped a beat as fangs erupted where eye-teeth had been.

A feral being replaced the polite and sometimes playful Erick I'd come to know.

He was manic, shaking and hissing long and low. He shut his eyes only to reopen them a millisecond later. Where his mesmerising irises had once been beautiful swirls of emerald and garnet, now sat two blood-red orbs.

I was a deer caught in the headlights of an oncoming car.

Erick lunged at me, stopping short by an inch as a blur slammed into him, launching him across the room to crash into the opposing wall.

The darkness faded, and through my dizziness, I saw a tall and imposing Jordan standing above me. He had, if even possible, increased in size.

Fangs clung to his bottom lip just as they did Erick's, and he crouched over me — but I wasn't afraid of him.

Shadows clung to the edges of the room, and I realised that it wasn't a result of my memories of the abyss—it was Jordan. That immense power emanating from every inch of him fuelled those shadows, giving them life.

I fought the oncoming exhaustion about to hit me like a freight train.

"Jordan, you need to stop. My mind can't... it won't take much more of your power and his rage. Please!" I pleaded.

I dared not touch him, fearing I would set one of them off.

"You will calm yourself, Erick. Take control of the rage riding you or I will knock you flat before I haul your arse through the door we came in. You are instinctively reacting to her power." Ignoring me, Jordan focused on Erick, his tone evoking images of boulders smashing together.

"You would turn on your King for a woman you barely know? You would betray me?" There was no humanity in that sentence or his once handsome face.

The changes weren't huge, but they were enough to blur those features I was slowly coming to love about him. His once round eyes were now pulled back ever so slightly, and his cheekbones protruded just that bit more, hollowing out his cheeks.

"No, I would never turn on my King, but I would protect the daughter of the one who saved my life. I would protect my chosen one."

"You mean you would defy my order and mate with her?" Erick seethed.

"No, she is not and never will be my mate, but you know as well as I do that there's more than just one version of a chosen one. You know our prophecies; you know the old stories," Jordan reasoned.

Okay, I must be closer to death than I thought.

I had no clue what he was trying to say, but judging by Erick's rather shocked expression, whatever he'd just referred to was a big deal.

*S*wirls of emerald returned to his eyes, breaking through the wall of red as his mind worked through Jordan's statement. "I don't understand, how do you know she's the chosen one?"

Erick's features slowly transitioned back to their original form as he calmed.

"Because of her ancestry, because of who her mother is. Why do you think I've been visiting the library at the mansion so often lately? Think, Erick, when have I ever visited our libraries or any library? Look, this is something I would prefer to discuss with you at a later date, but not here, not with Evanee lying on the floor, broken." Jordan's voice hitched, and he cleared his throat to hide it.

The shadows receded and Jordan's stance relaxed. He still didn't move from in front of me.

"You'll explain it to me now, Jordan. There are no secrets between us, brother," Erick demanded with a growl.

Jordan rose to face Erick, his shoulders set. "There are some oaths I will not break, brother, and this is one of them."

Erick approached, palms out in surrender. "I still don't understand."

"I can't answer your questions without breaking my oath. If you want answers, I would need permission from Reagan," Jordan explained wearily.

In the mirrored ceiling, I continued to watch the exchange between what I now understood were brothers more than King and servant.

Erick remained silent, prompting Jordan to continue with what brief explanation he could provide. "Look, I need to protect her; every fibre in my body is telling me to guard her with my life. I saw her power release, watched it wing its way into the night; but it's more than just seeing it." Rubbing at his face, Jordan murmured shakily, "I absorbed a small amount before my arse got nailed to the wall in the loading bay."

He did what now?

"So you absorbed some of her power. How is that significant?" Erick flung his hand in my direction as he spoke not even realising he had done it.

"You're not listening. When have you ever known a converted to absorb power? It's a gift only given to those born, not created. The Royal families are the only ones I know of that have the potential to do so." Jordan cursed quietly, before continuing, "It's more than that though. Her power, it calls to mine, it has since the moment I saw her at the party. It has nothing to do with me exchanging blood with her; that only strengthened the bond that was already there."

Jordan's feet moved, his enormous body pacing before mine, still protecting my horizontal frame without even knowing it.

"The incident at the morgue got me wondering why I felt so bonded to Evanee yet have no romantic attachment to her. I turned to the library, hoping it might have something in the ancient texts." Jordan turned and looked at me, changing the subject as concern flitted across his features. "Erick, we need to leave. We're tiring her out. She'll not handle much more of us being in her mind, and our bodies are growing weaker by the second trying to sustain the connection. I'll show you what I've found once we return."

Jordan dropped to his knee beside my head.

"You will not die; do you hear me?" Jordan ordered, and my lip quirked. "You'll rest and regain your strength and I'll return. We'll both be back to help you return to consciousness. I meant it when I said I would protect you. Don't make me an oath breaker. And please don't give your mother a reason to lay me flat on my arse. I have a reputation to uphold," he grinned at me.

With a soft snort of laughter, I nodded at him.

Jordan rose gracefully and stepped back.

Erick took his place at my head and turned his head to the side. "Go on ahead, Jordan, I won't be much longer."

Looking between the two of us, Jordan turned and strode out Erick's door.

As soon as he was out of sight I gripped Erick's forearm.

"Erick, you need to listen closely. You can't come back after this visit; do you hear me? Something is happening to me, and I'm not sure what it is. When that creature attacked me, it did something. Until I can discover what it did, you need to stay out of my mind. You both do, do you understand me?" My voice was hoarse, fatigue catching up with me at last.

Erick frowned, "I don't sense anything. What makes you think that thing did anything to you?"

"Why else would I be dying, Erick? The power I have would not decay my body to this point so quickly; it's always been a part of me I've kept shut behind that black door. It would never try to kill me no matter how pissed at me it is, it only protects me." With a barking couch, I grimaced at the pain. "You need to take my blood and tissue samples, specifically near the puncture wound on my back. Get the samples to Ellie and Brad. They've already got samples from the other bodies. Get scans done, although I don't think anything will show up on them. Has Bob come to visit yet?"

Erick nodded. "He's been coming and going for some time."

"What do you mean for some time? How long have I been comatose for?" I frowned.

Dread filled his eyes as he carefully chose his response.

"Evanee, you've been in a coma for nearly two weeks now. Jordan and I have been donating blood nearly every second day. This is the first time we've been able to reach you telepathically, and even now I'm the one holding the connection." Strain laced Erick's deep voice.

"Two weeks!" My screech would have been louder if my voice hadn't already been shredded.

"Mic luptător, you need to calm down. Your body is healing perfectly, thanks to our blood donations, but it is your mind that has been impenetrable," Erick reassured me.

"Erick, didn't you stop to think why it was impenetrable in the first place? Did you not stop to think that maybe my power, and I were the ones to put the barricades up in the first place?" I husked, exasperated. "Look, it doesn't matter. Find Bob, ask him to check with Ellie and Brad about my samples. My body is dying; I can feel it even through the erected barriers. If the previous bodies are anything to go by, it will be a painful death," I winced.

Fear flashed through Erick's eyes, creases forming at the corner of his eyes.

Erick opened his mouth to argue, but I silenced him before he could try to placate me. "Look, either you do this or get me someone who will. Hell, get me Tristan; the bastard would take great pleasure in confirming my prognosis."

"I'll do what you're asking. But we'll continue to give you blood, Evanee until you're able to regain consciousness," Erick tried to reason.

"You do what you feel you have to. Just get what I asked done, please. There's something killing people out there and it needs to be stopped."

His nod was stilted, and he stood with all the elegance and grace of a ballet dancer. Looking down at me, he frowned and knelt once more.

Pressing a soft kiss to my forehead, he whispered, "Hang in there. I'll find a way to get you out of this alive, I promise."

And then he was gone, and I was once again alone with my pain and a mountain of questions.

CHAPTER 18

After Jordan and Erick had left, I realised I was still in the autopsy uniform I'd been wearing the night of my attack. I summoned every bit of energy I could to erase all remnants of that night.

A turquoise silk nightie now graced my body, with a bed encased with Egyptian cotton sheets beneath me.

Hey, every girl needed to lie on Egyptian cotton sheets with nothing more than a slip of silk covering the essential parts at least once in their life.

My penchant for beautiful lingerie meant the world's thinnest spaghetti straps whose only reason for existence was to stop the piece from falling off now caressed my thin frame.

The back barely skimmed my backside; whilst the front dropped into a sharp V. The miniature slits on either side of the nightie allowed for effortless movement; thus, allowing my bare skin full access to the glory hugging the mattress.

Sleep came and went but stayed more often than it left. When I woke briefly, my reflection only hinted at the small progress being made on my body in reality. During my waking moments, I replayed the last time Jordan and Erick had been in my mind, and why my mind would portray them as vampires. I'd never seen or heard of vampires or the living dead other than as myths, so why would they appear in my mind?

Although, it would make sense if the two men were of the supernatural variety, considering they'd all been blasted through two walls and walked away without so much as a scratch.

Over and over the questions churned, with no logical answer in sight.

~

Something felt different.

My weary eyelids sprung open, panic dissipating when I realised I was still in the bed in my mind's room.

A slow smile spread across my face and I raised one arm, then the other. I even raised one leg, followed by the other to test how far I could push myself. When I still didn't breathe hard from the effort; a thing that wouldn't have even been possible before, I pushed myself up slowly.

The room spun a little, then righted itself. Deciding not to push my luck by getting out of bed, I was happy to settle with sitting up — I would try getting out at a later stage.

'They must have done something right out there, in reality.' I murmured.

Erick's energy slid over my body and I shivered, my head turning to find him in the doorway that connected us.

Tenderness softened his emerald eyes as he greeted me, "hey Evie, how are you coming along?"

"Hey, Erick. Do I look this skeletal in reality?"

His hesitation was all the answer I needed.

"Great. So, what are you doing here, anyway? Didn't I explicitly tell you not to come back?" I groused.

Erick padded across the carpet, his footsteps silent. Coming to a halt in front of me, he knelt before me so I wouldn't have to strain my neck to look up at him.

"You did, but I ignored your advice and come help you return to your body." His hands gently picked mine up, cradling them as if they were precious crystal. "It's time," he whispered.

A shiver of fear gripped my body, and I stared at him wearily. "What if I'm not ready to return yet? Don't think I don't know what's waiting for me. I feel the pain my body is experiencing, but it's dulled by the barrier. I don't know if I can face it full-force."

"We need you, Evanee. Your friends miss you. Bob and Steve are beside themselves, and I'm sure Steve has been consuming at least half a pack of doughnuts a day. Ellie and Brad have been pulling all-nighters and refusing to leave their lab until they've found something. I'm also scared your mother may carry through with her threat to dissect both the doctors and us with a butter knife if she doesn't start seeing results soon. And if that doesn't convince you," he added dryly, "you're the only one with enough insight to solve the murders. You know that."

I sighed and looked down. I was still wearing the skimpy nightie! My cheeks heated with embarrassment and I quickly yanked the covers up around myself.

"Good grief! Why the hell didn't you tell me I was still dressed like a hooker?" The turquoise material still sat in place, hugging my curves.

Erick grinned cheekily. "And here I thought it was for my benefit. The colour is breathtaking especially with the colour of your eyes and your white hair."

I attempted to look stern., but I had no doubt it probably wasn't working.

"Since when do I do anything for your benefit? Focus, please." I clicked my fingers, dragging his eyes from my cleavage to my face once more.

Smoothing down the fabric over my thighs, I sighed. "There's no point now in summoning up something different, not after you've seen just about everything."

"Not everything, Evanee." Heat and tension radiated from him, gold swirling through his beautiful emerald eyes.

My nipples drew tight, the material straining slightly against their peaks.

Down, girls. He isn't ours.

"Close enough, Erick. This is not how a woman behaves with the man who's interested in her best friend. I have more respect for myself and her. Now eyes up," I reprimanded him.

I should have left him to ogle my girls, because the heated gaze he turned on me had my insides doing a happy dance.

He frowned in confusion. "Why would you think I'm interested in Ellie? What gave you that impression?"

"How could you not be interested in her, Erick? She's intelligent, witty and has that rare combination of being beautiful on both the inside and outside. What man in his right mind wouldn't be interested in her? Plus, you were asking me all those questions about her. I wasn't born yesterday," I reminded him bitterly.

Okay, yes, I was slightly jealous, because some part of me felt something for this hunk of a male specimen. He intrigued me like no one else. His smile lit up the room and did funny things to my insides. His brain was something I wanted to pick. He continually saved me, which made me feel all warm and fuzzy but pissed me off at the same time. I didn't want to need saving. I'd been taking care of myself for so long, but it was nice to have someone care so much. My major trust issues and constant battle with the depression and anxiety were only ever a thought away. Despite all this, he'd slowly worn down my defences, and there wasn't a damn thing I could do about it.

"I admit the way I went about asking for information about her may have given the impression I was interested in her, and yes all the qualities you listed are spot on with Ellie. I'm not blind to them. And as it turns out, neither was Tristan." He said pointedly.

I looked at him blankly, and he continued with a grin, "I asked about Ellie on Tristan's behalf. I know the two of you don't get on very well, and he didn't feel it would be appropriate to talk to you about Ellie when you disliked him so much."

"Are you serious! Tristan... actually, now that you mention it, Ellie has been obsessed with the man since meeting him. Huh, who'd have thought Mr Stick Up His Arse would go for carefree and fun Ellie?" I mused.

"We don't choose who we fall for, Evanee. It's fate who controls our destinies."

"That's bullshit and you know it. We decide our paths in life, not some mystical force. And while we're on the topic of the mystics, you need to tell me just what the hell I saw when you and Jordan were last in my mind. There's no way the shit I saw was humanly possible, and I know I didn't make it up." I crossed my arms stubbornly.

"Now's not the time to be talking about what you thought you saw. Perhaps once you've woken in reality we will discuss it," Erick hedged.

I shook my head. "Uh, no. We will discuss it now, Erick, or I will continue to live in bliss in my little world."

No way in hell was I budging. He could flash his beautiful eyes at me all he wanted, but I wasn't giving an inch.

"Evanee, I said not now. We don't have the time," he growled, taking me by surprise.

"Did you just growl at me? You better not have," I warned with a growl of my own. "I've said it once and I'll say it again. You're not my Prince; your royalty means exactly this much to me." Placing my index finger just over my thumb I lowered it until it was mere millimetres from touching each other, emphasising just how little I gave a shit about his title.

Erick's shoulders hunched ever so slightly and he rubbed at his face. "Look, there are things I want to tell you, but I worry your mind would not handle it at the moment. When you're stronger, I'll gladly tell you everything."

And that's when it dawned on me, events from the past couple of months finally slotting into place.

I never saw him or the others during the middle of the day. He looked exactly as he had when he had left Murder Point Bay all those years ago. His touch hadn't burned me that night at the party; how could it, if he was what I suspected? There was his ability to communicate telepathically with me, not to mention that tiny demon display with Jordan recently. Oh, and how could I forget the lack of a heartbeat the night he'd held me close in the staff room?

"Holy crap, are you a vampire?"

Why didn't I see it sooner? Probably because I don't believe in that crap. Do you even know what you believe in anymore?

"Evanee… Please don't do this, I'm begging you. You need to return to reality; there have been another two bodies discovered since your attack and you're vital in helping us to determine who is carrying out these attacks, and what attacked you," Erick pleaded.

I paused for a moment, thinking about all the clues I'd missed. That he'd always left the morgue with an eskie fulled with something during my teen years.

Wait, did that mean Bob and Steve had known all this time and did that mean that my mother was a reaper?

Firm hands gripped my shoulders, shaking me gently.

"Evanee, I promise I'll explain everything as soon as you're back in your body, but we need to go now. Do you hear me?" The urgency in his tone snapped me out of my trance.

"Did you say there were more victims?"

"Yes, I did. Now, will you come back please?" He beseeched.

"Fine, but you better explain to me what the hell is going on with you. I mean it, Erick; don't you dare shut down on me when I get back. I'll kick your arse up and down the hospital, if I have to," I warned hotly.

It probably sounded hilarious coming from little old me, but I had one advantage, one he had only had a taste of so far—my power.

His lips tugged into a grin and he gave a small nod. "I'm a man of my word, mic luptător. Now let's go please."

Erick rose, holding his hands out to me, waiting patiently for me to take a hold of them. Shuffling a little closer to the end of the bed, I placed my hands to his.

"Thank you. Now we will have to sink back into your body. I'll be right beside you the whole way. I won't lie, it will hurt when you re-emerge, but Jordan and Tristan will be right there to heal you in case anything goes wrong. Do not let yourself slip into unconsciousness, no matter how painful it is. Stay conscious until I get back to you, okay?" Erick warned, his eyes never leaving my own.

"You make returning sound like I'll be greeted with sunshine and daisies," I snorted. "How can I resist an offer like that?"

The look he gave me shut my mouth. I knew I sounded like a brat, but truth be told, it terrified me.

Erick's body tensed for a second, before he murmured, "right, the others are ready."

Pulling me from the bed, muscular arms held me tight as Erick leant forward, laying a small kiss to my forehead.

Hugging me tightly, he whispered into my ear, "Big breath, mic luptător. Remember, I've got you."

With a tiny nod, I breathed deeply. The room darkened before it disappeared around us. Erick's essence cocooned my fragile soul, encasing us in a protective shield.

The barricade I'd erected appeared before us sooner than I would have liked. Envisioning a one-way plasma door, the grey watery substance shimmered into place.

The sight beyond the doorway had my soul shuddering with horror and fear. I hesitated only slightly, and Erick must have sensed my hesitation, as he tightened his grip, maintaining his pace even as the door shrank with my fear. He sped up and together we hurtled down, bursting through that shrinking door with milliseconds to spare.

A hideous screech erupted around me and in the distance. Pink feelers reached for us, but Erick was there, his flame erupting in quick bursts.

I slammed into reality, Erick's light dissipating before I drew my first breath.

CHAPTER 19

My eyes sprung open, and I stared at the greyish white ceiling for a few seconds before overwhelming pain slammed into me. Drawing precious oxygen in, I did the only thing I could to release some of that pain—I screamed.

I cried out for all the times I couldn't in the abyss. I screeched as my power slammed me to the bed, fighting something that attacked me from within. Tears flowed unchecked, my body arching off the mattress before arms shackled me to the bed, preventing my attempts to pull my hair out.

"Evanee! Damn it, look at me! It's Jordan. You need to focus. Breathe, princess, breathe." I could hear him yelling, but the screams wouldn't stop.

"What the hell is going on here? You all need to leave right now," a harassed voice yelled into the room.

"Get them out now!" Jordan ordered.

Yells sounded throughout the room.

"Evanee, look at me. You need to focus, baby. Come on, you can do it. Come back to us, my sweet girl." My mother's cool and gentle voice breathed over my sweat-soaked body, my power rising to greet hers like an old friend, yet my screams never ceased.

"Fuck, her eyes! Are you guys seeing this? Look at her eyes! I've not seen that since…" Jordan cut Tristan off before he could utter another word.

"Not now, Tristan. We have bigger issues to worry about. Come on, princess, don't make me get into trouble with Erick. You need to stop screaming before he gets back," Jordan pleaded.

Where the hell is *Erick?*

Panic set in, mixing with the pain. Again, my body bucked against the bed, muscular arms the only thing tethering them.

I felt his fiery presence before he entered.

The door to the room blasted open, slamming against the wall. Delirious with pain, my head flopped to the side, staring blindly at the man who'd convinced me to return to this cruel reality.

His eyes blazed around the room, taking in each person who held me down. Beautiful flames similar to the colour of the essence he'd surrounded us in not moments before hovered over his skin like a second layer. I wasn't sure whether it was my power that could see it or whether he was using his power for all to see. Pure rage creased his handsome features, his flame responding; surging outwards.

Drawing in a breath for my next scream, I hesitated when I felt it.

The darkness that had surrounded me in the abyss. That ancient power I'd kept at bay for so long — it was coming. The full force, no longer kept at bay by my slumber, rushed from within me. There was no telling what would happen once it hit, and that scared me even more.

Voice rose, melding together as they each tried to speak of the other.

My eyes locked with Erick's and I reached for the person who was supposed to have been here to help me. There was a loud thud of something heavy hitting the wall beside my bed before Erick ripped the drip from my arm. The pain nothing compared to what I already felt.

One second Erick stood at the door, the next he had my fragile body cradled within his sturdy arms. Bending ever so slightly, he jumped us over the bed before opening the window with a flick of his wrist.

Launching us through the window, we landed in the car park below.

He didn't hesitate; he took off at a sprint as if the devil himself was on our tail, trying to outrun something we both knew would claim me any second. There was no telling what that darkness would do to those surrounding me. Behind us, three beings fought to keep up.

There was no time left.

Skidding to a stop amongst a clearing surrounded by Grey Iron and Spotted Gum trees, Erick crouched down, his knees pushing dampened leaves blanketing the ground further into the dirt. Cradling my ruined body, he braced for something he couldn't possibly see or defend me from.

The world stilled, expanded, then shrunk back in on itself seconds before the full brunt of the darkness I had kept leashed for so long slammed through me. There would be no containing it this time; there would be no shutting it behind a thick door as I had before. No, it had felt freedom and it would not be held prisoner any longer.

Our bodies ripped apart as raw power slammed through Erick before retreating into me. He was nothing more than a crash test dummy hurtling through the air before slamming into a massive gum tree behind him, shards of wood lodging in trees and the ground either side of him. Flopping face-first to the ground, he lay unmoving.

Horror filled me as the sheer force of my power slid my limp body across sharp twigs and decaying foliage, turning any that made contact with my skin to ash. Finally coming to a stop, I lay motionless, staring up at the night sky.

In the distance, two sets of ancient eyes focused on me, a woman's manic laughter reaching my ears.

Glad to know someone's enjoying the show, 'cause I'm sure as hell not. I panted mentally.

I waited, knowing it wasn't over, despairing because there was nothing I could do to stop it or fight it.

"Do not fight it, sweet child. Let it take you and fill every part of your being. You are it and it is you. Work together, not against each other. To do anything else will kill you." A patient and wise voice filled the very air around me.

I recognised the voice at once — how could I not? It was a little hard to forget the voice of the man who had helped me three years ago.

A cloaked figure appeared over me, and I frowned at it, unsure if it was my imagination conjuring the figure up or if it was real.

The figure disappeared, and I blinked.

The man had been right once before, and I'd trusted him in my greatest hour of need. It would seem like I would do the same thing once again.

Relaxing my body as much as I could, I encouraged my mind to accept what was about to happen. There was no denying it any longer.

Movement to my left offered me a much-needed distraction. Gazing across at Erick, he staggered to his feet, shaking his head.

I smiled at him, trying for reassurance, and knew I failed miserably. Emotions I couldn't read chased each other across his handsome face before he sprinted towards me.

Behind him, Jordan and Tristan entered the clearing. The ghostly form of my mother emerging from the fog, twisting and churning at her feet beside them. Beautiful white hair streamed around her, her piercing blue eyes broken by white swirls.

She isn't human. The conversation I heard was real.

There was no time to analyse how I felt about this. The next wave was upon me.

Closing my eyes, I gave myself over to the power once again pushing towards the surface. It slammed at my body from within, vicious and angry, and I let it. My body lifted off the ground, then slammed back down, the impact blasting what little breath I had left from bruised lungs.

I was a puppet, the power now my puppeteer, and it snapped me upright. The cold of the dead rushed at me from every direction, before it poured down my throat to fill every bit of me.

The screams of the condemned pierced every bit of flesh with their anguish and longing to live once more.

Silence and stillness that only the dead could achieve finally replaced their screams, still pouring down my throat until I thought I could hold no more.

At last, the torrent of power slowed and my eyes snapped open so I gazed upon the four vampires below me. My mother knelt beside Jordan, silent tears streaming down her pale features.

Gentleness replaced the anger, and I extended my arms in that moment of tenderness, embracing the rest of what my power offered.

One by one, souls drifted into the clearing, their luminescence bathing the area in a gentle white light. They waited silently to be ferried to their ultimate resting place, for I was their ferryman.

In and in I sucked the power of the grave, of the dead, until there wasn't one part of me not filled with its cold stillness.

Around me, the world grew brighter and brighter before plummeting into a darkness so black, not even the full moon and stars could pierce it.

The darkness slid across the forest floor and back towards its source—me.

At last, stars twinkled above, as a gentle breeze whispering enticing stories of life and love reached my suspended body. I drifted to the ground, my bare feet hovering over the blackened forest floor.

Three sets of glowing eyes gazed at me in surprise, while Jordan dropped to his knees, his head down, hand over his heart. He didn't have to say a thing; his gesture spoke louder than words ever could.

Beside him, Tristen hissed, backing away as fear rolled off him in waves. Head snapping to face him, I watched him briefly, not liking his reaction one bit. With a flick of my wrist, he shot into the air, immobilised.

"Sheath those claws Tristan, or I'll sheathe them for you. Don't mistake me as weak because this body is fragile. The last man to make that mistake endured more than his body or mind could take," I warned.

Information trickled in from all around me, my power filtering what was and wasn't needed.

There was no one in this clearing, other than my mother, who posed a threat to me.

I waited patiently until claws that had stood in place of manicured fingernails retracted slowly. The glow of Tristan's eyes dimmed until they too returned to normal.

Satisfied, I released him, looking on with satisfaction as he thumped to the ground, landing hard on his arse.

"Mother dearest. You've been keeping some big secrets from me, haven't you?" My voice was strange even to my ears. I'd whispered the words, yet they'd burst through the clearing as if I'd shouted them.

My power and I were yet to settle into a more cohesive relationship, there were two of us living in this body after all. With each passing second, I could sense us gradually melding together to become one.

"I'm so sorry." Reagan's head bowed in misery as her hands clutched at her knees. "I wasn't sure you would end up with any powers, and when you did, I still wasn't sure what the extent of them would be. I know I should have told you about our ancestry, but I just didn't know how to. I'm so sorry."

Crying was not something I'd ever seen my mother do, and it was a sobering act.

"My powers over the dead have been getting stronger by the day, and you didn't know how to tell me I was—what was it you've all been calling us? Reapers? You lied to me," I hissed, hurt peeking through the power.

My mother's mouth opened and closing in shock, and I dismissed her.

Turning to Jordan, I smiled fondly at the man. He was no threat and never would be.

"You can stand now, Jordan," I smiled benevolently.

He grinned at me and rose to his feet. "I knew you were the one as soon as I read the stories. I knew the Queen foretold in our prophecies was you." Genuine happiness radiated from him brighter than the sun at midday.

My eyebrows drew up in surprise. "A light display and some parlour tricks are insignificant things, Jordan. I'm not sure what prophecy you're referring to, but be sure you've chosen correctly, ancient one, to do anything else may cost you dearly."

Words poured from my mouth faster than I could process the information pouring in from every direction. Images of ancient times and memories I'd never experienced funnelled in.

At this rate, I'll need a whole new filing system. There is no way I'll be able to store all this.

"I'm sure. This decision hasn't been made lightly. To second guess myself would be to second guess my instincts, and I never do that. I have sworn my loyalty to Erick, but I now swear my loyalty to you too."

Walking forward, he lifted his battle-scarred hands, waiting for my permission to proceed.

Head inclining ever so slightly, roughened skin scraped gently against the tightened skin of my temples before his soft lips touched my brow.

Power flared around us, mine cold and still as the grave, his solid and earthy. An instinct as old as time took over, my right hand whipping out to grip his left bicep, smoke emanating from where we were joined. Jordan hissed, a fear shinning within his eyes; yet, he never moved, waiting patiently for me to finish before taking a step back.

Looking down to where my hand had held him, there burned into his skin was the image of a scale, similar to the pendant draped around my neck.

No one spoke as we all starred at his charred skin, watching it heal before our eyes. Instead of healing over completely, the scales stood out as raised scar on his umber skin.

Distraction was my undoing.

Erick's power slammed into me, and he pounced out of nowhere, his hand latching on to my throat. My legs dangled limp and useless as he slammed my body into the nearest tree. Behind him, Jordan and my mother leapt forward, coming to my defence only to be kept at bay by Tristan.

"How dare you try to take what is mine? You will not corrupt my brother." Erick's rage was tangible, his body shaking with it.

He no longer appeared human. His skin had tightened around his eye sockets, his cheekbones just that bit more prominent. His once plump cheeks became hollowed out as his flesh lost any human qualities it'd held not long before.

"Erick, stop! You're reacting to her power; she has stolen nothing from you." My mother pleaded with him, hoping to break through the rage that now controlled him.

My pale skeletal hand found his wrist, yanking down hard on it, and his hand slipped from my already bruised throat. Out of the corner of my eye I caught sight of his other arm coming up, and I moved quickly to block it. My power surged, meeting his brutality head-on; and the fight for dominance began.

My leg smashed into his groin, and Erick grunted in pain, dropping to his knees. Grabbing a handful of his beautiful dark chocolate hair, he received another knee to the face; a satisfying crunch echoing through the night air.

I slammed my foot into his chest, shoving hard as it connected. Erick's body came to a skidding halt a few feet away. I leapt then, sailing gracefully through the air to land lightly over his midsection. Dropping to bruised knees, I straddled his waist, hyperconscious of my power and its dominance of my body and instincts. I'd been designated the passenger seat, my power now the driver. Normally I'd have fought harder to take control, but in this case, I let it. Fighting wasn't my strong suit, and Erick was in a mood to fight.

Thick fog rose around our joined bodies, seething, before rushing outwards over the charred foliage, looking for a live victim. The scuffling from Jordan and my mother being restrained cut off, cries of fury and frustration silenced.

The fog had found and latched onto the two undead beings, shackling them in place, their powers now rendered useless.

Reagan remained unaffected by it, which wasn't surprising considering it was a power she too contained within her.

A look from me stopped her short before she could intervene between Erick and myself. This was not her battle to fight, it was mine.

"One can't take what is freely given, Erick," I crooned dangerously. "Don't accuse me of theft, Erick, or I'll rip your balls off and walk away with a smile. I didn't ask for Jordan's gift of loyalty and devotion; I didn't, as you say, corrupt him. He gave it freely." Leaning close, I snarled into his face, which proved to be a rookie mistake.

The thing with vampires, I'd just learned, was that they healed quickly — too quickly.

One second Erick cradled his nose, the next his hands were on my waist, his eyes wild with the violence that raged within him.

My body shuddering in excitement, my power responded with its own fury. Cries of anguish and injustice from those taken from life too soon roiled within me, their need for vengeance loud. Tonight, I would give them what they sought.

Tonight, I would reap.

CHAPTER 20

Fog blanketed the charred foliage beneath and around Erick's body.

Ghostly hands reached through the miasma, begging for freedom from the veil beyond. Muffled wails of the long-departed echoed eerily through the night. The part of me not affected by the power wept for the sorrow and devastation felt by so many of the innocents trapped beyond that veil.

Erick's hands tightened at my waist, and the world spun as he flipped me onto my back with a bone-breaking thud. Clumps of dirt blasted in every direction like shrapnel. Pain ricocheted through my spine and I couldn't breathe for a moment.

Something sought me out; something inhuman and evil probed the wintry night air, looking for me. I slammed shields into place, my pain forgotten.

I took a deep breath and put my palms on Erick's chest, gathering the power offered freely from those beyond the veil and mother nature herself. Shoving him hard, Erick's body flew into the air before plummeting back down. Rolling at the last second, he landed in a crouch where my body had lain moments before.

I floated to my fee, ready to face my opponent.

"Evanee, stop! Please, you must stop or you'll damage your body further," my mother begged.

I glanced at my mother, but continued to gather power, black sparks spitting from my fingertips and drifting to the ground, sinking into the deceased foliage.

"Do not interfere, Reagan. I warned you the night I was attacked that this part of me would not be shut away forever, yet you did nothing." The hissed words came out of my mouth, yet I didn't speak them. Something other spoke through me.

"You are Evanee and she is you. Without her, you would dissipate, as would she," Reagan reasoned, her voice thick with tears.

"You think I don't know this? Who do you think has kept this body alive until now? What do you think will continue to sustain this fragile vessel as the life is sucked from it by the evil within? She is withering with each second that ticks by."

My mother gasped, before once again trying to reason with me. "If that is true, then surely this exercise will prove futile. You can stop this now, end this. Erick has done nothing but help; he's simply reacting to that primal part of him that recognises the potential for his death. He recognises the reaper within you."

I stared at Erick in silence.

She's right. Erick removed us from the hospital to minimise casualties. He came to us when I needed him. Erick's not the one you're angry at. I whispered to my power.

Sensing my distraction, Erick darted forward, a fist appearing seconds before it slammed into my chest. An audible crack followed by agony was all I needed to know that the human part of me would not make it out of this alive.

Snatching his wrist to keep it in place, we skidded backwards together. Blood trickled out of the crease of my lips. Turning my head to the side, I spat the build of blood within my mouth and smiled at Erick.

The smile didn't last long before Erick wiped it away with a solid fist to the jaw, the crack adding to the list of pain I already felt. Kicking out, my foot connected with solid flesh, and I released his wrist at the last second so he skidded backwards. I fell to my knees, my power drained.

Great, you go on back to your nice cosy little spot and leave me to deal with the mess you caused.

The power didn't respond. I noted that it didn't leave me entirely. Instead, it continued to supply me with just enough energy to keep my heart, lungs, and brain functioning.

"Stop! Erick, stop, please. It's me, Evanee," I gasped, unable to fight any more.

Swayed by the threat he perceived from my power, Erick didn't notice my please. Grabbing my arm, he pulled me backwards.

I winced as broken bones scraped together. Swelling had set in around my jaw, making it increasingly more difficult to get words out. Soon there would be no more talking.

"Erick fease. I shwear iss me. Ere's pease et me go." I begged through my locked jaw.

The fire and rage glinting in the depths of his eyes extinguished, and he blinked at me.

Horror and disgust replaced the rage and he let me go, stepping back. My body dropped limply to the ground.

Something scraped along my rib cage. The skin over my spine puckered briefly before lowering back to its original state.

I froze for a second before I lost all sanity.

It's in me. One of those creatures from the morgue is in me. Fuck!

I'd seen what it did to its victims, and the excruciating pain it had inflicted on its victims. I'd born witness to their despair as their souls were drained slowly.

Then I remembered the nest of tentacles Erick and I had blasted through to get back to reality. I'd watched the thing die, so how the hell did it get in me? Was this the evil my power had spoken of?

My swollen jaw trapped my screams, and I raked chapped fingernails at my pale blue, dirt-stained hospital gown, the ties at the back snapping. The movement in my spine came again, and this time shearing pain radiated from the back of my heart. My dirt-stained hands scratched my side in desperation, ripping the gown from body so that I lay naked. I had to get it out, it needed to come out.

I looked at Erick, summoning what little power I had left. My thoughts slammed into him in my haste to try to communicate telepathically. I couldn't risk going back into my room, not with what was inside me.

"Get it out! The creature is in me. Get it out now." I screamed telepathically.

Looking down at me, Erick's despair was replaced by horror once more when he realised why I'd torn my hospital gown from my body.

"Fuck, it's in her. Jordan, that thing's in her!" Erick bellowed.

Dropping to his knees, he rolled me over as slowly as he could, trying not to trigger the thing trapped within me. Jordan, no longer shackled by my power, appeared at our side, my mother not far behind him.

"That thing that attacked her, it's in her. Look there at her spine." As he spoke the creature stretched once again.

Skin rippled as my muscles tore, my screams muffled by my clenched jaw.

"Shit, okay, well let's cut it out then!" Jordan suggested.

Ignoring them, I reached behind me, continuing to try and claw the thing out of my back. Solid hands grabbed my bony ones, bringing them in front of me as gently as they could.

"We can't cut her here, she'd never survive. The fight has undone all the work you both did. She'll need more blood, hell, she might need a bite this time. If we cut it out here, we could disable her, if not kill her."

Tristan's calm voice was at odds with the scene unfolding before him.

"No, but I could. It's alive, right? Everything that exists can be killed, nothing is immortal. Stand back, I'm going in." Reagan's voice was quiet and firm.

My mother could command an army if she felt the need to. She was the strongest woman I knew.

My knees drew up into my chest as I hunched in a ball. I prayed silently to anyone that would listen, begging for it to end, even if that meant death.

My mother dropped her shields, something I'd only ever experienced once before, the day my father had died, and her power entered my body.

Her power was cool and steadfast, similar yet different to my own. It was disconcerting to feel her drifting through my body. It didn't take long for her to spot what was causing the issue, and I felt her mental shudder in my soul.

Moments later the thing's grip on my ribs tightened, pain shooting through my heart once more. The hands shackling my wrists held steadfast, never letting go, even as I yanked hard, crying tears of frustration, panic and pain.

It had to come out, I needed it out.

My mother's presence withdrew gently, her power subsiding, but never leaving.

"Back away from her all of you! Nobody touches her." Regan commanded.

Someone released my arms, the twigs scraping the undersides of them going unnoticed. Slowly, one by one, the group backed away from my naked form. The movement in my back continued once, twice, then stopped.

They left me panting, crying softly, silence once again descending upon the night.

As I lay broken on the dry earth, my mother's gentle voice rolled over me, offering little comfort. "I've never seen anything like what's in her. It's wrapped around her ribs and it's fused with her spine. It's impossible to remove. But I swear this thing is part-reaper. I tried to reap it, but it's somehow immune to me. It also doesn't have a soul. It has a barbed tail pointed at her heart, if we try anything further, it will pierce her heart. She'll die."

Rolling to my side, shudders rippled through my bruised and battered body. There wasn't any part of me that didn't hurt. I knew there was blood in my lungs; every breath felt heavy.

And here they all are having a nice little tea party while I lie dying.

'That's a bit dramatic, Evanee. You're not going to die. I'd never let that happen.' Erick huffed mentally.

"I'll give you dramatic, Erick. As I recall, you're the one who attacked me to begin with. My broken jaw didn't happen on its own." I raged.

Erick's face shuttered, but not before I saw the shame he felt. "Tristan, I need you to do a full assessment before any of us touch her. If she needs healing straight away, then we'll do it here, otherwise, I'd prefer to get her back to the hospital."

"Evanee," My mother's soft voice came from nearby, "I'm going to gently roll you over. It will hurt, but it's the only way Tristan can check what is happening with your internal organs. On three, okay."

It hurt too much to nod, so instead, I raised a finger from my clenched fists. If they didn't hurry, I would pass out soon. The adrenaline was leaving my body faster than air releasing from a slashed tyre.

Taking it as a sign to proceed, Reagan placed a soft hand below my shoulder closest to the ground, and another on my other shoulder.

"Can someone stabilise her neck and her legs?" Reagan snapped, the rustle of foliage above my head the only sign someone had moved to support my neck.

Together, they turned me over as gently as possible. Moans of pain were all I could manage, but they barely expressed the agony tearing through me. Lying as still as I could, I focused on my shallow breaths. Anything deeper hurt too much.

My mother's frigid hands wiped at the tears and stickiness coating my face.

Jordan shook out my torn hospital gown and laid it across my bare body, smiling reassuringly at me. At my head, Erick tried, but failed to hide the fear and anguish at seeing the damage done to my body.

The oddest sensation of someone drifting through my body was the only warning I got that Tristan was assessing me.

Coming back to himself, Tristan frowned, "She has an incredible amount of internal damage. I'm surprised she's even awake. You've undone a lot of the work you repaired, Erick."

"I did what any good Prince would do in the face of perceived danger." Erick muttered. "I had no idea she was coming into her powers, let alone that those were powers of a reaper. If I'd known…"

"That's no excuse," my mother interrupted. "You're ancient, she's just a fledgling. You could have held back if your pride hadn't been so wounded." Reagan spat.

She was in maternal mode, her outrage at my pain and regressed health fuelling her anger.

Erick hissed angrily at Reagan before turning to Tristan to snarl, "Does she need healing here or can she make it back to the hospital?"

"Evanee will need blood now," Tristan replied evenly. "She's in no condition to be moved. She has a collapsed lung, a minor scratch at the base of her heart and internal bleeding to the abdomen. Not to mention the broken jaw, cracked ribs, and sternum. Oh and torn ligaments throughout her body."

"Fine, I'll do the blood exchange here then."

Erick's decision final, he looked into my eyes, weariness darkening his eyes. '*Evanee, this part is for you* to decide. I can keep doing these transfusions, as Jordan and I have been doing for the past few weeks, and we will keep having to do them until we can remove whatever has infected you, or I can bite you before I give you my blood.'

'Bite me? What, you want to get fangy with my neck?'

Laughter burst from his tight lips, winging its way into the night sky. Goosebumps flared along my body, my hairs standing on end not from fear, but from the heat flooding my icy body.

Erick's thumbs strocked tenderly. 'Yes, it would require me to get fangy with your neck. However, it would not be a fatal exchange, merely enough to boost your healing capabilities. Blood alone isn't working; the next logical solution would be to perform the first bite. To bring you partially into my world. It requires three bites to bring you fully over, with the last one draining you. This isn't performed unless there's cause to do so, and the vampire is an ancient.' He spoke quickly, aware I was deteriorating.

My power was the only thing keeping me alive and conscious.

'Okay, so let me get this straight. You want to get up close and personal with my neck, then feed me your blood hoping to heal the damage you and this thing did to me. Not to mention the fact that you're all ancient, like Egyptian-mummy ancient. Did I leave anything out?' I clarified with exasperation.

'I don't think so. Oh, I'm not so old as that, though.'

'Oh, okay, well that makes more sense. Are you freaking kidding me? You were meant to tell me I was dreaming. You know what this probably isn't even real, anyway. I'm probably back in the abyss and it's screwing with my head again. I didn't have you pegged as the violent kind of guy. So you know what, go right on ahead and do your fangy thing.'

With a shaky sigh, Erick announced, "She's agreed to allow me to bite her before we exchange blood."

Protests burst into the night at Erick's proclamation.

"Sire, you can't. Think before you do this. You'd be tied to her." Tristan exclaimed.

Apparently, this was a fate worse than death, according to Tristan's horrified expression.

"Erick, think before you do this. To combine the vampire and reaper species in such a way is forbidden. You know this." There went my mother.

I noticed Jordan was the only one who hadn't said a word while the others had a meltdown.

"Enough!" Erick bellowed, his eyes glowing, as golden flames licked at his forearms. "Tristan, I hold rank here, not you. As to thinking about what I'm doing, I have weighed the consequences thoroughly. This isn't a spontaneous thought, but something I've been considering for a while now.

Erick's eyes shot to my mothers, and he growled, "You should have thought of the combining of our species before you asked Jordan to save her life and lied to me, Reagan. As for your other objections sure to come, it has been a while since I performed the first exchange, but I'm not a fledgling who would lose control." Staring hard at the vampires and reaper surrounding him, Erick continued, "Jordan, you will stand watch, both Evanee and her power seem to trust you. Now that she's embraced the Reaper side of her, I'm not sure what the outcome will be with a first bite."

No one spoke once he'd finished. I could only hear the crunch of dead leaves underfoot as Jordan stepped forward. I looked up at the mark on his arm, which had now fully healed. It moved against his skin, the scale once crooked, now balancing.

'Erick, not to distract you, but could you ask Jordan if he feels the tattoo moving on his arm? Please.' I whispered in his mind.

Eric looked towards Jordan's bicep. "Evanee wants to know if you can feel the tattoo moving?"

Jordan frowned. "Yes, I can. It's the weirdest sensation as if something is trapped just below the surface of my skin. The tatoo feels alive, but not. It's a hard sensation to describe."

"Will you allow me to test something?" Eyes never leaving the mark, Erick raised his right hand waiting for Jordan's permission.

Jordan nodded.

Fingertips sparking to life, golden flames flickered gently as he lowered his hand towards Jordan's bicep. Touching his fingers to the tattoo, Jordan's skin sizzled, tendrils of smoke rising into the air.

Fluttering took up residence in the pit of my wounded stomach. It was not long before the fluttering progressed to swirling and churning, the longer Erick burned the marking. My fingers twitched, tingling progressing from the tips of my fingers up my forearm to just below my elbow.

"Erick, stop," Reagan whispered in warning as she came to stand above my head.

"Interesting," Erick murmured, intrigued.

Instead of stopping, Erick intensified the flame, unaware obsidian sparks had ignited in my resting hands.

Nostrils flaring, I caught the familiar metallic scent of blood. I knew without needing to look that beads of blood now coated Jordan's brow, dripping slowly down his cheeks as he stood stoically waiting for Erick to finish.

That part of me that had fled after our fight streamed back to the front, screaming at me to stop Erick. He was hurting what was ours to protect.

Head flopping to the side, my eyes found Erick's. My arm shot out, and my hand found his boot shielded ankle, shackling it.

"Shit, Erick, stop now!" My mother's yell was too late.

Erick's head snapped down to look at where my hand gripped his jean-clad leg. The obsidian sparks cascading from my hand caught at the material—decaying it first, then starting on the leather hidden beneath it.

Erick yanked his leg back, finally ceasing the torture on Jordan.

'You will not harm him again, Erick. You do, and I'll remove one of your appendages in such a way that not even your little regenerative powers will heal it,' I spat.

'It was merely an experiment, mic luptător. Calm down, I was not hurting him without a purpose,' Erick tried to reason.

'I don't care, Erick, don't touch him like that again. He's mine to protect. He's my clipeum, my shield.'

I didn't even know how I knew that word, but it meant something to Erick.

He stilled, a look of surprise creasing his beautiful face. *'As he is mine to protect. He is my brother in arms, don't think you can steal him from me.'*

'We have had this conversation before, Erick Tenebris, and it didn't end well for either of us,' I warned.

'Hey, I'm still standing, you're the one with her cute arse to the ground,' Erick teased light-heartedly.

'Come a little closer and say that to me again,' I dared him.

Erick grinned but stopped needling me; instead, he knelt beside my prone body. He waited to see if I would lash out, and when I didn't, he gently touched my hand.

"If you're still okay with this Evanee, I'll perform the first bite now before anything else happens."

'Will it hurt?' I whispered.

It was extremely frustrating not being able to talk. Thankfully Erick could communicate telepathically with me, or things might have gotten interesting. I wasn't entirely sure I was up for a game of charades.

"Yes and no. It has a lot to do with the emotions of the vampire doing the biting at the time of the bite. If I meant you harm, then yes it would hurt. If I wanted to make it pleasurable, then I could," he explained quietly.

'Okay, let's get this show on the road so I can wake up and put this all behind me as the nightmare it is.'

"Everyone except for Jordan," Erick growled at the group. "Clear out. Make your away to the hospital. Tristan, you're on damage control. Unfortunately, I may have scared a few of the staff, and Ellie and Brad will be curious as to why I jumped out a window with their best friend. Bob and Steve already know the drill."

My mother's hesitation didn't go down well with Erick. It seemed she didn't take orders any better than I did. They stared at each other as she refused to move.

"I said go, Reagan. I will take care of her."

Her gaze fixed on Jordan, and she nodded, looked down at me before she turned to follow the two vampires into the darkness of the trees.

"Oh, and before you go, Reagan. Why would Evanee refer to Jordan as her clipeum? It's Latin, isn't it?" Erick enquired. "I know I've heard it before."

"Sorry, I do not understand why she'd refer to Jordan as her shield or mark him with our family's coat of arms. I do vaguely recall *clipeum* being mentioned in one of our ancient prophecies taught to us as children, but I never taught Evanee any of our family's prophecies. I'd need to look it up to see which one you are referring to."

Erick nodded. "Do that. The sooner we know what's going on here, the better."

The air before my mother wavered momentarily, before a doorway appeared, an unlit corridor on the other side. Stepping through, she vanished along with the doorway.

"Jordan, wait at the first ring of trees. Don't disturb us unless it's urgent." Bowing his head ever so slightly at the both of us, Jordan left.

And then it was just us.

CHAPTER 21

Erick scrubbed at his head, his head drooping low for a second.

His guard dropped for the first time, revealing the tiredness and loneliness he kept hidden. It surprised me, considering he had so many friends and family surrounding him.

'You look like shit.' I whispered mentally to him.

He snorted. "Always so eloquent with your words, mic *luptător*. How can anyone resist you when you talk so sweetly?"

'Hey, at least I'm honest.' I huffed at him.

If I could have shrugged, I would have. From the numbness and tiredness creeping in, it became obvious my body was shutting down. The creature was once again awakening; I could feel it stirring, sickeningly.

With a slight smile tugging at his pouting lips, Erick conceded, "That you are. Your heart is struggling, we must hurry if we're going to do this."

"*That'd probably be a good idea.*" Coughing harshly, my body heaved with the effort it took to regain my breath.

Placing an arm gingerly behind my neck, Erick angled my head further to the side, allowing for better access to my arteries.

'*Please be in a good mood. I don't need any more pain.*' I begged tiredly.

'*I'm so sorry I hurt you. It was instinct, not intentional. Not my proudest moment, I'll admit. I've never raised a hand to a women unless it's been during a challenge. Tonight should never have happened. I can promise you I'd never bite you intending to cause you pain.*' Erick murmured guiltil.

Too tired to respond, my eyes drifted shut, waiting for whatever was about to happen. Hints of citrus and vanilla teased my senses as he bent closer to my neck.

Breathing deeply, a tiny smile quirked my dry lips. '*You smell divine. The phrase 'I could just eat you' pops to mind.*'

I couldn't see whether he was smiling, but his response suggested he might be.

'*Funny, I was about to say the same thing to you,*' He growled softly.

Soft lips caressed that sluggish pulse along my stretched neck. Once, twice; before he inhaled deeply at the spot he'd been caressing, taking my scent into his lungs.

Even if I could have moved, I probably wouldn't have; that inhale reminded me far too much of a predator scenting its prey.

Inhaling once more, his soft lips caressed my pulse one last time, then the gentle scrape of sharp teeth triggered my fight-or-flight response, adrenaline flooding my body.

My body's reaction only excited Erick that much more, the hard bulge beneath me hinting at just how excited he was. His teeth scraped softly at that delicious spot again in reassurance and it no longer scared me.

Goosebumps broke out across my body, liquid pooling at my core with his soft caresses, but I was unable to relieve the pressure building between my legs.

My arousal drew a long low growl from Erick, and it vibrated against my neck, shooting right to my core.

His beast surfaced, the man pushed to the side. And I wasn't entirely sure how I felt about that. My objection was on the tip of my tongue when he bit down, my skin giving way beneath sharpened canines.

My body flooded with blinding pleasure, and my fingers curled, my arms limp at my side.

I'd have grabbed all that beautiful hair if I'd had the energy to move, but for now, all I could do was lie there, absorbing the thousands of fireworks exploding through my abdomen, tightening things below even further.

The need for relief consumed me until I was sure I would go insane. Teetering at the edge of that delightful precipice, I was ready to fling myself off into a world of bliss and carnal delight when Erick pulled back.

I hissed my protest from between my clenched jaw, frustration a kick to my already wounded gut.

His groan of pleasure brushed my body before he murmured, "You are too delectable, Evanee. I'll lose all sanity if I take any more."

I could say nothing. My body screamed at me, at him, for release. A sharp inhale sounded from above me forcing my heavy eyes to open. I looked into his face, his sensual smile emphasising his ruby stained lips.

"You need blood now. Your power is the only thing sustaining you at the moment. I don't think we want to find out what its limits are," Erick murmured.

Mesmerised by his hooded gaze and the colours swirling within those irises, my mind remained blissfully blank.

Raising his index finger, I watched avidly as his fingernail lengthened into a claw before my very eyes. Erick placed the tip at the edge of his wrist and tugged downwards, his skin puckering before it gave way, a crimson line appearing.

The realisation hit me then, as a thought smacked me in the face.

Oh shit, he wants me to drink his blood. He's not going to give me a traditional transfusion. He literally wants me to drink his blood.

There was no time for protest, and sensing my hesitation, he gently gripped my tangled hair as he placed that leaking vein to my lips.

My lips remained tightly sealed, and a growl emitted above me, warning me to take what he offered.

"Don't make me do this the hard way, Evanee. I have enough guilt on my concious tonight. I don't want to force this on you, but I will if I have to. You're too important."

When my lips remained tightly sealed, he snarled.

His patience was at an end, and as my head slipped back, he seized my fractured jaw, squeezing. Stars and black spots danced across my vision, the edges going fuzzier than they had been before. He took advantage of, pressing his wrist onto my lips.

Thick warm liquid pooled in my mouth, coating my tongue, but I refused to sallow.

"Swallow it, Evanee," he snapped angrily.

'Screw you, Tenebris,' I spat back.

"Fine, have it your way, but remember I warned you."

His fingers slipped over my nose and clamped it shut, and I was forced to decide between swallowing or suffocating. Self-preservation won out.

'BASTARD!' I cried.

Blood seeped down my throat; the healing instantaneous.

My jaw, ribs, and collarbone shifted with a *crack*, resetting themselves. I flinched at the pain, but it disappeared on my next swallow. My partially collapsed lung that had been labouring before, lightened, filling with precious oxygen.

The longer I drank, the hazier my brain got. My power rose to the surface once more, recognising Erick's power and something else, something I dared not inspect too closely—his essence.

Sitting up, I took his wrist with me. The flavour no longer metallic; instead, I now tasted those hints of citrus and vanilla I'd smelled on him as he'd embraced me. It reminded me so much of cheesecake filling. Thick and smooth, with hints of vanilla and lemon.

Within me, his essence caressed and stroked at my power, coaxed it to come and play a different game than the one before. Every part of me responded; my power, body, and mind.

This was what I'd wanted since he'd come to visit me in the morgue. Right in this moment, I wanted him—consequences be damned. I needed all of him.

Dropping his now healed wrist. I was little more than a blur as I moved to straddle him.

Large, firm hands gripped my waist; steadying and encouraging me.

I touched my nose to the smooth skin at his neck, inhaling deeply.

There it was again, that delectable vanilla and citrus. Licking the smoothness at the crease of his neck, frustration bubbled up when I couldn't taste what I had before. Fingers twining through his silky hair, I yanked hard, extending his neck until it was taut. I needed to taste him, to once again balance at the edge of that heady precipice.

Beneath my thighs, I felt Erick tense as he tried his best to restrain himself.

Nipping at his ear, my demand escaped in a hissed whisper. "More. Need more."

I didn't want patience, I wanted action.

"I'm trying hard here, Evanee. We go down this path and there's no telling where this will end. I'm trying to be a gentleman." His strain was clear, but I didn't care.

"I. Said. More." Biting down hard to emphasise my point, his gasp of delight pleased me immensely.

"Fine, you want more, I'll give you more—and then some," Erick hissed.

Creating a minor cut to his neck, I was on him before his hand had time to reach my waist. Licking at that tiny crimson line, my mewl of satisfaction drew a possessive growl from the man beneath me.

More. Must have more of him.

My blunt, human teeth sunk around the wound.

Erick's fingers tightened, bruising my emaciated hips. Dragging me closer, his left arm secured my hips in place, his other arm coming up to cradle my head.

My bare breasts caressed cotton and annoyance that he was fully dressed flickered briefly before vanishing beneath the intoxicating liquid his body held.

Gentle hands tucked the knotted hair at my neck to one side while I continued to suck. There was no brief moment of searing pain like before as he bit down; instead, I climbed that cliff once again, reaching for the euphoria that awaited me at the precipice.

The problem with being human, even part-human as I was, and ingesting blood, is that there's only so much blood you can swallow before the body tries to expel it. I'd reached that limit and was forced to release Erick's neck.

My hips arching into that hardness hidden beneath his jeans, the friction enough to trigger the release I sought so desperately. Pulling back at the last second, his punishing lips crushed down on my parted ones, drinking down the scream he'd helped to create.

Flying apart in his arms was beyond anything I'd experienced. In that moment of bliss, I wondered if I'd ever feel anything like this again.

Our hard kisses turned to gentle caresses as we sat entwined. A peace I hadn't felt in a long time settled over my sated body.

Pulling back slightly, I nipped at his luscious lips, licking at the spot to chase the sting away. My hands combed gently at his soft, dark hair. I fought the reality waiting impatiently to crash down upon us; for now, we were both happy to luxuriate within this bubble we'd created. There wasn't a single part of me that didn't want to stay ensconced in this world we'd created together.

Ever so gently Erick's head pulled away from mine, placing gentle kisses at my shoulder and neck.

Shivers of pleasure wriggled their way down my spine, goosebumps breaking out over my chilled skin.

A breeze drifted lazily over us, puckering my nipples and reminding me I was sitting on a man, semi-naked. It hadn't been an issue a moment ago, but then again, that was before reality had gone ahead and taken a knitting needle to our bliss bubble.

"We need to go," he murmured reluctantly between kisses. "Tristan feels it necessary to throw images of the hospital staff at me. They're getting antsy at not being given access to see you."

His chest rumbled against my bare one, igniting new tingles. Nipples once again puckered, begging for his attention. The orgasm hadn't been enough; my traitorous body begged the man between my legs for more. My panties chaffed, and the jeans Erick wore scratched at overly sensitive skin.

One orgasm will not be enough.

Sniffing the air, Erick groaned. His lips pressed kisses along the line of my neck until he reached just beneath my ear.

There was no way of hiding my attraction from him, not when he could smell it on me.

"I'd very much like to give your body what it's craving, but you need rest," he whispered seductively into my ear.

"Would you stop reading my thoughts? It's bad enough that you can tell when my body's turned on, never mind what I'm thinking," I groused, embarrassed by my body's reaction.

"I try, I do, but it's like Pandora's Box. I just have to see what's inside, even if it means dooming the world to your foul mood." Chuckling, Erick pulled back, giving me one last tender kiss before we drifted into the air.

325

Breath catching, my legs latched behind his back as I held on to him for dear life.

"A little warning next time. Not all of us have the nifty trick of levitation." Mortification roiled within me, and I tried desperately to hide my feelings.

"Ah, but you do. You were doing it before and during our minor disagreement," Erick chuckled.

"That was the power, not me. And if you call what we had a minor disagreement, I could only imagine what our fights would look like," I sniffed.

"There's a part of me that wants to find out, but the reasonable part of me agrees that we probably shouldn't find out. Now, you have two choices; I can carry you back like this to the hospital, with Jordan in tow, or I can give you my shirt and at least give you the illusion of modesty. What's it to be?"

Oh crap, Jordan's still here?

"Yes, he is. Now hurry and decide before I make one for you," he hastened me.

"Fine, I'll take your shirt. Please," I sighed in defeat.

"Wise decision. I wouldn't want to rip Jordan's eyes out for seeing something he had no right to."

Sliding my body down his, Erick moved in a blur, tugging his shirt over his head.

Legs wobbling, Erick's arms came around me once more.

I would need help to put my shirt on at this rate.

"Come again? I don't think you have the right to dictate who can see anything of me." I said incredulously.

"Evanee, my reactions where you're concerned at this point will be extreme. The first bite helped you would. However, that second bite and the way we exchanged blood changes things." Sighing at my confused look, Erick continued to explain. "I only meant for us to exchange a single bite and a small amount of blood, instead we exchanged more than double that. I meant it to be methodical, but things got a little more heated than either of us planned for." His brows pulled together as he continued. "Look, I've performed an exchange before; usually, it's clinical and straightforward. However, what we just did, well that changes things for me; it changes things for us. It changes the relationship we have. Now arms up, please."

Mouth shutting, I waited patiently as he gently pulled his shirt over my head, before gingerly helping me to place an arm in each hole.

Shirt firmly in place, Erick stared down at me. Releasing a frustrated breath, he cupped my icy cheeks in his now warm palms.

"I don't have time to explain the things I want to; we need to get back to the hospital. I'll explain it to you later, okay? But for now, if you could keep joking about your relationship with other men to a minimum, I'd appreciate it." He pleaded in earnest.

Eyebrows raising, I felt myself nodding before my brain had a chance to process what he'd said.

Erick scooped me into his brawny arms, my skeletal ones looped over his neck. The wind tickled my cheek and dangling feet as he took off out of the clearing.

We reached Jordan after a few seconds, and he nodded before we were off again, the world once again blurring.

My eyes drifted shut and my head rested against Erick's firm, warm chest. Feeling safe for the moment, I allowed myself to drift into a dreamless slumber.

No doubt I'd wake in the hospital bed to find this had all been some bad and weird dream.

A small part of me hoped not, though.

CHAPTER 22

Motes drifted lazily in the patches of daylight breaching the partially open blinds. My eyes acclimated to the light, and I watched the particles dancing merrily.

Judging by the amount of light coming in, I was guessing it was around midday.

Stretching gingerly, I winced when my back cracked.

I took in the room's sparseness, noting a single chair sat beneath the window, facing the direction of the outdated TV in the corner near the door.

Panic set in as I realised I wasn't in my bed at home. Gazing down at the sterile white blankets cloaking my stiff legs, I realized where I was.

"No, no, no. This isn't happening, it's all just a nightmare."

Combing at my hair, I checked for twigs and dry leaves, my relief at finding none short-lived when memories from the night before filtered through the panic.

Memories of a boxer clad Erick cradling my fully naked body beneath the warm spray of the shower as my mother washed the dirt and debris from me.

He'd sat on the closed toilet, holding me while my mother did her best to towel dry us both.

Afterwards, Erick had replaced me in my bed before lying beside me, spooning my body as he quietly told me a bedtime story from his childhood.

My mother had sat beside the bed, cradling my skeletal hand listening to Erick's story.

Ripping at the white blankets confining my body to the blasted bed, I finally swung my skinny legs over the edge. Ignoring the chill of the tiles beneath my feet, I stepped towards the direction of the bathroom, only to collapse in a heap.

Breath leaving my lungs in a whoosh, it took precious seconds as I remembered how to fill my lungs again.

Sucking at the air, my fingers clawed at the metal frame of the bed, dragging my useless body up the side of the bed until I could once again sit on the rock-solid mattress.

I concentrated, willing my wobbly legs into action as my heart calmed its racing beat.

Gingerly standing once more, I grappled with the chair under the window, shuffling my stiff feet towards it; sweat trickled down my forehead, my lungs heaving uncomfortably. This was proving a lot harder than it should have been.

Turning, I focused on the small cupboard near the door to the bathroom and plotted my course. It wasn't that great of a distance.

I can do this. I can do this.

Waiting for my breathing to even out, a gentle warmth stirred to life at the crease where my shoulder and neck met. Hands drifting over the area, I jerked when trembling fingers brushed two tiny puncture wounds.

Planned path be damned.

I launched myself from the olive chair, slamming into the cupboard before pushing off towards the bathroom. Smashing into the heavy white door, it slammed into the bathroom wall before bouncing back to hit me square in the face.

"Shit!" Yelling proved useless as the floor rose to greet me.

My shoulder connected with the tiles, tearing a grunt of frustration and pain from me. Not stopping, I rolled to bony knees, crawling towards the sink.

Clawing my way up the toilet, horror at the germs I was potentially coming into contact with faded into the background as I finally got to my feet and gazed into the mirror. My vision blurred and what little blood I had in my face drained.

It couldn't possibly be me.

The ash-blond waves that had been my crown and glory for years lay pasty and lifeless. I combed a shaking hand through the strands and large clump came away, drifting lazily to the floor.

My curves were now long gone. Shadows now lay in the hollows of my eye sockets, and my teeth had yellowed.

Taking it all in, I knew the woman staring back at me was dying. I didn't need my medical training to tell me that my body was giving up. I had used any possible source of energy my body could find to keep going.

The warmth I'd felt before grew hotter, drawing my eyes to the two tiny pinpricks at my neck. Turned out what I thought had been a nightmare, hadn't been one.

My brain remained blank, as I moved past panic and skipped right along to acceptance.

'I'm dying.'

'Mic luptător, why are you out of bed?' Erick's concern swirled through my mind.

Ignoring his question, I turned back to my room. Using the frame, cupboard, and chair as rest points, I eventually made it back to the bed. I wanted nothing more than to be back home again, but I had a feeling I wouldn't be released from hospital anytime soon. Not unless I checked myself out and left against medical advice.

'I'm dying, aren't I?'

Silence met my query, but it was answer enough.

'Well shit, never thought I'd be this young.'

'We're working on a way of getting that thing out of you, Evanee. You need to be patient,' Erick reasoned wearily.

'Oh yeah, you're working on it, are you? What have you guys come up with so far? Do you know what it is? How do you plan on getting it out without it shredding

my heart in the process or puncturing my brain because you know my walls will only work for so long?' I snapped, my fear overtaking any shred of reason I had left.

'We're working on it. I'll be there later this evening to give you more blood. The mark has not worked as I had hoped it would,' Erick ground out frustratedly at the turn of events.

'You think? Don't bother giving me more blood, why waste it on a lost cause?'

'Stop feeling sorry for yourself, Evanee. It doesn't suit you.' The snap in his voice whipped across my aching body. He may as well have been standing in the same room as I was.

'How is me not wanting to waste any more blood feeling sorry for myself? I'm the one dying, not you. You're already dead, aren't you?' I retaliated.

'I don't have the time for this, Evanee. I want to comfort you. But I can't do that and look for a cure at the same time. You have your mother, your friends, and me and my people looking for a way to save you.'

Useless tears sprang to my eyes, and I scrunched them shut.

'You're right. I'm sorry, please thank everyone for me.' Shutting him out. An emptiness remained in his place, one I regretted instantly.

The lonely and vulnerable side of me wanted to call him back, while the stubborn and independent side rejoiced at once again being alone.

Alone, that's how I would die. There would be nothing to remind the world I'd once walked this planet. In time, my friends and mother would move past my death, to remember the day I died as a sad, distant memory.

I'd gone through life quietly, avoiding contact with anyone who might have made me happy. It was my fault, and not one I'd make again given a second chance—despite my trust issues.

The door to my room swung open, distracting me from my depressing thoughts, as in walked the last person I ever wanted to see.

"Hello there, beautiful. How's my girl doing?" Desmond's sang merrily, his voice scraping against my sensitive ears.

I'd not had any contact with him since the party. I'd thankfully avoided him coming and going from work since then.

Not having Desmond, Cassandra and Jared in my life for the past few weeks had been bliss. There'd been no bitching and whining about what a dead-end town Murder Point Bay was from Cassandra. I hadn't had to put up with being creeped out every time Jared and I were left alone in a room together, his beady eyes watching my every move as if I were a specimen under a microscope. More importantly, I'd not had to fight off sleazy advances or delusions of a non-existent relationship from Desmond.

"Why are you here, Desmond? I don't remember asking to see you."

"Oh Evanee, always joking around," Desmond chuckled to himself.

Closing the door, he walked towards the bed, a vase full of white and red carnations, roses, and lilies shielding the front of his body. Panic gripped me when Desmond placed the vase on the bedside table; his thighs touching the bed, he placed a hot sweaty palm on my hand.

"I wasn't aware I was joking, Desmond. What do you want?" I snapped.

This was getting uncomfortable, and there wasn't a damn thing I could do about it, except move my arm from under his clammy paw.

"I thought I'd come and see how my best girl was going after that horrible attack you suffered. I'd have come sooner, but I've been busy covering your shifts. Tsk tsk. It's irresponsible of you to neglect your work, Evanee. We've had Bob sniffing around more than normal, which is really inconvenient," Desmond chided.

Is he serious? Could he be the reason Bob was called to investigate the bodies disappearing from the morgue?

There was something seriously wrong with this twit's head. He'd completely ignored both mine and Erick's threat from the party. I was regretting my behaviour towards Erick and his departure.

"Look I'm exhausted, Desmond, so say what you came to say and get the hell out."

Anger flashed across his face briefly only to be replaced by an evil grin stretching his thin lips.

Oh hell no! He looks like Bill Skarsgård's version of that damned demonic clown. All he needed was the outfit and makeup, and the look would be complete. *Okay, it's time to say bye-bye to the sadistic psycho now.*

"I must admit you being moved to Murdering Point Bay Hospital has proven a bit of an inconvenience for Jared and me. I suspect Bob and Steve may have suggested it after they caught me trying to sneak in to see you not long after your attack. Not to worry though, things have still progressed as we'd hoped."

Come again? What on earth's he talking about?

Before I could ask, Desmond continued talking. "We just celebrated Jared's approval for further funding. He made quite a significant breakthrough with the experiment he's been working on for the past two years."

"That's great Desmond, but why on earth would I give a damn about Jared and his experiments?"

He'd lost me carrying on about Jared and his success. I'd had nothing to do with Cassandra or Jared since the night of the party, and even before that my contact or interest in Jared and his work had been minimal.

"I would have thought you'd care, considering you're a part of the experiment." He taunted mockingly.

My shock at his words left me speechless.

Delight shone from the depths of Desmond's cold eyes as he added, "You really should have taken me up on my offer, Sheperd. I might have spared you all this pain. Well, some of it." Gesturing towards my frail, bedbound body, he continued gleefully. "Now, however, I will enjoy watching the light bleed from those fuck-me eyes of yours. I might even put in a request to perform the autopsy myself; it'll give us time to get to know each other the way we could've if you hadn't been such a stuck-up bitch."

I'd been right in assuming he was a sadist that first night I'd given him the tour of the morgue, I just never suspected he was anything other than that. Something in his speech triggered a memory of the night Brian had attacked me. Did he somehow know about the attack? Surely not; they had sealed the records.

"I'm not dead yet, Desmond. And I do not understand what you mean when you say I'm part of Jared's experiment." I prayed he didn't mean what I thought he meant by it. "Desmond, just what do you know about what's happening to me? If you know what's been attacking all those innocent people, you might find it in your best interest to tell me what you know. Trust me, you don't want my friends interrogating you," I warned him, thinking of Erick.

"You're in no position to threaten me, Sheperd. Ellie and Brad are no match for me or the people I know. All it'd take is for me to click my fingers and they'd be next. In fact, I may just put Ellie on the list. From what Jared has been saying, she's gotten on some very important people's wrong side lately, looking for a cure to that thing inside you. The thing is, there is no cure—only death. It's how Jared designed it. It's amazing to watch really, makes you feel like God in a way." He crowed with delight.

"You stay the hell away from Ellie, do you hear me? I mean it, Desmond, I'll rip your fucking heart out if you touch her." I spat before I lunged at him.

Desmond moved out of my reach easily, heading towards the door.

"Sheperd," he smirked, "you're in no position to threaten me. I'll be sure to give Ellie your best."

Shutting the door, Desmond's cheerful whistle shredded my ears drums.

My hand slapped at the bite marks as I thought of Erick. Concentrating, my head ached, as my energy wavered.

Grabbing the remote beside me, I hit the button for the nurse.

"Nurse, nurse! Hey, I need someone in here now!" My screech worked, and with seconds, two nurses bolted into the room.

With a shaking hand, I pointed in the direction Desmond had left, my voice wavering "That man is not to come within 10 feet of my room. He's just threatened me. I need a phone right now."

"Miss, you need to calm down. If you're concerned for your safety, we'll call security and get the police involved, but you need to lie back and rest." The female nurse reassured me.

"Screw resting, get me a phone right now or I'll crawl out this bed and find one myself. I don't need the police—I need to call someone, I need to warn them," I fumed.

"Miss, please you need to calm down or we'll sedate you," the male nurse warned.

"I'm not a threat to you or myself. I don't need sedation, what I need is to make a phone call." The male nurse pushed me back against the bed, as the female nurse hit the alarm, signalling for the on-call doctor.

I kicked wildly against the nurse's grip, but there was no escape.

"What's the situation here?" The brisk voice of the on-call doctor reached my ears, despite my struggles.

"She's having a psychotic episode, sir. She may need sedation before she causes any further injuries to herself."

"I'm not having a psychotic episode, you morons. I need to use the phone. Get off me!" I gritted out.

The doctor looked between the three of us, before jogging from the room. Re-entering, he carried with him a syringe and a small bottle filled with a clear liquid.

"No! Let me use the phone. Don't do this, they'll kill her. Please, I just need to use the phone for one second," I pleaded.

"Miss Sheperd, you need to rest. Your body has been through a trauma which has affected your reasoning. This is only a mild sedative, it'll relax you enough to sleep. You'll feel a lot better once you wake," the doctor reassured me.

He placed the needle at my arm, and the sting hurt more than I thought it would.

My limbs grew heavy, and a fog descended over my brain. Thinking of Erick once more, I searched for the new pathway he had created the night before. I had no idea what I was looking for but knew the moment I found it.

There, blazing a trail past the creature's web of tendrils, was a pathway encased in a golden glow. Latching onto it, I pulled hard. It was getting more difficult to think, the fog thicker now. I was out of time. I yanked as hard as I could on the cord.

The cord finally vibrated, signalling Erick's presence, but it was too late—I was out of time.

Darkness rose, and I wept in frustration and despair. It was too late, I was too late.

~

The sun sat on the horizon by the time the sedative finally wore off.

My brain was still fuzzy, but it was slowly dissipating. Looking to my left, relief brought tears to my eyes when I caught sight of Ellie tapping away at her laptop. She was immersed in whatever she was doing, as was always the case.

Licking dry lips, I tried to speak.

Clearing my throat when the only sound that emitted was a croak, I tried again.

"You're here. Thank goodness." I whispered with a mouth that felt as though someone had stuffed it with cotton wool.

Ellie looked up, and her gentle smile tugged at the heartstrings I usually kept in check.

"Of course I am, silly. Erick was worried something had happened to you when you reached out for him and wouldn't answer, so he asked Brad and me to check on you. Brad went to grab some snacks. He'll be back soon. Then we thought we could have dinner together," Ellie suggested with an encouraging smile.

My eyes darted to the darkening sky outside the window.

Dread gripped my stomach and my eyes darted back to Ellie in panic. "Ellie, what time is it?"

"It's after six. Why?" She frowned.

"You need to leave and go to Erick's place, okay," I whispered urgently. "Take Brad with you and don't you dare stop anywhere until you've reached his place."

Sweeping the bed sheets back, my legs swung over the side. *Too quick.* I squeezed my eyelids shut as I waited for the spinning to stop.

Ellie jumped from the chair, placing her laptop on it as she rushed to aid me.

"Evie, what the hell are you doing?"

Gritting my teeth against the fatigue and the pain coursing through my body, I hissed, "Get Brad on the phone now. And get your car keys."

"Evie, talk to me. What's going on?"

"Ellie, for once in your life would you just listen instead of arguing. Get Brad on the phone, now!" I'd never gotten angry with Ellie in the few years we'd been friends. That I was partially yelling at her in my rusty voice now alarmed her.

Pulling her phone from her oversized handbag, Ellie hit Brad's number before putting it on speaker.

My power surged to the fore, warning me something was coming, something not entirely human.

We need to leave now.

A tired voice answered, and I spoke up, not wanting to waste time. "Brad, where are you?"

"Oh Evie, hey princess. How are you feeling?" Brad greeted me cheerfully.

"Brad, I don't have time for niceties, just tell me where you are," I snapped.

"Okay. I just entered your floor and am near the nurse's station at the front. Why?" Brad mumbled in confusion.

"Look around you, tell me what you see," I ordered.

"Fine, Sherlock Holmes, calm down. The nurses are at their desk talking about some new doctor. There are a couple of patients watching TV in their rooms, but other than that, there's not a lot happening."

I exhaled shakily. We still had time.

Pointing to Ellie's laptop and bag, I motioned for her to pack her things, before pointing towards the cupboard. Her items would be safe in there for now.

"Hang on, a group of men just exited the elevator. They look like private security. Oh look, your best friend, Desmond's with them."

Alarm caught hold of my body, and I went rigid.

My voice shaking, I whispered urgently, "Brad, listen to me, keep walking and don't look back at them. Once you're around the corner, find the nearest room and hide. Do not leave this hospital until one of Erick's people comes to fetch you, do you hear me?"

"Evanee, what the hell is going on?" Brad's alarm at my order was a welcome relief that he was taking me seriously.

"Don't argue Brad, just do it. Keep your phone on silent and don't hang up. Once it's all clear, come and get Ellie's bag and laptop. It's in the cupboard. El, which room are we in?"

Ellie rushed around the bed to support my fragile frame.

"We're in 10A." Her voice was shaking as badly as mine was.

"Brad, have you hidden yet?"

"Yes, I have." His whisper confirming he'd done what I asked.

Ellie stood silently beside me, holding the phone to my mouth.

"I can't contact Erick or Jordan at the moment, and I don't know where my phone is. I don't have the energy to communicate any other way. The sedative is blocking most of my neural pathways." I cringed at the memory of the needle going into my arm. "The second I hang up I need you to message them and tell them I'm bringing Ell to the mansion. She's in danger. Desmond and Jared have picked her as their new target to infect."

I was hoping Tristan had somehow told them the truth about what he and the others were, the night they had jumped from my hospital room window; otherwise, this conversation would get awkward quickly.

I spoke over the top of Brad, as he tried to make sense of what I'd just said. "I don't have the time to fill you in on everything. Keep your head down until everyone's gone."

He didn't reply, but that gave me the answer I needed. They were close.

Ellie tossed her phone on the bed, knowing it would be easy to track. Having come from a military family, she knew exactly what private corporations and the government were capable of.

Leaving her phone and laptop behind, Ellie hauled my useless body against her slight frame, and together we approached the door. Ellie opened it silently and peeked around the edge before nodding the all-clear.

Hobbling down the hall as silently and quickly as I could, we made it around the corner just as the clomp of heavy booted feet sounded from behind us. Not stopping to wait, we circled around to the elevator near the now-empty nurse's station.

Security, my arse.

Anyone could come and go as they pleased. Case in point, the group invading my room.

We made our way to the lift and pressed for the ground floor. As the door slid shut, I glimpsed Desmond and his people coming around the corner.

The doors shut with a whoosh and I exhaled, relief flooding me.

A second later, I knew my relief was a mistake. I should have known better than to think I was in the all-clear.

The creature at my spine twitched — slowly at first, ramping up its movements the further we got from the group above us until I was sure it would burst from my back as it had done to the corpse in the morgue.

I doubled over, spit and bile splashing to the ground. Clenching my fists, my brittle teeth gritted together, fighting the pain. The pressure was too much as one by one, each tooth cracked, breaking off to fill my mouth.

The door to the elevator opened and a mouth full of broken teeth hit the floor.

"Shit, Ev!" Ellie screeched. "We shouldn't be doing this. You're killing yourself. Please, let's just call the cops. I'm sure they can protect us," she begged.

"You don't get it, Ellie. The group behind me aren't all human. You felt it; don't even try to deny it," I groaned.

We continued down the corridor, heading towards the exit.

"I don't know what you're talking about," she denied shakily.

"Don't lie to me, Ellie. We've never lied to each other, so let's not start now. I know you're not entirely human, I can feel it now. This thing in me is not happy to be putting distance between the group and us."

Startled, Ellie said nothing; instead, she pushed on out the doors and into the chilly night.

Reaching her little car, she unlocked the doors. Helping me into the front seat, she slammed the door shut, blocking the shouts of anger that had erupted behind us.

Sprinting around the front of the car, Ellie was through the door and starting the engine in record time.

"Go, Ellie! Now, go!" I screamed hoarsely.

Slamming it into drive, tyres screeched and the stench of burnt rubber filled the car. We catapulted forward just as a body slammed into the rear window, only to roll away.

Looking back, I caught sight of the man as he dropped and rolled into the gutter, lying still.

Yeah, that's going to hurt in the morning.

"Head towards the crater. You know the one we went swimming at last Christmas? Erick's place is in the mountains near there," I directed.

The drive was a good 30 minutes out of town, but I was counting on Desmond not knowing where I was heading. After all, he hadn't mentioned Erick was one of my friends, and I hadn't corrected him on it either. I hoped he might think we would head towards the police station or the city.

Laying my head back, my heavy eyes shut in exhaustion.

~

Ellie's panicked voice woke me from my dreamless state. "Evie, they know where we're going."

Ellie swerved around the bend, taking it too wide, forcing the car to swerve into the opposite lane.

I prayed there was no oncoming traffic, or we'd both be dead. There was no need to look behind me to know we were being followed; I could feel the infected closing in on us. The creature had begun to breach the defences I'd placed around parts of my brain.

"Ellie, it's me," I gasped, horrified by the serious mistake I'd made. "They're tracking me through this thing in my back. My shields are failing. Drop me off and keep going."

"Like hell. I don't know the way to Erick's place. I'd get lost and be screwed if they didn't track me down first." Sighing, I knew she'd be safer without me in the car, but she had a point.

Desmond knew I wasn't getting far in the condition I was in.

"Okay Ellie, in about 500 meters there will be a dirt road that leads to a picnic area. Turn there and floor it. It'll be bumpy as hell but go as fast as you can until you hit the picnic area. Hopefully, they'll drive past the turnoff. I highly doubt it though. We could always try to lose them in the bush," I directed.

Spotting the turnoff, Ellie slammed her brakes on and swerved onto the dirt road with reflexes I that hinted she was no ordinary human. Stones and dust caught in the tyres before spraying the trees and shrubs.

The sedative had worn off more, but my pathway to Erick remained blocked. He wouldn't be able to help me now.

"When this is all over, and if I make it, I'd like you to tell me what exactly you are," I hissed painfully as we hit a bump in the dirt road.

"Banshee," Ellie whispered through her clenched jaw.

"What did you say?" Holding on for dear life, I looked at her profile in the darkened interior of the car.

"I said, I'm a banshee," she said louder this time.

"Okay. Fair enough. If it makes you feel any better, I just found out I'm half reaper. I guess us ladies of death have to stick together."

Together we laughed nervously, unsure of how each of us felt about this recent revelation.

After driving a little further, I tried summoning my power. I would need all the help I could get for the next part of our journey.

"Ellie, I'm about to try something," I warned. "Whatever you do, don't freak out. Keep driving no matter what you see. I need you to know I won't harm you."

"Do what you need to do, Evie, I've got this." And there it was, her military upbringing rising to the occasion. Survive by thinking on your feet.

Looking at the road ahead, I focused inwards, coaxing that cold and ancient power that had been sustaining me for the past few weeks to the front. It glowed dimly in my mind's eye, almost drained.

I need you one last time, old friend, then we can rest. I coaxed.

Swirling lethargically, it floated towards the surface. There wasn't much, but it would be enough to protect Ellie and get me through whatever I would face next.

Bolstering my mind's shields, I prayed it would be enough to stop the creature from advancing any further.

Ellie hit the brakes violently, and we skidded to a stop mere millimetres from a cement bench. Jumping out, we bolted in the direction that would eventually take us along the walking track that bordered Erick's property.

CHAPTER 23

On and on we trekked beneath the star-speckled night sky.

The rough terrain and the pitch black of the bushland forced us into a brisk walk. Despite each of us having superior night vision, the shadows of the encroaching trees made it that little harder to see. We were careful not to brush against any of the bushes, to avoid leaving any evidence that we'd been that way.

Ellie trekked up ahead of me, picking our path just off to the side of the trail, her scout and military upbringing a Godsend in this moment. I followed precisely where she stepped.

"It's not far now, Ellie. You'll be safe with Erick and Tristan, they'll protect you." My ragged whisper pushed through cracked, clenched teeth.

"Evie, what the hell is going on? Why are we running from Desmond? Do you think Brad's okay?" Her breathless whisper drifted along with the breeze rustling the surrounding leaves, only just reaching my ears.

"Brad will be fine. The crucial thing is that you both survive. I need you to survive so you can help Erick and Tristan stop Desmond and Jared. From what Desmond said this morning, I think Jared is the one who created the creatures that have been killing people. You need to warn Erick that this is bigger than just humans, although I suspect he already knows this. You and Brad will have to work with Erick and his team on finding out just how much Aeternum knows about Jared's experiment."

Breathing heavily, I kept whispering, hoping what little information I possessed would somehow help put a stop to all the murders.

"This thing in me has multiple strains of different species. My power could detect the human and animal DNA easily, but it's the other strands that have me a little stumped. They're supernatural but because this is all so new to me, I can't quite process what supernatural DNA was added," I ground out in frustration. "My mother mentioned she thought she recognised the reaper within it, so you'll need to take a sample of my mother's and my DNA to test it against the creature. I'm hoping once this thing ejects, you guys can capture it and study it, maybe stop this cycle," I wheezed.

After another few minutes of hiking, I peered down the embankment to see a wooden post supporting a barbwire fence.

At last, Erick's property. Took us bloody long enough.

Tugging at Ellie's shirt, we veered off the track and down towards the fence line, picking a path through rocks, loose gravel and rotting vegetation. Approaching the fence on unsteady legs, we hunched down, climbing between the barbed wires. Clumps of my weakened hair snagged on the wire, ripping at the roots, as black blood pooled where barbs latched onto my bare arms.

On the other side, I took a second to glance over at Ellie; she wasn't looking much better than I felt.

Twigs crunching beneath booted feet alerted us to the position of Desmond and the rest of his group on the path just above us. Slowing down had cost us precious time, the distance between Desmond and us closing.

I stepped forward to start the journey down the embankment, underestimating the moisture of the foliage and the steepness of the embankment. My bare feet lost their grip and down I went, dragging Ellie with me. Together we slid down the embankment, smashing into rocks and barely withholding shrieks of pain. Limbs flailed every which way, and sticks scraped along my already bruised and battered skin as I tumbled for what felt like an eternity.

Ellie's breathless scream echoed over the crunch of dead leaves and twigs beneath my rolling body, seconds before I launched into the air.

Bracing for impact, I knew without a doubt I would hurt tomorrow if I made it to tomorrow.

I hit the ground with a resounding thud, air leaving my labouring lungs in one massive rush, and I lay still, unable to move for a moment. Taking stock of any serious injuries I'd sustained, my sigh of relief at having none was short-lived when my instincts screeched at me to move. The fall had gained us a few minutes in distance between us and the group above, but if we lay here any longer, those minutes would dwindle into nothing. They had surely heard us.

Lifting my head warily, I looked around, trying to identify landmarks to see where we'd landed. The slated roof of the monstrosity of a mansion Erick called home loomed ahead of us.

Pushing the pain from my head, I forced my tired body off the ground, crawling towards Ellie who lay panting centimetres from me.

"Ellie, you need to get up. We need to keep moving before they catch up to us. Come on El, you can do it. Don't make me do this on my own, I need you to help me, okay," I pleaded with weariness.

Getting to my feet, I breathed through the pain, while Ellie slowly rolled to her side, then to her knees.

Her moans of pain got louder as she got to her feet. Halfway up the hill, the unmistakable sound of branches cracking and grunts of pain drifted down the embankment.

Shit! We were out of time.

Grabbing Ellie's hand, I yanked her muddy arm, dragging her in the mansion's direction. Making it through the boggy field, we limped onto the soft dewy grass of Erick's manicured lawns.

The mansion sat on top of a hill overlooking tamed gardens, and untamed bushland beyond that. The house looked sizeable from a distance and was even bigger the closer you got, comprising two stories ensconced with a wraparound veranda on each level.

Three smaller buildings surrounded the main house, all atop the levelled hill. Steps led the way up to the main building, ascending gently with three gardened tiers providing rest points. I wouldn't make it up those three tiers. My body was already beginning to shut down, my power dimming with each step I took. It wouldn't be long before my power faded completely.

Hobbling as fast as we could towards the steps, Ellie and I pushed on, and finally, we began our slow ascent.

Our stumbling across the field and lawn had taken too long, looking back I saw our pursuers closing in on us.

I had no choice but to get someone's attention, or they'd get to us before we made it halfway up the stairs.

The creature out of my mind thanks to the knowledge imparted by the bodies I'd autopsied, but the people chasing us had no such knowledge.

Darting a look over my shoulder, I failed to see Desmond amongst our pursuers. Instead, what I saw sent chills down my spine. A variety of supernatural beings and humans rushing forward, their movements stiffened by the creatures controlling them.

I screamed at the top of my lungs for anyone who home. "Help! Someone help!"

My desperate screams weren't as loud as I'd hoped, and I fought the urge to cry helplessly when I saw no response.

We made it past the first tier and halfway up the second before my power spluttered. My legs gave out and body crashed to the ground, leaving me to stare helplessly into the starry sky.

My back arched, and pain scorched every nerve ending in my body, before bile and blood gushed out the side of my numb lips, dribbling down the side of my face and over my chin.

"Oh shit, Evie, get up!" Ellie sobbed. "Please get up! Come on, it's not far now, just one and a half set of steps to go. You have to get up," Ellie urged thickly.

Her petrified face hovered over mine, and Ellie split her attention between the field and me.

"Please, they're coming! I can't do this on my own. Please!" She begged

Trying as hard as I could, my body refused to cooperate.

In a moment of clarity, a thought hit me. Ellie was a banshee. Could that help us?

"Ellie," I groaned, "I need you to scream... Scream like you did at the party... Clo...close your eyes and foc.. focus on me, focus on my body. Focus on my organs shut... ting down the decay and death. Now scream," I groaned.

Getting words past numb lips was an uphill battle. I could no longer feel any of my extremities, my body redirecting precious blood flow to my heart and brain. I was dying and there was no way for me to protect the people I loved most in this lonely, wretched world.

How could I have failed them so terribly?

"I ca...can't, Evie. I can't concentrate," she sobbed.

Shackling her elbow, I transferred the pain I was feeling to her in a bone-crushing grip.

"Scream, dammit! Now!" I yelled in desperation.

Pale, bruised eyelids shutting, Ellie's features slackened before her lids lifted once more, her eyes darker than the night sky. Turning to face our pursuers, Ellie opened her mouth and released a heart-rending screech.

The high-pitched, hair-raising scream soared through the night sky to hit those assailants who'd made it as far as the middle of the field.

The effect was instantaneous as men and women, human and supernatural alike, dropped to the ground, their brains liquifying under the pressure of Ellie's screech.

Those further back fell to their knees, hands at their ears, trying in vain to preserve their already perforated eardrums.

That should slow them down.

My vision blurred with tears of relief and grief.

Ellie's screams went on and on until a figure scooped her up and sprinted her up the rest of the stairs. At last her screams stopped, and I knew she was safe.

Vanilla and citrus embraced me before powerful hands gently reached under my failing body.

The world was deathly silent without Ellie's screams.

Head lolling back, I squinted barely open eyes towards the field. An obsidian fog poured from the wilderness beyond, obscuring the group following us.

Echoes of chaos erupting from within the fog drifted up from below as Jordan charged through the survivors, slaying as he went. Cries of anguish and agony lashed me, as images of the dead begging to be ferried filled my mind.

Moaning at their distress, aching to give them what they so badly desired, overrode any self-preservation I had.

Erick launched into the inky night sky, screams of the dying floating away. The wind roared in my ears as shrivelled strands of hair drifted over my face, and the images of death drifted off with the wind. It left as suddenly as it had arrived, and with a gentle thud, we stopped flying.

Erick laid me gently on something wonderfully soft, but my eyes refused to open.

An equally soft blanket was placed over my frail body. Around me voices yelled and talked in rushed sentences I couldn't focus on; their words made no sense.

Erick cursed in a foreign language and silence descended over the room.

Coughing hard, the audible crack of my ribs may as well have been a bomb dropping in the room. It was deafening.

"Fuck, that was her ribs." I recognised Jordan's gruffness as he approached the bed.

"Hold her down. I will give her some blood to heal whatever is broken until she's strong enough for the transformation." Urgency laced Erick's tone.

"Can't you just perform this transformation or whatever now? She's dying." Ellie's tearful voice filtered through my coughing fits.

"Her power is all but gone. There is but a single speck left within her soul." My mother's presence rippled throughout the candlelight room.

Opening my eyes, I watched her step from the shadows. Her form may have scared most, a translucent ragged dress floating around her ankles and her deathly pale skin now white and glowing. Some might have mistaken her for a ghost.

"She depleted her power getting you to safety," Erick snapped at Ellie, "If I perform the transformation now, she won't survive it. Her body has already begun to shut down. My blood should regenerate most of what has shut down and heal any broken bones and bruises. I'll continue to give her blood each day until her power is enough to help sustain her through the transformation process."

Placing a wrist at my parted lips as he spoke, Erick's blood dripped onto my tongue, rolling down my throat. "You must understand Ellie, I won't be performing a blood exchange as I'm doing now. I'll drain her of all her blood before I replenish it with my own. We both need to be ready for this." The concern in his voice was palpable, and I struggled to stay conscious. "It's draining and is made even more dangerous because she is not entirely human. We don't know what will happen, or if the transformation will even work. There has never been a combining of species such as ours. But we are out of time and ideas, and I won't lose her." Erick's voice hitched at the end, and he cleared his throat sharply.

The bed dipped beside me, and Erick removed his now healed wrist from my cracked lips as he leaned over me. "Mic luptător, can you hear me?"

'*Yes.*' Responding telepathically was all I could manage at this point.

I was sure someone had replaced the packet of cotton balls from the hospital into my mouth judging by how dry and unresponsive it was.

Gently stroking my forehead, Erick bent closer, his beautiful green eyes staring directly into mine.

"I need you to listen to me carefully. I've given you just enough blood to heal the damage done to your body during your escape; it'll allow your body to function for another day. I will continue to give you some blood over the next day or two until your power reaches an acceptable level. Once I'm happy with where it's at, I'll perform what we call the kiss of death." Erick stroked at the tears leaking from both my eyes. "We've already performed the first two exchanges, leaving only one more to go. The bite combined with my blood will trigger a transformation that will bring you into my world. I need to know you are okay with me doing this. I won't not do it without your permission." He continued stroked my brittle hair as he waited for my response.

'*I'm beyond help. Just let me die.*' I sobbed at my failure, the pain having worn my determination down. Peace was now the ultimate prize.

"I'm afraid I can't do that, beautiful. I've grown rather fond of our sparring sessions and chats. There's something between us. I'm can't let you die," Erick whispered with a smile.

Do you think I'm beautiful and worth being stuck with for all eternity? Beacause, you know it'll be eternity right or until one of us is staked or reaped?

"You've become a bit of an obsession for me. I can't seem to get enough of you," Erick confessed. "There'll be hell to pay later with my people and yours, for combining our species; but, when it comes to my soulmate, I don't give a shit about the consequences," Erick declared passionately.

My mother's and Ellie's gasps reached my ears, as did Tristan's profanities.

'Stalker much? Fine, but Erick, you better make it worthwhile, soulmate or not. Whatever that means.'

"It means there is no life for me if you die. I refuse to walk this earth without you in it. The conversion can be painful, but considering the pain you've been in for the past month, I have a feeling you'll be able to handle it. As for making it worthwhile, I'm sure I can come up with something that satisfies your criteria," Erick chuckled.

'All right then. I guess the answer is yes. You'll just have to get used me walking this earth a bit longer I guess.' I teased tiredly.

Erick leaned forward to press a gentle kiss against my forehead. *'Thank you, mic luptător. Rest now, beautiful. I'll be right beside you when you wake.'*

Eyes closing, I finally allowed myself to slip into the darkness.

CHAPTER 24

My eyes snapped open, and I blinked in confusion. I lay on my side with my reflection shimmering and shinning back at me, almost as if I were looking at a reflection in the water.

I recognised the vanilla and citrus aroma in the air instantly and knew before turning that I'd find Erick behind me. Lifting his weighted arm from around my waist, I moved onto my back as a grumpy Erick moaned softly beside me.

His body tensed before his eyes snapped open.

He appeared just as confused as I felt. I tried to recall the last memory I had, and my mind stuttered briefly before memories of Ellie and I running through the dark state forest drifted to the surface, followed by a brief flash of Erick's face hovering over mine, kissing my head, before everything went dark.

"Where are we?" Erick frowned, then rolled to his back, looking at what appeared to be a small dome above us.

"Funny, I was going to ask you the same thing. The last thing I remember is you kissing my head, and the world going black," I answered with a frown.

I reached a tentative arm up to touch the shimmering dome above us, stopping short when I realised my arm was no longer skeletal and had returned to its previous size. Jerking my arm down, I examined the rest of my very naked body.

I looked and felt renewed. It was incredible.

I reached up once again, delicate fingers skimming the dome above me. It was solid and cool to the touch, reminding me of solid glass. Sparks of rainbow colours rippled where my fingers touched and I jerked my hand back in shock.

"Did you see that?"

I didn't take my eyes off where my fingers had touched the dome, and in my peripheral vision, I saw Erick's hand reach up beside mine.

"I did," he murmured huskily.

Laying his hand flat against the glass, a much larger wave of sparks rippled outward from his palm.

"It's odd, I recognise the blankets and the bed we are lying in — it's my bed at the mansion, but I don't recall being placed in here." He gestured to the dome.

"What do you remember?" I asked distractedly.

Looking around, I tried to find an exit, only to come up empty-handed.

"The last thing I remember is performing the kiss of death on you, which appears to have gone well. I exchanged blood with you, after which I allowed my body to shut down, so I could recuperate from the exchange. I haven't slept the sleep of the dead in nearly a year, maybe a little more."

Erick pushed a little harder at the surface, testing for weaknesses.

"Good to know. Judging from my apparent health, it seems I've joined you. Is this what usually happens during a conversion, though?" I gestured to the dome.

"I'm not sure I've ever heard of anything like this," Erick murmured. "You've definitely converted though. You'll notice your teeth soon."

I ran my tongue along my upper teeth, my tongue gliding across the sharp teeth he'd mentioned.

The high-pitch of a female's voice from above stalled our conversation. "Well isn't this sweet? Just look at you two love birds nestled together. I must say, this is very impressive."

A thud came from beside me and I jumped, scooting back into Erick with a hiss. His arm came across my abdomen as he drew me closer to him to protect me from whatever or whoever had just spoken.

"Oh, you don't have to worry about me, lovelies. I'm not here to hurt you. I wanted to admire my work in person. It's rather spectacular, don't you think?" She drawled.

That feminine voice sounded familiar, and I suddenly recognised it as the same one I'd heard the night I'd been attacked in the morgue. It was the same one who had laughed when Brian had attacked me all those years ago.

"I know your voice, but I don't know who you are." My weariness only seemed to amuse her as she giggled lightly.

"Who am I? Well, let's just say I'm someone who's taken a liking to you and have been watching you develop and evolve since before you were a twinkle in your parents' eyes," she mocked.

My skin prickled at her response. Why, and how in the world had she been watching me since *before* I was born?

"Do you have a name or even a face that we can put to the voice, or are you going to make us guess?" Erick growled.

Tinkling laughter came again, raising the hairs along my arms.

"Now that's a bit of a lengthy story, but let's just say your families and I go a long way back. I'd say to the dawn of man in your family's case, Evanee. I have quite a few names actually, but you can just call me Fate," the woman chuckled as though amused by her response.

"Fate! As in the Fate that predetermines significant events in a human's life?" Erick's fingers tightened against my ribs.

"The one and same. But darling, I don't just deal with humans, I deal with all beings. Kind of like the head of her family does. Where did you think all those prophecies lining your sacred libraries came from?"

A feminine form stepped forward, obscured by the warped substance of the dome. She didn't come any closer, and my eyes strained trying to glimpse her face, but she was just a blur.

"Head of my family? I'm not sure who you're referring to as I've never met either side of my family."

My father lost touch with his extended family after his mother and father's death before I was born, and my mother was only just reacquainting herself with her side of the family.

"I was referring to the big man himself. I believe he would be what the humans refer to as a great-grandfather." Fate stated matter-of-factly.

Remaining silent, Fate laughed maniacally as she realised neither one of us had any clue what she was talking about. I stiffened with the realisation that there was something not right about her.

"That's right... your mother still hasn't told you everything, has she? She always was a stubborn woman. It made for interesting viewing the day she defied her lineage to marry and mate with a human. Then again, I had a helping hand in that little gem." She sounded proud, whereas I was growing more confused than ever. "One of my more brilliant moments, if you ask me," Fate giggled.

With a dramatic sigh, Fate explained, "You're not just a reaper, darling. You're descended from the big man himself, *Death*. Phew, just thinking of that man gets me all hot and steamy." Fanning herself, the area where her head should have sat dispersed before slowly floating back to reassemble itself in what might have been her face once again.

I couldn't hold back my snort of incredulity, which slowly morphed into outright laughter.

Erick didn't move or say a word.

Fate truly was insane.

"What are you laughing at? You'd better not be laughing at me, child, because if you are."

The cloudy figure of the woman coalesced the closer she got to the dome.

Fate's solid figure leant over the dome and she hissed, "I will make what you have been through the past few months look like sunshine and daisies, you brat."

Stiffening at her rage, mine rose. Realising now wasn't the time, I shrugged apologetically at the crazy lady. "Sorry. Look, I wasn't laughing at you, I was laughing at the craziness my life has become, and by the looks of things, my undead life isn't going any better than my first life did. I'm trapped in a dome-covered bed with what I'm assuming is a naked man, who has no clue what happened after he converted me. Next minute you come along and tell me my great-grandfather is the big, bad Grim Reaper of all Reapers. I wasn't laughing at you, just the hot mess that is my life."

Calm descended over her seething features, now visible through the dome, and Fate smiled slightly. "Oh, I see. You're not trapped in there, by the way, you're asleep."

This women's bipolar. Either that or she has some serious mood disorder.

One second, she was ready to rip my head off, the next she looked likely to suggest we sit down to tea and cookies.

With a benevolent smile, Fate traced her index finger along the top of the dome as she said, "I've taken pity. I've decided to give you a bit of a helping hand with your current predicament."

What predicament?

"Listen carefully. Before you return to your body, I will implant a premonition, kind of like the one I planted that night Erick came to visit you in the morgue, Evanee. Did you like it, by the way?" Fate's voice hitched with enthusiasm.

"What premonition?" Erick spoke up for the first time in a while, but we both ignored him.

"Hang on, are you talking about that little daydream I had where he had that stunning woman bent over the chair?" I clarified.

"What woman? What chair?" Patting Erick's arm to silence him, I waited for Fate's response.

"The one and the same. I was trying to give you a sneak peek of what was to come. How did you not understand that from the premonition I sent you?" She threw up her hands in exasperation.

How was I supposed to know it was a premonition? I'd never had one in my life, not to mention the fact that the only thing I got a good look at was the woman's hair and body.

I'm sure my body has never looked as good in person as it did in that dream.

"Silly girl. Now, the two of you take note of exactly what's in the premonition, as it'll be the key to your salvation. Oh, and a little head's up, Evanee is not the only one who underwent a bit of transformation. You both did, my sweets," she winked before ploughing ahead. "There has never been one such as yourself, Evanee. Half-human and half-reaper, you were a contradiction of life and death in one little vessel. You now find yourself in the unique position of being both reaper and vampire."

Looking over my bare shoulder at Erick, she addressed him. "You would think the two would go hand in hand, yet there will be those who will not feel this way. Take heed." Erick nodded, his hands tightening possessively around me.

I realized then that he was probably already aware there might be threats to not only me but himself in the near future.

"All vampires inherit a power upon their human death or birth. For you, Evanee, these powers will be amplified by your pre-existing power and genetics. You'll both become more. Exactly what, even I'm not sure yet, but it will be exciting!" Fate's voice got higher the longer she spoke.

Interpreting our silence as acceptance, when to be honest my head felt as if it was about to pop off and rotate 360 degrees. The crazy lady clapped her hands gleefully.

"Now, we are out of time. Remember what I told you two. Pay attention to all the details in the premonition, and you might survive what's coming. Oh, and if you see your great-grandfather, do me a favour and let him know how helpful I was, okay. Also, don't forget to slip in just how fantastic I'm looking. The man has no idea what he's missing," Fate pouted.

The room plunged into darkness. Colours and images flashed before my eyes as I plunged headfirst into the world's worst nightmare, Erick right beside me.

~

A fire consumed me as my heart stuttered its first beat.

The pain was instantaneous, a red sheen of sweat coating my body. The creature at my spine fed hungrily, a succubus draining the very life from me. My heart struggled to continue beating with the minimal blood flow, as the creature continued to absorb what little blood I had left in my body from my feed the night before.

Images of something large and hideous appeared within my mind, transmitted through one of the tendrils that had infiltrated me. Thanks to the premonition Fate had bestowed upon me, I now knew this was the initial virus—the Queen. She was Jared's pet project, the one who'd spawned the creature that had infected me.

Searing pain beneath my ribs dragged me back to the present as the creature's claws pierced a lung and scratched the back of my heart. Unable to take it any longer, I screeched, releasing every bit of pain I felt, the hopelessness of the situation, and the anger of being so vulnerable.

Arching off the bed, firm hands clamped down on my arms, holding me as the agony passed.

Finally, all movement stopped, and my eyes opened despairingly to stare into Erick's haggard face hovering over mine. Anguish creased his handsome features.

It had been a two weeks since we had risen. I'd been unable to tolerate being around anyone other than him as I struggled to control my heightened senses and unquenchable thirst.

Tugging at the pillow beneath my neck, I pulled it over my head. Crying softly, I prayed it would all end, prayed that my new life would be more than just endless pain and overstimulation.

Erick and I had not talked about our shared experience with Fate, we'd not discussed plans of action or what had happened after he'd performed the kiss of death. We'd not had visitors, except those who brought fresh blood supplies upon each waking. Erick had not left my side, choosing to remain there despite the many messages Tristan delivered daily. There was only silence, as Erick allowed me to adjust to the changes I was going through.

The pillow shifted up a fraction and he placed a unit of blood at my lips. It was Erick's way of telling me it was time to feed. Sipping slowly at the bag, I fought the urge to gulp it down as I'd done the first few risings.

With a gentle tug, Erick removed the pillow from my face and smiled reassuringly at me as he stroked at my now snow-white locks.

Removing the empty bag from my grip, Erick dropped it in the bin beside the bed.

"I think I might be ready to try talking now." I croaked raggedly.

"That's good to hear. I've missed hearing your voice. Would you like to shower and change into something new?" His whispered, and I was grateful for it; the pounding in my head threatening to shatter my momentary calm.

"Yes please."

~

Feeling more refreshed than I had in days, I took a seat opposite Erick in front of the fireplace, the warmth now alien to me.

"I thought perhaps, if you're ready, that we might have your mother and Jordan visit for a while? I know they're both eager to see you," he said cautiously, unsure of how I would react.

"If you think I'm ready. It'd probably be a good idea to get some clarification on some things Fate spoke of. Although, I'd prefer it if we didn't mention the premonition. The less everyone knows, for now, the better," I murmured with bone-weary tiredness.

Nodding in agreement, he looked towards the double doors. Seconds later they opened and in stepped my mother and Jordan. I continued to stare into the flickering flames, not wanting to face the woman who'd lied to me my entire life.

Sensing my hurt and anger, Erick rose to his feet, greeting my mother and Jordan.

"Erick, thank you for having me. I appreciate the hospitality." Reagan spoke formally from somewhere behind my chair.

"It's no trouble at all. Please take my seat. Jordan and I will stand," Erick's replied with the same formality as my mother.

My mother stepped into my peripheral vision before taking a seat in the chair opposite mine.

Jordan's sizeable frame blocked my view of the fireplace before he bent to look me in the eyes.

"How's my favourite vampire going?" He whispered with a slight smile.

I shrugged my answer, not knowing how to respond to his query.

"You're doing better than I did," he reassured me in his deep rumbling voice. "It took me weeks before Erick allowed me to leave the dungeon in Romania. That's where Erick converted me." He whispered reassuringly.

Looking to his bicep, the image of the scale I'd gifted him caught my attention. Reaching forward, I gently caressed the moving scales; that ancient power I'd possessed before my conversion rising to greet Jordan like an old friend.

I smiled, comforted by the knowledge that at least one thing from my previous life hadn't changed or left me.

"It's good to see you, Jordan," I greeted him cautiously.

"Likewise, Evie." With a wink, Jordan rose, moving to stand beside Erick.

Looking at my mother, I studied her, watching her shift uncomfortably.

"You lied to me, why?" I didn't bother trying to hide the hurt and betrayal I felt, asking the question that had been burning in my mind for what felt like forever.

"I had no way of knowing you would inherit my powers, and by the time you did, I didn't know how to explain it to you without having to tell you about the Messorem family history. Choosing to raise you to be human was the most difficult—and probably the best—decision I've ever made."

When I didn't respond, Reagan sighed. "The supernatural world is full of so many dangerous beings. Reapers are not loved by the supernatural community. I've always put it down to the fact that we remind them of their mortality. There isn't a creature alive we can't reap, other than gods, and even then, rumour has it that Death himself can reap them from time to time." Clasping her hands together, Reagan sniffed delicately as tears trailed down her pale cheeks. "I didn't want to expose you to that prejudice at such a young age when you might never have inherited any powers. I'm so sorry, I did what any mother would do for her child. Protecting you was the only thing I've ever felt good at doing, and even then there were times that I felt I'd failed to do even that."

Seeing her honesty and her tears, my resolve to stay mad softened as I contemplated what I might have done if I'd had children. The truth was, I'd have probably done the same thing my mother had.

"So it's true then, that you are the descendant of Death himself?" Erick voiced the question I'd been mulling over since Fate had mentioned it.

I thought back to the night of Brian's attack, and that night in the forest, when I'd finally been forced to accept all of that power living within me. I'd heard a masculine voice and I thought I'd seen a cloaked figure, but it hadn't been Erick or any other male I knew. Could it have been him—my great grandfather?

"Yes, but how did you know?" Frowning at Erick's question, Reagan looked between Erick and me.

"Let's just say it wasn't an accident Evanee and I met, or that she was converted. You could say it was—preordained," Erick answered dryly.

I snarled.

Fate really is a bitch.

'Careful mic luptător, you never know who might be listening,' Erick warned.

I nodded, then allowed my mind to go blank in case he was right, and Fate was listening. We weren't sure of her full powers.

"What I'm about to tell you does not go beyond this room or the people within it. It is a family secret, and to divulge it would put my family at significant risk," Reagan warned ominously.

She looked at each of us; once she satisfied with our oaths of silence, she continued. "Most people believe that all reapers are Death's creations. While this is partially true, it's also a lie. Death needed to protect his offspring, namely my father, aunts and uncles, from the supernatural community. Who my grandmother was, none of my generation truly knows. Death created the reapers you, Erick, and the other supernatural community have heard of and perhaps even met, as a diversion of sorts. They were tasked with assisting my grandfather to collect the souls of the dead and bringing them before him to be ferried to their final resting place."

I remembered those souls; they'd called to me the night of Erick's and my battle.

"If Death's supposed to ferry the souls, then why did they call to me the night of my fight with Erick? I've been releasing souls for the past couple of years now, and I've never been to or seen Death while I sent these souls on their way," I entlightened my mother.

Reagan rose sharply and paced before the fire.

"The last time my family saw my grandfather was not long after I was born. He gave me his blessing, as he has done for every newborn within our family. This blessing allows us to access a part of his power, and any gifts he wishes to bestow upon the child. I was the last of my family to receive this power before my grandfather cut off all communication from the family," Reagan frowned but continued her story. "When Death stopped communicating, parts of my family's powers started dissipating, so that the only thing they can now do is accept the souls of the departed and assist them in finding their resting place in the afterlife. Relics belonging to our family have lost their power, and my grandfather's scythe has disappeared from the vault. That night in the forest shocked and terrified me." Wiping a stray tear from her cheek, Reagan's eyes glazed over as if she were reliving that night.

"Why's that?" I cringed, the memory still vivd.

"You are or were part human, and vulnerable to so much. I feared that power would destroy you. I've felt nothing like what you experienced that night, sweetheart. Death wasn't around when I was little, so I have no way of knowing what his power felt like. I've said nothing about that night to my family, and until I've had time to think it through, I won't. I'm worried about how they will react, and that the lot of them will descend upon this place to study you, Evanee. I don't know how you now contain the powers lost to them. The only thing I can think of is that you somehow came in contact with my grandfather, but surely I'd have felt him?"

Reagan stopped pacing to stare at me.

"You'd not even scratched the surface of your powers before Erick converted you; now, well, no one knows what the outcome will be. I can sense your reaper trapped just beneath your skin, and baby, it is beautiful. So beautiful." Wiping at her eyes, my heart hurt at the pride and adoration in my mother's voice.

"You said your family had lost their powers, does that include you?" Erick had picked up on her careful wording just as I had.

Great minds think alike.

"No, it does not include me, yet." Reagan fell silent, unwilling to part any more than she already had.

The room descended into silence, each of us burdened with our thoughts.

Jordan cleared his throat uneasily. "There's something else though, something none of us has talked with either of you about since you woke."

"What is it, Jordan? Spit it out," Erick ground out, his body now rigid.

"Something happened after Evanee transformed. As you know you went to sleep alongside her, which isn't that uncommon given how much energy you spent during the exchange," Jordan shrugged. "But, uh, what you don't know is that you two were asleep for, um, nearly a month," Jordan spoke slowly as if he were unsure how Erick or I would react.

"What!" Erick exploded.

I guess I know why Jordan didn't want to start with that bit of news.

Erick's yell sent Tristan bolting through the bedroom doors.

"Erick, please calm down. Everything's taken care of," Jordan reasoned. "Tristan and your aunt have been managing your affairs while you rested." Looking to me, Jordan cringed, "Evanee, I'm sorry, but for your safety, we had to declare you deceased."

They did what?

Spluttering, I didn't know what to say.

What would happen to my job, my house? What about uncle Bob, aunty Marg, Steve, Ellie, and Brad? Did they know I wasn't dead?

Sensing my rising panic, my mother spoke up. "Evanee, it's okay. I took over ownership of your house, all your bills are sorted. Bob, Marg, Steve and your friends are aware you're still alive. They came to visit you while you slept. Ellie and Brad never stopped researching for a cure for that creature inside you. Bob has been overseeing the rebuild of the morgue since you accidentally destroyed it. Luckily no one was injured during the explosion," she reassured me.

I hadn't thought about the morgue and my forensic nurse, Mel, who'd been there at the time of the explosion. That I hadn't, saddened me. The morgue had been somewhere I'd felt at home, where I'd felt accepted. Was it becoming unimportant to me?

"Tell them the rest, Jordan." Reagan interrupted Erick's mutterings, and the room fell silent, Erick's steely gaze fixing on Jordan.

"During your sleep, none of us could reach out to or touch you," Jordan shook his head, his gaze weary, "The next evening when Tristan came to see if you'd awakened, Erick, and he found you both encased in a dome or cocoon of some kind."

Rubbing the back of his neck, Jordan stopped talking, unable to go on.

"What he doesn't want to say is that each one of us tried to get through the outer shell, but with each

379

attempt, we had our arses blown across the room," Reagan smirked. "Interestingly though, with each rising something new would happen to the both of you. Some days we found you encased in onyx and electric blue flames, the next we found you encased in gold and garnet flames. One evening a light fog filled the inside, hiding your figures from us mostly, but at one point we all could have sworn your bodies morphed into something other. Something not entirely human in form. We can't be sure exactly what, as the outer layer of the shell was too warped."

Erick moved to stand beside my chair, and I gazed up at him. Worry creased his brow, and he laid a heavy hand to my shoulder.

'I think that answers whether our meeting with Fate was a dream or real.' Erick's statement echoed my thoughts.

'I guess it does. So that would mean there's a chance for me to be free of this thing in me.'

'I believe so.' There was hope in Erick's eyes, a hope I was hesitant to indulge in until I knew for certain the creature was out of my body.

"Can anyone tell me the whereabouts of Jared and Desmond?" Erick looked between Jordan and Tristan.

"Ellie and Brad returned to the Aeternum Science Laboratories not long after we declared you dead to keep up with appearances. They've seen Jared fleetingly; however, he spends most of his time in one of the laboratories there." Reagan explained.

"And Desmond, what's that piece of shit been up too?" I looked at my mother and then to a rather ashamed Jordan.

"I'm sorry, Evanee. We lost him. He disappeared the night you left the hospital. I've checked at his house, and the morgue, but he left the city the night he attacked you at the hospital. We found his name on one of the flight manifests to Brisbane." Jordan hung his head.

Looking at my mother, her steady gaze told me she'd thought the same thing I was thinking.

Dread curled within my stomach, my slim hands gripping the chair.

"Why does Brisbane keep coming up? First Brian, and now Desmond. You don't think they're connected do you, mother?" I croaked.

Fear squeezed my insides at the thought of Brian and Desmond possibly knowing each.

"Who is this Brian and why are you so worried about him and Desmond knowing each other? You've mentioned him before." Looking between Reagan and myself, Erick demanded an answer to a story that was intensely private and hard to talk about.

Now that I was bound to him there would be no hiding that rotted door within my mind from him, there would be no hiding my past.

I knew the latch would snap in time, allowing those wretched memories to burst forth.

'It is something I'd rather not discuss in a room full of people, Erick. Recalling that memory is difficult for me, the nightmares are too much to bear, even after all these years.'

'Any other time I would afford you the space and time to reveal your secrets to me. But I need to know Evanee, if not because of the bond we now share, then because it could be useful in locating Desmond,' Erick pointed out.

'Fine, but not with everyone around, please. Especially not Tristan. We are not close enough for him to know all the details of my past.'

Rubbing gently at my shoulder, I looked up to see Erick nod his understanding.

"Tristan, I'll speak with you once Evanee has gone down for the day. I want a detailed update. Jordan, work with Reagan in locating Desmond. I believe Detective Bernard might be helpful. If Desmond arrives back in Acrasin or Murder Point Bay, I want him watched at all times. No one is to touch him. Carry on monitoring Jared and his habits," Erick ordered, his tone brooking no argument.

I quickly added one additional request. *'Could you please have someone guard Brad and Ellie? Desmond or Jared might come after her. Desmond said she'd pissed off some people in high places trying to rid my body of this creature.'*

Erick gave a small nod of agreement before calling out to Tristan.

"Tristan, one more thing. I want someone with Ellie and Brad at all times. If they can't have someone in the lab with them, they can come and work here at the mansion. Have they been able to get their hands on a specimen?"

"No, they haven't. They've been analysing blood samples Evanee and Bob have given to them. I believe they have made some progress with some DNA strands, mostly human and animal. Reagan was correct in suggesting there might be reaper DNA strands. They found DNA to support this in the body Evanee was autopsying at the time of her attack in the morgue. The other bodies had no such DNA, however," Trisan relayed with brisk efficiency.

Dismissing Tristan, he bowed his head ever so slightly before exiting the room. Reagan and Jordan followed suit.

The room descended into silence . At last, we were alone, and I was grateful for the break. The visit had been more taxing than I'd thought. But one thing kept swirling around in my mind.

Why did only one body have Reaper DNA, and not the others?

CHAPTER 25

Stepping through the portal, I marvelled at the fact that I'd been able to create something so extraordinary.

Thanks to my mother's guidance and teaching, I'd mastered creating and stepping through a reapers' portal to various locations around the mansion. I'd welcomed the challenge of learning this skill to distract me from the boring and snail-paced days at the mansion. The past two weeks had tested my very limited amount of patience.

My mind drifted back to that night, two weeks ago, when I'd finally relayed the secret I'd kept so well hidden to Erick.

He hadn't taken my confession about Brian's attack as I'd hoped he would.

I'd watched his eyes widen in shock before anguish had crept over his face, his fisted hands tightening the longer I spoke. Reaching the end, I'd revealed how I'd gotten my revenge, or at least how my power had. It was then that Erick had placed a barrier to his mind before he'd allowed a stoney mask to settle over his face.

He'd stormed from the room as soon as I'd finished.

I'd stood watching Erick's retreating back when Jordan had come barrelling in, a look of horror and confusion on his face at the sight of the pink tears trailing my cheeks.

Looking back now, it was comical watching the big guy look around for someone to tell him what to do, while I cried hysterically, blabbering, "He lied. How could he lie to me?"

Jordan had been forced to ring my mother, who had had to come back from wherever she'd been reaping. We'd lain on the bed, her holding me like she'd done when I was a child after I'd had a nightmare. A concerned and now seething Jordan had sat beside me, stroking my hand until I'd passed out, and the images had finally stopped.

Erick had returned the next rising, but I'd physically kicked him out of the room, bellowing for Jordan as I spat prophanities at the man who'd broken my heart.

Since then, I'd not seen or spoken to Erick until he'd received intel that Desmond was at last back in Acrasin City. Breezing into the mansion's library without so much as a greeting, Erick had paced before me until I'd put my book down.

Satisfied he had my attention, he'd brought me up to date in what had to be the fastest debrief in history.

"This is it. Fate stated in we would know the moment to strike. I believe this is it. I'll ask Ellie and Brad to send an email to Jared insinuating they have evidence showing he infected you and others. They can instruct him to meet them out front of the science and research department. Brad and Ellie can only get us in so far, and then we'll need to use Jared's ID card." Cold and calculating Erick was all I was getting, and that was fine with me.

"Thank you. I'll take what you've said on board and plan accordingly. Now get the hell out, before I throw you out on your arse again." I dismissed him.

It didn't taken long to organise a plan of my own with Jordan. He agreed to come as my backup. He'd even approved of bringing in Brad and Ellie, who had agreed with Erick about utilising their passes to help me gain access to the department.

I left Erick and Tristan out of the loop; I didn't need them interfering, not when Erick and I could barely communicate.

Tired, hungry, and in a world of pain, my life now passed in a blur. I'd lost my life to some arseholes' pet project, and my friends were in danger because of it. I was pissed, and I was done playing nice.

Sealing the portal shut behind me with a simple thought, my bare feet left slight impressions in the cold dewy grass as I slowly glided towards the hospital.

Looking around, I couldn't help but appreciate the beauty of the city and the lights surrounding the hospital, especially after being cooped up for the past two months.

Life and laughter embraced me, whispering tales of families and friends gathered for the evening. To think I'd been one of those people content to go about my daily life.

Not anymore. You have a manmade supernatural creature sucking the life out of you each rising, and your great grandfather is the one and only Death. Time to woman up and make this thing your bitch.

Squaring my shoulders, I twirled my wrist, summoning a light mist. It crept over the damp grass, swirling gently around my ankles—the power I'd once rebuffed rising to greet me.

Scenting the air, I released a peaceful sigh into the crisp night. A new resolve in place, I knew what I needed to do.

I'd woken this evening to find a rather peculiar gift at my side—a short-handled scythe. Looking down at the weapon in question, I marvelled at how easily it had become an extension of my arm.

I'd not told anyone of the man who'd saved my life on at least two occasions. Why? I couldn't say; but, I now believed it had been my great-grandfather giving me a bit of a helping hand.

My suspicions were confirmed when I'd found a short note attached to the scythe.

My gift to you. It needs a new master and friend. D

Electric power zinged through the blade, vibrating with glee at once again being held. It begged to take a life, to feel fresh blood dripping from its tip.

It was a thing of beauty. The handle was encased in the softest leather that had already moulded to my grip. Emeralds, onyx and gold glinted eagerly, forming a border around the top half of the leather. It was perfect for the dramatic entrance I was about to make.

Crossing the gardens, the mist I'd summoned thickened around my ankles, parting only slightly with each step. I could see wisps of my snow-white hair over my shoulders, drifting lazily in the cool night breeze.

A stunning powder blue slip my mother had placed in the closet at Erick's mansion, caressed my thin frame. The soft Viole material caressed my bare breasts, with slits either side of my legs reaching my mid-thigh. The halter-neck front tied at the back of my neck, with the back open and scooping up at the hips. Both my legs and arms were free to move without restraint. I had no doubt the dress would look out of place to the people I was about to meet, but I there was more than one reason I'd chosen it.

Strolling calmly towards the side of the science and research department, I rounded the corner, my gaze zeroing in on the people arguing at the front of the building. I stood quietly in the shadows for a moment, observing the group before me.

As requested, Jordan had collected Ellie and Brad, who were in a stand-off with an irate Cassandra. I hadn't expected to see her here this evening, but what the hell, the more the merrier. Desmond stood beside a stone-faced Jared, shuffling slightly, looking from Jordan to Erick and Tristan. The presence of the two vampires surprised me, as I'd purposely not told any of them what I had planned for this evening.

Studying the group, my eyebrows rose. There swirling within each of them were their souls; something

I'd not been able to see before my conversion unless I was within my mind.

I studied Ellie and Brad, noting the pure effervescent white orb with streaks of varying shades of blue, and a sliver of light pink that was Brad's soul. Ellie's soul held no shape, swirling chaotically as shades of pearl, sapphire and a speck of onyx intermingled. Looking to Cassandra, Jared, and Desmond, I noted the discolouration in both Jared's and Desmond's souls. Their souls were the colour of rotten eggs with black and red veins swirling chaotically. Cassandra's soul was still fairly pure aside from the red and grey swirls that had slowly replaced the pure blue swirls over time.

My, my Cassi, what have you been up to?

My presence went unnoticed by all except Erick and Jordan. That Erick was now my sire meant he'd always know where I was; he'd always have a direct connection to me, as I would to him.

Separating from the crowd, Erick strode over to where I stood, his piercing gaze taking on my choice of clothing.

'Evanee?' Erick growled mentally. *'You look stunning. I'd have thought a dress might be an impracticle choice of attire for tonight events? Is that a scythe you're holding?'* He frowned, his eyes skimming over me once more.

'Considering you already know part of what will happen this evening, I'd have to say yes, this dress is the perfect choice for tonight's festivities. And yes, it's a scythe.' I snapped at him, my anger lashing him mentally so that the corners of his eyes tightened ever so slightly.

389

Erick rubbed at the back of his neck, while emotions I couldn't quite decipher flashed within his eyes.

'Care to let me in on your plans for tonight, or should I just order Jordan to tell me?' His tone was neutral, which only frustrated me even further.

I'd thought he might have understood or at the very least sympathised with me about that night with Brian; instead, he'd rebuffed me and made me feel as if I were a monster not worthy of his presence.

Temper flaring, I ignored his question; instead, I kept my focus on the situation at hand.

Stepping to the side, I looked past him to where the others still stood arguing.

Jordan now faced my direction, his hand over his heart, as he inclined his head slightly in acknowledgment of my presence. Tristan, Ellie, and Brad all looked in my direction, not yet seeing me.

"What are you all looking at?" Cassandra snapped impatiently, her need to be the centre of attention saddening me.

Her years of being invisible within her family and at school had nurtured the trait.

Squaring my shoulders, I stepped through the mist, scythe at my side.

"They're looking at me, Cassandra," I drawled.

Horror bloomed across Desmond's face as anger lit Cassandra's eyes. I focused on Jared's expression, noting his curiosity and fascination. No one spoke or moved, realising the enormity of what was happening.

That's right bitches, I'm baaack. I sang to myself.

"What, no words for your old friend? Desmond, darling, you look as if you've seen a ghost. No words for your girl?" I snapped, baring my teeth at him.

Desmond's face paled before it turned an interesting shade of green.

"Cheer up, will you? Tonight's a good night. At least," I lifted the scythe before me, my index finger following the curve of the blade, "it is for some of us."

"So that's why your mother kept delaying the memorial. You couldn't pick up the phone and call to say you're not dead? It's been two months, for goodness' sake, and what the hell is that thing in your hand?" Cassandra all but screeched.

If Cassandra had cared, she'd have reached out to my mother or Uncle Bob. She hadn't.

Ignoring her, I addressed the group cheerfully. "Shall we go in?"

Strolling towards the group, I looked at the cameras at the front of the building, glad I'd had the foresight to ring Steve and see who was on security detail. Luckily for me, it was him. I'd brought him in on my plans for the evening under the condition that under no circumstances was he or anyone else allowed near this side of the hospital. I'd send someone to let him know once the chaos was over and it was safe to leave. There would be no casualties but the ones I chose tonight.

I gestured towards the opaque glass sliding doors. Brad and Ellie, followed by Tristan, walked ahead, scanning one of their ID cards to open the secure sliding doors that sat at the front of the glass walkway.

Situated slightly apart from the hospital, the building had a walkway over a drain that had been transformed to resemble a creek bed that allowed water to run naturally through it during high tide or the wet season. Lush greenery surrounded the building, giving it a harmless appearance, except to those who knew the experimentation that took place within.

Jordan propelled Desmond, Cassandra, and Jared into action by Jordan, despite their objections.

That left Erick and me alone.

Looking towards the direction of the morgue, I could just see the yellow tape prohibiting entry. Repairs were still in progress within the morgue and dressing room. The pathology lab hadn't sustained too much structural damage during my attack, other than a hole in the shape of three tall men.

I'd chatted with Bob on the phone one evening while I'd been waiting for word on Desmond. Apologising for the damage I'd caused, Bob had laughed it off, saying the place had needed a facelift.

Erick's whisper distracted me from my thoughts.

"Are you going to tell me what the plan is for tonight? I might be able to help in some way."

Like you helped after you stormed out of the room when I told you about Brian. I don't think so, jackass.

'I heard that. Can you at least tell me where you got that thing? It's not your average looking scythe.'

Tearing my eyes away from what had once been my home away from home, I looked up into Erick's face. "The scythe was a gift from my great-grandfather. And you'll soon see what I have planned, Erick."

I fought the urge to laugh at Erick's slack jawed expression. Instead, I stepped forward, not bothering to try to act human or tamp down my new speed as I appeared just behind Jordan, Erick not far behind me.

Following the group inside Aeternum Science Department, Ellie and Brad let us through until we reached the back area of the lab which was sealed off by yet another set of security doors.

"Here we are. Jared, be a darling and flash your card for me, please. I'd get Ellie or Brad to do it, but apparently, they don't have clearance," I crooned sweetly.

"I'm afraid I can't do that, Evanee. None of you has clearance. Anyone of you could be exposed to some highly infectious diseases." His cocky attitude only heightened my anticipation for what was to come.

I grabbed Jared's upper arm and pulled, his feet dragging uselessly along the ground, as I yanked him over to stand before the security panel.

"I'm not worried about infectious diseases," I hissed impatiently. "Now you'll open this door, Jared, or you'll become well acquainted with my temper."

Shaken, Jared wordlessly raised his card to the panel with shaking hands, and the heavy-duty matte-glass doors opened with a sigh.

"See, that's better, isn't it? Right, in we go, everyone," I smiled.

I held onto the back of Jared's shirt as he made to leave.

"Not you, Jared, you can hang back here with Erick and me," I whispered huskily into his ear.

The group moved forward in silence, with Jared, Erick, and I following behind them.

"Which lab are you keeping her in, Jared?" I whispered into his ear, causing him to jump as if I'd bitten him.

"I don't know what you're talking about, Evanee," he murmured stubbornly.

Listening closely, my heightened hearing picked up on the sudden increase in his heart rate.

Oh, he knows exactly what I'm talking about.

"I won't ask twice," I warned.

My grip on his arm tightened dangerously.

"Okay, okay. It's the smaller laboratory at the end. Lab 3. That door to the right is the viewing room," he confessed with a trembling voice.

Approaching a small door beside Lab 3, the group parted like the dead sea, making room for Jared, Erick, and I to step through.

"Open the door," I ordered.

Jared shook his head, his olive-toned skin paling before my eyes as he stammered, "No."

"You will open this door, Jared, or I'll have Cassandra choose which bone I break first. After I've broken that bone I'll move on to the next and then the next, until you do as I say," I hissed into his ear, waiting for him to respond.

I could have taken the ID card from around his neck, but making him squirm felt a lot more satisfying, especially after all the pain and grief he'd caused.

"You wouldn't do that to your best friend," he sniffed haughtily.

Again, so cocky for someone whose night would only get worse.

"Ex-best friend, Jared, and wrong answer," I hissed. "Cassi, darling, we're going to play a game." I smiled sweetly, probably enjoying this a little too much. "The game's called 'pick a bone'. All you have to do is pick a bone somewhere on Jared's body. Go on, give it a go. Oh, and I'd advise you to pick something small."

"What if I don't want to play this game, Evie?" Petulance held her shoulders rigid, though her face was stark white. The pathetic wretch of a girl.

"Just pick a damn bone, Cassandra, or I'll choose one," I spat.

Pointing at Jared, Cassie's hand shook. "Okay, fine. Wrist, I choose wrist."

"Delightful," I crowed.

Moving fast, I released his upper arm, taking up his wrist to snap it with little effort. The crack of bone was something familiar to me.

To the side Ellie stepped back into Tristan, while Brad watched on, a satisfied look lighting his face. I guess I wasn't the only one who disliked Jared enough to inflict pain.

"Evanee, what are you doing?" Erick stepped forward cautiously, wary of the unfamiliar person he was seeing.

Jordan didn't move, knowing and understanding my need for vengeance. As my shield or clipeum he would protect me if he felt I needed the help; otherwise, he trusted my judgement, which was rather refreshing.

My head snapped to look at Erick, and snarled, "Back the fuck off Erick, this isn't your fight." I faced Jared once more, and snarled, "Open the door, Jared, or we keep playing,"

I didn't have to ask again.

Retrieving his security card from around his neck, he slammed it against the security panel, the door sliding open.

"Good boy. Off you go into the viewing room. You too, Cassandra. The two of you get to have front row seats. I'll be taking your security card now, thank you." I slipped the card from around his neck, and he tripped over clumsy feet as I shoved him inside the viewing room, Cassandra dashing in after him.

The room was like the viewing room at the morgue, except for this one being used by top executives and scientists of Aeternum Ltd.

Against the left wall stood a massive two-way mirror spanning the entire top half of the wall. A good-sized lab sat before the window in all its sterile magnificence.

"Ellie, Desmond and Brad, you guys are with me. Erick, you, Tristan, and Jordan can wait in here with Jared and Cassandra. If he moves, Jordan, snap another bone, will you?" Jordan nodded. Satisfied, I continued, "Oh, and under no circumstances are Cassandra or Jared to leave your sight, Jordan."

Jordan cracked his knuckles with a broad grin, and I rolled my eyes at his theatrics.

Beside me, Erick stood unmoving. "What about you? What have you got planned for the lab? Fate only showed us how to remove the creature, nothing else."

He wasn't giving up.

"I'll be having surgery, Erick. I can't think beyond removing this creature. You can't comprehend the pain I've felt—and continue to feel. Once this thing is gone, you'll be rid of me. We'll all return to our old lives as if none of this ever happened."

Anger flared across Erick's face and his hands clenched. Realising he was fighting a losing battle, Erick turned, shaking his head as he retreated into the viewing room with Tristan and Jordan.

I gathered the left-over members of my party and ushered them to the lab doors just down the hall.

My scythe hummed quietly, begging for a chance to reap something. While my birthmark spasmed the closer we got towards that door at the end of the hall, warning me of impending danger.

The creature at my spine bowed and lashed at my heart in a warning, and I halted briefly, hunching over to wait for the pain to dissipate. Red droplets formed across my bare skin, the crimson liquid seeping through the front of my dress. No one said a thing as they waited from me to regain my composure.

"Son of a bitch," I panted before straightening to slap Jared's ID card against the panel.

Entering the lab through the decontamination room, I didn't bother suiting up as I moved onto the room beyond.

Gazing around the lab, I noted the steel bench similar to the one I had in my morgue in the centre of the room.

The outer edges of the room held more steel benches with shelving on one wall. Boxes of gloves, syringes, needles and alcohol swabs filled the shelves; while boxes of test tubes, sample jars and other assorted sample tools littered one bench. Another bench held the latest testing equipment and a computer.

Strolling over to the far wall, I selected an instrument trolley nestled between the two benches. I placed my scythe gingerly on it and dragged the trolleys towards the centre of the room, placing them on either side of the gently sloping steel table.

"I wouldn't touch this unless you have a death wish." Speaking to everyone and no one in particular, I breezed towards a set of drawers that likely housed various implements.

Opening draws and shutting draws, I located and withdrew the scalpel I'd need for my procedure.

I'd stored the premonition Fate had implanted within my mirrored room, guarding it against the creature's probes. So far, my barriers to my room had held up—both before and after my death. With the creature's tendrils breaking through my failed barrier to my brain itself only. As a result, I'd not been able to travel to my room of mirrors as frequently as I'd have liked, for fear it would follow my path.

"If I could please have everyone's attention," I announced loudly. "I've asked most of you here for a specific reason this evening. Jared and Desmond being men of science, I thought you might like to get front row seats to the unveiling of two new species." Keeping my tone neutral proved a little harder than I'd expected.

Rage consumed me, thinking of all the months of pain I'd experienced, and the innocent humans and supernatural beings that'd been infected and lost to one of these creatures.

"What is she talking about?" Cassandra's wariness elicited a grin from my slowly drying lips.

I would need nourishment soon, but not before this thing was out of me.

"You'll see. Now, Desmond, I'll need your help, and yours as well, Brad and Ellie, in retrieving the specimen. If you could all prep yourselves for surgery, that would be fantastic," I addressed them cheerfully, despite my inner turmoil.

Ellie and Brad didn't hesitate, already knowing they would be cutting into me. They hadn't been happy about it, considering neither of them was trained, medically . I'd reassured them they couldn't kill me or paralyse me unless they intended to stake me through the heart. Jordan had confirmed that myth about vampires was true when I'd checked.

"Chop, chop. Come on Desmond, move it. I have a lot to do tonight." Clapping at Desmond, he scurried off like the rat he was, hurrying back into decontamination room to join Brad and Ellie.

Turning in the viewing window's direction, my gaze fixed on the covered cylinder tank to the left of the window.

I'd purposely ignored it, not wanting to set the creature in my back off again. It appeared harmless and insignificant and had likely gone unnoticed by those who frequented the lab daily; but for those who knew, it was anything but insignificant.

Thanks to Fate, I was one of those people.

Strolling back to the table, I joined Ellie and Brad at the steel table in the middle of the room. Desmond took his sweet time at the sink, doing goodness knew what.

"I need you guys to listen to me closely," I whispered, quickly explaining to them what exactly was in that cylinder.

It'd be the key to everything we were about to do.

"Now Ellie, you'll be the one to cut me. Make a large vertical incision along the top of my spine, don't cut too deep, just deep enough that you should be able to see my spine. Don't stress about any damage you'll be doing to me, I'll heal. We need to be quick," I reassured her.

"How will we know when it's safe to cut?" Ellie's irises bled black, hinting at her anxiety and affording me a glimpse of the banshee buried within.

"I'll tell you." I gripped her arm, squeezing it lightly. "Right, this next part is important, your lives will depend on you following what I say."

~

The next few moments passed quickly. I sat on the cold table, my surgical team at the ready. Brad stood at the cylinder, prepared to unveil its contents, Ellie stood on the other side of the table scalpel in hand, while Desmond meandered at the side closest to the door, trying not to be involved at all.

If I followed every step of Fate's premonition, we should all survive this. *Should.*

"Just how did you figure out how to remove this thing from your back, Evie?" Ellie whispered nervously, and I felt bad I couldn't tell her how I knew.

I worried divulging Fate's interference until I'd discussed it with my great-grandfather, might ruin things. I was still at a loss as to how to contact him though.

"All I can say is Erick and I had a little help from on high. Guys," I sighed, a pang of remorse hitting me at their expressions on their faces. "don't look so worried. Everything will be fine as long as you do exactly what I told you."

My heart constricted at how brave they both were, considering the amount of drama that had befallen our lives of late.

'Do you remember everything from the premonition, Erick?' Looking towards him, I watched him nod. *'Take care of Ellie and Brad when it happens, won't you?'*

'I can do that. But when this is all done, we need to talk about what happened the evening I fled,' Erick replied huskly.

'Are you kidding me? You decide now is the best time for us to have a heart to heart about your bloody tantrum the other evening?' I snorted with incredulity.

Swivelling, I maneuvered onto my stomach, my face coming to rest against the cold steel of the table. I didn't wait for his response; instead, I closed my eyes.

'Evanee, look at me, please. Look, I'm sorry. I' sorry I stormed out likeI did, it wasn't through any fault of yours. I know now isn't the time to talk about this, but we need to talk about it once this is all over,' he pleaded.

His apology felt sincere, but it did nothing to satisfy the hurt part of me.

'You made me feel like nothing more than the dirt beneath your boot. You caused more pain at that moment than this creature has since it infected me. I trusted you with something insanely personal, hoping you would understand and sympathise with the guilt and hurt I'd suffered these last few years. You said you wanted to be with me for eternity, and when the going got tough, you bolted.' My throat tightened with the tears I fought to hold back.

I couldn't say anything more, it hurt too much. A single tear trickled down my cheek and I dashed it away.

'Mic luptător, please don't cry, you're breaking my heart. I meant it when I said I was sorry, and that it wasn't your fault. All I can say right at this moment is that I was overcome with the enormous amount of emotions you were feeling. It was as if it were happening to me. I worried I might scare you with the reaction I felt coming on, so I ran. Please forgive me,' Erick pleaded.

There was nothing more I could say at this point. I either accepted his apology or I needed to walk away from him. There could be no sitting on the fence with this.

'I won't tolerate bullshit apologies and repeat performances, Erick. I need someone I can trust, not empty promises and pomp.' Squaring my shoulders, I

braced myself, turning my head to face him and the rest of the audience.

Desmond, the dipshit, shuffled, looking bored.

Oh, I'll be giving you plenty of action in a minute, jackass. You're about to meet Karma, and she has a very special message for you.

"Look alive, Des. You like girls in pain, right?" I taunted.

I recalled the glint in his eyes at the cries of pain from the female forensic assistant that day they had charged me with his induction. The glee in his eyes at seeing me confined to the hospital bed in pain had further confirmed my suspicions. Desmond was a sadist, and I had no doubt there had been other women who'd suffered at his hands.

"Maybe I do. How would you know?" His voice matched his soul, rotten to the very core.

Nearby I saw Brad tense, hands clenching into fists—ready to do some damage, given half the chance. Judging by the thunderous looks of the three vampires behind the viewing window, they wouldn't be far behind him.

"I have a fantastic memory. I believe her name was Danielle," I said thoughtfully.

Ignoring the flicker of surprise in his eyes, I calmed all my thoughts, and gathered my emotions, drawing them inwards before pushing them to one side. What I was about to do would be too much for the emotions and the beliefs I'd had all my human life.

Finally, safely tucked away, I crooned at the darkness hovering patiently just below the surface, allowing it to flood my psyche. Eyes opening, my right hand snapped out, and the scythe slid across the table and into my waiting grip.

Gasps rose from the humans within the lab and the viewing room. Glowing gently, the weapon hummed impatiently, begging to taste blood.

"I told you she was special. Didn't I tell you there was more to her than you could see?" Jordan's voice held pride and excitement, snapping my attention back to the room and its occupants.

"Yeah, yeah you were right, we were all wrong. You want a medal or something?" Tristan's snapped back, annoyed at being called out.

"Will you two shut the hell up? She needs to concentrate," Erick snapped.

His voice held no emotion, yet I felt his worry through the connection we shared; the connection that he'd kept blocked until now.

"Brad, now please." Nausea welled up as the words left my mouth.

The squeal of wheels wobbling across the polished concrete floor signalled Brad's return with the tall cylinder tank. He stopped at the top right corner of the table, beside my head.

Closing out all sounds and all movement, I focused on the object directly in front of me. Ribs aching where claws scraped viciously at them, the network of tendrils encasing my brain pushed harder at the barrier I had erected around the parts of my brain not affected.

Tears of agony stained my cheeks, fresh blood seeping through my pores.

"You can do this, mic luptător," Erick's open palm slammed against the window as his yell boomed through the lab.

I gripped my scythe harder and looked at Brad.

"When I tell you to, Brad, remove the cloth and get out of the way," I sobbed through the pain, worried I'd pass out before we even began.

This was as ready as I would ever be.

In the night, howls of creatures approaching the lab drifted through my brain in response to the creature at my ribs, and its proximity to the queen. I didn't have to worry too much about the lab being infiltrated by the infected just yet, as I'd foreseen in my premonition. The door was slightly more reinforced than the viewing room door and they'd still need to make it through the decontamination room after that.

Gripping my scythe for reassurance, I craned my neck to look at Brad and get a glimpse of what lay beneath.

"Now!" I croaked.

Ripping the cloth from the tank, Brad dropped it and stepped back. Ellie and Cassandra gasped, while Brad paled. The vampires never made a sound. Instead, they studied the creature, storing information away for later.

What was interesting, but not wholly unexpected, was the lack of response from Desmond and Jared. There were no gasps of surprise or cursing beneath their breaths as Brad was now doing.

I guess I wouldn't react either if I'd created the thing.

CHAPTER 26

Horror and disgust churned my shrunken stomach at the sight before me.

From behind the viewing room window, Erick shut our link down with a resounding clang, but not before I felt his rage and helplessness.

There in all her rotten glory was Jared's initial creation, the Queen herself. She shared similar features to the creature that had exploded from the body of the corpse I'd been examining all those months ago, with a few notable exceptions.

Instead of a flat and see-through body like the others, she was at least 120cm long and 30cm wide. The thing reminded me of a witchetty grub on steroids. Where most of her offspring resembled jellyfish in texture and colour, she had a putrid yellow tinge to her and could not shield herself like the one that had attacked me, which I found odd. She had no tail, unlike her offspring, but she had six legs. Eggs floated around the tank, waiting to be plucked and implanted.

The thing truly was hideous.

The pain radiating from my ribs, spine and brain ceased, as the creature stilled in the presence of its Queen. Fate had been right.

I nodded to Ellie, and she moved closer, touching the tip of the scalpel to the left of my spine. A trickle of blood followed the path of the blade as it parted shrivelling skin.

I hissed long and low, my hand gripped the metal table, and the sound of groaning metal ricocheted off of the walls.

My head dropped to the side in time for me to see Erick's fist smash into the wall beside the viewing room window. Rage shone from the depths of his glowing emerald and garnet eyes.

I panted through the pain, my body screaming for blood. My thirst reared its insidious head and the heartbeats of every human within the lab hammered at me, enticing me. Inside the tank, the Queen squirmed and twitched, rearing back and thudding her blind head into the glass.

The bitch knew what was about to happen, and there wasn't a damn thing she could do about it.

Pale crimson tears trailed down my cheeks, the metallic scent of blood permeating the room, overriding the pervasive smell of chemicals. Ellie never faltered, only stepping back once she'd completed the incision. She held a mirror to the incision. Trying to move as little as possible, I twisted my neck to focus my eyes on the mirror glimpsing the incision.

There at the top of my spine lay the docile creature, exposed and unable to move.

The creature twitched at my spine and I screamed. Muscle and tendons tore, wasting more of my precious blood. Stars danced across my vision, but I fought them, knowing this was my only chance.

Lifting my finger from the hilt of my scythe, I signalled for Brad and Ellie to skedaddle.

Brad caught my signal and withdrew quietly, taking Ellie with them towards the far-right wall. They were a safe distance from the viewing window and the table, as I'd requested.

A still clueless Desmond stared at my back in horrified fascination—and perhaps a bit of enjoyment.

Right hand reaching to my back, I ran the tip of the scythe lightly along the posterior of the creature; but instead of dying like any being with a soul or essence might, it screeched, jerking and twitching as if I'd syringed acid along its back.

Deep within the tank, the Queen responded with a screech of her own, writhing and lashing at the glass once more.

Pain and fury echoed into the night from the spawn closest to the hospital, as they picked up their pace, heading toward their Queen.

The creature within me released its hold on my ribs just a little more, its tail bursting from below my ribs, serrating the skin across my side and up to my spine. I screeched in agony and I lay unmoving on the cold steel table.

Another thud came from within the viewing room, and I didn't need to look to know Erick had slammed his fist into the wall once more.

When the creature didn't evacuate my body, I fought the darkness dimming my vision and reached back once again, dragging the tip of my blade back down the same spot as before.

"JUST. GET. OUT," I screamed with frustration.

Another screech exploded through the air, and the creature finally released its grip entirely, expelling from my back. Crimson sinew and gore arched through the air, the soft splats of muscle and tissue hitting the ground reaching my ears. Laying still I waited for some of the pain to subside before I pushed myself onto hands and knees, the rip at my side opening a little more.

Ugggh.

Harking, I spat up dark blood. If I'd been human, that would have been a terrible sign. Mind you, if I'd been human, I'd have been dead already.

Desmond's high-pitched scream beside me was sweet music to my ears.

"Karma's here, you jackass, and she didn't come empty-handed," I crocked painfully.

There was a reason I'd asked Ellie and Brad to stand as far from the operating table as possible. I hadn't been confident that I could kill the creature while it was still in me and suspected it may eject under threat.

My hand shook violently as I grabbed a bag of blood, biting into it. Blood sloshed down my chest as I drained the bag in seconds, uncaring that I was being a slob. Reaching for the next bag I ripped into it, watching Desmond as I sucked down the contents.

The wounded creature was now visible to all in its moment of weakness. I was now latched onto Desmond's neck, its tail arched high in the air. Nobody moved or breathed as they watched that tail slash down, piercing his clothing to penetrate deep within his back, his screeches of pain and despair now muffled by the creature covering his mouth.

It took only 30 seconds, and I felt myself healing even as I watched Desmond's demise. My wounds stitching together at my side, my internal organs healed with every forced pump of my heart.

Finally taking pity, I slid off the table. Bending over a kneeling Desmond, I studied the creature. That darkness that belonged to the reaper within me whispered at me to reap it. Trusting that ancient power, I brought the tip of the scythe to the back of the creature gripping Desmond, whispering one word. "Die."

I slashed downward, marvelling at the lack of acid or blood as the blade struck. Instead, there was only ash left behind as the creature disintegrated.

Desmond crumpled to the floor, now free of the creature.

Smiling in relief, my head snapped up to look at Erick. I caught a glimpse of my eyes in the glass's reflection, and I noticed for the first time that my eyes were glowing.

"Her eyes." Tristan's awed whisper made my smile widen a little more.

At my feet, Desmond's unconscious body seized as the egg within him attached to his spinal cord.

Is this how my body responded?

His body finally went limp and Desmond stirred with a moan before he bolted upright, his hands slapping uselessly at his face and neck.

Waiting for his initial shock to dissipate, I caught his attention.

"Desmond, Desmond, you shouldn't have come after me. Did you think you could get away with your sick, twisted games forever?" I said cheerfully, watching his face morph from fear to blind rage as I hit a nerve.

"You bitch! What have you done?" Desmond shrieked.

"Now, now, Desmond, didn't your mother ever tell you not to call people names?" I chided him.

"Fuck you, slut. You deserved everything you got and more. I should have just killed you straight up like Brian wanted," he spat venomously.

Shock replaced my smile, and seeing it, Desmond gained a little confidence.

"And the light switches on. I was wondering if you'd remember him. My *cousin* isn't doing so well now. Whatever you did to him has spread. It's eaten his legs and has slowly crept upwards. It was up to his navel when I saw him the other day. The doctors don't expect him to last out the next 12 months."

I ignored him, looking past his head to Erick, his face set with grim lines behind the viewing window.

'I had no idea it had spread, or that it would...' I stammered.

'He deserves what's happening to him and more. Don't you dare feel guilty over his suffering,' Erick declared.

Erick was right, Brian had been rotten to the core. It appeared his body was now beginning to reflect his soul.

"Brian got what he deserved and more," I hissed. "I see the rotten apple doesn't fall far from the tree in your family. So, what, you concocted this elaborate plan and asked dipshit back there to help you seek revenge on the women who bought justice down on your cousin's head? That's an awful lot of work just to kill little old me. Did you tell Jared about your family dramas, and him being the great friend he is, suggested he use me as a guinea pig for his little project, wrapping it up as killing two birds with one stone?" I prodded.

Desmond's hesitation and confusion gave me pause and had me wondering if perhaps there was more to the story than I was seeing.

Staring into Desmond's eyes, I took a second to think. What if Desmond hadn't told Jared who had hurt his cousin?

"Desmond did you tell Jared the name of the woman who hurt Brian, or did he already know who I was?" I murmured.

Eyes widening in realisation he'd been played, Desmond looked back to where Jared stood soberly, giving me the answer I needed. "Wow, you really are as thick as your cousin. Looks like you got played. That's all I needed to know. Looks like you've served your purpose," I whispered silkily.

My eyes grew cold, and I hissed long and low. Fangs bursting forth, I had him by his throat, dangling inches above the ground before he could blink.

"What the hell are you?" Desmond gurgled.

Clawing at my partially transformed skeletal hand, his fear rolled off him, the aroma delightful. It reminded me of smooth, rich dark chocolate.

Mmm, delectable.

"You want to know what I am, Desmond? It's simple really—I'm your death," I murmured silkily.

Striking faster than a pissed off taipan, I removed my hand from his neck milliseconds before burying my teeth into his carotid artery.

Hot liquid burst over my tongue, and I gulped it down. Slapping his flailing hands away, I gripped his shoulders, the handle of my scythe digging into his shoulder. Taking what my body needed, I reared back, ripping out a chunk of his neck with my movement. Arterial spray landed hot and sticky on my chest, the warmth dripping down, soaking my dress.

Spitting the flesh out, I launched a limp Desmond at the viewing window. Glass shattered, spraying the audience in the viewing room as Desmond's corpse dropped uselessly to the ground. Cassandra's screams cut short when she fell backwards in a faint, dragging a pale Jared with her.

Erick, Tristan, and Jordan stepped back, not fazed in the least. I watched as Brad and Ellie quietly made their way to the now shattered window. Tristan and

Erick didn't hesitate, reaching over to grab Ellie under her arms before hauling her up and over the jagged shards of glass at the window's edge. Brad followed next.

Once I was sure they were safe, I made my way to where Desmond's corpse had landed. Crouching down, I used my power to search within in him until I found what I was looking for — his soul. There within his chest sat that delicate orb waiting to depart. Reaching down into his chest, I gently removed the orb, holding it in the palm of my hand.

"Say hi to my great grandfather from me, will you? Oh and tell him I said thank you for the gift." Flinging the fragile orb up, I thought of Death, not as a state of being, but as a person.

The orb disappeared from my sight.

Standing, I relaxed for a second, taking a moment to enjoy my freedom. Hearing Cassandra lose her lunch in the viewing room made me smile.

"That felt rather good. Judging by the ruckus coming from outside the glass doors down the hall, I think now would be an excellent time for you, Erick, and Jordan to hop on into the lab and give me a bit of a hand. Spare the humans if you can, maybe just knock them out. They'll prove more resilient than usual, given they're all infected. The vamps, well they'll heal, so go hard. Brad, reinforce the door."

I glanced at Tristan. He stood at the window, torn between doing his duty of fighting by Erick's side and his instinct to protect the woman he'd fallen in love with. His internal struggle manifested itself externally, his shoulders rigid as he adopted a side stance.

Erick didn't need asking twice, and he threw his leather jacket off before jumping over the wall to join me. Jordan followed suit, the set of scales on his bicep no longer balanced, but leaning to one side.

Stepping up to Tristan, I muttered. "Erick and Jordan will be fine without you this one time. I can see your indecision, and I can understand if you may not be ready to acknowledge your feelings for Ellie just yet. Judging by your loyalty to Erick, I imagine you've rarely, if ever, followed your heart. Now is your opportunity to go with your heart, so don't waste it."

For once the great and mighty Tristan was at a loss for words. He had turned to stare at Ellie, who stood with her back to the wall and Brad positioned protectively just slightly in front of her. This was my olive branch to him; it would be up to him if he accepted it.

"Can you handle this, or should I get Jordan back in there?" I really didn't have time for his indecision. I had a job to do.

Shaking his head, he stepped away from the shattered window. The poor bugger looked as if a truck had just hit him. In a funny way, he probably had.

"Tristan, remember no killing the humans. Use Brad, he has a background in martial arts and will be useful against the humans." Moving towards the middle of the room, the lab door rattled ominously. *I'm out of time.*

"I need you both to buy me some time, the liquid needs to drain before I can get to the Queen." Not bothering with any more explanations, I grabbed hold of the tank, dragging it towards a metal drum in the corner.

I knew it would be risky putting myself in a corner with no escape, but it would be easier to defend while the tank drained.

Seeing a metal drum near the sinks, I positioned the tank over it, smashing the glass with the hilt of my scythe. The pungent smell of acid wafted up from the liquid gushing into the drum, making me glad I'd opted for the drum instead of the drain.

The lab doors finally gave way as the first wave of infected people rushed inside.

Without hesitating, Erick slammed his fist into the head of the first person through the door. Jordan was beside him, sending a human flying into the nearest wall, the man's body slumping down, out cold. *Ouch, he's heading straight to ICU for a few weeks after this is over.*

More bodies rushed through the door, three barrelling past the guys. Two were vamps, the other human.

Oh crap!

Grabbing the human female by the throat, I let my vampiric instincts take over as I brought my head forward, smashing it into hers. She was out cold as I tossed her left towards the furthest corner near the viewing room. Widening my stance, arms loose, I mimicked the pose Erick had adopted before the assault. Scythe humming, I faced the last two vamps who'd made it past Erick, not wanting to fight them. There'd been enough blood spilled by me tonight.

"Evening. Look, I really don't want to have to hurt or kill either of you tonight. Can't we just talk things through, or better yet, let's go get a drink?" Ignoring me, the female rushed forwards, a snarl on her lips. *Yep, that didn't work.*

Meeting her in a low tackle, I stood, flinging her behind me, only to realise my mistake when I heard the thud of her body hitting the tank. Looking back at the tank, the woman's head had lodged firmly in place, her screams muffled as the acid ate at her skull. It didn't take long before her corpse dropped to the ground, allowing the acid to pour freely onto the smooth surface of the floor.

I launched onto the nearest table, papers and glass jars scattered in every direction as I landed.

"Acid on the ground guys, watch your step." Not heeding my warning, the second vamp made his way towards me, uncaring of the acid fast approaching his booted feet. Unable to move, I watched as he slowly dissolved with every step he took towards me. He fell forward, no longer able to balance, toppling face-first into the burning liquid.

I turned from the sight. Instead, I looked at the tank. There at the bottom lay the Queen. It would be hard to reach her from my current position, and I had a feeling she wouldn't stick around long. She would need a host or liquid to survive. Shifting slightly, I looked on as she readied herself to launch.

She was aiming for Erick.

Leaping across tables, I landed lightly on the edge of a metal sink just near the tank. Keeping my blade down, the creature and I observed each other. It was then that I sensed something familiar about her. The vampire part of me recognised the vampire within her.

"Sucking the life from the host wasn't a flaw, it was part of your design. But where did Jared get Vamp DNA from, and why don't you have reaper DNA like the creature that attacked me?" Head tilting to the side, I studied her.

Recognising the danger she was in, slits opened at her back, and what could only be described as wings unfolded. They were double the size of her, and clear, with vibrant blue veins. Multiple thin feelers erupted, extending a few centimetres from the outer shell of her body.

"You have to be the ugliest thing I have ever seen. I'd say you need a makeover, but bitch there is nothing in this world that could fix you," I baited.

A long rattling hiss erupted from the Queen as she changed direction, launching herself at me.

Throwing myself at the nearest table, I took a second to assess the room, looking for the best way to get to a dry part where I could stand without getting burnt. By now the acid, along with all the eggs, had made it to the drain at the centre of the room. The drain would at least stop it from reaching the rest of the room where Jordan and Erick still fought. *I could launch in their direction, but that would only put them in danger.*

Sensing my hesitation, she made my decision for me. Turning towards Erick, she once again readied herself to launch at him.

This just isn't my bloody day. It's been swell, I guess. Time to promote myself to hero status.

Pushing off the table, I sailed high, crossing over the top of the creature. Conjuring thoughts of death and decay; my arm extended, the edge of the blade scraping along the creature's sinewy wings and across her back. Unlike the transformed creature that had been trapped within me, she exploded instantly, turning to ash. With no reaper DNA in her, the bitch of a creature was no match for the blade or my power.

Staring down, I watched the ground grow closer, liquid rippling in anticipation.

This is going to hurt.

CHAPTER 27

I braced for impact, and a body hit mine mid-fall, spearing us over the steel table and into the back wall. Dust and cement exploded as we smashed through the wall and out the other side onto the manicured lawn. Laying on top of my rescuer, dust and debris settled around us. I sniffed the air, and a familiar scent teased my senses.

"I hope I'm not crushing you?" Pushing up with one arm, I braced against Erick's chest, staring down into his glowing eyes.

"You could never crush me, mic luptător. Besides, someone needs to keep you out of the trouble you keep getting yourself into," Erick groaned.

He reached up with a dust covered hand to tuck my hair behind my ear.

"Hey, I just saved you from being a mutant creature's bitch. Where's the respect?"

Rolling his eyes in exasperation, Erick sat up, forcing me to slide off him. Kneeling before him, I looked at the blade still clasped in my hand, turning it from side to side, inspecting it for any damage. Releif that I hadn't dropped it, and that it was still in perfect condition rippled through me. If Erick noticed me staring at the blade, he said nothing.

Erick chuckled, muttering, "I have a lot of respect for you, Evanee."

His dusty fingers reached up to cup my cheek. Leaning forwared, Erick's full, crimson lips hovered over the top mine.

"Thank you for saving me," he whispered across the top of my lips.

I frowned when his lips continued to hover over mine. It hit me then that he was waiting of me to move. He was allowing me to take control, encouraging me to define where our relationship went from here.

Closing the distance between us, my lips feathered across his before I pressed them firmly to his.

A groan ticked the back of my throat, and my hands rose to cup his face.

Erick's hand slid across my hips, pulling me closer to him as his other hand slid into my hair. His lips never moved from my mine. Feeling his restraint, I shoved my hands into his hair, my nails scraping along his scalp so that he groaned.

Growling at his continued restraint, I lifted my lips and gently bit down on his swollen bottom lip.

It did the trick, obliterating that careful restraint of his. With a growl of his own, our open mouths crashed together. The hand holding my waist slipped down to cup my arse, Erick's fingers digging into my flesh. Our tongues danced and clashed, our passion released at last.

Erick pulled back first, and I groaned at the separation.

Nipping at my pouting lip, Erick smiled sensuously, "I'd love nothing more than to hide out here in the gardens, kissing and talking about the distance I stupidly put between us, but we're needed back inside the lab. Jordan is in there on his own. And Tristan, is probably having a meltdown at the fact that I just busted us through a wall."

I giggled, and Erick smiled before he pressed one last tender kiss to my lips.

Still buzzing from the adrenaline and euphoria of removing the creature from my back, I rose with Erick.

"Fine," I huffed with mock indignation.

Erick's masculine chuckle came from not far behind me, as together we stepped through the hole in the wall. Careful not to touch the acid, we used fallen debris as stepping stones.

~

We stepped through the whole in the wall and into chaos.

Bodies littered the floor, while a humming Jordan kept himself occupied by dragging the unconscious closest to the acid to safety. Tristan stood at the window his lavender eyes focused on the hole we'd just stepped through. With a quick nod to Erick and me, he turned back to Brad and Ellie.

"Jordan, you good with the wounded?" I called out.

"Yep. I gotta say, you sure know how to show a guy a wonderful time." Rolling my eyes at him, he chuckled before continuing to whistle while he dragged bodies into the decontamination room.

He's incorrigible.

'Tell me about it.' Erick chuckled beside me.

Hopping onto the nearest metal table, I pushed off, sailing through the air once again, this time landing unsteadily beside Jordan, whose arm shot out to my shoulder to steady me.

Erick landed lightly beside me, his hands reaching around my waist to steady me.

"I think my landings need some work." I blushed.

"You'll get there," Jordan shrugged.

With a nod, I yelled at Brad to open the viewing room door. Turning toward the exit, the three of us exited the lab and decontamination room and headed towards the viewing room.

Stepping inside the doorway to the viewing room, I focused on Jared sitting beside a very pale and tearful Cassandra.

"Now that that's all taken care of, I can finally focus all of my attention on you, Jared," I crooned.

Cowering, Jared held Cassandra to his side, and I had to give him credit. The man really loved her.

"What the hell is wrong with you, Evanee? How could you do that to poor Desmond? He didn't deserve that. You're… you're nothing but a… a monster!" Cassandra screeched.

I cringed, her screech grating at my sensitive hearing.

"Oh, shut it, Cassandra. Anyone ever tell you how annoying your voice is? Everything about you is annoying. Goodness only knows why I put up with you for as long as I did. Oh, and that sack of shit you're harping on about had it coming. I was only helping Karma along," I gestured toward the lab, and to where I'd last seen Desmond's body.

The blood coating me had dried, and I could feel it cracking with even the slightest of movements. It wasn't a pleasant feeling.

"Now sit your backside down while I have an intense chat with your boyfriend," I orderd.

Dismissing her, I focused on Jared. "You've been a busy little bee haven't you, Jared? Creating new species, infecting both humans and supernatural creatures. Tell me how secured supernatural DNA?"

"I don't know what you're talking about," Jared sniffed, his eyes flicking up and to the right.

The miserable shits lying.

"Bullshit, I sensed it just before she attacked, and my mother sensed it in the creature that was in me. Where did you get the DNA from, Jared?"

When he said nothing, Erick stepped forward, pulling him up off the floor.

"Answer her, now," he snarled into Jared's face

"They gave it to me before I came here," he stuttered, refusing to meet Erick's gaze, "with another lot delivered five months ago."

"Who gave it to you? I want a name right now." Stepping up beside Erick, I stared at the man dangling uselessly before me.

"They didn't leave a name, only instructions. I was to use the first se of samples to build the initial virus. Once I'd perfected the transfer and incubation of the virus, I needed to locate you, Evanee. That was it, until a five months ago, when I received a fresh set of DNA samples. There was no label, only the vial and instructions to add it to one of the eggs from the Queen before placing it in a test subject."

"That must have been the one that infected me," I shared a shocked look with Erick. "And you have no idea where the samples came from?"

Watching Jared shake his head, I let out a frustrated sigh.

Another dead end.

'Not necessarily. We know it has to be someone working for Aeternum, we just don't know who, or why they seem to want you dead,' Erick reasoned.

'Other than Brad and Ellie, I don't know anyone else that works for Aeternum, Erick. I mean other than Brian and Desmond, who the hell would hate me that much that they would willingly sign me up as a test subject?'

'We'll find out, mic luptător. In the meantime, I suggest we take Jared with us and see what further information we can gather from him about Aeternum and his experiment.'

"Was all this before you met Desmond?" I needed to be sure I was right about Desmond being played the fool.

"Yes, when I found out he worked with you and had some personal vendetta against you, I saw a way to get to you. If it all went south, I'd just pin it on him."

"I thought he was your friend?" I scoffed, my eyebrows rising.

"I would never willingly associate myself with a sadist like him. When he set his sights on Cassandra, I couldn't let him have her. He'd have broken her, and she's too perfect and beautiful for that."

"And what, the other countless women weren't? You're a piece of shit, you know that? You're no better than he was. It's astounding that you're not even the least bit sorry about the lives lost to your experiment." His shrug made something within me snap.

Hello anger, my sweet dear friend. Let's have some fun.

Things ended badly when my temper came out to play, but in this case, it really didn't matter. Embracing it felt glorious, like a hug from an old friend you hadn't known you'd missed.

I lunged for Jared. Removing him from Erick's grip, I had him against the wall before anyone, including the vampires, could blink.

Staring at Jared, he looked down at me in terror, as he gagged for air. I sneered at him, but lowered him until his feet touched the ground. Jared's gasps for breathe echoed in the room.

"What are you?" He wheesed, eyes wide.

"I'm glad you asked. You see your friend, Desmond, asked me the same question, and I'll give you the same answer I gave him. I'm your death." Stunned silence met my admission, and I continued. "But not today. Erick has a few questions for you, and you will give us answers whether or not you like it."

Releasing him, Jared slumped to the floor, his legs useless.

'*He's all yours, Erick. It might be a good idea for Tristan to escort Jared back to the mansion before I rip his throat out.*' I growled mentally.

Erick nodded, turning to Tristan, who was hovering protectively in front of Ellie and Brad.

He repeated my request, then added, "Please erase Cassandra's memory of tonight and send her home."

With a nod, Tristan did as asked. Stepping up to a petrified Cassandra, he gazed into her wide eyes. Cassandra's eye went blank and I turned from the sight.

Ellie and Brad kept their distance, and I stepped toward the window to hide my cringe at the weariness in their eyes.

Erick took command of the clean-up, his commands soft but clear.

Looking back at the lab, I noted Desmond's body had dissolved entirely in the acid, which now covered a good portion of the floor.

The battle for my life and sanity finally over, and I was exhausted.

"What a mess," I sniffed back tears of tiredness.

Running blood-stained hands through my hair, I considered what else I needed to do, when Erick came to stand behind me. I could feel his uncertainty about where we stood, despite our earlier kiss. Deciding now was as good a time as any to take a leap of faith, I pressed back into him.

Erick's arms wound around my midriff, securing me to him as he spoke into my hair. "Mic luptător, it's finished. You're free of that creature and can now look to the future."

Laying a gentle kiss against my head, he pressed his face against the side of mine.

"There are wounded people outside to deal with. The humans need to transporting to the Emergency Department, and the others need to find somewhere safe to rest until tomorrow evening," I fussed, adding things to what seemed like a never ending list.

Erick looked up and leaned back slightly, without removing his arms from around my waist addressed Brad.

"Brad, could you please call Steve and ask him to contact Detective Bernard. Let Steve know Bernard should bring backup; that there are injured people in here."

With a nod, Brad pulled his mobile phone from his pocket, his fingers flying across the screen as he walked out the office.

Ellie looked to me, and for the first time I noticed her eyes had bled black, as they'd done the night we'd been chased. With a stiff nod, she trailed carefully after Brad, her body as stiff as a ramrod.

I frowned, but shook my head.

One thing at a time.

Turning in Erick's arms, a crunch at my feet drew my eyes down, and I noticed the shattered glass on the floor for the first time.

"There's broken glass on the floor," I frowned lifting my foot to see smeared blood. "Why didn't I feel that?"

Erick glanced down, then dipped and lifted me into his arms, and made his way into the hallway.

"I'd say it's a combination of shock, fatigue and your healing abilites."

Sliding along Erick's body, exhaustion beat at me as I faced Jordan. "Are any of the supernatural beings able to walk out or will they need help?"

All I wanted was a hot shower and a bed. I could barely hold myself up.

"Some are out cold, but most are fine. They need to feed, but that's not unexpected," Jordan responded.

"Right." I mumbled, then raised my voice, shouting over the group before me. "Listen up! You need to get your arses out of here before the human authorities and medical staff arrive."

Looking around, stunned faces stared at me. No one moved.

"Am I speaking in riddles?" I exclaimed. "I said start moving!"

"I don't think so, lady. We don't take orders from you." A short female vampire stood, staring at me in defiance.

Oh, for crying out loud. Not tonight, I don't have the time or patience to deal with this shit.

'If you're going to stand at Erick's side, you must use a firm hand. They won't follow someone they think is weak.' Jordan's deep voice floated through my mind.

Shocked, I realised this was the first time Jordan and I had spoken telepathically. It felt different to the way Erick and I communicated, as if I was using a different pathway.

'*Jordan, I'm standing in a dress covered in blood and gore. I look like Carrie after the pig's blood, and you're telling me I'm still not scary enough for them to listen to. I used my big girl voice and everything.*' I whinged.

'*You just went through what most would equate to torture for the past how many months. You killed an evil creature and kicked the arse of one of the sadists who targeted you. I've seen you kick Erick's arse while a creature sucked the life from your human body. Show them that woman. Asking nicely doesn't work in our world. Dominance reigns here.*'

'*For fuck's sake. This is just ridiculous. I'm tired and I just want a shower and sleep.*'

He shrugged his shoulders, and I sighed at the ridiculousness of it all. Pulling my power to the surface once again, an icy wind whistled down the corridor.

They wanted a show of power, fine, they'd get one.

Electric blue and onyx flames licked at my hands, before it crept over the scythe. I stepped over bodies, careful not to touch them. Judging by the look on the conscious supernatural beings' faces, my eyes were now glowing.

"What's your name, little girl?" I hissed.

"I'm not a little girl," she muttered, but her rebellious gaze was fading. "Jenna."

"Jenna? Listen up, you ungrateful bitch. I just saved your arse and everyone else's in this room. The very creatures who were controlling your every move and sucking the life from you are now lying dead within you. Now, you have ten seconds to get off your arses and get the hell out, or anyone not moving dies," I seethed.

"Oh please, parlour tricks don't impress us. We all have powers. Besides, I didn't see you hauling bodies out of the lab—that was all Jordan." She folded her arms across her chest.

Looking to Jordan and then to Erick, the realisation dawned that if I wanted to give the two of us the slightest chance, I'd need to show his people I was worthy of standing by his side.

Studying the vampires, I realised all living creatures had a soul or essence, even the living dead, as contradictory as that sounded.

Where human souls were orbs, supernatural creatures' souls were more transparent and held no shape. A vampire's soul was no longer pearl, but purple. I'd seen it in Erick and the others.

Looking to the vampires I was familiar with, I noted how they each had varying shades of white, yellows and blues in amongst that swirling purple. Each had a speck of black, which I guessed meant the same as it did in humans. They'd taken a life at some point.

Looking around the room, my eyes sought out the vampires both awake and unconscious.

My eyes landed on a middle-aged looking male vamp, crouched over a young human male no older than seventeen. He looked innocent enough until I looked at his essence. Every instinct in me screamed he was pure evil. His soul was pitch black with slashes of red and not a hint of purple in sight.

You'll do nicely for my demonstration.

I appeared at his side, and he stood to meet me. His cocky expression was clearly in an attempt to hide the lust and hunger rolling in waves off him.

I looked deep into his eyes and something unnerving happened the longer I stared. His life as both a human and a vampire played before my eyes. It took seconds to watch an innocent child turn into a bully, then a killer, and then onto a serial killer. He'd spent his undead years killing at leisure, his victims of choice males, aged between fifteen and twenty. Any good he'd possessed had disappeared in his human childhood.

"You'll do nicely."

My transparent hand slid into his chest, and I gripped that foul thing that was his tattered essence, yanking it out. His eyes went dull, and I opened my hand, releasing his essence into the air, allowing it to move on to whatever awaited him beyond. Personally, I was hoping for whatever he considered as torture.

Reaching up, I grabbed a fist full of hair, and holding his head still, I spoke. "Justice is served for those who could not seek it."

I slashed my scythe across his neck, severing his head just below the chin. His body turned to dust before it hit the ground, including his head.

Turning towards my audience, now watching in stunned silence, I blew his ashes from my hand.

"Be warned, I will play judge, jury and executioner when needed. I'm fair, but don't mistake that for weakness. If I need to wade through your bodies to prove a point I will. Now get up and get the hell out of dodge," I ordered calmly.

No one spoke for a moment. Then chaos erupted as fallen comrades and strangers were picked up and speedily removed from the lab and hospital grounds. Once the hall was empty, I rolled my neck, sucking my power back within me.

"Well, that's one way to empty a room. I must keep that in mind for the next party I'm forced to attend," I murmured tiredly.

"Evanee, what have you done?" Jordan's worry startled me.

"You said they needed dominance, not kindness, so that's what I gave them," I said, exasperated.

"Ah, I didn't mean perform an execution." Worried, Jordan looked to Erick before looking back at me.

"Okay, either come on out with it, or I'm going home."

"The council or king's approval are needed before an execution can be performed. To do one without formal notification is what you might call illegal and punishable." Tristan looked ill as he spoke.

"Well hell, why didn't anyone tell me? It's not like he didn't deserve it. The guy was a serial killer not to mention a paedophile, I was only ridding the world of someone who should never have been converted. I intend to pass on the whereabouts of his victims' bodies to Detective Bernard." My voice rose the longer I spoke.

"This is not the time or place to discuss this. The human authorities will be here soon." Erick's voice was firm. "Tristan, take Ellie, Brad and Jared to the car. Jordan, take care of the cameras and any electronic devices, then meet us in the parking lot. Evanee, let's go, now." Authority was one thing Erick did very well.

Stepping over the bodies of sleeping humans, I approached Erick cautiously, worried I'd just undone what little progress we'd made tonight.

I'd reaped two souls this evening, one a vampire, the other a human. He might have said I'd done nothing wrong that night with Brian, but he'd still walked out on me afterwards.

I braced for the possibility he might do the same thing again.

Erick's face softened, and he held his hand out to me. "It's okay Evanee, I'm not angry with you. I'm not going anywhere. This just means we will be meeting the council a lot sooner than I had hoped." My free hand landed in his and he squeezed it reassuringly before he explained. "They'comprised of our eldest vampires, both born and created. They govern disputes and advise the king, my father, when needed. There is more, but I will explain it later. It was inevitable, given your genetics, conversion, and link to me, that I'd need to bring you before them. This incident will complicate things, but we'll discuss this at home, okay?"

Erick leand forward and I tilted my head back to look him in the eyes. His free hand cupped my face and his lips caressed mine.

Pulling back silently, we stepped forward, our movements a blur as we came to a stop out front of the security room. Checking in on Steve, I was relieved to see he hadn't been affected by the evening's drama. Hugging Steve, I promised to visit him once things had settled down.

Turning to Erick, I smiled as the realisation that I was free really hit home, along with the realisation that we had never had a relationship where he wasn't saving my arse, and I wasn't giving him sass.

Making our way to the car park, I noticed Tristan hovering beside an exhausted Ellie, while Brad leaned against the car, silently staring into the distance. A petrified Jared, sat in the backseat of the large SUV his eyes darting between Tristan and Jordan.

My eyes darted to Jordan, who stood grinning at his phone, as his fingers flew across its screen.

Frowning at the SUV, I realised it wouldn't be big enough for all of us.

"Where's your car parked, Erick?"

"I didn't bring a car. I flew."

My gaze flew to his and I gaped at him. "Come again? You guys can fly? Hang on... could I fly too?"

"Yes, those of us who have enough power and who are old enough can fly. That was how I got into the mansion the night you fled the hospital, don't you remember?" He frowned down at me, but I shook my head, only just remembering that night. "Well I did. You're still a fledgling, so you will need another fifty years at least before you can even contemplate anything as energy-consuming as flying."

Well that sucks. Not to worry though, I'm not completely useless.

"Where did you park your car?" Erick asked, looking around the parking lot.

I smiled, not divulging my little secret just yet. "Before I tell you where it is, do you want to make a friendly bet?"

Looking confused, Erick shrugged. "A friendly bet? Yeah, okay, why not? So what's the bet?"

"I bet I could get us home faster than any other mode of transport, including flying vampire style." Grinning cheekily, I waited for him to consider what I'd just said.

"That's not possible." He sounded so sure of himself.

Stepping back from him, I thought of the mansion and the hall just outside the bedroom we'd once shared. The image clear in my mind, I summond a portal large enough to accommodate Erick's height. A white light flickered dimly, before it expanded to give of glimpse of the dimly light hallway beyond.

I giggled at Erick's slack jaw and wide eyes.

"I told you I could get us home quicker than anyone else," I smirked.

Returning my smile, he clasped my free hand. "That you did. What did you have in mind for payment?"

In my other hand, my scythe hummed happily, sedated after tonight's reaping.

"Hey, no fair! How come I don't get to travel like that?"

Giggling at Jordan's outrage, I crooked a finger at him. "Come on then. Don't say I never did anything nice for you."

I indicated for him to step through first.

Obliging me, he took a step forward. Laughing, I tugged at Erick's hand, pulling him through to the other side.

Stepping into his arms, the portal sealed shut behind us, the world drifting away as his mouth once again descended upon mine. The time for gentleness was long gone. Erick's desire scorched my cool lips, breathing life into my newly healed body.

I might have a hostage to question, a Vampire Council to face, and a long overdue family meeting to attend, but they could wait. For now, I intended to appreciate my new life, with a group of people who had started as friends and strangers, but I now considered family.

I was once moribund, but now I'm the living dead.

Born and raised in South Africa until the age of 17, Tammy S Petersen now resides in beautiful Far North Queensland, Australia. She has been a storyteller since a young age but had never explored writing creatively until the birth of her first child in 2014.

After taking a Creative Writing course in 2015, she fell in love with the challenge and creativity associated with fictional writing.

Moribund came about after one of her crazier than normal dreams that then blossomed into the first book in the Evanee Sheperd series. After taking a short break from writing in 2017 for the birth of her daughter, she soon sat back down to complete Moribund.

In between reading and writing, she loves to hear from readers and authors alike. Visit her website: https://tspetersen307.wixsite.com/website

and Facebook page:

https://www.facebook.com/tspetersen307

for the latest news.